odd hours

odd hours

ania bas

WELBECK

Published in 2022 by Welbeck Fiction Limited, an imprint of
Welbeck Publishing Group Based in London and Sydney.
www.welbeckpublishing.com

All characters and events in this publication, other than those clearly in the public domain, are fictitious and any resemblance to real persons, living or dead, is purely coincidental.

A CIP catalogue record for this book is available from the British Library

Hardback ISBN: 978-1-78739-949-5
Trade Paperback ISBN: 978-1-78739-950-1
Ebook ISBN: 978-1-78739-948-8

Printed and bound by CPI Group (UK) Ltd., Croydon, CR0 4YY

10 9 8 7 6 5 4 3 2 1

Mamie i Tacie

1

A large, 24/7, unethical supermarket, late on Friday night. Gosia Golab sits at checkout number fourteen; she is three hours and seventeen minutes into her shift. The next tea break is forty-three minutes away. Strip lighting melts her make-up. She is thrilled. The man of her dreams is choosing her lane again for the fourth time this month. He looks nothing like Andy, her cheating ex. Even the way he fidgets while waiting in line is striking. Oh my god, he is speaking to her.

'Why don't you have more checkouts open?'

She responds with a bright smile that she hopes won't be mistaken for corporate politeness.

'It's our policy to encourage customers to use the self-checkouts late at night.'

He glances at his phone.

'It's barely eleven o'clock.'

She leans over the conveyor belt, exposes her breastbone, picks up a bottle of upmarket bubbly, scans it.

'Forty-two pounds and thirty-five pence, please. Do you happen to have your loyalty card?'

He produces a neatly folded plastic bag from under his arm-pit and starts to pack his shopping away while she gives him his green points. Always the same amount, sixty-nine. One day he will understand the deep hidden meaning and it will make him fall in love with her instantly. He will go through all his receipts just to be certain of her devotion. He will gallop to the checkout with at least two bunches of £5.99 roses. He will go down on one knee and express himself in the most straightforward English: 'Marry me.'

Then he will go down on her in the staff toilets and they will live happily ever after.

That fat guy with the loud voice is here tonight too. He is exposing his hairy belly while piling reduced-price potatoes onto the conveyor belt next to a double line of fizzy drinks. But then he clasps his hands together, makes smooth arm-waves and proficient wrist-flexes and speaks to the man of her dreams.

'Ooh, champagne! Someone's having a party. Any spare invites?'

The man of her dreams shoots him a quick, puzzled look and walks away, his white headphones nestled firmly in his ears. There must be international news on, a thought-provoking interview with a heart surgeon, or possibly one of the greatest arias (according to a Google search), 'La Forza del Destino', playing.

'Fancy-pants, always too busy to chat,' says the fat guy.

'Pardon?' Gosia is not impressed.

'Look at him. Look at that posh nelly!' He points his sausage finger in the direction of the exit. The double doors close and the man of her dreams is swallowed by the darkness of an inadequately lit car park.

Gosia sighs.

'Why would you have a go at him?'

'Me?' The man spits a little onto her weighing area, leans over attempting to clean up with his sleeve. She is quicker and removes his saliva with a cloth. He straightens his back and pulls his jeans up. 'He's the rude one. Didn't say thank you to you, didn't notice me, and acts like we've never met. But you know what? We use the same showers at the gym. I can't look that different with my pants on.'

'Five seventy-two. Do you have your loyalty card?'

2

Saturday morning. A small room with cream walls in a ground-floor flat with shared access to the garden but no access to the internet. Furnished with all the essentials: a single bed, a poly-cotton wardrobe, a multipurpose laminate chair in punchy orange, a tall and narrow chest of drawers and a single floating shelf alongside the window. A small mirror on top of a cabinet and three black notebooks on the shelf. A cobweb hugs the cylindrical lampshade. A heap of clothing sits on top of the chair. In the single bed among the sheets lies Gosia, naked. She makes herself come.

Key in the lock. The front door opens with a squeak and the rustling of plastic bags and two sets of heavy steps fill the flat. Gosia dries her fingers on the sheets. She is angry. Calm and collected, she told Lyndsey last month, 'Bringing boyfriends home on my only day off is a no-no. I need some rest.'

'Sure thing. Mark your days off on the calendar in red and he won't be here.'

She did. He is.

Lazy pop music streams through the flat. The air fills with the odour of frying onions. This is it. She will go to the kitchen and say, 'Leave now! I told you I need to relax. I've had another forty-five-hour week. I don't want to see your *boyfriend* here when I am trying to collect my thoughts. This is my day off.

When will you learn to respect my time? Since you started dating this wannabe detective you don't give a toss about anyone else. Grow up. Don't you have better things to do with your life than pretending to be in love?'

They will take their frying pan with sizzling onions and vacate the flat. She will calmly switch off the gas.

She puts on yesterday's clothes, starting with her socks. By the time she gets her top on, the air reeks of burnt, cheap meat. She needs a wee before she can confront them. She sprints through the corridor and bangs her head against Kev's arm as he exits the kitchen.

Lyndsey shouts through the music, 'Join us for food!'

Kev adds with a chuckle, 'Enough grub to feed a whole army.'

'Thanks, but I think I'll have cornflakes.'

She really needs to wee. Kev aims for the loo. They take the next three steps to the bathroom door in unison. She reaches the handle first.

He says, 'I'm desperate for a dump. Been carrying it with me all morning.'

She gives him a cold look. 'Well, you should've left it in town then.'

He forces his way through the door. 'Gosia, you're funny!' And locks it behind him. She turns away, defeated.

Lyndsey grabs her arm, drags her into the kitchen and whispers.

'You'll never believe it. Kev took me out for breakfast to this posh place on the high street. He booked the window table! I think there's something bigger on the cards. He keeps putting his hand in his pocket.'

Gosia raises her eyebrows and crosses her legs.

'Adjusting his balls?'

Lyndsey continues in a heavy mutter, shifting her body from foot to foot.

'I think it's a ring. We went past a jeweller last Sunday and he was pretending to look at the watches, but I know better. I pointed at this big, fat diamond ring and I said, "Those sorts of rings are great accessories for any outfit," and he says, "It goes with your eyes," and I say, "You must be joking," and he says, "I am not," and I say, "I always wanted one," and he says, "Dreams sometimes come true," and I say, "What's your dream?" and he says, "A Rolex."'

Gosia looks at her with sympathy.

'Maybe he wants to ask you for a loan?'

Lyndsey adds canned tomatoes to the pan and scratches the Teflon with a fork. Kev comes into the kitchen, his right hand firmly stuck in its usual place, his jeans pocket.

'It's a no-go zone. Total carnage!'

Gosia flares her nostrils.

'Did you use the spray?'

He looks at her, puzzled.

'What for?'

Lyndsey adds thoughtfully, 'Air fresheners give you cancer. It was on the news last week.'

Gosia wants cancer. She heads for the loo. That prick dried his hands on her towel again. She flushes the loo, picks up the aluminium bottle, walks the length of the room and sprays. Carcinogenic droplets fall onto her skin while she cleans the toilet seat with bleach.

'Complete losers, both of you,' she mutters to herself. 'Kev, you'll never be a detective! Your bouncer career is for life. And you, Lyndsey, you can drop your aspirations to apply acrylics to the nails of famous models. Beautiful women do not want people who have nothing to say anywhere near them!'

She will calm down, dissipate her urge to hit them with a toilet brush, walk out and face them both.

But now, she pees.

3

A small, council-run library. The room is packed with self-conscious teenagers full of acne and agitation queuing for their computer slots. A small group of boys on phones play games involving the spilling of virtual blood. Gosia has run to get here before the school crowd and she sits with damp armpits at the last and most exposed computer in the room. She logs into an online poetry platform and reads comments under her poem.

This time she nailed it. Writing about her ex, Andy, usually made her hyperventilate or sob, lose control and break something small and useful (a candlestick, a glass, a pencil). No more. She is ready to move on. She's found a person to move on to. This poem is closure, archiving Andy away together with his cheating smile and disgusting wife.

R_M wrote: 'What a load of self-pity. Get a self-help book, don't write poetry. You give me eye-ache! Apart from poor writing this makes for a poor story. Do we have to constantly read about female experiences? Give us something we can ALL relate to or actually better still just stop!'

Derek_Admin wrote: 'Keep our poetry platform free. Donate now.'

Rich_M wrote: 'Poetry written by women tends to present one-sided stories of broken hearts and sulking souls. Love affects us all and is a universal topic that only a few poets manage to convey without making it sound cheap, worn and flat. I suggest you read some Shakespeare for a start.'

Woman_with_a_moustache wrote: 'Ignore douchebags. Keep writing.'

RichardMutton_PoetForDarkTimes wrote: 'Better poem about love here.'

Love story

I hate love stories
Since my boyfriend left me for a pregnant woman

Their entanglement started
When I had a bit of a tough time

I did see their text messages
Love Fuck Love Fuck Love Fuck

They didn't feel bad or sorry

He took away my motivation
To be a good person

He moved in with her
When she was due

There is a gap in my teeth
That I try to fill with meaning:

I deserve better, plenty of fish, third time lucky

4

Lyndsey's room has pistachio walls and is rammed with old furniture that wouldn't pass for vintage. Large wardrobes with slimming mirrors, two bookshelves filled with DVDs and a floor lamp with a purple fabric lampshade sandwiched in between the furniture. A dressing table full of lotions covers half of the window. The remaining inches of the wall are Blu-Tacked with postcards from desirable destinations. A large double bed takes up the majority of the floor space, a fluffy blanket in pale pink draped across it. Gosia sits on the floor. She reads.

Sunday. I lost 1lb.

During breakfast as I was spreading jam on my toast GG told me that Vincent was killed in his kitchen. I was shocked. I often look at his house. It's large and pretty with big bay windows and a pear tree in blossom – something me and Kev dream about.

GG reckons that Vincent was found with a knife in his chest. A normal kitchen knife. I had a knife in my hand, and it wasn't sharp, but it had a pattern on the side and I had a dark thought about stabbing GG in her thin arse.

I asked GG who did it but didn't think she'd know. GG said it was the cleaner, and that it wouldn't have taken much to bump him off. Her voice was cold. It just rolled off her tongue.

I was shocked and had to hold onto the kitchen table while she just bit into her tiny apple. She always eats around me.

GG reckons the cleaner was the only person who had keys to Vincent's house and the knife had her fingerprints on it.

Cleverly, I told her that maybe that's because the cleaner looks after the place and it must be full of her DNA. Maybe the cleaner was the target? I actually felt smug as I said it. I saw a story like that on TV. GG gave me a 'You must be joking' look and asked about the prep for my holidays. I know all she wants to know is if I fit into my new swimming suit. Last week, I went mad and bought one three sizes too small. I'm going to only eat bananas and eggs five days a week. I want to see my bikini line when I look down this summer, it saves me so much money if I can do all the waxing myself.

Kev keeps telling me how much he loves my muffins, so I don't want to be stick-thin like GG. No wonder guys are not interested in her, she is flat like an ironing board. Kev thinks she's gay.

I told her that we booked our hotel and Kev has already printed a guide to five must-see places. I can't wait.

Gosia puts the diary where she found it, under Lyndsey's pillow, straightens the blanket and walks out.

5

A poky post office that fights to stay open by diversifying income streams: a metal rack with greetings cards, a bookcase filled with stationery, and a photocopying and scanning service. There are two innovative approaches. In one corner, a mobile phone repair shop is run from a half-table by a short, smiley man. A rainbow of plastic phone holders is displayed behind his head and a small selection of affordable second-hand mobile phones are exhibited on bleached paper in the bay window. He uses kinked leads to connect phones to his two-generations-old laptop.

In the other corner, a young, heavily tattooed woman offers face-painting services. Creased A4 photos of different designs are Blu-Tacked to the wall, the majority of them variations on popular superheroes and cute animals. A ring binder with the full offer travels between the queues.

Six square metres of the remaining floor space is a spaghetti junction of human mass, people queuing in different directions for different things. Everyone's talking.

Gosia waits for her turn to pay her utility bills. A monthly ordeal she doesn't dare to execute from the library computers and risk compromising her online security. She endures the queue full of old, needy people, who clearly come here for a free conversation. She's been waiting twelve minutes so far and only one person has been served.

Her phone rings. It is a jolly, old-fashioned ringtone that turns people's heads. The black word 'Mother' shines on the grey screen of her ancient mobile. Mother only calls if it's urgent. Gosia takes it.

'Hello?' Gosia assumes her outdoor speech, that of a shy and reserved person, a voice that, she hopes, will disappear amid the throb of the post office.

'Gosia, we need to talk.' Mother's loud voice seeps out of the speaker, attracting the attention of a middle-aged woman in front. Mother is on an inhale, ready with her next sentence. 'Your father and I are getting divorced.'

The seven words are like a series of bullets from a machine gun, piercing Gosia's thin layer of inner stability.

'He moved out and he's not moving back.' Mother delivers her words in the thick voice of someone who is coming round from a slight overdose of their favourite sedative.

The woman in front tilts her head to hear better. Gosia recognises the hungry side-gaze of the sensation-seeker and nearly makes a move for outdoors, but she is paralysed by the thought of needing to come back and rejoin the queue. It has finally started moving.

She shields the mouthpiece with her hand, turns sideways and asks, 'What happened?'

'He is not a man worthy of my love and attention,' says Mother. She has practised her lines, probably rehearsed them with Aunt Clara. 'I should've trusted my instincts earlier. Expelled him from my life years ago. It's an overdue spring-clean.'

Her parents never pretended to be in love. Their marriage, like a business deal, manifests itself through outdoor and indoor rituals: daily TV-watching, weekly churchgoing, the monthly trip to the tip, the annual garden party and a holiday at a seaside resort just after the season (to avoid high rates).

They do everything else separately: shopping, eating, sleeping. Their bedroom, two single beds pressed against opposite walls, is demarcated by a heavy rug pinned to the floorboards.

Gosia has a vague memory of them being close and maybe even smiling, but since 'The Calamity' the atmosphere in the family has changed. The fog of misery is permanent.

Mother often calls Dad names: loser, idiot, fool, dunce. Occasionally prat. Often twit. Sometimes muttonhead. Today she adds a new one.

'Your father is a liar and I don't want to see him again.'

'What did he lie about?' Gosia whispers.

'About everything,' Mother fires back.

Gosia wilts.

Mother and Dad together make home. A place she thinks about at times of distress. An actual location with a stable postcode, that elevates the gloom of a wobbly and unpredictable future. Somewhere to escape to, somewhere to go. Although she wouldn't want to stay there for long.

Her childhood room was repurposed long ago, but there is still space: the pantry, the understairs cupboard, a lean-to. The main thought forming in her injured mind is, Are they going to sell the house?

'I've decided I'm going to sell the house,' Mother says.

The middle-aged woman turns sideways for a better view and clearer access to Gosia's phone, badly hiding her interest in Gosia's parents' drama and the collapse of Gosia's support structure. She issues Gosia a half-smile, concerned and understanding, with a 'Life is so unexpected, keep strong' undertone.

Gosia turns to leave. She hopes for a swift exit but people, like bollards, stand in her way. She barges into a man selecting an envelope. She lifts her leg to avoid a buggy and then there is a slalom around a teenager with a dog and a woman with a shopping trolley. She evades their gaze, ignores multiple tut-tuts.

She is out, in the sharp, cough-inducing air of a failing high street.

'But Mother,' she presses her back against the brick wall by the out-of-order cash machine, searching for words that would offer a pause or a reset, 'what happened?'

'Gosia, I told you,' Mother snaps, her breathing heavy and agitated. 'You are always on his side,' she adds, her voice hurt. 'He lied to me, Gosia, and I don't want to have anything to do with him.'

There is an uncomfortable silence filled with distant ambulance sirens and the noise of cars.

Mother recovers, her voice now even.

'See you on Sunday. Bernie's coming too. We'll talk some more, but now I have to go.'

Mother hangs up. Gosia hesitates. Should she call her sister? Would Chrissy be able to talk freely with Mother on the other side of the wall? No.

Dad's lies must be the size of a prominent mountain range to cause Mother to risk the public failure of a divorce. Has he had an affair? Got deeper into debt? Committed a crime?

She stops herself from a courtesy call, Mother's accusation of her allegiance ringing in her ears. She opts for a polite text message, punches the buttons: 'Hi Dad, how are you?' and stares at her screen for the next ten minutes. Finally, there is a clunky reply:

'I'm OK. Come see me when you are next home. Will need your help. But. Don't worry. Nothing to worry about. Love, D'

6

A small, council-run library. The crime fiction and sci-fi sections act as a buggy park. Six children, three mothers and one father queue for accessible toilets. The children's area is congested with toddlers and their guardians. A young woman sings and claps: 'Mary had a little lamb; Its fleece was white as snow; And everywhere that Mary went; The lamb was sure to go.'

Four computer desks situated in the middle of the room are not being used. Gosia sits by a fifth, nearest to the window. She wears soft foam earplugs for everyday use. She hasn't slept. During the night her limbs shook as her breath accelerated. Her cold sweat left yellow patches on her mattress protector. In the bleak hours of early morning she passed a loose stool. She googles 'remedy for anxiety'. OurDailyBread.org provides an answer:

'The remedy for anxiety, of course, is to trust in our Creator, Jesus Christ.'

Aunt Clara trusts Jesus more than her family. That's why she shares her pension with the parish. Google offers a cheaper remedy – only £38.95 for the High Complex Calm Tonic. It doesn't sound like a lot for a peaceful mind but it only buys a 50ml bottle; it wouldn't last a week.

The young woman sings: 'Twinkle, twinkle, little star; How I wonder what you are.'

Further search results take her to the politics section of an American daily newspaper:

'In truth the only remedy for anxiety is personal and has little or nothing to do with homeland security. Depending on the kind of person you are, one of the following steps might help:

1. Talk to someone who really listens. Share how you feel and ask for realistic feedback.
2. Avoid talking to people who fan the flames of worry.'

Gosia doesn't have much luck finding real listeners. The majority of people she knows sit comfortably in the second category: her mother, her sister, her brother, her flatmate, her aunt, her colleagues, her ex-colleagues. This only leaves three people: Dad, Anna and Andy.

Dad's reply left her deeply worried.

Gosia and Anna are not on speaking terms and there is an Anna-shaped cavity in Gosia's body. They were friends. They understood each other. They shared secrets. Anna would always tell her if she had salad stuck in her teeth. She would never leave her in the bar on her own. She always replied to her texts.

Andy broke her heart and then told her not to contact him again.

'Hi Andy, long time no see. I know you told me not to contact you again, but this is different. My parents are divorcing and I'm turning thirty this summer, not even sure if anyone remembers. Do you? I found this list we wrote during our last holiday. It has all the things we were going to do before thirty. Have a baby, buy a car, own a flat, visit Paris, swim in the ocean, go on a hot air balloon ride. Reads like a dream. Don't worry, I am not asking you to get back together. I just wondered if you have time to meet up and share a piece of my birthday cake. Take care, Gosia x x'

She presses send. The young woman sings and claps: 'If you're happy and you know it, clap your hands.'

There is an immediate response from Andy's account.

'Leave my husband alone. Margaret'

7

A small room with pistachio-coloured walls, dotted with postcards. The room bursts with furniture and tat. Gosia sits on a large double bed covered with a terry throw in pale pink. She chose this over a night at the cinema (alone). She reads.

Tuesday. I lost 2lbs! But I am sick of hard-boiled eggs.

The police came in asking about Vincent. I told them what a sweet old gentleman he was, always, 'Hello, how are you, miss, have a nice day.' And he let me eat his pears.

But GG told them all about his late-night visitors, young women in high heels and see-through dresses arriving in taxis. In groups of two or three. Pissed and falling all over the pavement. I didn't think this was appropriate (or accurate). Why not let Vincent rest in peace?

She also told them about the cleaner, that she was young and foreign, and that Vincent once shouted at her. I suggested that the cleaner probably stole from him and told them again what a charming and calm man he was.

I could tell it pleased GG, to tell all that to the police. But she didn't tell them that she used to clean there too. I bit my tongue.

GG even took a card to call with more details if she remembered anything else. Sure she will. She remembers exactly how much money I owe to the kitty and whose turn it is to clean the bathroom. She remembers everything.

I told Kev all about it and he decided to start his own investigation, says he's going to get to the bottom of things.

Vincent's son turned up. He looks nothing like him. Muscular, tall and slim. He never visited before. Must live far away and be a busy person. He took all the furniture but chucked all of Vincent's other stuff. And there is a large 'For Sale' sign attached to the porch.

GG said he only wants his money. But it was her first running across the street to search through Vincent's boxes before the clearance people showed up. I found fourteen DVDs and a couple of really nice designer shirts that Kev can fit into when he loses a stone or two. GG made multiple trips but only came back with one of Vincent's pictures. She hung it above the toilet! A very pretty framed sunset with a couple by the seaside, with cliffs and a boat in the distance. Kev says it makes him want to piss for longer.

I've known her for years but still GG is so hard to get. I never know if she is happy or sad. Kev thinks she needs a good shag. I've learnt not to say too much. There are things that clearly upset her. She goes to her room and slams the door.

Anything to do with Andy is a no-no, and anything to do with Anna is a no-no too. Andy, fair play, he left her and got married the next month. I can never mention how cute his babies are. But Anna? They were inseparable! And now they aren't even friends on Facebook!

We all met stewarding at a dreadful summer festival, stuck for hours in a car park in the pouring rain. Andy was making us all laugh and Anna was sharing her endless supply of flapjacks. I thought Andy would go for Anna but it was GG who caught him in her net.

I wax Anna all the time and even give her mates' rates, but she doesn't talk about GG. It's like GG was never around. Shocking really, as I was always jealous of how close they were, drinking from the same straw and wearing matching tops on a night out. But that's GG for you, she can destroy the strongest of friendships.

Gosia puts the diary where she found it, in a shoebox under the bed, straightens the pink fabric and walks out. Lyndsey moved in just as Andy moved out, almost two years ago, and since then money is permanently missing from the kitty. There are soapy smears on the bathtub. It is not her turn. She marks in red her days off on the calendar. Draws a little flower around the circled number and writes GG. A coded reminder that in a few months it is her birthday.

8

A shabby semi-detached house on a treeless street in a small town only fifty-five minutes from London on the fast train. The number 137 is painted in pink nail varnish on a grey front door. On the drive stands a selection of bins and an aged Nissan. The window ledges are filled with dwarf daffodils in full bloom. Gosia presses a buzzer.

A woman in an apron opens the door.

'Finally, you're here! Chrissy miscarried last night. She's not herself, all nerves. Just don't ask her about it. Can't stand another discussion about the *pressure* I apparently put her under. Could you look after the twins? I'm exhausted! And Bernie is *finally* bringing his new fiancée. He texted me her name.' Mother takes a mobile with large buttons out of her apron pocket. Gosia stares at the floor, hides her moist eyes.

'How do you pronounce it? Itchybeer? He sent no pictures. I worry she might be foreign. She'll sit next to you. I've made pie and crumble. A roast for seven people is out of the question. Give us a kiss.' Gosia leans over, her mother shouts. 'Oh, look! Bernie's here. In a black cab. Good lord, she's taller than him. Bernie! Bernie!'

A short, stocky man in formal clothes exits the car with a multi-coloured bouquet in his hand, a prominent M&S sticker glued to the foil. A tall, stick-thin woman in a skimpy black dress and killer heels is by his side. Both of them are heavily tanned.

'Bernie! I haven't seen you for months! Look at my boy. So brown!' Mother walks out in her slippers to meet them.

Bernie extends the flowers in her direction.

'Ma, these are for you.'

'Oh, Bernie! You shouldn't have! Flowers! How wonderful! What a glorious selection.'

Bernie grins.

'Ma, this is Aitziber.'

'Oh, nice to meet you, Itchybeer! I've heard a lot about you! I'm so pleased you could join us for tea. Gosia, run to the kitchen for a vase.'

Gosia doesn't move, Bernie points at her.

'This is my sister, Gosia.'

The fiancée offers her hand in a practised way that exposes her diamond ring. 'Gosia, the thin sister?'

Gosia looks at Bernie.

'You must be the tall fiancée.'

Aitziber laughs.

'I'm addicted to high *hills*. Bernard doesn't mind, don't you? Women in flats look so boring.'

Bernie looks up into his fiancée's eyes. Gosia looks at her trainers. Mother looks at Bernie. Fiancée looks ahead.

Mother breaks the silence. 'Come in, come in. You must be hungry. I made pie, your favourite, Bernie! Itchybeer, I can give you the recipe, my dear. It's proper Irish food. Bernie would kill for this pie when he was a boy.'

'Oh, I don't cook,' Aitziber says lightly. 'I can't face kitchen after a long day at work. Bernard doesn't mind, don't you?'

Mother stops in the doorway.

'So, who cooks?' She directs the question to the fiancée.

Bernie replies.

'We eat out a lot. Aitziber likes oriental cuisine.'

Mother persists.

'And when you are in?'

Fiancée concludes, 'Oh, we have takeouts.'

Mother is speechless.

Gosia leads the way down the corridor and asks, 'And what do you do for a living?'

Aitziber replies happily, 'I'm a shop assistant, in a bridal shop. I fit wedding dresses.'

9

Monday. Hazy and early. A commuter train to London. The train is fifty-five minutes from the destination and is packed. People in tailored clothing who left their houses in charming villages and abandoned their cars in multistorey car parks sleep, eat their early-bird breakfast deals and check their emails. Laptops are open, iPads and iPhones swiped.

A man with a manicured beard makes a phone call. He starts a trend, others swiftly join in.

'Print three copies of the report I've just sent through.'

'Make sure Williams reads it before he goes to sales.'

'Sort out my flight for tomorrow, for as early as you can.'

'Get me Harriet on the line when she arrives.'

'Pack Alfie a banana.'

'Forward the spreadsheet to the board.'

'Allocate extra funds to the project.'

'Get Martha something nice, twenty quid tops, though.'

'Organise a meeting with Boris. This week. No buts.'

'But why is my mother calling you to arrange that?'

Gosia's pressed into her seat, all crumpled and stiff after a night on the sofa in Mother's living room. She sits next to a woman applying make-up from scratch, a bit too much foundation, eyelashes heavy with mascara. The woman moves on to reading a glossy magazine.

On every page are pictures of semi-famous people who have lost weight, gained weight, made babies, divorced, worn the wrong dress. Gosia reads along for a bit.

A guy to the right analyses spreadsheets on his tablet. An older man by the window leafs through a newspaper featuring adverts of Gosia's supermarket and a gym chain. At the bottom of the page is a free home-delivery coupon next to a pert teenager promising a new-found confidence in your body.

The crowd shifts further in at the next station and she feels someone's piercing gaze on her. She examines her thumbs before slowly lifting her head. It's a woman, mature, creased face and heavily pregnant. A 'Baby on Board' badge pinned to her left breast. She gives Gosia a stare that lifts her out of her seat. Gosia shifts her feet to the aisle and lifts her bag into her arms, while the woman takes her place, manoeuvring herself into the seat and exhaling like a whale.

'Gosia?' A voice trills from the depths of the carriage. Gosia freezes.

She hates being singled out like this; her odd Polish name spoken out loud across the many shoulders. She has always wished she was a Mary, a Lucy, a Jane. Her siblings don't carry their foreign origins as bluntly as she has to.

She turns around slowly. It's Picky Becky in a sensible navy-blue dress, pushing through the suits to get closer. In high stilettos, she wedges herself between the two men opposite Gosia.

'I knew it must be you. Long time no see! What are you up to these days?' she bellows.

Becky gives her a wry smile, her pout weighed down with lip gloss.

Gosia shields herself with her bag and responds politely in a forced whisper.

'I'm well, thank you. How are things with you?'

Becky has no such hang-ups; she takes pleasure in sharing details from her predictably successful life.

'Oh, same old, same old. We just moved to a larger house, I got promoted at work, Julian started prep school and Jimmy and I have no idea where to go on holiday this year. Any suggestions? I hear the Basque country is becoming quite a destination.'

Clearly Becky must still follow Bernie on Facebook. Gosia only learnt yesterday that Bernie's fiancée, Aitziber is Basque. She contributes her limited knowledge, at a whisper.

'The food is supposed to be delicious.'

'So, you haven't been yet?' Becky barks, eyes glimmering with joy.

'Not yet,' Gosia replies.

'I bet neither has Bernard. He always hated flying.'

Becky says it using a voice suggesting that this fact alone could ruin a solid relationship.

'I hear he's *finally* getting married.' Her comment cuts through the remaining pocket of air between them like a razor. 'Mum told me your parents are going all out and downsizing to give him a proper party.' Picky Becky pierces Gosia with her eyes, scanning for answers.

'Um-hum.' Gosia avoids her gaze and looks at Becky's right cheek instead, paying close attention to an area enhanced with blusher, an area that she would like to smack.

'It's so last decade. These days it's all about boutique weddings in remote locations, involving only the closest family.' Picky Becky delivers this with satisfaction. 'But I guess you Irish folk and Polish lot like it large and loud.' She ha-has theatrically.

Gosia holds her right hand with her left, suppressing a rabbit punch.

The wedding has been discussed only briefly, Mother insisting on a 'proper Irish affair' and Aitziber describing, in impenetrable adjectives, a traditional Basque ceremony that seemed to include dancing in the streets.

'But I'm paying for it,' Mother had erupted mid-meal.

'And that's why we are getting married in England,' Aitziber had replied coldly.

After that, they had collectively chewed and nothing was said about Chrissy's frequent sobs and endless trips to the loo. Mother had dispensed Ibuprofen into Chrissy's hand too frequently. The twins had sat under the table, holding onto Chrissy's legs. Gosia had waited for a good moment to whisk her sister off to a quiet corner, to hug her, to speak in private, to mop up her pretty wet face, but that moment had never arrived.

Dad's Polish side had not even been mentioned. There was also no discussion about the sale of the house, but Gosia had spotted some paperwork, 'Equity Release' printed in bold on top, hidden behind the bread bin. She had also spied a perfectly fine bouquet of flowers, red roses, in the bin, foil still wrapped around the stems. She had suspected they were an olive branch held out to Mother by Dad.

The train arrives at her stop in Zone 3. Gosia squeezes forward, getting ready to leave.

'My stop,' she says.

Becky lifts a card out of her leather handbag and deposits it, with her manicured hand, in Gosia's palm.

'Would love to catch up. Give me a call. Maybe lunch some time? There are tons of delightful cafes around Bank. My treat!'

Gosia must be a loser in her eyes, not good enough to even clean her office, but Picky Becky was always thirsty for gossip and her connection to the Golab family runs deep. She is invested.

Gosia nods and steps onto the platform. She always leaves the train three stops early to make the rest of the journey on the bus to save her pennies.

She is on time to catch the number 29 and travels in the opposite direction to the morning traffic. The bus driver is singing a song, a couple at the back are having a row, a bloke with an old polystyrene cup in his hand is sitting in a seat for the pregnant and disabled. He stinks. There must be a group of school children upstairs. Their feet thump as they run between the seats.

Gosia sits at the front and considers Becky's card. Her job title includes, among other words, 'start-up', 'executive' and 'manager'. Picky Becky is an old acquaintance, childhood neighbour, Bernie's ex, greedy cow and a burden. Gosia won't be lunching with her but she keeps the card anyway.

The morning mist lingers, and she watches the streets. She is not in a mad rush; she starts her shift at 10 a.m. The driver comes to the chorus, 'No woman, no cry!' He smiles, shows his teeth with a prominent gap at the front, gets to the next stop and with a shake of his head welcomes a passenger with a tatty shopping trolley. She is home.

10

A busy library. An argument by the counter over charges for the late return of new-release DVDs. A resentful customer throws his card at the librarian and leaves. People watch.

KarenStevensWrites wrote: 'Fresh and new perspective. I identify as middle-class, so I greatly appreciated this new point of view although I stand by my choices that include a mortgage, children and a fair bit of exercise! Is that a middle class only approach though? I perceive it as universal.'

R_M wrote: 'Working class poet! Ha! Wish you went to Uni now?'

Woman_with_class wrote: 'I enjoyed the narrative nature of this poem. Great structure and good repetition. Defo a poet to watch!'

RichardMutton_PoetForDarkTimes wrote: 'Quality poetry here. New book of my poems out soon. Would like a copy? Pre-order here.'

Rich_M wrote: 'Is it enough now to identify as a "working class poet" to gain instant recognition? Mediocre at best.'

Middle Class People

I don't tell middle class people
What I do for a living

They don't comprehend low pay and long hours
Somewhere between primary and secondary school
They made sensible choices

I don't envy middle class people
Their cars, homes, children
Accessorised with mortgage, veg box and a nanny
False stability, deceptive reassurance that
You made sensible choices

I don't ask middle class people
For advice, for help, for a loan
On their way to the promised land via Pilates
But I don't swim there
I made a sensible choice

11

A large, unethical supermarket open 24/7 (10 a.m. to 4 p.m. on Sundays). The cereal aisle is congested with a late delivery. An organic muesli variety and gluten-free puffs are frantically packed onto shelves. Gosia stacks up the cheap and cheerful cornflakes range, she dents each thin cardboard box with her thumb. She distributes some of the boxes straight into people's hands. She prefers tills and the separation of the conveyor belt between the bodies, hers and others.

The aisle is full of dangers. Pinched bottoms, a full-frontal attack from a man who tried to press his bollocks into her back as she reached for the top shelf ('Do you want a hand, love?'), a child who vomited carrot and chicken onto the floor and massaged some of it into her calf when she tried to clean it up. Stale breath. Poking.

She is not in the mood for a chat when the man of her dreams walks into her aisle. She never sees him here this early. He looks perplexed and is evidently perturbed by the commoners gathering around the cornflakes. She knows what he needs. She abandons her task and walks over to the fit and healthy section, reaches for quinoa and acai berry porridge and delivers it into his hands.

'Looking for this?' she says with a coy smile.

He removes his earplugs, scans the box and then her. He gives the box back. He lifts his mouth corners, moistens his lips and almost smiles.

'I'm looking for decaf organic coffee beans. Hundred per cent arabica. Strength five. Ideally Ethiopian.'

She knows what he wants. He bought that coffee a month ago. She tosses the porridge among the Choc-Pops and gently touches his sleeve. 'Come with me.'

He follows. She can feel the imprint of rich cotton left behind on her index finger. She can almost smell his menthol breath on her neck. They walk together. They are a team. She leads.

The hot beverages aisle is under attack. A large group of pensioners queue for a sample of instant coffee from a taster table.

'Doris, this smells delightful!'

'Could I have two, my love? These cups are awfully small.'

Silly Molly, the Saturday girl, with big eyes and a small brain, gives coffee away willy-nilly and doesn't notice that the pensioners are cheating. They queue more than once, add heaps of demerara to espressos and hide extra sugar packets in their coat pockets. Molly distributes coffee with her beaming smile and enthusiastically repeats, 'Only one ninety-nine a jar.' The greedy pensioners look carefully at the label and loudly express their views.

'Hazel, you can get thirty cups from one jar! If you use half a spoon that's sixty!'

'It has fifty per cent less caffeine, you won't shake!'

Gosia makes a parting through the group with her hands. With surgical precision, she aims for the top shelf where top products at top prices are stored. From a wide range of brands she selects an Ethiopian arabica from a sustainable plantation, 100% organic,

100% fair trade. She turns around with a killer smile, but the man of her dreams is not behind her.

The old bags must have eaten him up, trodden on top of his ironed trousers and destroyed his immaculate haircut. No, she spots him. There he is. Standing in front of Silly Molly and sipping instant coffee out of a miniature cup designed for a portion of ketchup. He is smiling towards Mr Brown-Swinton, an elderly fellow with a grand past and clearly a troubled present who spends his weekends between the sampling tables and the supermarket cafe. Gosia approaches. Brown-Swinton holds the man of her dreams' other hand in his long welcome.

'And then this young man cracked a bone in my spine and . . . MIRACLE! I could walk again. I am telling you, Doris, nothing finer has happened to me since 1966 than a visit to this man's clinic.'

Brown-Swinton shakes his hand a few more times, winks and helps himself to another mini coffee cup from the stand.

'Well, thank you, Mr Swinton, always a pleasure to bump into a happy customer. Good to see you and,' he turns his lips, eyes and forehead towards Molly, 'thank you for the drink. I will take a jar.'

The man of her dreams scans the crowd. He locates Gosia, locks his eyes with hers and blinks meaningfully. She holds onto his coffee and lifts it to her chest, making sure the bag is in his eye-view, her bosom providing an enticing background. His lips part again, and he lifts his hand extending two fingers into a peace sign. She is quick to grasp it: he needs two bags! She quickly returns to the shelf to fetch it.

When she is back, Brown-Swinton is raising his hand with a cup in the air as if to toast.

'Ah! Our Molly here treats us to delicacies every week. We had delicious cheese bites with an extravagant dip just the other day. We're here to support Molly's efforts. It's a small community, something new to try and lovely people to talk to!'

Molly laughs.

The man of her dreams throws the cup into the bin.

'I really must dash. Clients are waiting. Once again, thank you. Goodbye!'

He turns to leave. He walks towards Gosia, first inserting his earplugs. That podcast about sustainable ways of living, an audio recording of a classic Russian novel (Dostoyevsky? Tolstoy? Pushkin? – that's what her library had on offer) or a life-affirming concerto by Debussy, 'Fantasy for Piano and Orchestra', is back on. He extends his arm towards her. His hand, like a toy grabber in a slot machine, lifts up the coffee bags from her palms. He pauses briefly to mouth 'THANK YOU'. The intensity of his breath, saturated with vanilla notes, nearly makes her swoon. She leans towards him and he gently pats her shoulder, sending prickles down her spine. She exhales, ecstatic as he winks at her. It is a sexy wink that makes her want to take her clothes off and lock them both in the broom cupboard. As she recovers, with one hand holding onto a display cabinet, he heads for the empty, under-five-products self-service lane, swiftly pays for the coffees, dumps the jar in the food bank box and promptly leaves with his beans in hand.

Brown-Swinton is in full swing now: 'Magician! That's what I would call him, not chiropractor. You must go to his clinic, it's just down the road, near the park. Molly dear, what are we having tomorrow?'

12

An empty library with extended opening hours for the Easter revision period. There is a heavy reek of urine in the air. Gosia sits by the screen, breathes into her roll-neck.

KarenStevensWrites wrote: 'Writing about love is never easy. I can sense your struggle. Portraying the subject of love can be difficult and I enjoyed how you concentrated on his skills, good heart and positive attitude, not his body – which would be typical for poems about love interests written from a male perspective. A very interesting attempt although there is room for improvement.'

RichardMutton_PoetForDarkTimes wrote: 'Read my poem ABOUT REAL LOVE here.'

Woman_with_experience wrote: 'Intriguing!'

R_M wrote: 'THERE IS MENTION OF A CHEST! A female gaze objectifies too. Pathetic.'

TORM3NT wrote: 'It will wear off.'

The Man of My Dreams

The man of my dreams doesn't fall for cheap tricks
He always has freshly baked bread in his basket

ODD HOURS

The man of my dreams has hands that do good
He regularly buys cans of beans for a food bank

The man of my dreams has a large heart
His shirt tightens on his chest when he keys in his pin

The man of my dreams says thank you like I love you
I watch his lips for more.

13

A small bedroom crowded with objects. A heap of tops in sizes L, XL and XXL are piled up on the bed. Gosia perches herself on the dressing table between the foundation pots. She reads.

I lost 2lb but gained it back over the weekend. Not sure why. I didn't let myself go. We only had a burger each and I avoided the sides and had the smallest of ice cream portions with barely any chocolate in it.

Vincent's son came round for a chat. I kept him by the door. And he leaned forward. Said he wanted to have a private chat.

GG appeared behind me and invited him in. But she didn't ask me first. This is a man we know nothing about, he could rape us both and leave and no one would know.

She even asked him if he wanted tea, but he didn't want any. He sat, although she did not offer him a seat and we were both standing.

He wanted to talk about his dad's house. It's for sale because he doesn't need another property in London, and they had viewings but nothing came of them because of bad press and people talking that it was a murder. It wasn't, he told us. It was an accident.

GG asked what happened. He hesitated and asked if he could be totally honest with us, and GG said yes.

I nearly said that GG knew Vincent well, that she cleaned for him before that Bulgarian cleaner arrived, but he started to talk.

First he said it was self-defence. Then he said the evidence was inconclusive.

His dad made some comments to the cleaning lady, she misunderstood, her English wasn't very good. He approached her, maybe grabbed her. She was confused, a bit scared, thought he was attacking her, maybe attempting a rape. How could he, he was eighty-two. But it doesn't matter now.

He told us that he was not pressing charges. That his dad had had incidents with women in the past, that he was a character, liked women and women usually liked him. It's terrible that he died like that, but it's important to stop calling it a murder. An accident like that shouldn't be pushing the price of the house down below market value.

He asked if we could help with that. If people knock on the door and ask questions, could we say it was nothing sinister? He sent letters to newspapers. He just wants to straighten things up, not ruin the sale.

I felt for the man, so I said sure. Vincent was a nice guy, all smiles and manners. I can't believe they let that woman off with no trial and like a million years in jail.

GG did not even nod. Vincent's son stood up and shook my hand. I closed the door behind him. GG locked herself in the bedroom and I wonder did she help, did she sharpen the knife?

Had to repeat it all to Kevin word for word, so he could include it in his investigation file that's getting bulkier every day. He's done tons of research already. He went round for a viewing of Vincent's house behind my back to see the site of the murder and take good shots. I know he kept it secret to protect me, he knew I would cry my eyes out looking at Vincent's floors.

Andy and Margaret surprised me too. They wrote a book! It is all about how to have a happy life. It covers everything: work, money, friendship and what they are so good at: love. All professionally done and available on Amazon for tablets but I thought about getting a printed copy. These are 'on demand' and Andy complained the cover doesn't stick well to the bulk of the book. That put me off, as it's pricey. I'm waiting to see if he gives me a discount, as I'm one of their case studies! It was so refreshing to spend an afternoon doing Margaret's nails and talk about what I want from my future. She thinks I should go freelance but that would be such a ball-ache. Me? A businesswoman? Kev thinks it's mad too. I'd rather be employed by a fancy spa.

That supermarket where GG works is always full of people, it must be a good place to pull but GG is still single. It's been two years now since Andy left and she still hasn't moved on and is unpleasant to be around. Kev thinks she's Catholic but doesn't want to admit it.

Gosia puts the diary back into the yellow box with 'Photographs' written on the side on top of a wardrobe, and leaves.

14

A council-run library at lunchtime. The reading area is heaving with people eating: prodding pasta salads with plastic forks, munching on triangles of bread and cheese. There is a decent queue to a self-checkout machine but plenty of free computers. Gosia has been here for ages – she lied about the nature of her research to a staff member and got a free half-hour extension.

The online search didn't take long; she pretty much found the book immediately. The title, for a start, is sickening: *The Bulletproof Guide to Sorting Out Your Life: Work, Money, Free Time, Family, Friendship and Love.* All the supporting reviews are clearly fake and by friends. 'This book has changed my life – Anna' reads one. Gosia isn't fooled. How could it? It was released last week! 'Thanks to these pages, I've finally decided what I want to do with my life – Kev', 'Days after reading this book, I found true love! – Lyndsey'.

It doesn't take much to figure out that the book has been self-published. The cover design includes three types of font and an oversaturated picture of Andy and Margaret on their wedding day. All the reviewers can be traced to people Gosia knows, has heard about or is vaguely aware of – Andy and Margaret's family, friends, extended network of colleagues, ex-flatmates and neighbours. A printed copy costs nearly fifteen quid and a digital version only three but requires an expensive tablet, an object apparently 'Frequently bought together' with the ebook itself.

Gosia's mouse cursor hovers over the box to close the browser.

She is not going to spend money to spy on Andy's life and good fortune.

She is done with him.

It is a closed chapter and she is ready to move on with her life.

She is in love with someone else.

There are other books she could read.

There is nothing new she could learn from Andy.

There is NOTHING she wants to learn from Margaret.

She spots a hyperlink.

So, Andy and Margaret have also created a dedicated website using a free blogging platform. The same garish picture welcomes the visitor; it spins when the mouse cursor hovers over it. There is a tab titled 'Try before you buy' that attracts Gosia's eye. The page includes a 150-word excerpt from the book that outlines its groundbreaking concept to 'Not just fix one area of your life but tackle them all together.' An approach that, Andy and Margaret assure the reader, 'Will lead to eternal bliss through the six perfectly balanced elements of a good life: work, money, free time, family, friendship and love.'

The Bulletproof Guide to Sorting Out Your Life:
Work, Money, Free Time, Family, Friendship and Love.
Introduction

You may not admit it to yourself, but you want it all: interesting work, good money, lots of free time, a happy family, fulfilling friendships and everlasting love. We wrote this book because we know what you are going through! You may have a great relationship with your mum and plenty of time on your hands, but you usually run out of money by the middle of the month and suspect your boyfriend is a cheater. We know how it feels when life is not quite what you expected. But we found a way to fix it. How? Read on!

Margaret worked all hours. She was a workaholic and would align all aspects of her life to fit her work pattern. She was jolted out of it when Andy arrived on her ward.

Andy suffered from debilitating depression. He was deeply affected by his previous, toxic relationship. His confidence undermined . . .

At the bottom of the page is a big button that takes Gosia to an online shop where she can purchase the book as a PDF for a fiver via PayPal. Her blood is boiling and her head spins but she must resist. She can't give them the pleasure of becoming their reader.

15

A small front garden fenced off with a sprawling dog rose, occupied by plastic bins, a metal bike shed used to store a buggy and a rickety wooden bench pushed against the wall. The nearby gas meters tick and hum.

Gosia tentatively sits on the bench, pressing firmly into her feet, anticipating a fall. She supports herself with her left hand; the right is pressed to her head, holding a phone. It is her fourth phone call today, her fourth attempt at a calm conversation with Chrissy, but she is constantly crying into Gosia's ear. Gosia listens, occasionally murmuring soft sounds that make little sense together: 'shh', 'I know', 'ohh'. Her body stiffens with each of Chrissy's gasps for air. Because she doesn't know. Her own experience is limited. The noises Chrissy makes add up to a tune of loss Gosia is glad she hasn't encountered herself.

Chrissy's speech is distorted.

'I've just. Lost a. Baby. And we'll. Have to. Move out.'

'Mother might not sell after all. She loves having you all around.'

Gosia has done her research. 'Equity release' doesn't require moving, and she knows exactly where the received lump sum is going to be invested. She read on for long enough to understand that her own inheritance might amount to a sum enabling her to buy a plastic cutlery set rather than a down payment. She hasn't slept.

Her body shook with internal rage, a commotion within her chest, a recurring thought of strangling her brother. She had eventually calmed herself down. It's not his fault that he's Mother's favourite.

'Where is Dad?' Gosia asks as soon as Chrissy's sobs subside.

Chrissy clears her nose and throat and speaks from afar, her phone resting somewhere on her lap or a nearby surface.

'Where's who?'

'Dad!' Gosia repeats, impatient now. She didn't get to ask that question on Sunday. She was mad with Bernie acting as if it was totally normal for their father to be absent, his seat taken up by his son; for Chrissy to be in spasms; for Aitziber to draw wedding plans with her diamond finger; for Mother to be spending ten grand on a one-night event.

Chrissy lowers her voice, as if sharing a secret.

'At the allotments.'

'What the hell happened?' Gosia had witnessed a number of her parents' rows but none of them had such dire consequences.

'I don't know,' Chrissy whispers, 'what *exactly* happened. But it was just after a parcel from Poland arrived. It was for Dad, and Mum opened it. Whatever she found in there made her go mad. Dad left the same afternoon.'

'Did he say anything?' Gosia prods.

'Just lots of "I'm sorrys" and then he took that box and left.' Chrissy exhales.

'Have you seen him since?' Gosia asks.

'Are you mad?' Chrissy is nearly inaudible now. 'I live here with my children! Do you want me to go on the street? I can't live on an oil rig with Duncan!'

They both go mute. Contacting Dad is a mortal betrayal. Mother won't have it any other way. Chrissy's life enabled by residence in two out of three bedrooms in Mother's house makes it too much to lose.

'But he must've been back,' Chrissy adds. 'His things keep disappearing. First his raincoat and wellies, and then the toolbox.' She pauses. 'On Saturday morning, when Mum was out, Dad came through to the kitchen. He took some clothes and a blanket.'

'How do you know?' Gosia wonders if Chrissy might have helped.

'He spoke to the boys. Told them his visit was a secret. It took some work, but they shared the secret with me.'

John and Paul adore their granddad, who taught them to call him Ja-Ja. They play with him like he is a horse, a climbing frame, a target, a drawing board, a clown.

The days are longer, warmer and drier, but the nights are still cold. The shed at the allotments has no wood burner or electricity. There are only some basic facilities: a compost toilet shared with other users, an outdoor tap. The structure itself is mainly used to store a wheelbarrow, some ancient spades and rakes, a rusty barbecue. Gosia shivers. She can't recall if there is a window or if the shed is large enough for a grown man to sleep in it.

'What can we do?' asks Chrissy.

'Nothing.' Gosia makes up her mind. No point bringing Chrissy into it. Mother can get anything out of her with one pointed look or a threat to not pay for a weekly food bill. 'They have to sort it out themselves,' she adds, to cover her tracks.

'But he's our dad!' Chrissy gasps, on the verge of tears.

'Mother must have her reasons. Whatever Dad did there is no point getting in between them,' Gosia concludes authoritatively.

Chrissy mewls. 'I'm so. Scared. And I. Lost a. Baby. And. What if. I have. To move. Out?'

Gosia softens, issues more calming noises at a low frequency, creating a phantom shoulder for Chrissy to cry on. She rocks gently to the tune of someone drilling the road, that first intensifies and then abruptly stops.

16

Gosia logs in.

Kevin Harris via mobile: 'Piss off London'

6 people like it.

Anna Walker says, 'Move out!'

Kevin Harris is now friends with Margaret Bark-Knight and 3 others.

Kevin updated his relationship profile to: 'In a relationship with Lyndsey Oates'

35 people like it.

Andy Knight via mobile: 'Finally dude! So happy 4 u 2!'

Gosia logs out.

17

A moderately busy library with a comparatively good selection of crime fiction on a fairly sunny day. Gosia sits by the computer, hands on keyboard. She tolerates the noise.

TheBestOf_Suzie wrote: 'I know men like that and I'm petrified of them. I'm also very worried for my daughter (she is not even two).'

Rich_M wrote: 'I'm deeply concerned that this poem is freely available to read on this prestigious poetry platform. It is a call to harm and it should be removed.'

KarenStevensWrites wrote: 'The depth of this poem is not apparent on the first reading. I'd encourage you to be precise though. *Doodah* is open to misinterpretation. See *Rich_M's* comment above. I assume you mean *sharp words* not *sharp knives*.'

Vultures

Bad men do not grow out of it
Hold hands on tits
Without invitations

Beyond good looks
and stiff tools
Against the rules and regulations

They come in all shapes, sizes, ages
Tube drivers
Shop managers
Neighbours

Sharp doodahs teach them a lesson

18

A large, unethical supermarket open 24/7, promising to price-match all branded products. Gosia is blocking an entrance to the self-checkout area with her weedy body. With her firm gaze, she's encouraging customers to wait in line until she calls 'Next' and points at the free machine. She is only metres away from a customer service desk that is unseasonably quiet. At the desk Obscene Doreen is teaching Silly Molly how to issue refunds. Molly sweats. If she completes the training and retains the information she might be moved from her tasting table to a better-paid job. Gosia suspects Obscene Doreen has already hinted that, to fast-track her promotion, Molly should let the manager put his hand under her skirt.

Gosia freezes. The man of her dreams approaches the desk with a bag in hand. Doreen and Molly pause the training and push their bosoms onto the counter.

'Hello, hello,' Doreen puts on her sweet voice solely reserved for customers that she fancies, 'how can I help you today?'

The man of Gosia's dreams empties the bag. It's a linen set from their top organic cotton range, in light blue, and a limited-edition copper saucepan with lid.

'Hi, I'm returning these,' he offers to the narrow gap between Doreen and Molly's arms, clearly aiming his request at Gosia. He extracts a carefully folded receipt and his credit card from the soft leather satchel suspended from his shoulder.

Gosia abandons her location and moves behind the counter.

'The purchases didn't satisfy you?' Doreen takes the items from his hands, as Gosia squeezes past her large backside and gives him a weak wave.

'It's not the quality that I expected,' says the man of her dreams and taps his card on the counter. He must not have seen Gosia yet.

Doreen passes the goods to Molly.

'Please check these haven't been used and we'll process the refund.'

It is clear from where Gosia stands that the linen set has been removed from, and then squashed back into, the plastic sleeve: all four corners are creased, and a piece of cardboard covering the pan is kept in place by a large piece of parcel tape. She would swap places with these sheets, with that pot, to be handled, touched and squashed by his hands. Molly lobs both items straight into the returns box and picks up the receipt.

Gosia lifts a large box of till rolls onto the counter and pretends to search through it. Her eyes migrate to the man that she's made the occupant of her heart. Yes, there is an obvious discrepancy between them. His cashmere top jars with her washed-out polyester blouse; his careful haircut clashes with her unkempt ponytail of split ends; his shopping habits do not match hers. His job brings him clients that boast about his skills in supermarket aisles; her job allows her to take home out-of-date yoghurt for free.

Are they too far apart in life? Gosia shakes her head. They have a special connection. Like now, his gaze migrates to her and she holds it. He narrows his eyes, moistens his lips. He likes her; he wouldn't do that if it was not the case. Him touching her arm last week in that erotic way confirmed his interest. If it was her issuing the refund, things would be different and their bond even stronger. Gosia finds herself parting her lips; she would take him into her mouth and offer him his money back. Silly Molly is making a meal of it by tapping numbers into the machine instead of scanning the receipt.

The man of her dreams exhales, shifts around and removes a piece of lint from his sleeve. His leather satchel is open and, in its gape, Gosia spots a book, its title in thick red letters: *A Quick Guide to Eliminating Negative Thinking.*

So there it is, another thing they have in common apart from this strong sexual pull – readiness for self-improvement. That's a solid foundation for a new life together. Something they can work on, develop and support each other with.

The card machine beeps and starts printing a confirmation slip. Molly exhales loudly as Doreen pulls her V-neck top down further.

'There,' she says, 'refund complete. Anything else we can do for you today?'

'No,' he says, his eyes on Gosia.

Doreen follows his gaze.

'You done here?' She pulls out the box from Gosia's grasp and puts it with a thud on the floor. 'The queue is a mess.' She points Gosia towards the congestion by the self-checkouts; people breathing down each other's necks and attempting to push their trolleys down the 'Up to 5 Items' lanes.

When Gosia looks back, he is gone, and Silly Molly lays her upper body flat on the counter, dreamily following the trajectory of his footsteps.

'I've done it,' Molly says, tears of joy in her eyes.

'You forgot to give him our names and didn't ask him to fill in the satisfaction survey online,' Doreen snaps at Molly, and pushes Gosia into the crowd.

19

A blustery, dry day with a promise of sun and a blanket of clouds above the community allotments. Patches of cultivated land are separated by decaying fences, some wooden, some mesh. Neat beds are ready for sowing, the fruit trees are in blossom, newly erected bamboo tepees are secured with twine and greenhouses are filled with seedlings carefully arranged on trays. The odour of manure and the heat rising from upturned compost heaps fill the air. Colour-clashing springtime tulips fill the borders, their petals exaggeratedly long, thin and ready to wilt.

Gosia scurries along, hood up, a supermarket bag in her hand filled with food that doesn't require refrigerating. Purchased with her 20-per-cent-off staff card: peanut butter, tins of mackerel and beans, instant soups, tea and coffee, nuts, rice cakes and crisps. She also bought a newspaper, a packet of matches and a loaf of bread.

The allotments look deserted, the work for the day complete, chairs folded and sheds closed, but she remains vigilant and walks efficiently towards the far corner where her father farms a generous piece of land. He took it on a couple of decades ago, just after 'The Calamity', when he needed somewhere to hide from the debt collectors. Since then he ploughs, digs and hoes at the soil, concerns himself with fertilisers and mulching, grows fruit and veg, brings baskets of it back home and sells some to the neighbours. Sometimes, on Saturdays, he runs a stall at the market. He came up with his informal veg box scheme long before you could order them online, but he is beginning to be muscled out of the market by websites and young people lurking outside stations with flyers. Last summer, the number of informal subscribers had gone down to twelve. He only covers local streets, peddling around them with his cart. He only takes cash. He only makes money in season.

Gosia gets to the gate and looks around. The shed looks freshly painted, its green body camouflaged with the foliage of evergreen bushes. The door is wide open, an old-fashioned wooden deck-chair set up outside; the barbecue frame next to it twinkles with a dying fire. The greenhouse has been cleaned of moss, shelves neat, trays displayed. She walks in. The gate opens with a gentle squeak, its hinges oozing with grease. She walks the length of the land all raked and ready, soil ripe for seed, past the fruit trees and currant bushes towards the gaping door of the shed.

'Dad?' she says, half expecting to find him hanging in there. Goodbye letter pinned to his chest, his face contorted, garden twine wrapped around his neck. She only spots the swept floor. Some fabric folded in the corner. A cardboard box.

'Gosia?' His voice comes from somewhere outside. She turns back but he is not by the raspberry bushes, nor by the compost pile.

'Dad?' she says again.

'Up here.' The voice is above her head. Her dad with a hammer and a roll of felt in hand lies on his belly on the roof slope. 'Won't be a minute. Just fixing a leak!'

He disappears again on the other side of the shed. Gosia walks around, towards what looks like an outdoor washroom. A metal bowl on wooden logs, a bar of soap in it, an old towel suspended on a line next to drooping pairs of socks and pants.

She spots the ladder resting against the shed and her dad's body, smaller, thinner, hammering down the felt with small pins into the far corner. It takes seven and a half minutes and then he starts moving carefully down, one leg at a time on the ladder, felt squashed under his arm, the hammer secured behind his belt.

He comes up to her, smelling of fire, wind, tar and soil.

'Gosia!' He hugs her tight, wraps his hands around her, lifting her slightly off the ground. The bag with shopping attached to her hand lifts up with her. Her other hand gives him a tentative squeeze.

'Cup of tea?'

She nods. He goes back to the shed then comes out with a camping stove, a camping kettle, a mug and an old battered tin, and sets it all up on a log by the deckchair. He rubs his hands.

'It won't take a minute. It boils in a flash.'

'How are you?' she asks.

'All good, all well.' He smiles his confident smile, with bright teeth below his moustache. 'The spring is here!' He points to the grey of the sky, the blossom on the trees, the dying tulips.

'Mother said you are divorcing.' She has no time for the weather, for gardening advice, for musings about the colour of soil. 'She wants to sell the house.'

He sighs. Shakes his head.

'Gosia, you mustn't worry. Your mother is upset.' He picks his words carefully. 'She needs some time without me.'

'She wants to divorce you and sell the house,' Gosia concludes. 'She is livid. She wants the rest of her life without you.'

Dad sighs, looks away, towards the kettle that still hasn't boiled.

'What happened?' she asks.

He indicates for her to take a seat in the ancient deckchair, its fabric body bleached and worn. She sits down, awkwardly. The wood creaks gently. She finally deposits the plastic bag on the dirt.

Dad disappears into the shed. Comes out with a fishing stool in one hand and a single teabag crumpled up in his other. He brews the tea for them both from the one bag and offers her the mug while he takes the tin for himself. No milk, no sugar. She sips enough to burn her tongue.

'Nothing much happened,' Dad says, his face innocent. Gosia's throat is boiling.

'There was a parcel for you that Mother apparently opened. She must have learnt something.' She pauses, makes an opening for his version, for his story. But he holds onto the tin, his calloused hands oblivious to the heat. 'Dad, did you cheat on her?'

He just shakes his head.

'Did you lose any more money?'

He smirks. The Calamity wiped him out.

'Have you done something wrong?'

She catches his eye. There is a firmness in his gaze now and she knows she's touched on something sore and unresolved. She chances it.

'Have you hurt someone?'

He empties his lungs like a convict.

'Gosia, it's between me and your mum. Please leave it alone.'

'But we are all affected!' She is shouting now, her voice resonates in her chest. 'Chrissy worried herself sick to the point she miscarried, and Bernard sees it as a chance to fund his lavish wedding and honeymoon!' Her whole body shakes. 'You live in this shack, you sent me a text asking for help and Mother is on permanent edge, ready to punch someone. And there is no home to go back to. So how can I leave it alone?'

Father touches her knee, rubs it a bit too hard.

'I'm sorry. I know it must be hard. But when I was your age . . .'

She knows what's going to come now. That story of independence, self-sufficiency, adventure; establishing himself in a foreign country. She doesn't listen to it any more. That story stops in the golden age. Mother and Dad buying their house on a quiet street in a lovely town, having babies. He never talks about The Calamity. She fires it at him now, before he comes to the conclusion of his narrative.

'But you lost all that money. If it wasn't for the house being in Mother's name, we would have grown up on the street. And now she is going to sell it so Bernie can have his wedding for two hundred guests, and you can't do anything about it.'

Dad withdraws. His voice is distant.

'I wish I knew what to do, I wish there was a signpost that told you how to turn things around. Life really is a constant surprise.' He smiles.

The clouds cover up more of the sky now, lowering themselves, layering up for rain. It's getting late. She needs to make it back home. She stands up.

'Brought you some things.' She points to the bag abandoned by the deckchair, its shiny plastic now dirty with soil. 'Do you need anything else? Dad?'

He lifts his head. Defeated. His voice small and embarrassed.

'Would you be able to lend me some cash? For a month or so?'

He has never asked her for money. His request is a shock, an unpleasant jolt she tries to cover up with an even voice, her innards out of tune.

'Sure, how much do you need?' She searches for her purse, squashed in the bottom of her rain mac pocket.

'Only a hundred pounds,' he says flatly. 'Only' amounting to a third of her weekly take-home after tax.

She keeps her eyes on the purse.

'I have twenty-three pounds fifty on me,' she says to the polyester lining. 'But you can walk with me to the cash point.' There is one a mile away. In the wrong direction, away from the train station.

'That will do for now. Just need to buy some seeds.'

She hands him the cash. Leaves herself her lucky penny and makes a move towards the gate without a hug. She waves weakly from behind the fence. Her dad with a handful of notes and coins, his body glued to a fishing stool, a battered tin in hand, doesn't wave back. She walks away. The rain is moving her along, covering up her tears with raindrops. The shortest way to the station leads through the street by the family house and she hesitates by the drive, loiters for a minute behind the old Nissan.

20

A council-run library, first thing in the morning. Gosia is one of two users who showed up for 9 a.m. The other person, a dry-faced man that Gosia knows is called Blake, is a morning regular. He always aims for the best computer, shielded from the eyes of librarians, has two memory sticks in the USB ports, a credit card in front of him and a wry smile on a face covered with red patches of peeled skin. They exchange a courtesy chin nod by the front door and Gosia, although she has arrived first, lets him through the door to claim his favoured spot.

She approaches him with six pounds in coins on an open palm.

'Could you buy me something online? My card is blocked,' she lies. 'It costs a fiver so I am offering a bit more to cover your efforts too.' She looks him in the eye.

Blake blinks and extends his hand; the inside of his palm is red and sore.

'Sure. Send me the link.' He pockets the money and writes down his email address on a scrap of paper: blake_is_always_right@mail.com

That was a breeze. Gosia had considered different options for getting the PDF without making it obvious to Andy and Margaret that she is reading their book. It took a bit of thinking to come up with approaching Blake; his obvious porn addiction is what made Gosia think he wouldn't mind helping.

She sends Blake the link and, within minutes, receives the PDF as an attachment forwarded to her account from his. It is exported at low quality, the cover pages, graphs and chapter names pixelated but she can just about read the text.

'What a load of bollocks,' says Blake. 'People pay for this?' He laughs. The PDF is wide open on his screen. 'Listen to this,' he adjusts the pitch of his voice, '"This book is the bulletproof way to get the life you want with minimal effort. It only takes a few simple shifts, a bit of knowledge and fresh ways of thinking to have it all."' He shakes his head. 'Bulletproof! Who wrote it? Ex-army bloke? I mean, who would ever fall for this?' He clears his throat. '"We will give you easy-to-implement ideas, answer your toughest questions and share how we tackled the same problems."'

He looks at Gosia, lifting his eyebrows.

She doesn't react.

'Oh my god. It just gets better, I mean, worse. '"This book is a practical guide, follow it step by step. Nothing in it requires expenditure, just your time and commitment to complete all 300 steps!"' He roars. 'They don't dare to mention that fiver that you have to throw at this badly laid-out pile of shite.' He turns in his seat, faces Gosia's chair. 'You don't look like a person who needs any of this.'

'It's for research,' Gosia volunteers.

'Are you working on a PhD on moronic self-help books? The whole genre is a load of bollocks. Plenty of material for you to choose from, I guess.'

'Some of it helps people to improve and work through their shortcomings and fears,' says Gosia. Her mind migrates to the red letters on a white cover that she had spotted in that soft leather satchel. She has already clicked through the PDF and sent a selection of chapters to print and just waits for a quiet moment to go to the librarians' desk to pay and collect. Printing the whole book is out of the question now she has funded Dad's seed purchases and is expected to help him out some more.

Blake sticks his hand into his pocket trousers and extracts a pound coin.

'Here, keep it,' he rolls it back across the desk to her, 'and invest it in something sound. I recommend gold.'

21

The Bulletproof Guide to Sorting Out Your Life: Work, Money, Free Time, Family, Friendship and Love. Step 1: How to Do What You Love

Want to sort out your life? Act on it! You shape your future. You do NOT let it shape you.

How do you do it? You follow your heart and your gut, while listening to your thoughts. You sync your body and mind.

Where do you start? First, acknowledge what you are best at. Love cleaning but work in accounts? It might be time to swap spreadsheets for starting that boutique cleaning business you have been dreaming about since your A levels. Great at growing house plants but spending days waiting tables? Swap your exhausting job in a restaurant for one at a garden centre!

Hold on, we hear you say. How do I work out what I am best at?

We get you. Andy spent a decade driving an underground train before realising that what he was best at is talking to people – and you don't meet many of them stuck in a dark tunnel! Margaret was born with a strong sense of wanting to help people, but it took her a while to recognise what style of helping she wanted to do before finally leaving her exhausting job as a nurse.

How did we get there? We carefully and patiently observed what we loved and what we hated. It is a simple device that costs you nothing but your time and attention.

Let's try it now! On the following page we have prepared two lists for you. Simply write down what you love and what you hate.

It is important that you don't rush this process. Don't read ahead until you are done. Acknowledge that there is no point pursuing the unknown: you must first see the life you want in front of your eyes. Then you can go and get it.

We've made all the mistakes so you don't have to. Andy had been through a rocky relationship that left deep scars on his psyche. Getting him out of the depression ravine took a long time, lots of pills and plenty of expensive therapy hours. Spare yourself the expense - read this book and NEVER fall for the wrong person.

By the time you finish this book, you'll be living your perfect life: earning a decent wage doing what you like, surrounded by real friends and family and enjoying your downtime in the arms of a person you truly love.

Remember, it is important that you tackle it one step at a time in the order suggested by us. No point rushing to find the love of your life if you haven't sorted out your finances first! Trust us! Let the journey begin!

I love	I hate
e.g. Working on my Japanese zen garden	e.g. Customers who always try to return things without the receipt
e.g. Blowing people away with my interpersonal skills	e.g. Extended periods of time alone in the dark, driving tube trains

22

A damp afternoon in a small park with loosely scattered trees and benches, and muddy paths. The loud guy from the supermarket loiters by a murky pond. He picks up an empty can, a crisp wrapper. A gymbag hangs on his shoulder. The ducks fed on Kingsmill are frightened by his dancing, a series of foot kicks to the sides. Some fly away. He moves with his handful of rubbish towards a path. He can't see Gosia, who walks behind the overgrown bushes. She slows down. She is much faster than him. She keeps her phone by her ear in case she needs to fake a conversation. He triple-sidesteps and disposes of the rubbish in the bin provided by the thoughtful council. He misses and bends down, exposing a rash on his lower back, as she reaches the bottom of the park and hides behind a tree. He walks past her and she follows him all the way to the doors of a local sports centre. That's the third time she's spotted him walking in there, the only gym in a two-mile radius.

She wants to walk in, pin him to the wall and check that this is where the man of her dreams showers after workouts. She can't. She can't be late.

She turns around, picks up speed and arrives just in time to be hurried into a small beige meeting room. Glass of water for her. Cup of coffee for him.

'Thank you for coming, Ms Golab, and for your interest in our chiropractic clinic. As you know, our business is rapidly growing and we are looking for motivated, dedicated, passionate individuals who wish to advocate good posture and general well-being. So, let me ask you, what made you apply for this position?'

Gosia inhales and, in her head, begins counting to ten to boost her mental strength and composure, silently ticking off the reasons on her internal list.

1. Since my childhood I always wanted to be a nurse. This didn't happen.
2. My entire career has been in retail. I work for a major supermarket and on a daily basis I interact with many individuals, some of them weird.
3. It is about making sure the customers are happy and returning.
4. But I realised that all I do is make people buy. And buy. More than they need or want.
5. However, I met the man of my dreams in that shop. He never takes advantage of the offers. He sees through them. I've heard that he works here.
6. So when I saw the advert in the window, I thought, This is it. I will meet him here and our relationship will flourish. This place is all about healing and bodily awareness. It's a perfect backdrop for love.
7. I don't want to watch a mother of five have to feed her children value pasta any more.
8. I keep working nights. This makes my skin sallow. I've read this is due to bad lighting and refrigerated air.
9. I want more from my life. You offer £10.50 per hour. That's over two pounds more than I am getting now. I will be able to save up for a holiday. I haven't had one since breaking up with my ex.

The man gives her a reassuring smile just as she gets to ten and she is finally speaking.

'My friend Lyndsey had terrible back pains. She has a sitting type of job. Beautician. She came here three or four times and the pain was gone. I thought that was a small miracle. When I saw the advert, I told myself, I want to work for people who *actually* make others feel better.'

The man nods approvingly.

'Do you have previous experience in a public-facing role?'

She looks thoughtfully at the multi-edition print of a seaside sunset hanging above the man's head. It matches the one in the cafe up the road.

'I work at the supermarket, as a cashier. I face people all day long. I have been there five years now. I think it is time to move on.' She forgets to add the practised lines about teamwork, dedication and developing relationships.

The man puffs his lips.

'Do you know how to use Microsoft Office software? Databases? We need someone with excellent IT skills and a great presence. Someone who has a welcoming smile and a beaming personality. We're looking for someone people-centred. Someone who can reassure our customers from the moment they enter that their back problems will be solved!'

'I know how to use computers. I did the emergency staff rota and other admin tasks when my manager was on sick leave. I colour-coded Excel spreadsheets to make them easier to follow. This is now company policy throughout the chain.'

He looks bored.

'Fascinating! Thank you for your time. We'll get back to you.'

In the space between her shoulder blades, she feels she is not going to get this job. All her hopes are now on the sports centre.

She enquired about the role just the other day. A young girl at the reception, dressed in pink hot pants and a tight top, told her she stands a chance.

'They want someone fit, young and resilient. This is a community gym and you deal with a lot of weirdos. You have to wear these Lycra tops and your bonus is linked to the sales from the FitShop. How many pairs of goggles, white socks or shorts do you think people buy when the prices start at fifteen quid? So I'm out of here. I lasted a year! Got a job in a travel agency. I think I know you. Your face looks familiar. Are you a member here? The membership is free to employees, but I never use it. My manager doesn't either. Apparently you can get pregnant from sitting in a jacuzzi. Anyway. Good luck.'

The girl had given her a top tip: add a hot passport photo to your CV, as the shortlist is done by head office and the managers there are only concerned with the shagability of applicants. A new, shiny shot in full make-up, blow-dry, plenty of bare flesh, lips parted. She truly went for it, hand-delivered her enhanced CV before she could change her mind. The picture made her look and feel cheap. But what wouldn't she do for love?

23

A small square in a poky town overlooking a car park, a train station and a pound store. The wind blows and a woman calmly watches her toddler wriggle and scream on a patch of grass, as people walk silently by on paved walkways.

Gosia can see him from the window as the train pulls into the station, sitting on a bench, arms on knees, durable plastic bags folded by his foot. She walks fast towards him. She wants it to be over before anyone recognises her. What a stupid place to meet. Bang in the middle of this gossipy town.

When he called from the landline in her mother's house, he insisted on this location, conveniently central and near the shops that are open on Sunday. If Mother finds out he keeps going back to the house, she will change the locks, and maybe blame Chrissy.

'Hi, Dad.' She aims for a neutral voice as he lifts his head and straightens up. He looks scrawny, cheeks hollow, shirt crumpled up and trousers stained with grass. Like a beggar, a drifter, a rough sleeper. Her mother will never take him back.

'Gosia!' He smiles with all his teeth and pats the bench, the spot just next to him. She sits down and he squeezes her shoulder for hello. He doesn't attempt a hug, he speaks to the space ahead of him, but, even so, she can smell his bad breath.

'I don't know how to thank you, Gosia. It's temporary. Another month or so and there will be salad and fruit. I'll pay it all back.'

So he wants it to be quick too. She is grateful he doesn't waste time with small talk. She roots about in her bag and lifts out a brown envelope, giving it to him like it's drugs.

'The frost wasn't kind to the trees or the broad beans.' He squeezes the envelope, assessing the amount with his thumb.

'Two hundred pounds, just as you asked.' She tries to say it matter-of-factly, bank manager style, tension removed from her voice.

The phone call had surprised her. Mother never uses the land-line to call mobile numbers. So she had assumed it would be Chrissy in need of an explanation of what a 'lifetime mortgage' or 'home reversion plan' is. The phone had rung during her lunch break, just as she was about to microwave her home-made, bottom-of-the-fridge soup, so she took it. Dad's voice a whisper, asking if she could come by, meet him in town, lend him money. He needed a little bit more cash, he had said.

A two-hundred-pound loan to Dad means a number of things. No hot drink at the station this morning, no fresh fish for dinner this month, no top-up for her mobile, no stain remover, no 3-ply loo roll, no toys for John and Paul. Each visit to an ATM erodes her carefully built sense of being able to cope.

'That should last till the end of the month,' Dad says, and she quickly calculates – the month ends in two weeks. He smiles gently. Looks at her, sideways. 'Meet you here again?'

'In two weeks?' she asks, and grips the bench. 'Meet you here and bring more cash?'

He nods.

'I think another three hundred pounds will see me through till first crops.'

THREE HUNDRED POUNDS she shouts in her head. Is she a milking cow? A gold mine? A piggy bank?

'Sure, Dad,' she says, and the anger suppressed in her gut now pulsates in her temples, circulates around her body, making her hot and dizzy. 'Same time, same place,' she adds and stands up to walk to family dinner. Today she will ask to take leftovers home, and she will put a couple of loo rolls from her mother's supply into her bag. She might steal a tube of toothpaste too.

Her father lifts his palm in farewell and she gives him a weak wave as she walks away, kicking at the loose stones, mad with herself.

Next time she will demand answers before she hands over the money. Next time, she will be firm: no explanation, no support. Next time, she will make him sort it out with Mother.

24

A shared kitchen covered with zesty blossom designer wallpaper from the 'Harmony' range, birch extendable dining table pushed into the corner and surrounded by three chairs. Sink, hobs and worktops all in a row, supported by a cupboard, an oven, a washing machine and a small fridge. Opposite, a worn dresser covers the entire wall. Mismatched plates and cups displayed on the shelves. A single window with a view of a tiny garden used by the next-door tenants, filled with plastic toys and an abandoned tent. Gosia and Lyndsey sit at the table and eat breakfast. Lyndsey narrates between mouthfuls of cornflakes.

'Are you sure about this? Fitness centres can make you really depressed. Kev stopped going 'cause the men were mean to him and laughed at his cellulite. Not that you have any. I remember going once and it wasn't nice at all. Everyone wears these tight-fitting leggings and eyes you up, and I feel sooo self-conscious when I have to expose my arms. The instructor was like, "Shake your booties, ladies, shake your thighs, shake it all." It was actually fun until I saw these girls pointing at me in the mirror. They were jerking like they had fits or something, and I thought to myself, I am *not* going to be their entertainment, and I didn't go back. But I will, you know. As of Monday, I'm trying out this ten-day fruit diet. I'll go back and wear the blue and yellow fitness set I bought last year, you know, the one with the sweet little frills. Their eyes will pop.'

Gosia nibbles on muesli and glances at the wall calendar. It's Tuesday.

'Why wait till Monday?'

Lyndsey points at the box in front of her.

'I still have cornflakes to finish off and two packs of pasta and a pound of mince. I can't have it lying around when I'm only supposed to be eating apples.'

'Give it to Kev.'

Lyndsey's eyes sparkle.

'We're going to diet together. Kev has his exams next month. He needs to lose a few pounds here and there. And it's nice to do something together, you know. It's the best thing about our relationship. I say to him, let's go on a diet, and he's like, awesome! And I'm like, "Let's try the fruit one, it sounds tasty," and he goes, "I l.o.v.e tasty diets." And we laugh. You know, Kev is so understanding. Remember the beetroot diet I went on? I lasted a day and a half. It was foul. Can't imagine anyone sticking to it for longer. And he says, "Lynds, why are you eating this rubbish, have some of my burger," so I did and felt instantly better, like a human again.'

'I think I am going to take the job.' Gosia has already signed the contract.

Lyndsey adapts her voice and sounds like a reasonable adult.

'I know it's better money and you'll meet new people, but think about what you're leaving behind. Your supermarket is so good to you. All those Christmas vouchers, your manager is laid-back *and* you can take reduced-price yoghurts home.'

Gosia persists.

'I don't want to retire by the checkout, and I should get fit and toned if I want to find a man. Not everyone is as lucky as you.'

Lyndsey goes soft.

'Ohhh, Kev is a real gift. My mum says so. Need to make a move, hun. Have to put acrylics on at half ten and I've got two waxings later on. It's so full-on.'

She moves to the sink to wash up.

Gosia decides to have a square of chocolate with the last few sips of her coffee. She unfolds the gold leaf slowly and purposefully.

'Do you want a piece?'

Lyndsey takes her body to the doorway.

'No thanks, hun, I packed a Milky Way for lunch.'

'You sure? It's your favourite. With nuts and raisins.'

Lyndsey pauses.

'Oh, go on then. Just one row.'

She swallows after two jaw moves. Gosia dissolves the square in her mouth and speaks to her cup.

'I needed that. Going for a walk. Good to have some energy to make it to the park and back!'

Lyndsey turns her head.

'You're not at work today?'

Gosia points at the calendar.

'Day off. The joy of shift work!'

Lyndsey's eyes go small.

'Oh, how lovely. I never have Tuesdays off! Kev will be here in a bit. Hope you don't mind. He's going to finally put this shelf up for me. It needs proper drilling. But since you're out it won't disturb you, will it?'

'It won't be a long walk.'

Lyndsey throws her hands in the air.

'It's just one shelf.'

'It's my day off.'

Lyndsey ambles to the door.

'I need it up.'

'I need some rest.'

Lyndsey's left leg migrates to the corridor.

'I can't do it myself.'

'You must be joking!'

Lyndsey looks at Gosia.

'I can't call it off. He borrowed the drill from the club manager.'

'I can't change my day off. And I have a long shift tomorrow.'

'I have to go.' Lyndsey lifts her right leg with a grunt, grabs her bag and leaves without a goodbye.

25

A 24/7 fitness centre with fluorescent lighting. The large reception area, manned between 8 a.m. and 10 p.m. Monday to Saturday, is occupied by mustard-yellow, leather-effect tub armchairs and purple coffee tables. A selection of vending machines stands by the wall: cold drinks, hot drinks, healthy snacks, power snacks, chocolate and crisps. Three extra-large plasma screens advertise forthcoming classes alongside success stories: *Donna lost 4 stone in 4 months. She did it with us!* The prime location by the main door is dedicated to an overpriced FitShop selling goggles, socks, shorts, swimming costumes, flip-flops and high-performance vests, alongside shiny fitness magazines and tacky merchandise: calendars, hair bands, fridge magnets and a running logbook.

Gosia sits behind a U-shaped reception counter in a tennis outfit. She has quickly settled in. A low, V-neck Lycra top wraps snugly around her padded bra. She is fully engaged in her new favourite pastime: completing a psychology quiz from a women's magazine. The magazine is from the FitShop. It's priced at £5.99, so she avoids marking it with her pen. She has no intention of buying it. The quiz is going to help her decide if she is happy with who she is.

1) What do you see when you look in the mirror?
B: Your blemishes.

2) Which of the following could you adopt as a symbol of your inner self?
B: A locked wardrobe.
3) People close to you tell you that . . .
C: You have a charming smile.
4) What kind of love seems the most long-lasting to you?
B: That of a child for its father.
5) You're asleep. What's your worst nightmare?
B: Swimming towards an island without ever reaching it.
6) Stimulants such as tea, alcohol, tobacco, etc. are:
B: Mood-enhancers.
7) You are out one evening when you meet someone and fall for them. They say they'll phone the next day but they don't. You assume:
B: They must have met someone they like more.
8) Imagine a person leaning on the parapet of a bridge. Suddenly, the bridge crumbles and the person falls into the water. They can't swim. What do you do?
B: Move away. You can't swim either.
9) You're getting out of a taxi to go to a party when a child who is walking past squashes their ice cream onto your outfit. You haven't got time to go home and change. What do you do?
C: Shout about how angry you are.

The results are comforting:

Mostly B: LOVE YOURSELF MORE
You need to be reassured about how you look, whether by looking in mirrors or by assessing how others see you. It's your physical appearance that you're in love with. You are

attentive to the impression you make on others and you like people to be envious of you. You have a big ego and you are working towards one main goal: to prove your worth. Your egotism also serves as a defence against reality. But hasn't anyone ever told you that you pay excessive attention to how you look? You want other people to remember you in a good light, as a pleasant person with an interesting personality. Invest in your inner look. Love your insides. Sometimes instead of combing your hair you could read a thought-provoking book!

Her ego is not that big, not as big as Anna's. But since the falling-out she has stopped comparing herself to her. Anna's ego was the size of a distribution centre: it enabled her to see herself as beautiful, intelligent, talented, funny and trustworthy. Although she also had oddly shaped ears, believed in UFOs, worked as a PA, repeated the same jokes to the same people and stabbed Gosia in the back. Their time together was usually about making Anna's ego even larger. They wore matching tops so Anna's boobs could look more substantial next to Gosia's pea-sized breasts; they shared Gosia's rum and Coke so Anna could hold onto her 'no drinking for a year' challenge. At the time, Gosia didn't mind and never thought she was Anna's personal doormat.

Now Gosia compares herself to Janelle, her colleague, and Sasha, the manager. They both practically live in the gym and in their spare time only talk calories, workouts and detox. Their diets consist of 'water-based food', like kale, spinach, cucumber and celery. They drink Evian by the gallon and nibble on blueberries and almonds. She feels fat and baggy next to them. All three of them are also single, so what chance does she have in their company?

'There is a man in the ladies-only area.'

'Pardon?'

'THERE IS A MAN IN THE LADIES-ONLY AREA and he's upsetting my friend.'

Gosia reluctantly breaks from her daydream and follows a young freckled girl to the Ladies' Zone. That annoying guy from the supermarket is using the treadmill and telling jokes to a neighbouring group of women on rowing machines. His loud voice echoes around the room.

'Straight people always ask me why I have such good fashion sense. Do you know what I tell them?'

'Noooo . . .' the ladies at the back chorus encouragingly.

'Darlings, I didn't spend all that time in the closet for nothing.'

The women shake their boobs as they laugh.

'Wait for this one! What do you call a straight pride parade?'

'Dunno?'

'A traffic jam.'

The women hoot, their thighs wobble from side to side. None of them are rowing any more; a couple silently escape the room.

Gosia steps in.

'This is the Ladies' Zone, so I'm afraid you'll have to leave.'

He addresses his audience.

'But we're having a great time!'

Gosia persists, 'But this is the Ladies' Zone. You have to leave.'

'Ah, what a shame! I was actually on the lookout for a men-only zone. Do you have one?'

One of the rowing women shouts, 'In the sauna!'

They all laugh, and he winks in their direction.

'Good idea, I'll go let off some steam!'

The laughter grows louder. He exits the room, swaying his arse as his audience whoops behind him. Gosia follows him out.

He is not smiling any more.

'Pet, don't run to your boss, it'll just ruffle her feathers. I was only having a walk around, looking for a friend.'

Gosia crosses her arms.

'I'll have to put a warning on your membership card.'

'I pay a fortune for that membership!'

'So do the women who wish to access the ladies-only zone.'

He scratches his side.

'Look, it's a lovely day and there's no need to be upset. I'm on a little personal quest to find my friend who hasn't shown up for a while. I'm concerned! Wouldn't you be if someone you expected to be at the rowing machine wasn't there? Please just tell me if my friend is in and I'll stop my search.' He flutters his eyelashes.

She walks back to the U-shaped counter. He follows. She pauses in front of the screen.

'So, what's the name of your friend?'

He rests his hand against the counter.

'Vijay.'

'Vijay who?'

'I don't know his surname.'

Gosia lifts her head.

'It doesn't sound like you're very close friends.'

He softens his tone.

'Acquaintances. We've only just started getting to know each other . . . How many Vijays could there be in one gym?'

'I'm afraid I can't help you.' She clicks confidently at the keyboard.

'But what if you are stopping me from forming a meaningful relationship? Vijay could be my destiny!' He presses his hand to his heart.

She pronounces her words carefully: 'I'm going to call my manager.'

He sighs.

'Forget it, pet. If Vijay comes in tell him that I miss him.'

He walks out humming a tune and swaying rhythmically.

Gosia puts Vijay into the search box. It comes up with two profiles. One, an elderly man who hasn't visited since last summer, and one with a picture of the man of her dreams. Until now, she's searched only up to the letter E. Her heartbeat quickens and fingers tingle as she prints his entire profile, which is technically illegal.

26

The Bulletproof Guide to Sorting Out Your Life:
Work, Money, Free Time, Family, Friendship and Love.
STEP 291: How to Find the Love of Your Life

People think that falling in love needs no practice, that the heart will open itself to the right person at the right time and you will live happily ever after. This is a fairy tale sold to us by Hollywood that brings with it numerous disappointments. Love, like anything else, requires practice. You get better at it the more you do it.

Instead of going on a date with a person you like, only to discover that you lack the skills to keep them interested, losing your chance to win their heart, we propose a new approach – practise dating! There are plenty of options out there: internet dating offers you easy access to people you can practise on so you can get very good at it. Only when you are confident in your abilities to win hearts should you proceed to date people you actually fancy, people who are worthy of a place in your heart and mind.

Try different approaches when you date. What usually works well is giving your subject plenty of breathing space, letting them talk about themselves while listening intently and aligning yourself with their interests and desires. Try it – but don't despair if it doesn't work straight away. Practice means practice! Margaret had dozens of dates before she honed her skills.

Make sure you keep clear boundaries. For example, remain elusive about your address. You do not want the wrong person to fall in love with you and follow you around. Andy learnt it the hard way. He is still stalked by his ex, who he ended up wasting long, torturous years with before realising that she was only meant to be his practice run.

We have prepared a useful sheet below outlining our favourite 'winning hearts' methods. Try them all and note down your achievements as well as your mistakes. Give it a few goes and watch your confidence grow and your skills sharpen as you become irresistible.

Name of subject	**Method**	**Achievements**	**Mistakes**
e.g. Toby	e.g. Listening intently to your subject	e.g. Toby paid the drinks bill in full	e.g. Gave him the impression that I too love ice hockey, so now he only wants to discuss this
e.g. George	e.g. Encouraging your subject to talk; asking questions	e.g. A quick drink after work was quickly followed by an invite to dinner	e.g. I drank too quickly while he spoke, and as a result kissed him first and put my hand on his thigh, which he politely removed

Name of subject	Method	Achievements	Mistakes
e.g. Lionel	e.g. Discussing areas you have in common, such as living close to one another and shopping in the same places	e.g. He has good connections at the local deli and has offered to source me a lifetime discount card	e.g. I gave him my address and now he sends me a mini-cheese board every fortnight (too much dairy causes bad wind), despite me not wanting to see him again

27

A small, council-run library. Rows of shelves of crime fiction, sci-fi and romance stand by the accessible toilets and children's area. A large DVD collection with a notice next to it: *New releases £3 per night, other DVDs £1 per week.* A solitary photocopier in the corner with a Sellotaped sheet on the top: *OUT OF ORDER.* Five desks with computers in the middle, screens exposed to passers-by. Humming ventilators and rapid mouse-clicking noises accompany an odour of sweaty feet.

Four men and Gosia sit by their monitors. She logs on to a dating site for the first time. She puts only basic information on her profile: '5' 4'', slim, 29, blonde, blue eyes, GSOH, seeks man 25–35, for friendship and maybe more.'

She uploads an image of herself in a swimming costume. She repeats her newly acquired mantra 'only for training purposes'.

Mr_wunderbar is the first one to write. He attaches a picture of his cock. She considers replying with a single word, 'Perv', but she settles on, 'I know your wife!'

DannyBoy contacts her next. He pastes into the message his entire 'About Me' section:

'Don't read the next sentence. Oh you rebel, I like you. About my short and humorously insignificant life: I don't have kids, I don't have ex-wives, I don't have debt. I am half Dutch and half

Russian. Like a cross-breed dog . . . I am able to accept that you had close male friends before you met me, no jealousy here. Drink tonight?'

She hesitates. She is looking for the right man to practise on. She needs more than just being able to hold Vijay's attention. Gosia analysed the history of his gym attendance in great detail. He is clearly a busy man with a tight schedule as his gym visits rarely last more than forty minutes – the length of a mind-broadening podcast revealing how science benefits from closely watching nature. The only factor Gosia can determine is that he goes through activity spurts. Three visits one week on consecutive days and then nothing for a fortnight. The erratic nature of his gym-going must correspond with pressures that life puts on him. He does not look like a man who is not committed.

But with a lack of any predictable pattern of days or times of his visits, there is no clarity to when exactly she should stand behind the counter looking her best while welcoming him to the fitness centre. Gosia knows she needs to be Vijay-ready all the time. She needs to rehearse her dirty laugh, she needs to become an experienced kisser, she needs to communicate 'lust' with one sway of her hips!

She adds 'passionate' to her profile between eyes and GSOH. SirMarco responds immediately.

'Ciao Bella, glorious figure, imagining putting whipped cream on you right now. Prosecco is in my fridge, where are you? I invite EasternBeauty and LuluXXX too. Hot night ahead. Contact me now!'

EasternBeauty's profile shows an Asian woman in a see-through dress. Her nipples large like doorknobs. LuluXXX has a picture of her buttocks on her front page, naked and well lit. Both women have put under hobbies list: Escort.

Ben_33 sends a brief note.

'I'm a great guy! I guess that's the most important thing to know about me. I'm passionate about my work and currently working on a great indie project. I like swimming and spending holidays on the beach. Just like you, I guess. I work a lot but also make time for fun and meeting new people. How about a drink this Saturday? 7 p.m.? Are you around?'

She is not. She has an evening shift. He sounds normal. She likes him. There is a single picture of a pair of green flip-flops floating in a pool on his page. She can swap shifts; Janelle already owes her two. She has this pretty, slutty dress that she looks nice in. The computer freezes and a red box with black text informs her that she has a minute left. She replies 'Yes' before her time is up. She gathers her stuff. The obnoxious guy with the loud voice stands behind her. His hand is already on the chair's frame. He gives her a smile.

'Well, I'd go for SirMarco – at least the guy's honest! That Ben sounds like the boring type who'll make you pay for his beer.'

She can't believe it.

'I can't believe it! How dare you read my private stuff?!'

He laughs a little, sits in the chair and puts his codes in.

'I didn't mean any harm, pet, I was just waiting for my turn. I can teach you a thing or two if you like. I'm an online Casanova!'

28

A large pub with original fixtures and fittings, a display of stuffed pheasants, three large TV screens with the same sports channel on, and an old wooden bar with a young, bored, underpaid bartender pulling pints. Small round tables and stools line the walls. It's busy. Ben_33 turns out to be white, tall and blond. Wonky nose, thin lips and pale blue eyes a bit too far apart. Good enough to practise on.

He has a sense of humour and a part-time job at a call centre: 'It's a temporary solution. I'm really an actor.'

His weeks are allocated to supporting customers across the UK: 'A great way to practise a variety of regional accents!'

And auditions: 'I was in that car commercial last year. You know, tall men lifting cars above their heads? I was lifting a red car. Seven seconds, five times a day, prime TV exposure for nearly eight weeks! Great campaign but I wouldn't drive a Renault!'

He drinks pints like water and lets her pay for each round: 'I'm broke.'

His weekends are currently dedicated to a low-budget, independent, experimental film production.

'I play a villain. It's a great part. I kill an old woman – it's revenge, because the son she gave up for adoption when he was three pays me to do it. It's a proper psychological thriller. Very provocative. I spent weeks preparing for the role. I talked to people who had difficult relationships with their mothers. The director is only seventeen! Young talent, and his dad is paying for the whole thing. Joseph Bailey, you'll see, everyone'll be talking about him soon. He's doing it alongside his A Levels. Prodigy!'

After the third beer, Ben_33 reveals that his family lives north of Swindon, parents retired, sister has two kids and younger brother works all hours. They all live in a three-bedroom house with a small garden. He was lucky to get out. His siblings regret their choices. His sister's husband left her for someone younger. His brother did badly with his GCSEs and a local bakery was his only option.

He doesn't want to overshare but, 'It's so depressing when I go back. Jess just wants to dump her kids on my lap and go out, Dave works double shifts to keep his job. Mum and Dad basically hate each other. They fight over anything. They never have money to visit London.'

Ben_33 shares a flat with three other actors. They also share contacts and opportunities. Very supportive. She must meet them.

'It's a party pad! And we swap information like, all the time. Just yesterday Rich told us about the auditions to this new sitcom and we all fit the criteria for the main character: young male! TV is a fantastic place to start. It's great exposure and you get fans straight away. All the big names on the big screen started off in TV.'

Ben_33 moves his hands a lot when he speaks. His eyes are constantly sweeping the pub.

'You have to be aware that directors and agents might spot you at any time. You might be trying on jeans at Topman and that's enough, someone notices your stage presence and offers you a part.'

He admits he sometimes just walks around Leicester Square on premier nights.

'Great vibe! People screaming, flashing cameras in your eyes and red carpets everywhere. I know it will be me one day. Walking the carpet, waving, giving autographs. I can give you one now. I like to practise.'

He can't find a pen in his pocket, takes a gulp of his lager and stretches his thin lips into a smile.

'How about you?'

Ben_33 is a bearable subject, he's showered and the aroma from his mouth suggests he frequently uses mouthwash. He has Vijay's build and height and Gosia looks forward to trying out placing her hand on his neck, resting her body against his chest. She confidently aligns herself with his interests.

'I love the cinema. But I don't go too often. There are rats in the one just up the road. You can hear them running around and nibbling on popcorn. I don't have a TV. I worked in a supermarket for a while to figure out what I want, and now I'm at a fitness club.'

Ben_33 sweeps the pub again with his pale blue eyes.

'Amazing! So many actors have personal trainers. Keeping your body in good shape is crucial. No one employs overweight actors, unless you're Jack Nicholson or DiCaprio. Did you see his double chin? I couldn't believe it! That fold makes him look sooo old. Luckily my metabolism is fast! I can eat chips every night of the week and nothing shows. Sadly I don't have time for sport. So busy with work and auditions. The only time I run is to catch a bus.'

Ben_33 looks at his watch.

'It's getting late and I need an early night. Got a seven o'clock start tomorrow – we're filming the post-murder scene in the park.'

Gosia leans forward and speaks straight to his ear, making sure the heat from her mouth warms up his earlobe.

'Shall we go to mine?'

29

Library noise in the background, a screen in front of Gosia. She doesn't notice anything else.

Woman_with_body wrote: 'I can see how you pulled the female body apart. I can sense your recent experience of being objectified and reduced to three parts. Well done for this expressive poem. Chilling!'

KarenStevensWrites wrote: 'This poem doesn't appeal to my taste but I appreciate your formal experiments. It made me think of an early work of mine, titled *Romance*, that you can read here.'

Rich_M wrote: 'I am appalled by the quality of this work. Reduction of the male figure to only two words suggests this is all that women can see in a man: penis and penetration. Yet another work that will give youngsters the wrong idea of the complexities of sexual experience; sexuality should not be reduced to this.'

Bosom, Bottom, Front

Knockers
Orbs
Baps
Tits
Boobs

Cock Fuck

Rump
Bum
Rear
Arse
Crack

Cock Fuck

Pussy
Muff
Minge
Snatch
Hole

Fuck Cock

30

The Bulletproof Guide to Sorting Out Your Life:
Work, Money, Free Time, Family, Friendship and Love.
STEP 18: How to Get What You Need From Other People

We often find ourselves in situations where we believe that our well-being rests in the hands of other people. We convince ourselves that our boss, our parent, our friend hold us back from the things we need and want, that we are kept away from pursuing our desires and achieving our goals. This is a lie. The sooner you realise it, the better it will be for you.

YOU and only YOU keep you from what you want and who you want to be. With us you can quickly learn how to get what you need from other people to become the person you want to be.

Sometimes, other people have information that allows you to proceed to the next step. Maybe you are seeking funding to start your new dream business? You need to find the right person and gather information that allows you to access money – this might be a phone call to your bank manager or a visit to your wealthy aunt.

Once you have worked this out, you need to practise being convincing. No one wants to release money to people who are not worthy of having it. Your bank will never give you a loan if you do not have a convincing business plan. Your aunt will never dig into her pocket if you show up empty-handed and do not compliment her on her new haircut.

How to be convincing? You have to first of all CONVINCE YOURSELF – if you do not believe in yourself, no one else will. You have to be sure your plan will work, that your ideas are sound, your estimates accurate and your solutions viable. You can't hesitate, can't allow for an inch of space for uncertainty. Once you believe in your power to be who you want to be, you will become this person.

Being convincing has always been Andy's weak point. He found himself in a relationship with a toxic partner who was undermining his abilities. Andy's ex would constantly tell him that he would be useless as a freelancer, unable to keep on top of the admin related to self-employment. He believed her. It took a year of hard work to undo it. Margaret was encouraging Andy throughout to repeat his mantra: *You are a natural-born businessman.*

How to convince yourself? This simple exercise works wonders and gives you great results within a few weeks, although occasionally you may need a bit longer. Every day, stand in front of a mirror and repeat slowly, while you look into your own eyes, the mantra that serves you, whatever this might be in your context.

Your Aim	**Your Mantra**
If your aim is to pursue a new career	You are a natural-born businesswoman
If you aim to find the love of your life, you first have to love yourself	I love you, you gorgeous creature

Your Aim	Your Mantra
If you are aiming to better your financial situation	You deserve to be rich more than anyone

Do not proceed to the next step until you have convinced yourself. If you are not 100 per cent sold on you being able to achieve what you want, no one else will buy it.

31

A 24/7 fitness centre with fluorescent lighting. Three extra-large plasma screens advertise the latest success stories: *Miranda lost 3 stone in 3 months. Her husband didn't recognise her. 'I'm a new person!' She did it with us!* Gosia stands behind a U-shaped reception counter in hand-me-downs from Janelle: an 'Acceleration' cycle top and Lycra shorts in devil red. She wears matching lipstick. She waits.

Sasha is due to leave for her weekly creative management course in ten minutes. She usually stays for lunch to hover over tall, handsome men with no wedding rings on. Janelle will soon bury her head for hours in monthly stats and key performance indicators.

Gosia chooses a light, cheerful playlist to match her mood. There are at least two hours ahead punctuated with little or no distractions. Plenty of time if she wanted to rent the changing room to, say, a local fashion studio who would no doubt love to use it for a photo shoot. Or she could make membership cards for all her family, or even walk around in the designer hooded merino wool top worth £150 from the FitShop.

But for now, she works on convincing herself.

She is taller, thinner, with longer and fuller hair. In the near future, she will stand around a market filled with colourful produce in a beautiful town by the sea. It looks just like a poster she sees regularly, hung in the window of the local travel agent, that advertises the joys of the Croatian coast. Gosia will wear a body-hugging dress in juicy orange and platform sandals. Her left hand will carry an ultra-suede handbag with wooden handles, her right hand will be accompanied by the hand of the man of her dreams. They will look great together. She just has to get what she needs.

The time is right. Sasha leaves. Janelle closes the door to the office. Gosia adjusts the tone of her voice and starts her practice.

'Good morning. I'm calling from the FitYou Sports Centre. May I have the pleasure of speaking to Mr Vijay Kumar?'

She lets the stale air out of her lungs and takes a deep, three-part breath.

'Hi! I'm calling from FitYou. Is Vijay around?'

Her larynx is relaxed, her heartbeat stable. She flexes her fingers and dials the number. A young optimistic female voice responds.

'Straight Back First Chiropractic Clinic. Amanda speaking. How can I help?'

She cannot find her voice.

'Straight Back First Chiropractic Clinic. Amanda speaking. How can I help?'

Gosia inhales.

'Hi. I'm calling from the fitness centre. Looking for Vijay Kumar.'

'I'm afraid Mr Kumar doesn't work here any more, and our clinic can't keep covering his membership fee.'

'But . . .'

The voice ignores her. 'I've already sent the cancellation form to the centre manager. And as I said, we can't be responsible for any outstanding charges.'

'But . . .'

'And NO, I'm afraid we don't have Mr Kumar's current phone number. I suggest you contact him via post. Is there anything else I can help you with today?'

Gosia thinks on her feet.

'No.'

The voice happily announces: 'Thank you for calling Straight Back First Chiropractic Clinic. Goodbye!'

The line goes dead and she puts the phone down. She will have to connect with Vijay in person. She has his address. She will check it out. She will find the right moment. She will approach him at the right time, with the right words, on a sunny day when people are more inclined to be in a good mood, ready for love. She will be irresistible, she will be his match. She is worthy of him.

32

A small bedroom full of clutter. The wall of postcards is gone. In its place there is a web of string connecting a number of words on yellow Post-its: victim, suspect, motive, evidence, location. The arrangement and state of the duvet cover suggests it was recently visited by a wild boar. On the floor, by the free-standing lamp, sits Gosia with Lyndsey's diary in her lap.

I gained half a stone or maybe my scales broke or the reduced-fat jacket potatoes with tuna, sweetcorn and mayo are not reduced-fat at all! I've been having two in one go. Having a really stressful time before our trip away!

Vincent's son came in again. I was just leaving for work when he knocked. I thought it was the postman and rushed for my delivery. The new range of nail varnish with glitter still hasn't arrived. But no, it was Vincent's son and he wasn't happy. He said that someone had spread nasty rumours about his dad, some awful fibs about his life that must be a figment of someone's imagination.

He asked if I had any idea who it could be. That they are ruining the good name of his father. Apparently, there is plenty of revolting stuff online. Outrageous, filthy lies and some pictures that supposedly show wild parties at his dad's place.

He said he needed to know who did this and he needed to deal with it right now.

I thought to myself that it could be GG's doing, but she wasn't in and he didn't let me interrupt him. He said that when he catches the lying, poisonous person, he will put an immediate stop to it, that they wouldn't have a pretty mouth to spread any more evil gossip. He added that the house has already lost value because of all this mess, and he has run out of ideas of how to stop it. Then he left. No bye, no nothing.

I left GG a note and I thought long and hard about what to write. I put something like, 'Vincent's son called. He's not happy.' I was sure she would read between the lines, sense that there's trouble coming. She's clever like that. But she just left me a note back that said, 'His dad died. Not being happy is normal.'

I didn't want to confront her. She always twists my words and would make it all my fault. I left her another note: 'He wants to find the person who tells lies about Vincent online. Do you know who that is?' and GG wrote back, 'Are you his PA now?' This is what she said to Margaret when Andy left and didn't answer her calls.

Margaret came to collect his things just as I popped in to properly view the place. She was only taking away valuables that Andy recklessly left behind. GG asked her, 'Are you his PA now?' I don't know where she got it from; Andy's been a tube driver all his life.

Margaret carried it all out: a laptop, a router, a coffee machine, a microwave, a 4-slice toaster, a high-speed juicer, a flat-screen TV, a DVD player, a toolbox, a hoover, an electric fan heater, a radio, folding garden armchairs, a ceramic fruit bowl, a soap dish, a woven carpet, a china tea set. GG didn't stop her and she didn't help. Margaret was a good seven months pregnant then and I'm sure GG wanted her to have a stillbirth or worse. Margaret, bless her, did it all by herself, put it all in her car and drove off. Then she sent for a man with a van to collect the sofa and a coffee table. Andy said she gave birth two weeks early because of the strain. GG must have been livid to see the engagement ring, big like a muffin, shining on Margaret's finger.

It must have been hard for GG, but it meant there was some space for me when I moved in and converted their living room into my love nest. GG should be grateful I offered to take the room, saved her from sharing with a total stranger. Andy was advising me against it but the rent was cheap, it was close to work and I needed somewhere I could bring a boyfriend. I knew what I was signing up for.

How GG can still live in this flat, I don't know. Kev thinks she's immune to it all. He said GG behaves like a psychopath and only then did I finally tell him about GG's revenge on Andy. He couldn't believe it. She really went to town with that professionally made stencil. It was an obscene advert and it had Andy's mobile number underneath.

I told Kev that she sprayed it all over the walls of the male toilets of all the pubs I know, and then some more around the neighbourhood. It made the news in the local newspaper. Andy had to get a new number. Once when he was drunk, he mentioned the 137 voicemails he'd had from sleazy types telling him what they would do to him. He cried in my arms, and Andy never cries.

But he should thank GG really. Without that experience, he would have never been granted an eight-week sick note and he would have never written that book with Margaret.

It is inspiring to see what people can do when given some paid time off. Not just bum around and watch TV all day. Kev and I could write a book together too. It would be about food and the joy of eating together, simply titled How to Eat *so it appeals to a wide crowd. Margaret told me that it's all in the title. If the title appeals to people, they will buy the book. That's why theirs is selling so fast. Everyone wants their life sorted, fast and for good. Everyone wants to eat too.*

Kev has officially started investigating Vincent's murder. He's so clever. He did the mapping of who and why, like on films, on my bedroom wall. We are now officially together. It took some prodding but Kevin finally updated his relationship status on Facebook. What it will need next is just a small change from 'in a relationship' to 'engaged'.

Kevin now worries about me when I am alone with GG. I told him that I can defend myself. I'm sure GG regrets what she did to Andy. After all, they gave her the maximum fine.

I actually think GG has recently mellowed. She wears a lot of Lycra but seems different. She brought me a pack of FitShop mints and offered me a discount to join the gym.

Or maybe her mood is to do with that actor? I couldn't believe when I heard the noise, but the banging of the headboard against the wall in the night can only mean one thing. Then, early, I heard steps in the corridor so I pretended to need a wee and walked out. And there he was. Ben. An actor! Up early and heading to work. But he hasn't been back since. Kev thinks GG doesn't know how to make a man come.

Gosia puts the diary away in a tote bag hanging in the wardrobe between knot-wrap mini dresses in rusty colours, and leaves.

33

A 24/7 fitness centre enhanced by a newly installed water cooler – fluid straight from Wales. Fluorescent lights shine steadily onto Gosia, who wears cheap burgundy yoga pants made in China. She has arranged, on a metal rack, a new delivery of fitness magazines and now she fills out a quiz to learn if she is at ease with her sexuality:

1) During sex I feel fine about asking my partner for anything I want, either vocally or with my body.
   Mostly disagree
2) I like to fantasise about different and unusual ways of making love.
   Mostly agree
3) I often think about my body during sex (does s/he find me attractive? Am I desirable?)
   Strongly agree
4) I like reading erotic fiction or erotic graphic novels that stimulate my desire.
   Mostly agree
5) I start to worry if my partner shows no interest in me for a few weeks.
   Strongly agree

6) I don't like it when my partner shows me affection in public.
   Strongly disagree
7) If I had a problem of a sexual nature, I would talk about it with my partner.
   Mostly disagree

LET YOURSELF GO. You are comfortable with your sexuality but in some situations you are reserved or reticent, and you might have difficulty communicating. If you're young, that's perfectly normal. It often takes time to grow into your sexuality. Perhaps you are putting the brakes on because you're afraid you'll go too far, or perhaps you experience your emotional and sexual life as if you were just an observer. Sexual pleasure and love can increase self-confidence so let it happen!

There is something in it. Every time she hears Lyndsey and Kev shagging behind the wall she imagines herself levitating above them, observing their sweaty backs, panting into each other's collarbones and hearing their muffled utterances.

'Suck my dick.'

'Grab my tits.'

His loud groans make her imagine him ejaculating onto Lyndsey's stomach before he collapses onto the bed. She uses his finger to come and moans into his armpit. They carelessly stain the sheets with their fluids and fall asleep.

Sasha, her manager, walks in. She checks for dust in the far corner of the U-shaped reception area, takes in a new display of endurance tops and bottoms, helps herself to Welsh liquid and speaks to Gosia.

'Janelle will cover for you. We need to talk.'

Gosia is alarmed. She hasn't talked to Sasha alone since the interview earlier this spring. Her month-long probation period comes to an end this week. Did Janelle report that badly handled complaint? Gosia refused to reimburse a customer who asked for a Mars bar, got it, ate it and was annoyed it wasn't Snickers. Or it might be about the moths that moved into the merino collection and have eaten three tops to date. She is careful not to browse websites and only sporadically logs on to her Facebook account from work. She duly uploads pictures of success stories on social media and endorses customers who like them. It could be about Vijay. She breached data protection laws and stole his address. She walks to a designated chair in the manager's office and feels her best-before date expiring.

Sasha sits down and talks to a sheet of paper.

'In your CPD plan you said fitness training. Are you still up for that?'

'Me?' Gosia's voice is small.

Sasha lifts her head.

'You. It wasn't that long ago. You filled it in when you joined, so I wondered if you were still interested? Unless you've changed your mind and now want to pursue, I don't know, reflexology or go back to retail. Things change. They shift in unexpected ways.' Sasha makes elaborate moves with her index finger. 'Take Janelle. She came here after a failed drama course all up for fitness, willing to expand on her body and voice training and then turned around and said she wanted to work with spreadsheets! All those accounting courses would drive me batty but she said she enjoyed it. So here we are.' She gives Gosia a long and careful look. 'Maybe fitness stopped interesting you. I won't be disappointed if you choose another direction. Lots of women go for massage, beauty therapy or, like me, management. So, how are things with you?'

Gosia allows herself to breathe. A picture of three young, sweat-free figures spinning on stationary bikes with smiles as wide as the English Channel hangs above Sasha's head. She's been through it once. In her previous job. With a clammy manager, pig face in a suit, mucus oozing out of the corners of his snout. He kept asking for her progression plan and frequently squeezed her knee, only to cut her pay for 'imperious aspirations', 'truculent attitude' and 'lack of commitment to the business aims' when she refused to join him for an after-work drink. It left her weak-hearted, baffled and ashamed. She never shared with him her well-preserved dream to one day be able to afford her own flat and live on a low-impact and high-salaried part-time job that would leave her enough time to do other things: lie on a sofa and read a book cover to cover in one sitting, bake fancy cakes or go for aimless walks.

But there is a mole on Sasha's face that makes her look genuine and kind. Not like her ex-boss, that vicious animal covered in weals, who took 70p an hour off her pay together with a slice of her self-esteem. She still wishes him nasty things.

Sasha's different, she doesn't assume things. At the interview she asked how she should pronounce Gosia's name.

'Gosh-ia' said Gosia. This led to a conversation about them both having Eastern European roots, eating sauerkraut and being able to roll their Rs.

'I like Zumba.'

Sasha checks the sheet.

'Your training could include that. You can choose from all sorts of options. You have to cover the basics: aerobic, strength, balance and flexibility. But then you can choose from a longer list: Body Pump, Groove FX, Body Synergy. Zumba is also included.'

Life has never offered dreams wrapped in cellophane complete with ribbon. Gosia tilts her head. 'How much would it cost?'

'It's a new scheme subsidised by head office and costs are covered, but you'd need to commit to delivering training sessions in community settings. It's all about developing new talent and bringing fitness opportunities to people who don't normally exercise: focus is on over-55s and young people at the risk of obesity living in small towns where we are due to open new branches.' Sasha pauses. 'You'd need to travel out of London.' She exercises her index finger some more. 'But after that you'd become a personal trainer and could work with whoever you wanted.'

She likes Zumba and what it does to people. Both pudgy and thread-like women come back for more, pat each other's bottoms, shave their armpits and put eyeliner on. They find something they thought they'd lost.

'I'll do that.'

'Great. Done. We'll be hosting the majority of the training sessions here and the course starts in two months as long as we enrol enough eligible people. Might need your help with this one.' Sasha's fake nail points at Gosia. 'One of the match-funding requirements is enrolment of a minimum of twenty per cent of local male students from diverse backgrounds. I thought you could target our customers with local postcodes. Could you work on that? Make some flyers? Talk to guys coming through the door?'

Gosia's eyes light up.

'Sure!'

Sasha puts the papers down. 'Perfect! I'll send you a link to an online form and you can just get on with it.'

There's no music to match her jubilant mood. Happiness prickles her cheeks. She stands by the door not moving a muscle but full of words.

You are the boss I've never had.

You are my hero. I owe you so much.

This is my passport to a better future. How can I thank you?

I never thought a boss could be anything but a soulless bastard.

You reignited my faith in hierarchical structures.

I am elated. You made my day.

Sasha is typing fast. She lifts her blonde head, her eyeshadowed eyes.

'Yes?'

Gosia asks, 'Will my pay be affected?'

34

A clammy afternoon in an airless small town outside London but located not as far as to be outside Birmingham. A heavy silence in a fuggy dining room in a semi-detached house. Mother, Chrissy, Gosia and the twins sit by a modern, white, high-gloss dining table with chrome details, and eat a formless lunch from durable, microwave- and dishwasher-safe plates. There is a scratch of knives, jabbing of forks and the muted laughs of little John who pokes little Paul. Mother hushes them with a frosty stare and turns to Gosia.

'So how is this training supposed to work? You'll all be exercising after work, in a group?'

Gosia had outlined the concept of the fitness training as a career development to her mother a little earlier, while peeling potatoes. She shared her news as soon as she arrived, in the hall, standing in her trainers between damp umbrellas and muddy wellies. Her mother just craned her head and said, 'M-hmm.'

'I guess so. But there are other elements too. I will have to learn about nutrition and anatomy.'

Mother purses her lips.

'What is there to learn? Eat three meals a day. Have a morning and an afternoon snack. It's all common knowledge, and I taught you that already!'

Gosia keeps her eyes on the beige food.

'So many people let themselves go these days and then diet and exercise to excess, only to let themselves go again,' says Chrissy. Post-baby fat that she attempted to lose using three separate dieting methods from random magazines sits under her top, each venture adding a solid stone to her frame.

Mother arranges a neat mushed heap on her fork and asks thoughtfully, 'Is it well paid?'

'Not to start with.' Gosia is still studiously maintaining eye contact with cheap china. 'But some people make a good living out of it. Some do stuff in magazines or videos for the internet or as part of big live events. A few work with celebrities. Some are celebrities themselves.'

Mother produces a crisp laugh.

'Well, you don't have to worry about that!'

Gosia's chest compacts.

Money is tight. Dad's loan requests come in monthly. She parted this morning with three hundred pounds in twenty-pound notes. Her exchange with Dad lasted just over a minute. She asked him how he was, he asked her back, but neither gave answers. His forearms bony, his skin sallow, his trousers filthy. He wanted another favour: a bag of clothes from his cupboard, some jeans and shirts, maybe a jumper, to be left out in the garden, by the back fence, before it gets dark. Gosia hasn't yet figured out how to disappear upstairs, pack the load and move it outside without Mother or Chrissy noticing. She will have to persuade them to go for a walk, convince them to enjoy the summer solstice outdoors rather than in front of the telly. She sighs; the course will eventually get her a pay rise. She won't have to eat rice with peas all week.

'Guess who I bumped into at the shop yesterday?' Mother's voice lightens. Her social collisions at the out-of-town supermarket the size of a two-runway airport are always seen as unexpected events.

No one dares to make a bad guess.

'Well?' Mother encourages with her sweet voice.

'Aunt Clara?' says Gosia.

'Oh, Gosia,' Mother takes a sharp intake of air at her pathetic attempt. 'You know that I take Aunt Clara to shop with me. We don't bump into each other. We go there together.'

Everyone chews a little bit too hard.

'Your school friend Rebecca!' Mother triumphs. 'Such a lovely girl. She married the Witfields' son Jim and they have an adorable child, little Julian. Such a good boy, he was helping Rebecca with the shopping and he's only a year older than the twins!'

Mother gives Chrissy a pointed look. John and Paul have already slid silently down their chairs and now sit under the table holding onto Chrissy's legs, patiently waiting for the dessert that on Sunday usually arrives promptly.

'She does this well-paid job supporting new business talents and they just moved three doors down from Melissa and Jeremy.' Mother is lost in her account, living a dream: 'Melissa is in love with her grandson and little Julian adores her to bits, "Granny can I have this, Granny can I do this." Little sweetheart.'

Mother's fondness for Picky Becky has been escalating ever since Bernie dumped her. She refuses to refer to her as Bernie's old flame, as if the relationship never happened. It is now clear to Gosia that Picky Becky was considered the perfect match for her brother – a local girl with high aspirations and a devotion to her family. Mother has successfully readjusted how Picky Becky fitted into her life, making her a blueprint for her own daughters. Gosia can't think of anything worse. She shivers.

John and Paul must be playing a thumb war; the faint noise of little boys with squashed digits travels to the surface.

'Even Aunt Clara was impressed. She proclaimed Rebecca a perfect daughter. Committed, successful and down to earth. I must say there is nothing snooty about her, although she's clearly married up.' Mother's eyes are stuck in the middle distance, halfway between the shopping Mecca and the dinner table. She has a benign smile on her lined lips as she says, 'Lucky for some. We have to make do with what we've got.'

35

The Bulletproof Guide to Sorting Out Your Life:
Work, Money, Free Time, Family, Friendship and Love.
STEP 43: How to Resolve Unfinished Issues

You are making great progress. Things should be starting to fall into place, people are doing what you want them to do and you feel energised by what the last forty-two steps have taught you.

However, by now you have probably noticed a collection of thoughts gathering at the back of your head, thoughts that stop you from fully enjoying your achievements. If you look at them closely, you will realise that they all relate to unfinished issues, some of them decades old, dating back to secondary school, if not nursery.

You thought they were gone but they bubble to the surface as you cleanse your mind and prepare yourself for your fantastic new future.

Usually when these thoughts emerge from under the carpet, the tendency is to push them back. This is not an approach we champion here. Now is the time to resolve them. Take them out into daylight, look at them closely and sort them out once and for all. It is hard but it is worth it! For Margaret, it was a relationship with her older sister that needed addressing. They shared a room when growing up and the build-up of negative emotions reached its peak around Margaret's GCSEs. This is when Margaret couldn't study as her sister kept her up all night talking about her boyfriend. Margaret ended up getting rather low grades as a result of her sister's heartache and her journey to her (at the time) dream career as a nurse was jeopardised.

Margaret never consciously realised that she held negative emotions towards her sister until she herself reached this step. She wanted her sister to know what a difficult and stressful time it was. She also realised she wanted to protect her own children, who also shared a room, from a similar situation. What did she need to do to put it right? She met up with her sister and shared her feelings as honestly as she could. She then made a decision to move house so her children had more space physically and mentally for their development.

What did the resolution to this unresolved issue look like? It took the shape of a coffee and cake meet-up that Margaret's sister paid for once she realised how much pain she had caused - and a bigger house in a nicer area for Andy and Margaret's children to grow up in.

As you can see, something as deeply buried and, on the surface, irrelevant as 'my bad GCSE grades caused by my sister' was actually an important issue linked to cramped living conditions and Margaret's worry about her children's future.

Now it is your turn and time to act. Look your demons in the eye, it is worth it. Remember, don't proceed to the next step until you resolve your unfinished issues.

36

A small council-run library with extended opening hours only possible thanks to volunteers. A large poster on the bathroom door reads: 'Pop in after work. Open till 8 p.m. on Mondays!' The reading area is in use by two people napping in the armchairs, rucksacks sprawled out at their feet.

Gosia is at her favourite screen and on extra time, immersed in the draft of an email she has been working on this evening. She wants to put things straight and get them sorted. Propelled by Step 43 and her urgent need for money, as well as some parts of her life finally falling into place, she writes.

Dear Anna,

You still owe me £25 for your fake tan. Could you send me a cheque or leave cash with Lyndsey next time you wax? (Put it in an envelope with my name on it, so Lynds doesn't confuse it with her tip.)

Remember my misplaced attempt to show Andy what a shit he was back when he left me? You stopped talking to me after that and I admit that I overreacted.

Humiliating him in that way was plain stupid. He wasn't worth it and it took a year to repay the fine.

The worst thing is that I put you in the middle of it. I am sorry for that. I should have told you what I really needed that stencil for.

I wish I'd seen it earlier. I didn't think you would leave me too. And I find it hard that you are best buddies with him now. But I wish you all the best, in everything.

Take care of yourself.

G x

Gosia reads through it again. She is happy with the tone. The letter comes from a place of strength. She wants her money back and she wants her conscience clear. Anna made it plain that she would never forgive her for making her a fool and an unsuspecting middle person, but Gosia doesn't want forgiveness, she wants a clean start. She wants the gap left behind by Anna sealed; she has leaked too many tears down that drain.

It feels wrong to send it via email. She copies the text to Word, chooses a calm and friendly font and hits print. She takes 10p to the counter. The librarian is filing complaint forms and a volunteer customer service assistant, whose badge announces her as 'Vicky, Here to Help', is staring at the screen as she says, 'I would send it as two separate letters.'

'Excuse me?'

'I think you should send it as two letters. "Give me my money back" first and then the apology.'

Gosia looks at her.

'Just want to help. I think you'll end up printing it again, so I'm saving you 10p.' She turns the screen to Gosia, 'Start from here again, as a new letter. "*Dear Anna . . .*"' – She points at the empty line between '*tip*' and '*Remember*'. 'I'll print both pages for 10p, so you see, it's genuine advice and not a rip-off.'

Gosia still holds 10p in her hand; her body goes numb.

'I'll leave it as it is.'

'Vicky, Here to Help' types fast. Then the printer hums gently in the background. The sheets pop out.

'Here you go. Both options. Both together as one letter and as two separate ones. I put the second version in green ink. It soothes people's eyesight. A demand for money doesn't come across as negatively as it does in black. Green makes it more pleasant. It will work with the apology too. If you don't like it you could always go for blue.'

Gosia stiffens. She pays, takes the sheets and doesn't give 'Vicky, Here to Help' even a single nod. She walks back to the computer, exposed. Her personal matters discussed out loud by a random person, young and stupid, who clearly knows nothing about pride, preservation and privacy. The sheets weigh her down.

37

A wet July day. A damp living room in a semi-detached house just fifty-five minutes on a direct train from central London. On the heavily scratched, oak-effect coffee table with a separate shelf for magazines stands a small, shop-bought round cake. There is one candle on it. It's not burning and has already been used. Next to it is a Colin the Caterpillar cake, eight lit candles arranged in two neat groups of four.

The room is completed with two sofas with freshly bleached throws on top, a vacuumed, multicoloured carpet with thick pile that dampens sound and provides a soft surface to walk on, a large flat-screen TV that is on and muted, and three large potted plants with leaves missing. The remaining corner is filled with toys in various shapes, sizes and colours and of varying degree of use and damage. Mother sits on a larger sofa in an apron. Gosia and Chrissy stand above the twins, who are playing on the carpet. The women sing.

'Happy birthday to you, Happy birthday to you, Happy birthday John and Paul, Happy birthday to you.'

The boys don't join in. One of them smashes the tower block made from Duplo with a teddy bear's head. The other one races a small car on railway tracks.

Chrissy shouts, 'Come and blow the candles now!'

They accelerate the play.

'Do as you're told,' Mother instructs.

They politely approach the table, one with a car, the other with the bear, and they spit on the candles. The women clap.

Mother starts cutting up the cake into generous portions. Gosia and Chrissy take seats. The twins eat it with bare hands. Chrissy takes a spoon. Gosia removes half of the portion onto a clean plate.

Mother sighs.

'Stop this diet. You are paper-thin. Who will want you with no fat around your hips?'

'Mum's right, Gosia. You look unhealthy.'

'I am fine. There are two birthday cakes to eat. I am leaving some space for mine.' Gosia eats a spoonful, looks away.

Mother continues.

'You'll only attract mean men with this body. Round women get rounded men, family-minded, hard-working types. Thin ones get all these deviants – bankers, politicians, actors and whatnot.' She looks up to the ceiling for inspiration to extend her list. 'I want you to have a decent man.'

'Could we stop now, please?' Gosia is two bites into her cake. The twins smear the cream on their tops.

Chrissy massages Gosia's thigh, tries to catch her eye.

'There's no harm in talking about it, Gosia. It's your birthday and you're not getting any younger.'

'Lord knows how lucky we are that Christine isn't like you! I couldn't stand it if both of you were so carefree. Who am I without the grandkids?' Mother shakes her head. 'You are thirty now, THIRTY. Time is ticking. TICK-TOCK.' She moves her finger from side to side. 'They said on TV how rapidly female ovaries shrink once you hit thirty-five and you can have deaf babies, mutants, or none at all.' Mother is crossing herself. 'I thank God every day that Chrissy married after school.'

Chrissy shifts in her seat. 'Well, nothing to thank God for, Mum. Twenty-five with two sons, no job, husband working away and I'm here, living with my parents.' She looks at Gosia again. 'You're doing all right, you're independent.'

Mother presses her lips and cuts another round of cake, and hands the slices out. The twins immediately crumble it in their hands and throw it at each other. Chrissy bites into her portion. Gosia refuses a top-up. Mother eats it herself.

'How's wedding prep going?' Gosia says lightly.

Mother straightens her back.

'Oh, really good! Itchybeer's abroad this month so I've asked Bernie to send me the copy of the seating plan. I told him that Aunt Clara must be at the main table, otherwise they can forget it. I'm pleased they're having a church service. Aunt Clara's on the case sourcing the right priest. She says the new young one from her parish is ravishing. Oh, the dresses! My lord! Itchybeer went for pretty pastels. You'll look stunning, Gosia, I told Bernie to tell Itchy to order size 10 for you, so you can plump up a bit.'

'How's Aunt Clara?' Gosia asks.

Mother perks up some more.

'Oh, she's fine. She was sorry she couldn't be here today. She has her choir practice every Saturday afternoon and they've a new hymn to learn. You know, that choir's her life but she left a birthday gift for you. Let me fetch it.'

Mother leaves. The kids pack the cake bits into the toy lorry. Gosia squeezes Chrissy's hand.

'Are you okay here?'

'Oh Gosia. It's a godsend. I don't think I would cope without Mum. Not ideal with one bathroom but, you know, we make do. The boys can't wait to see Duncan but that's another month. He calls, and sure, it helps, but it's not the same. What can we do? He'll be back for eight weeks and we'll try again then.' Chrissy's eyes go wet.

'You sure about that?'

'I want it so badly. Like crazy. And I want a girl. I'll try till I get one.'

Gosia looks her in the eye.

'Chrissy, do you really want to be popping them out till you get a girl?'

'But we are perfectly capable of having one. I want her to have Duncan's hair and dimples. And the twins are going to school in September. I could do with some distraction.'

'Get a job?' Gosia offers.

'You are such a feminist, Gosia! I really don't think I know what I'd like to do. I like being a mum. Feeding them, playing, going for a walk. I love being on baby time. I can't bear shifts and things. And what job would I get? I'm not fit for a till job. Not like you.'

Gosia looks away.

'I'm not on a till any more.'

Chrissy is confused.

'Oh yes, it's a counter, right? Being good with customers and money? I'd never be able to do all that. I got a D in maths, have no experience and would call everyone "love".'

Mother bursts into the room with three wrapped gifts.

'Here we go! This one is from me. This one's from Christine and Duncan, and this is the one from Aunt Clara.'

Gosia unwraps them in the same order.

Pink oven glove with felted polyester layer.

Maroon faux leather gloves.

Another oven glove, pink with white and yellow Hawaiian flower print.

'Oh.' Mother stares at the tropical flowers. 'Aunt Clara said it was tea towels, so I thought I'd match it.'

'Don't worry.' Gosia begins to fold up the wrapping paper.

They all shift in their seats. Gosia methodically tries all the gloves on. Chrissy grabs the matches and in a smooth move lights the single candle on the small cake.

'Come on, boys. Let's sing a birthday song. It's Aunt Gosia's birthday as well.' In a squawking voice she starts, 'Happy birthday to you!'

38

The Bulletproof Guide to Sorting Out Your Life: Work, Money, Free Time, Family, Friendship and Love. STEP 73: How to Celebrate On Your Own Terms

Are you stuck again in an Indian restaurant fighting indigestion after a second helping of rich curry? Are you dreading the fast-approaching moment to pay the bill for all twelve people around the table who are doing you a big favour by joining you on a bank holiday weekend to celebrate your wedding anniversary? 'How did that happen?' you ask yourself. Why are you here plunging even deeper into debt to spend time with your friends' spouses who bore you to death? You would rather go for an affordable option: a visit to a cinema to watch a romantic comedy with your partner and feed each other popcorn.

It is time to curtail expensive and expansive social obligations to celebrate on your friends' and family's terms. It is time to stop spending obscene amounts of money to be social. You do not have to be part of an entire hen-do weekend in Malaga. You can join the bride for a coffee at Heathrow before take-off and wish her a sunny stay. This way, you still show that you care and that you are a good friend, but without the need to sell your kidney on eBay to fund the escapade. Not to mention a whole weekend that you now have to yourself to pursue your goals and move your life forward.

The Malaga story is true. Margaret couldn't afford a lavish, all-inclusive, yoga retreat that her friend organised to please the bride. Margaret opted for a thoughtful and affordable way of celebrating her friend getting married – she posted ahead of time a 'Have a great time' card and Skyped the girls from the comfort of her flat while they were cramped together next to a tacky swimming pool in a seventies resort, clutching plastic cups filled with warm Prosecco. She knew then and there that she had made the right choice.

The savings of time, energy and money that this step affords you are often life-changing. The moment you realise that you CAN and SHOULD celebrate on your own terms usually brings with it a huge sense of relief. If the tightness in your chest goes once you have completed the table below, you will know that these unwanted, opulent social occasions that you feel pressured to be part of, are what was causing it. It is time to celebrate on your own terms!

Social obligations	**How do you celebrate them currently?**	**How do you want to celebrate them?**
e.g. Best friend's hen do	e.g. An expensive trip abroad lasting the whole weekend	e.g. An affordable celebration (a drink?) lasting an evening

Social obligations	How do you celebrate them currently?	How do you want to celebrate them?
e.g. Colleague's birthday party	e.g. A day-long celebration inclusive of expensive lunch and overpriced entertainment	e.g. A small contribution to their birthday present collection fund at work, combined with a brief but thoughtful note in the work birthday card
e.g. Buying gifts for extended family at Christmas (or other relevant cultural celebration)	e.g. An expensive gift or gift voucher for each relative, which is often of higher value than what you receive in return	e.g. An agreement not to buy each other gifts this year and instead to each bring a food dish for a family meal proportionate to their relative wealth within the family (higher earners to contribute meat-based mains, for example)

39

A small seaside town on the South Coast. Forecast for showers with spells of sunshine throughout the day and a stormy evening. Sea temperature: 15 degrees. Air temperature: 19 degrees in the sun. Body temperature: 37 degrees.

Gosia is feeling a bit hot and a bit cold. The sweaty patches under her armpits are now easily 10cm in diameter. This is her only top. Shirts in the nearby shop read 'Keep calm and drink beer' or 'Sunny bitch' or 'My sister went to the seaside and all she got me was this lousy T-shirt'. They are all priced at £15 each. The pebble beach is filled with groups of masochists jumping in and out of the water and screaming 'Fucking cold!' or 'Freezing!' or 'Love it!'

Gosia sits on the concrete steps, sweats and listens to the sea. She is tired, she caught the first train and the journey took ages.

The joint birthday party did not last long. She excused herself before the twins' bath time. Went to see Dad at the allotments, received a handful of strawberries as her birthday gift and departed minus one hundred pounds to help him out as 'the crops were late'. Since April she's loaned him nearly a thousand pounds. April was also when she last saw Vijay and that memory is fading fast.

Once home, Gosia fell asleep on the sofa, in an odd position, fully clothed with the sheets of *The Bulletproof Guide* crumpled by her side. She left the house before dawn and binned her new supply of oven gloves in a charity container in town. When she asked herself what her dream birthday would look like, her inner voice whispered 'seaside'. She would normally hesitate, swat away a silly little thought like that and stick to cleaning her windows. This time she made her way to the train station and purchased an expensive day return to a desirable location on the South Coast. Her fingers tingled as she keyed in her pin.

'Do you come here often?' A man, old but not repulsive, shirt half buttoned up, new vibrant fabric with busy flowery pattern on it. Short shorts. Tanned. Droopy muscles. Crooked teeth. Smiley.

'Pardon?'

He comes closer.

'I asked if you came here often.'

'First time.'

He sits next to her.

'Not tempted to dip your pretty toes in the sea?'

'No, not at all. Too cold for me.'

He looks in her eyes.

'Why would you come all the way to the sea and not even touch it?'

'I like it from here. It looks good. Tame.'

He laughs a short, crisp laugh.

'You should've seen it on Valentine's Day. The sea decided to kiss the land. It covered the pub, swept the beach away as well as two dozen boats. Proper bang!'

'So I've heard.' She hadn't heard a thing.

'Did you see any pictures?' He takes out an old iPhone, keeps it a metre away and thumbs through the images. 'Look at that!' A grey foamy wave covers the seafront. Next. Grey. Large droplets on the lens. Next. Haze. Next. A foamy wave above the pub.

'Nice! You captured it all.'

'I'm Rod.' He extends his hand.

'I'm Jane.' She shakes it. It's clammy, like hers.

'Jane. Nice strong name.'

He has a front tooth missing, smells of salt and seaweed and didn't shave today. His chest is hairy, and large moles cover his left arm, like an army of resting creepy-crawlies. He is too old for her, not much of a dating subject, not much of a challenge. But she could do with a shot of whisky and a bowl of chips, and she doesn't mind a hand between her thighs. There is a pub just 300 feet down from the promenade and there is a free table tucked in the corner, away from the families with two children, away from their Sunday lunch.

He knows everybody, shakes hands and kisses cheeks, holds her by her waist. He buys her a JD and a bowl of scampi, and later pays for a seafood platter and shots of tequila. Compliments her breasts. Asks her questions. Makes her laugh. Men her age never do that; they usually just want to know if she removes her pubic hair before they decide to take her pants off.

Families leave and the pub fills up with drinking men and women. A yachty sort in expensive anoraks and leather loafers. The sea turns rough and it's raining. She checks her watch. Her last day return leaves in thirty minutes.

'Stay the night.' He licks her ear. His hand deep in her pants.

'Do you have a spare sofa?'

He laughs.

'And I do a great breakfast.'

'OK.' She smiles, grabs her bag and goes to the ladies.

She leaves the pub through a small window just above the loo, scraping her hands and knees. She gets on the train two minutes before departure.

She is pleased with herself. She took what she wanted. She was desired, complimented, cared for, listened to and touched. She liked being Jane.

She doesn't think much about him once the train starts moving. Two birds with one stone: birthday on her terms, and some practice in keeping a man waiting. She found his story amusing, a failed musician exiled to a small seaside resort where a local pub lets him play his substandard songs about love, or worse. He thinks he can pull. He might think again.

40

The reading room of a local library, currently in use by a Residents' Association meeting. Nine people attend, debate is heated and loud. The Chair is pulling his hair out. Three out of five computers are in use. An older woman in a red jumper, a man with dirty fingernails and Gosia are immersed in the screens. They all have earphones in.

Rich_M wrote: 'The usual, and by this I mean bad. A story of a man for once. Unsurprisingly biased. I've had enough of this feminist-cheap-word diet that we are fed all the time. It pollutes the world of poetry and should be banned. How come this is one of this portal's "Poets to Watch"?'

TheBestOf_Suzie wrote: 'This poem touched a scar in my heart. I was only 17 when I met a guy like this. We were only dating for a few months but it was enough for him to squish my aspirations and turn me into his personal cheerleader. For years I felt like I had nothing interesting to say. It took a decade of therapy to understand what happened and to find my voice again.'

Woman_with_a_point wrote: 'How unsurprisingly that for *Rich_M* "he" is a synonym for "human being".'

RichardMutton_PoetForDarkTimes wrote: 'Poetry about human experience here.'

Wannabe

Wannabe has been musician
Told me a story of his life
In great detail
So I could appreciate his moment of fame

He came from a small town
Guitar was his only toy
Bought second-hand
He got his big chance at the age of nineteen

At a local venue
Where people point fingers at the ceiling
To any song
He played a set before Roxette

People went literally mental
There was sex on the dance floor
Rock and roll
Free beers, girls on his lap, pats on his back

Now he is livid that young people
Have it fast and easy
Record deals
Money and glory before they get wisdom teeth

41

A 24/7 fitness centre with a large display board advertising new classes and a rare opportunity to be a part of a subsidised personal trainer course delivered in partnership with the local council, the Job Centre Plus, a national organisation for the improvement of health and well-being and a 30-min-activity-a-day campaign supported by the Mayor. Gosia bathes in fluorescent lights while cutting freshly printed and designed in-house 'last chance to join' flyers with a pair of slightly blunt scissors. Bouncy hip-hop tunes are keeping clients motivated and focused on their personal targets. The annoying guy with a loud voice bobs towards the counter. He gives Gosia a small wave to attract her attention.

Gosia holds the scissors ready to cut.

'Good afternoon and welcome to FitYou, how can I help?'

'Ah, I had this beautiful dream. I woke up taller, slimmer and with a new career on my hands.' He chuckles.

She looks at him, thin-lipped, and patiently waits for more.

'So, I thought this must be a sign that I should enrol.'

She doesn't get it.

'To the course that you're about to start.' He points his index finger at the stack of flyers she has patiently cut into irregular squares.

'I see.' This must be one of those moments that Aunt Clara would refer to as a gift from the gods. They need at least one more man on the course to be eligible to start it. Does it matter that he grates on her? His presence alone irritates her. Is it because of his smile? He always smiles, especially on a dull day. Maybe it's his voice? Booming and rowdy, always too loud for the circumstances. Maybe it is because of his absurd interest in Vijay? Or is it the moves? He always seems to sway or tap his way across the floor as if dancing is his default. If she tried that in public she would be nervous, embarrassed and feel like a fool.

'It's excellent news that you would like to consider joining a personal trainer programme.' She takes a deep breath. 'There are some forms to fill in, that you could do online or right now, on paper. You need to show us some documents: ID, proof of address, your current employment status. There is a requirement to write a short personal statement. Just an outline of what you hope to achieve as a result of the course and what is motivating you to join it.'

He empties his pockets. Crumpled-up sheets appear to be a current gas bill, a council tax form and a letter from the Job Centre. He adds a debit card in a shiny plastic wallet.

'Will that do?'

She prints a form. Puts it in front of him together with a cheap biro.

'Here you go. Fill this in and bring it back.'

'My handwriting's awful. I'm better at typing but I used up my library internet allowance for the day.'

'There's always tomorrow,' she says brightly.

He sighs. Looks around. Points at the empty reception area with his hand.

'It's not like you're having a busy time.'

Gosia says nothing.

'Are you waiting for the magic word?' He taps his fingers on the counter. She cuts two more uneven squares.

'Abracadabra!' He laughs. 'OK, OK.' He takes a deep breath. 'Please. I'm saying PLEASE. Could you *please* help me to fill out this form so I could submit it today? *Please?*'

She puts the scissors away.

'Part of the programme requirement is to run ten classes in community settings. These will be outside London and you won't be paid to deliver them.'

He is tense.

'Fine. Whatever. Ten. Doable.'

She straightens the crumpled sheets. Grabs the form. Fills it in meticulously, frequently referring to his documents and occasionally asking him questions. He lives in a tower block on a sprawling estate somewhere on the other side of the high street. He is only thirty-four. He has an account with a building society. He identifies as white, working class, European and male. He wants an active job that is people-facing and doesn't require him to stand by a conveyor belt or spend hours glued to a chair in a call centre. His name is Steve.

42

The Bulletproof Guide to Sorting Out Your Life: Work, Money, Free Time, Family, Friendship and Love. STEP 11: How to Pursue Your Dreams

We all do it! It might be when you flip through a magazine and insert yourself into the pages of the perfect life of other people, thinking, *If I only had a car like this, hair like this, a house like this, skills like this*. You waste valuable time on daydreaming. You think that a perfect life is outside of your reach, beyond your control. Think again! You hold all the tools; you just need to use them. It is simple: instead of daydreaming, you need to learn to pursue your dreams.

Andy always wanted to write a book. He daydreamed about it, about the font, about the number of pages, about who he would mention in the acknowledgments. The shiny cover was vivid in front of his eyes, but he hadn't written a book – yet. He was excellent at making up excuses: he didn't have anything interesting to write about, he didn't have any valuable insights that would be of interest to others, he had no time to dedicate to such pursuits.

It was Margaret who introduced Andy to the importance of a routine and the magical powers of perseverance. She suggested they spend each Sunday morning working on his book: they would go to a nice cafe, order lattes and croissants and talk about ideas. Within weeks, it became obvious that he really did have strong material – the content of this book! They did not drop these important, Sunday-morning brainstorming sessions, as they both recognised this is where the best stories were generated, but they did spend an additional two evenings a week writing it all down. Word by word inserting it into Word.

In Andy's case, he needed a buddy and a collaborator to pursue his ambitions, but you can achieve the first step outside the house of daydreaming by yourself. The useful table that we have prepared below is all you need to get started and keep at it.

Nobody won the lottery without purchasing a ticket first. You can't achieve what you want if you don't work on it!

Dream	**Routine**	**Perseverance**
e.g. To write a book	e.g. Develop ideas on Sunday mornings; write two evenings a week regardless of other commitments such as social visits and childcare	e.g. Keep going until you have 90,000 words
e.g. To start your own business	e.g. Invest two evenings a week to create a sound business plan	e.g. Commit to and invest in building up your business – consider applying to a TV show where business people select companies to invest in, to raise profile

Dream	Routine	Perseverance
e.g. To find a husband	e.g. Be frequently present in places where cultured single men hang out: classical music concerts, 'Chinese for beginners' classes, tennis clubs	e.g. Meet new people and be eloquent, entertaining and enigmatic; once you are certain that you have found the right man, follow our advice outlined in Step 292

43

A warm and sunny July evening on a calm and quiet street on a hill. Terraced houses glued neatly together, each with a miniature front garden filled with compost bins, herbs on windowsills and padlocked plastic bike storage sheds. People walk up the hill weighed down with disposable shopping bags from a nearby supermarket. They disappear behind front doors painted in statement colours.

Gosia, in large sunglasses and a grey, forgettable dress, walks around the neighbourhood. She found the right house an hour ago but there was no sign of life indoors and no obvious place to loiter where she wouldn't attract the neighbours' gaze. She paces parallel streets, walks up and down the hill twice, spends some time studying the timetable at the bus stop, watches people getting on and off, reads announcements displayed on the community noticeboard.

She spots a neighbour from the house on the left. A young woman in a tailored jacket pushing a pram and cooing to a pink newborn. She spots neighbours on the right. A mother and son, or maybe a woman with her young lover. They leave the house and walk close together; he caresses her arm.

Gosia is about to give up when a bus arrives at the bottom of the hill and people pour out. She sees him straight away; she has spent the last three months waiting for this moment. She takes him in. Confident walk, an ironed shirt with a crisp collar, precise haircut, his cross-body bag gently bouncing along. She slowly begins to follow, keeping to the opposite side of the road and pretending to look ahead.

The man of her dreams whistles, searches for keys in his trouser pocket, opens the door and bends down to collect a letter from the doormat. A cat, a fluffy sort, appears by his foot, and he pets it gently, lifting it up into his arms and softly closing the door behind him.

She stops and exhales, faking interest in the neighbours' rose bush, touching the thorns. It's 7.38 p.m. So, this is it. He really lives here, behind an azure door with a silver number 11 attached above the spyhole, on the well-to-do side of the railway tracks, on the hill, in the sun, with a stunning view of the city and instant access to fresh, unpolluted air. She closes her eyes to enjoy the gentle breeze and the warmth. This address must come with a special microclimate. Where she lives, on the other end of the high street, beyond the park, in the dip, they've had a terrible summer.

She can see herself moving in behind the cloudless-sky door. She would not bring much. She can't think of many objects she owns that would go with the interior. There must be wooden floors, duck-egg-blue-coloured walls, a fireplace, cushions and throws. She is willing to shell out on a new tea set in imperial blue to match the curtains. The cobalt-blue glaze of the cups will accompany them at breakfast.

She sighs with delight and is about to leave when she spots another man, tall and muscular, in jeans and a T-shirt walking up to number 11, opening the door with his own key, disappearing into the mouth of the corridor. A flatmate? A mortgage in this location must be too much for one person. She could make friends with him, find out more about Vijay. His likes and dislikes. Little things that bring him joy. She checks her watch. It's seven forty-two. They finish work late.

She will come here again. She will persevere. But now, she walks home.

44

A kitchen with Zesty Blossom Harmony Range wallpaper in the glow of a single naked 50W light bulb. A small pot boiling on the stove, a washing machine spinning. A white cup and a white plate from the Basic Matters Home Selection in the sink. An extendable dining table extended. On it, a half-empty glass of water and an open letter.

Gosia takes in the contents of the envelope: a cheque in her name signed for the value of £25 and a card with an embossed 'GOOD LUCK' on it. The colour of the paper, a shade of green, matches the fake puke from popular cartoons. Inside the card, there are five lines of text written in the neat, careful handwriting of a measured and well-rehearsed response.

Dear Gosia,

Please find enclosed a cheque for the money I owe you.

Pleased to hear you've finally understood your mistakes and hope things work out for you.

Regards, Anna

Lyndsey's out for dinner with all the people who were once close to Gosia. Anna must be cooking her special meatballs in a rich tomato sauce. Andy will bring a trifle.

Gosia can hear the neighbours.

'Liar!'

'You make me sick.'

'I've had enough. I'm done. You hear me?'

Quick footsteps on the stairs, a door bangs and then Gosia drowns in the neighbour's sobbing. There is no rhythm to the convulsive gasps. It sounds exhausting, just like it was for her.

Back in secondary school, Gosia made stencils as part of an art week that didn't include the usual visit to a local museum where her class would normally fool around pretending to gather answers for a heritage trail designed for six-year-olds.

That year, they had masterclasses with an eager young artist who pretended not to hear the group's foul language directed at the size of her bottom.

The artist was short and her face became covered in red blotches when she stood at the teacher's desk and meekly asked for everyone's attention. Gosia stained her uniform badly with printing inks that week.

On the last day, they made stencils for posters about issues they cared about. Nobody took it seriously. A large selection of rushed, badly stencilled penis-like depictions polluted the girls' toilets for weeks. But Gosia made a mental note of what the artist said: that art is like a personal weapon, a tool to protect and fight for one's rights.

When the size of Andy's infidelity became apparent and she felt squashed and humiliated beyond repair, the weak voice of the young, self-conscious artist started haunting her. She couldn't sleep for days.

Anna had worked in a small, family-run company making laser-cut stencils. She always complained that these mainly included arrows and large signs for car parks, with only the occasional diversion. Gosia played her badly. Sent her a request to design and print a stencil for her 'mother's new business idea': handmade woolly items. A modest size that could be folded easily into a handbag and read, 'Call now for a really good sock', followed by Andy's number. She paid the full rate for it including next-day express delivery and spent an evening customising the crucial 'o' into a 'u'. The internet offered her a number of fluorescent paints in 500ml cans and she decided to dedicate an entire weekend to spraying the stencil on as many male toilet doors of chain pubs and sordid bars as she could find . . .

⋆ ⋆ ⋆

The night is warm and she leaves dressed for a party: short skirt, fitted top, biker boots. Her oversized bag, full of cans and the cut-out neatly folded into a tea towel, hangs prettily on her shoulder. She puts lipstick on, Andy's baseball cap and has a few shots of neat rum before leaving the house.

The first toilets are in their favourite pub on the corner, with wooden stools and a generous courtyard where they spent a number of evenings swirling warm wine in cheap glasses. This is where Andy first told her that he loved her. This is where Anna puked on her shoes. Gosia gets into the men's toilets to a cacophony of hoots and whistles. She locks herself in the only cubicle and works fast. Cut-out held in place with a strip of masking tape, a quick shake of a can, a hiss of the spray, a stink of the paint.

The squalid bar by the flyover is nearly empty so she stencils the wall above the urinals in three separate places and in three dizzy colours. She walks into The Goose, with its bouncers, live gigs and violet lights in the loos. Her short skirt attracts a hairy guy at a urinal. He moves towards her without washing his hands and puts both of his shovel palms on her buttocks. She turns on her heels, sprays his top and ignores his growling yells.

She finds her way to The Blue Lagoon, famous for the ease of getting drugs from the bartenders. Everyone in the toilet is high so she stencils both sides of the wall by the sinks. The music deafens her thoughts. She sprays to the beat. Careful and diligent to include the whole number and not smudge it.

She gets a taste for it and, fuelled by a lack of sleep, cheap wine, the thin light of the dark night and her endless internal rage, she stains a few garage doors, the side of a newly rendered building on the high street and the brick wall of the local cemetery.

It took Anna a full week to connect the dots, swallow her pride and provide the evidence. By that point Andy was already in touch with the police and had visited Gosia in person on a few separate occasions just to call her 'deranged' and 'a barking mad bitch' to her face without any solid proof.

Gosia had to do hours of community service washing off her own illicit words from all the seedy toilets in a mile radius. She had to divide her fine into months of instalments. Anna's letter doesn't surprise her really. Gosia has almost scrambled out of that hole but sometimes, in the biting darkness of moonless nights, she still thinks that she doesn't want to be associated with herself.

But now, with the cheque in hand, she makes a promise not to lose friends and not to let people treat her badly again.

45

A busy event in the library's reading area. A local MP responds to questions from the packed floor. Maps, pie charts and spreadsheets of planned road closures and new developments circulate the room. Gosia is the only logged-in user. She stretches her legs.

Woman_with_good_advice wrote: 'I find the last two lines infantile, too telling: "know-go-grow". Otherwise I enjoyed the tight structure that you worked with. There are some unfortunate moments: "have it easy" or "pretty", or "nice". I can see that you are trying to use the language of clichés to your advantage but I am not sure if you have succeeded.'

KarenStevensWrites wrote: 'I love "a slice of cake, a bit dry, our lives with a boring cast", I don't think you could put it better. I enjoy what you are trying to achieve here: high and low being connected in an interesting and provocative way. I find the last two lines very compelling. "Walk to the river" is a beautiful metaphor with many cultural references. I personally wouldn't change it.'

Derek_Admin wrote: 'Keep poetry platform free. Donate now.'

Rich_M wrote: 'A load of unreadable sh*te.'

RichardMutton_PoetForDarkTimes wrote: 'Poetry that speaks to heart and mind here.'

Friend

My friend didn't have it easy
She dealt with my issues
Shared too many fizzy
drinks, left behind wet tissues

My friend didn't have it pretty
She saw me curse and fret
We talked love, life, nonsense, gritty
Words, that made us cry and sweat

My friend didn't have it nice
We shared an uneven past
We didn't dare dream big, a slice
Of cake, a bit dry, our lives with a boring cast

My friend didn't stand by me
She said I've gone too far
And I will let her be
Wave goodbye, au revoir

It's empty and dark now but I know where to go
I will walk to the river, touch the water to grow

46

A dining room in a semi-detached house in a small town just within London's commuter belt. All the seats next to the modern, high-gloss dining table with chrome detailing are occupied. Six women wearing white cotton gloves sit and glue pink bow ribbons to shiny, brilliant-white cards. The finished invitations pile up in the middle. Gosia sighs and checks the time. Mother scolds her with a biting look.

'Tea break?' trills Chrissy.

Nods of approval around the table.

Mother takes over.

'You know the drill. Drinks in the living room, so we don't mess these up. I'll put the kettle on.' She heaves herself off the chair and walks to the kitchen.

'I think this bow isn't straight.' Aitziber lifts up a card that Gosia has just added to the heap.

Women look at the card, at Aitziber, at Gosia.

'I think it is.' Gosia tilts her head to inspect.

Aitziber grabs a ruler, puts it underneath the bow.

'See? Wonky! I don't want wonky.'

Aitziber's eyes fill up with tears and Maria Luz, her best friend and confidante, gently pats her arm.

'Just mark it as mine. I don't mind wonky,' Gosia offers.

Aitziber grabs a fountain pen stored in a small metal case, specially purchased for the occasion. 'Who should I name on the invite?'

'Well, me, of course.'

Aitziber prods.

'Are you not bringing a date?'

Gosia dabs a little glue and firmly holds the tiny bow in its designated place on another card.

'I might. Just put it down as me with a guest.'

Aitziber checks her spreadsheet.

'That makes it 124 guests.' In her large, even, round handwriting she puts on the wonky card 'Gosia Golab & Guest'. She ticks two numbers off her list, seals the envelope and writes Gosia's name on it.

'Do you want me to post it?' Aitziber holds the envelope in mid-air.

'No need.' Gosia smiles. 'I prefer delivered by hand.'

Aitziber stiffens.

'Bernard told me that is the Polish custom, but we won't be adhering to it. There is no time. The wedding's too soon to drive around to everyone. We have too many guests.'

Gosia looks for support to the others around the table and says in a slow voice:

'That's not what I meant.'

But she feels a little stab underneath her ribs. Her family never visits. They never helped with any of her moves. She left home at nineteen with a small, heavily used suitcase on wheels. Dad dropped her off at the railway station, gave her money for her first week in a cheap dorm, infested with bedbugs and pickpockets. Mother's only question, 'Are you sharing with girls?' Dad asked if she wanted a penknife. Aitziber's words pierce the scab on her hurt feelings.

'You can give it to me now. I really don't mind,' she bluffs.

Aitziber extends her hand with the card over the table and arranges her lips into a smile.

'Here you go, Gosia. It would be a pleasure to have you at my wedding. I hope you can share this important day with us.'

Gosia grabs it.

'Thank you. I'll be there, and I'm really looking forward to being your bridesmaid.'

Aitziber raises her eyebrows.

'Excuse me?'

Gosia looks at Chrissy and their cousin Viola, who is visiting specially from Poland, apparently to help get things ready for the wedding.

'Bridesmaids. Mother keeps telling me about the pastel dresses that you want us to wear.'

Aitziber raises her voice.

'There must have been a mistake. There is only one bridesmaid.' She points at her friend. Maria Luz goes red. Mother walks in.

'Tea and cake in the living room.' She dries her hands on the apron. All eyes are on her. 'What is it now?'

'The bridesmaids . . .' Chrissy starts, but Gosia takes over.

'Nothing. Just a misunderstanding.'

Mother looks at them all.

Aitziber continues in a high pitch.

'I told Bernard three times. One bridesmaid, one best man. We are not going to have the crowds in our picture. It is a Spanish wedding. He doesn't mind. Don't you?'

Mother sits down.

'Good lord. I just want my daughters to be part of the day, Itchybeer. You'll be sisters soon. I just thought it'd be a lovely way to bond. So we all have fond memories . . .' She looks at Viola, for the first time today without hostility in her eyes. 'Your mum was my bridesmaid. She loved it to bits.'

Gosia is not sure if Viola follows; her English vocabulary is limited and she tends to smile and politely agree to things.

Aitziber is not amused.

'But it is my wedding!'

Gosia is using her soothing voice, the one she specially developed for needy and capricious customers.

'As I said, it was a misunderstanding. Maria Luz is your bridesmaid and we will come as guests. Thank you so much for the invite.'

Chrissy adds, 'Cake, anyone?'

Viola gives her a shy smile. Chrissy and Viola stand up and leave the room, Maria Luz and Aitziber follow. Mother inspects the cards. Gosia scrapes the glue off the glove.

'There's no need for matching dresses, for all the bridesmaids nonsense.' She talks with her head down. 'It's about Bernie, not us. Just let them do it their way.'

Mother sighs.

'How can you have this attitude? It breaks my heart. First proper wedding. In a church. All the family will be attending and you are not even a bridesmaid!'

Gosia is glad Chrissy doesn't hear this. Her sister got married in a town hall, aged nineteen, and had a reception in the basement of the local community centre that lasted two hours and was attended by twelve people. Mother didn't pay for any of it, her hatred towards Duncan evident in every grimace. Duncan's parents did not make it down from Scotland and his brother turned up slightly drunk.

'The invites aren't even out yet. It's all a bit of a rush.' Gosia lifts one card from the heap on the table, presents the proof. 'The family may not even show up.'

She knows she touches a sore point. A buried memory, heavy like a foundation stone, that her mother carries with her wherever she goes. The memory of her own wedding that took place almost thirty-one years ago, when a large part of her family did not show up because she was marrying a Pole.

Earlier in the day, Gosia found a D8 form hidden behind the bread tin, the *Application for a Divorce* line poking out. Her mother had filled out most of it. In Section Six, *Give the reason for your divorce or dissolution (the facts)*, Mother ticked Option Two: *Behaviour: The Respondent has behaved in such a way that the Petitioner/Applicant cannot reasonably be expected to live with the Respondent.*

'Tea's going cold,' Mother says.

47

A cloudless evening. The sun weakly sticks out from behind tall trees at the edge of the allotments, ready to dip. The path is well trodden, the grass underfoot flat, surface uneven, damaged by the wheelbarrows.

The plots of land are lavish and green; apples and pears hang heavy on branches, slowly turning yellow and red. Cabbages expose their pert hearts. Beetroots poke out from the soil and work on their bulk. Runner beans strangle bamboo sticks, the pods ready to split.

A crisp smell of freshly cut grass, a sickly aroma of rotting berries, and the sweet scent of the freesias that line the rickety fences hit Gosia in her nose. Viola is walking by her side, pointing at things, calling them Polish names: *jabłoń*, *ognisko*, *działka*. As if she is trying to unlock something in Gosia's brain. Viola's bag is heavy on Gosia's arm. There is no way to wheel it on the dirt. Viola carries her backpack, nearly as large as her, the straps digging deep into her shoulders.

'Is she planning to move in?' Mother had whispered to Gosia over lunch, pointing at Viola's bags abandoned in the corridor.

There is no one about. Gardeners long gone to their homes, to husk, hull, pod and preserve. The patches of land raked, tools put away, veg watered.

They approach her father's field, a front gate wide open, empty. Flimsy, single-use wooden boxes for fruit line the lawn, some of their slats broken or missing.

Dad can be seen at the back, turning compost, a pitchfork in his weedy hands. He is clearly not expecting their visit.

Mother had sent Gosia to go and find her father to 'take care of the problem'. Gosia had pretended she didn't know where to look.

'Go to the allotments,' Mother had barked. The box of ripe fruit and veg carefully scrubbed of soil had lain deserted by the kitchen door. Mother had not wanted to touch it. Gosia had helped herself to the blackcurrants and the raspberries when Mother was not looking.

There was no room for Viola in the house, Mother had announced. She had stopped Chrissy mid-sentence, forbidding her to offer to sleep with the twins.

'Hi, Dad!' Gosia shouts, to give him some warning, time to abandon the putrid mound and wash his hands before coming their way.

But Viola is fast to ditch her rucksack on the ground, and she walks towards Gosia's father like a nymph, leaping on the grass, her quavering voice repeating, '*Wujku! Wujku!*' You would think they mean the world to each other; you would think they share more than blood.

Gosia follows, bewildered by the welcome. By her father lifting Viola off the ground and spinning her in the air once, twice. By the shriek and the quality of their speech, fast and rough. By Viola cuddling into her father's chest like a child when Gosia is fairly sure that Viola must be nearly her age.

Her father extends his hand, welcomes Gosia into the embrace, but Gosia only squeezes his palm and keeps her distance. From where she stands she can smell him: dry sweat and decay.

'*Herbata?* Tea?' Her father says, and Viola nods her head eagerly as if she was kept dry-mouthed all day.

Dad goes to the shed and Gosia follows. She wants to have a peek in that box, the box that told her mother that Dad behaved in such a way that she cannot reasonably be expected to live with him any more. Dad blocks the entrance, looks at her with surprise.

'I can make tea and you can catch up with Viola,' she offers, her voice not betraying her intentions. She holds her breath.

'You better get the seats ready. I will have a whole month with Viola, and you, I guess, have to head home soon?' he asks.

'A month?' The question escapes her mouth before she can tighten her lips.

'A month,' he nods. 'She wants to practise her English and help me with the garden,' he says, searching for tea and mugs in the darkness of the shed.

Gosia can spot a camp bed neatly folded in the corner, kept apart from the tools. On an inhale, the shed smells of lavender, mint and thyme. Large bunches of them are drying above her head.

Dad has upgraded to a larger gas campfire and a new barbecue and he offers tea made from a teabag each. That's what her money bought him; she bites her tongue.

Viola is head-deep in her rucksack, trying to get something out and struggling. Dad urges Gosia with a firm press of his palm on her arm to give Viola a hand, and gently pushes her out of the shed.

Viola pulls out metal poles, and a roll of deep green cloth, and then there is an air mattress and a pump, and a thick, goose-down sleeping bag. She is going to camp! Gosia's head spins. Viola quickly assembles her tent. It's a small, one-person structure that she pins with the pegs to the ground between the gooseberry bushes, away from the path, concealed by the growth. She offers Gosia a foot pump and the mattress. Gosia takes her time to connect the vent, to fill the folded fabric case with air while Viola digs to the bottom of her backpack, extracts a towel, toiletries, a pair of flip-flops and a pair of wellies, a torch, a pack of batteries and a raincoat. Her bag on wheels is full of neatly folded clothes and fits snugly in the corner of the tent, like a wardrobe.

Gosia has never camped because her mother always hated it. They would usually rent a cabin by the seaside, just after the season, making them all miss a week of school. It would be fish and chips for tea and a daily argument. It would rain a lot. The cabin was small and her parents' voices were loud, so she would press her fingers into her ears as far as they would go and she would read to herself out loud from a book about characters with adventurous lives. She realises that camping would have made these holidays a lot worse.

Dad brings the tea and Viola drinks it like it's an elixir, making satisfied noises after each sip. It makes Gosia sick, the gratitude seeping out of Viola's body. That look of a needy dog, thankful and indebted for a rug to sleep on, for leftovers to eat. Viola's face, normally twitched and deformed by rapid eye movements or a lip tremble, is still and symmetrical, content and calm.

'I must go,' Gosia says. The sun is low and she does not want to walk back in the dark. The Saturday-night train will be filled with a rowdy crowd, heading to town for an all-nighter. She did not anticipate enduring that today.

'See you soon!' Viola offers in her stilted English, wrapping her hands around Gosia's neck, giving her a loud kiss on each cheek.

Dad walks her to the gate.

'What is this mess for?' She points to the boxes scattered on the lawn.

'Good to move veg around. Finally selling some, but it's slow-going. Loads of people are on holiday and only a few of my regular clients are about.'

'Are you all right for cash?' she asks, her stomach clenched. She gave him one hundred pounds on her birthday and nothing since. She gives herself an internal punch for opening up to more.

'I could do with another loan,' he whispers, clearly not wanting Viola to hear.

'How much?' She is squeezing her thumbs with her fingers, delivering just enough pain to stop her from screaming.

'Four hundred.' He doesn't hesitate. It's not a slip of the tongue. 'It's temporary,' he adds. But she doesn't believe him.

'All right. I'll bring it up next time I'm in town.' She says, defeated. This will empty her cash ISA even further, and she can't afford to dip into her overdraft.

'And wait, I need you to have something.' He walks back to the shed, his steps urgent. He disappears into the opening and emerges a few moments later with a brown bag in his arms. He approaches with a smile and hands the bag over. It's heavy.

'That's for you,' he says and kisses her on the cheek. The smell of rot travels to her nostrils. She holds the bag like a baby, careful not to drop it, and walks with it in her arms all the way to the train station. Maybe this is his way of sharing his secrets?

On the train she spreads out over two seats and slowly opens the bag. It is full of new potatoes.

48

A small bedroom congested with furniture and tat. A web of brown parcel string links up words, line drawings and an article cut out from a local newspaper with a picture of Vincent in his front garden, his smile wide and bright and, next to him, a pear tree heavy with fruit. A large title: 'Killed In His Own Kitchen'. A yellow Post-it stuck to the article with 'Victim' written in black pen. Below, another Post-it with the word 'Suspect' accompanied by a list of three numbered names: 1. Bulgarian cleaner 2. Neighbour 3. Unidentified visitor. The bed is covered in clothes still on hangers. By the entrance, pressed against the doorframe, Gosia stands and reads.

I lost 3lb during our holiday. We had fizzy water all the time and only one Diet Coke a day. Or two at the most. We swam loads in a lovely heated pool with a jacuzzi corner. It helped that the food was awful. Bland cereal for breakfast. No bacon, no sausages. Salad and grain for lunch. For dinners they served white fish but grilled with no batter and steamed green leaves. The worst all-inclusive in the history of my holidays. I gave them one star in my review.

We went hungry for the first twenty-four hours and then found a KFC around the corner and normally shared a bucket for lunch and had double ice cream after dinner. It kept us going. But the weather was amazing and we both have a great tan. I show it off wearing my tight white shorts. Hard to be back though.

Anna called as soon as we touched the tarmac and said GG wrote to her. Anna asked if I knew what was going on. It left me speechless, so I told her I knew nothing. GG is a secretive person with a twisted mind. She befriended Kev on Facebook as soon as he and I started dating. Her profile is empty and I can't see any of her pictures.

It's only thanks to her sister's wall that I know a thing or two: a picture of GG's pathetic bday party, mention of her brother's wedding. I said to Anna, GG might be worried who to take to the reception. We all heard about her family from Andy – a nightmare! I would want a male arm I could grab with all the judging aunties lined up by the bar.

I asked Anna what the letter was about, but she said nothing and changed the subject.

Kev is going strong with his investigation. He gathers all the evidence and puts it up on the wall. It looks well pretty too. All of the lines and Post-its. He made drawings of the murder scene based on the article alone! He has three suspects and wants to interrogate them all. I want to help out but he says we have to be canny about it. He wants to start with the Bulgarian woman, get her to come and clean his flat, have a conversation as she scrubs the tiles.

I said to him that I'm not going to leave him alone with her, and he said she's only a woman and he can floor a large bloke with a proper knife in his hand if he needs to.

I know I shouldn't worry but I do. She might be faster than Kev, or he might not notice her slipping drugs into his tea, or she might come with someone else. I just don't trust foreigners.

Gosia puts the diary into a used jiffy envelope, slides it back under the dressing table and leaves.

49

Gosia logs in.

Kevin Harris added a new photo. 'Grub with mates. Thanks chef!'

14 people like it.

The picture shows Andy with the twins in his lap, exposing his crooked teeth. Margaret crouches by his feet, holds the hand of one of the children and looks lovingly towards the ceiling. Red-cheeked Anna stands behind, with one hand on her belly – she must be suppressing her IBS symptoms. A man Gosia has never met stands on Andy's other side with a glass of beer in mid-air and halfway through the 'Cheers!' Next to him, barely in the frame, is Lyndsey's cleavage, part of her leg and the side of her face.

Andy Knight via mobile: 'Party animals!'

Lyndsey Oates via mobile: 'LOL'

Margaret Bark-Knight via mobile: 'What a night. Good to c u all!'

Anna Walker via mobile: 'Really loved our evening together. Must do it more often.'

Kevin Harris, Margaret Bark-Knight, Andy Knight, Lyndsey Oates and Bruce Woodcock like it.

Gosia peers at Bruce. He looks like Anna's type, all hair and torso. Gosia logs out.

50

The Bulletproof Guide to Sorting Out Your Life: Work, Money, Free Time, Family, Friendship and Love. STEP 123: How to Tell People How You Feel

We are conditioned to be nice. This is not a bad thing in the majority of social situations: when negotiating the price of your new car, for example. But sometimes, keeping your feelings to yourself can cause long-standing damage to your psyche that will take years to work through, not to mention all the emotional energy that you will have to spend on it.

Life gets easier (and you can preserve a lot of energy for more important things) when you tell people how you feel, when your friends and family do not have to second-guess your state of mind. You may want them to be able to read your mind, to detect that you are in a bad mood from the way you launched a used teabag into the bin, but this just leads to endless frustration. Do not think that people can see your emotions in the way you interact with inanimate objects.

Andy, in his previous relationship, found himself often wondering if his ex (let's call her Gloria) was happy or not. Gloria was a solemn person with a dour face. She would arrange cutlery in an odd manner on the table and Andy was sure there was a code to how the spoons and forks were laid out but he never managed to crack it. He was always second-guessing her emotions and found it exhausting to continually have to figure out if she was in the mood for a walk, a coffee or a conversation.

It was a breath of fresh air for Andy to meet Margaret as she voices her feelings openly and loudly, never leaving you in doubt of her emotional state. It makes everyone's life easier if you know whether your beloved is happy or angry with you.

Letting bad feelings accumulate leads to rows about nothing, where an emotional balloon bursts because of the smallest, silliest thing that has nothing to do with the stockpile of bad blood.

How not to let bad emotions accumulate? Burst that balloon early, or ideally do not fill it at all.

We advise you to follow these three principles for communicating your emotions:

1. **Tell people how you feel.**
2. **Use straightforward language to do so.**
3. **Do not leave any room for speculation.**

Once, Andy was running late and didn't inform Margaret. When he arrived, thirty minutes behind the agreed schedule, Margaret was not simmering in her anger or stuffing it in an emotional sock for later. She openly told him how she felt in a few sentences along these lines:

'You are thirty minutes late and you did not warn me, therefore, for the last half hour, I have been worrying myself sick that you might have died under the wheels of our neighbour's sports car. It might sound fatalistic but I can't help thinking the worst when I am kept waiting. In the future, I want you to call me to let me know that you are going to be late and give an accurate time of arrival. This will keep me calm and I will also be able to spend my time doing something more productive.'

Margaret's openness about her mind going into the dark space of worry and anxiety allowed Andy to understand that he causes her anguish when she doesn't know where he is. Andy simply keeping Margaret informed of his whereabouts resolved the issue, as opposed to Gloria's approach of long silences, mysterious utensil arrangements and heavy sighs.

Now it's your turn. Tell people how you feel and watch your relationships flourish!

51

A corridor in a 24/7 fitness centre filled with a group waiting for a class. People in breathable Lycra fidget on cheap, wood-effect flooring that bows and creaks underfoot. Many rest their backs against the concrete walls painted sterile white; some bash with their thumbs at the phones that can't access 4G. Harsh overhead lighting accentuates the dark circles under everyone's eyes.

Gosia stands back a little from the group and scans the crowd. They are all waiting for their introduction class. The corridor is heavy with the breath of future personal trainers. She is tapped on the shoulder.

'Hi, pet!' That loud guy that follows her around extends his arms ready for a hug. 'I got in! All thanks to you.'

He throws himself on her, embraces her rigid chest, pats her shoulder blade.

She gives in, pats his back in return and whispers into his ear, 'If you call me *pet* again, I will cut off your balls.'

He laughs.

'Feisty woman! Sadly, you aren't my type and I'm not into S&M, but I can give you a number . . .'

'I mean it.' Her voice is stone cold.

He takes a step back, gives her a tentative look, pulls at his cotton tank top.

'I'm sorry. I just don't know your name. Steve, I'm Steve. Should've asked you before!'

He sounds genuine. A drop of saliva is gathered in the corner of his mouth.

'Gosh-ia.'

He clears his ear.

'How do you spell that?'

She rolls her eyes.

'G-o-s-i-a,' she takes a deep breath, 'although you're supposed to say "nice to meet you" or something along those lines.'

'Sure thing, very nice to meet you. After all this time! I feel like you've been following me around.' He smiles. 'Wherever I go, I bump into you. Thought social services sent you to check on me. Supermarket, bang, there you are. Library, surprise surprise, who's using my favourite computer? And then here. Bloody hell, in MY gym! Are you planning on showing up at my dance class any time soon? I promise, I won't act surprised.'

He looks at her again. It's a glance she knows from the builders down the road, always commenting on the size of her arse as they mix cement. They scan her head to toe, taking in her body as if it were a dummy in a shop window display.

Something loosens up in her. She feels in control. She doesn't mind the crowd in the corridor tightening behind her back. She's taken too many of these looks without a word of complaint. She is ready to bite.

'Don't you ever look at me like that again.'

He panics, looks confused.

She repeats, spitting each word out.

'Don't. Give me. That look.'

He looks around.

'What look?'

'This one.'

She takes his body in, slowly. Starts at the top of his balding head, scans the irregularities of his face, lingers at his chest, pointedly ogles his torso and fatty breasts that are larger than hers. She takes pleasure in assessing his pudgy belly, short shorts pinned around his crotch, chunky thighs, dark curly hairs on his calves, enlarged veins, small feet in old trainers, white socks sticking out, wrapped around the ankles. She wouldn't.

'God. You give me the shivers.'

'It doesn't feel great, does it?' She moves towards him. 'Imagine getting it five times a day. Random locations, random guys.'

He looks at her towering over him.

'Flipping heck. I'm sorry. I just looked at you as I normally do. I'm not here to pull you. Relax! I'm gay. And I didn't mean to offend you.'

His body suddenly feels weak and wounded. She steps back.

'I didn't mean to attack you.' But she hums with anger, the hair on the back of her neck bristles. She breathes through her mouth, squeezes her hands into tight fists. 'I don't usually risk being punched or labelled a frigid bitch.'

He irons his hair with his hand.

'Don't worry. I'm not into manhandling people. And I don't think you are any such thing. You're helpful. I just wanted to say thank you, really, for saving my life. I would've had to start working at the biscuit factory, packaging custard creams if it weren't for you and this training. I'm bloody grateful. New life ahead of me.' He lifts his hand up in the air, pointing at the door of the training studio.

Gosia follows his gaze. The door opens with a squeak and a five o'clock Body Pump group glowing with sweat spills into the corridor, pressing everyone against the wall.

The heat gathered in her throat is slowly melting.

'Glad I could help.'

He assembles a sterling smile and offers his hand.

'Friends then?'

It is a warm male hand with hairy fingers and clipped nails. She shakes it.

52

A sunny Saturday, promising a long, unruly queue for soft ice cream in a cone. A cramped greasy spoon situated on the edge of a commuter town, away from the centre but near an industrial estate and a sprawling development. The new houses look like cardboard cut-outs.

In front of the cafe sits Dad's trailer, fit to be horse-drawn. A decade or so ago, he spent a whole summer modifying it so it could be operated by bike. 'Organic Food Forever' is painted in large, lopsided letters on the side. The trailer is filled with empty boxes, some loose veg and a tote bag.

Mother has always laughed at Dad's food business.

'Your daddy is busy with his OFF fruit and veg,' she would snigger, although it all functions under her name – The Calamity didn't allow for her father to run a legitimate enterprise. Mother must have some remaining grains of conscience stopping her from shutting it down.

Here they are, occupying a window seat, deep in conversation. Their heads above steaming plates of eggs and beans. They look like a family, like a couple of people who get on.

Gosia walks in and the bell jingles. The place is full and reeks of cheap fat and chips. She wants to gag. They lift their heads and Dad smiles, extends the third seat, a stool, from under the table.

Viola says, 'Good afternoon,' BBC presenter style, all consonants and vowels pronounced.

Gosia settles and when a waitress comes up to the table, she regrets she agreed to meet them right here, in this bloody caff.

'Gosia? Long time no see,' says the waitress, as Gosia recognises, in the creased, oily face and stout arms, her classmate Jessica. 'Your dad said you would be joining. What a surprise!'

Jessica was always known for three things: her ability to drink a pint of beer in one go, having a third nipple that she would show off to boys for money and her love of gossip. Like a server farm, she is able to store an endless amount of rumours, potential scandals and titbits overheard in a church pew, a lunch queue or by the gravestones. Gosia feared her at school and always kept her distance. She would be careful where she looked and who she talked to when Jessica, with her hungry eyes, was scanning the room.

Now Jessica is looking at her, trying to learn all that she can from Gosia's clothing, hairstyle and the lack of rings on her fingers. In her hand she is clutching a greasy cloth and cleans the crumbs off the table as she asks, her voice light and innocent, 'Helping your dad and Viola with preserves this afternoon?'

Dad smiles his praiseworthy smile, all teeth out, and cheerfully nods.

'Anything to drink? Anything to eat?' Jessica encourages.

'Can I get a glass of tap water, please?' says Gosia. She can't waste money on the bottled sort.

'A glass of tap water?' Jessica repeats with a squawk. She laughs and her bosom shakes above Gosia's head. 'No wonder you're as thin as a rake. Would you like a bacon butty with your glass of water?'

Half the cafe is laughing now. Jessica is strolling to the counter, receiving high fives from some wide-chested men two tables down.

'How are we?' Gosia asks, keen to change the subject, keen to leave.

'We had a very good day at the market.' Dad's voice is delighted. 'Sold out! Thanks to Viola.' He points proudly at his niece, who chews carefully, her face warping. 'She is a natural with the customers and has charm not many people can decline.'

Charm? Viola's posture is one of a beaten dog, shoulders folded over her chest. Her face oddly flexed, arched and curved. The twist in her lips more evident when she speaks, her facial muscles kinked. Gosia only once saw her mutate into a different kind of girl; that first time in Dad's allotment, when her features relaxed and her body straightened.

'We made a small fortune!' Dad adds. 'Viola suggested we make some preserves, and those sold before we even finished unpacking.' Dad lowers his voice. 'Don't tell anyone, but we made the jams and chutneys from rejects!'

Gosia wonders if the knowledge of the manufacturing conditions would not cause more of a concern. She imagines Viola and her dad boiling fruit on the campfire, flies included for higher protein content.

Gosia touches her bag. She has another brown envelope. The requested four hundred pounds issued across two days from two different ATMs. She has never carried this much cash with her. She questions if she should offer it, since things are clearly going well.

'So we are going to upgrade our set-up and make more money. We decided, Viola and I, to invest today's income into more equipment to double production.'

'I see.' Gosia's voice is vacant.

'And I thought Viola deserved a treat!' Dad gently pats his niece's forearm. 'A day in a big city with the best guide I know!' He points at Gosia, his face stretched into a smile.

'A day with me? In London?' Gosia's bewildered. She keeps her voice low while her water is delivered.

'From the best source in town,' Jessica says, 'our holy tap!' She chuckles and walks away, swatting a fly with her cloth.

Viola excuses herself and disappears into the back of the room, duly following toilet arrows to the backyard.

'Do it for me,' Dad pleads, 'she's been working so hard and I want you two to get to know each other.'

'You could have warned me.' Gosia is bitter.

'There was no time to give you a call.' He is lying, and she knows it. His mobile number is not responding. It's been too long since the last top-up.

'I will take Viola to town if you will sort out this mess with Mother,' she says firmly, like she means it.

'It's not that easy, Gosia.' Her dad tears a napkin, white, thin and coarse, into tiny pieces.

'OK then, I will take Viola to town if you tell me everything, if you tell me what happened.' She feels smug as she gives him options.

Dad exhales. The scraps of napkin gently lift up in the air, travel the length of the table. Some fall to the floor.

'Please take Viola to town, and then we will talk.'

'For one day,' Gosia sets conditions. She hoped for a quiet Sunday to visit Vijay's house, make herself a consistent part of his day. Her presence in the vicinity of his home allowing for a friendly chat by the rose bush, an invite for a coffee, a kiss. Not a day with a distant cousin who barely speaks English.

'And the money?' Dad asks. 'Have you brought the money?'

She extracts the fat envelope from her bag. He takes it, opens it, removes the money and puts it in his wallet. The banknotes fill up the worn leather. He keeps the wallet under his palm on the table by the empty plate, near the smeared cutlery.

Viola walks back, settles in her seat and Dad ceremoniously extracts fifty quid and moves money across the table towards her.

'For your London trip,' he says in English. And follows it up with long, shrill words in the language he never cared to teach his own kids. His eyes dance and Gosia can take it no more.

'Let's go. The trains will be packed.'

She stands up, puts her bag on her shoulder. Viola is slow to follow. Dad urges her with his hand. He stays behind to sip the dregs of his coffee from an obese mug.

Viola collects a tote bag from the trailer and waves vigorously at Gosia's father, stuck on the other side of the glass, pressing his calloused palm on the windowpane, moisture glazed over his eyes. Gosia's jaw clenches. She wants it to be over before it has even started. She is going to keep it simple: get back to hers, eat dinner, get some sleep and get to town early tomorrow to do the 'tourist route.' Then she can forget all about it.

53

A hot Sunday afternoon in a well-kept park with white and green deckchairs, ready to rent by the hour, stacked into neat towers. The trees offer free shade to tourists exhausted by the delights of the city. Flocks of them sit on the dirt and eat overpriced ice cream bought from a hut erected by the side of the children's play area. The queue for frozen goods is long and twisted; the length varies from fifteen to twenty-seven people. Tourists play it safe. Vanilla is the most popular choice. It takes under four minutes to eat one scoop.

Gosia and Viola lounge by a bush, in a small spot of shade that moves with each quarter of an hour. They obediently follow it with their bums. Their foreheads, necks and knees have turned red from the unexpected September sun that erupted fully by lunch-time and scorched them both. Viola's shoulders are covered in small, painful-looking sun blisters. Gosia blesses her choice of top. Their feet are swollen from covering miles of tarmac.

The day started well. They shared a bed and, to Gosia's surprise, she slept well, cuddled into the wall, careful not to pull too much of the duvet her way. They had a simple breakfast of egg on toast, a cup of black coffee each and left to catch an early bus to town. Their conversation was limited to essential exchanges.

'We go now,' Gosia would say, and Viola would answer, 'Yes.'

'We eat now?' Gosia would suggest and Viola would answer, 'Yes.'

'Look at this,' Gosia would point to a monument, a bridge, a church, a building and Viola would stop, shield her eyes from the sun with her palm, observe carefully and thoughtfully the mass in question and smile at Gosia when she was done.

Neither of them took pictures. Neither of them wanted to loiter for too long in large museum rooms packed with commoners looking at paintings of wealthy people, purple, red and gold oozing from the canvases.

They window-shopped, they water-gazed, they smelt foods at markets, they ate the soggy sandwiches (cheese and pickle) that Gosia had made in the morning.

They had sat for a break on a bench overlooking the Thames with its surprising beauty and glamour.

'You lucky,' Viola had said, breathing in the air, a mix of river breeze and traffic fumes that tumbled down from the bridge. She had gaped right across to the other side, filled with tall buildings, and then looked below at the receding tide, revealing a brown, puddle-strewn beach. She had gripped Gosia's hand, narrowed her eyes and said:

'We go now.'

They had walked down the steps to the edge where filthy, slippery stone met the mushy sand. Viola had stepped on it, half of her foot submerged. She had kept going until she reached solid ground a few metres down, near the rocks. Gosia had followed, more out of a sense of obligation than delight. She had stupidly worn her work trainers, pristine white: mud would embed itself in the fabric.

Viola skipped to the edge of the water that was moving away, revealing more of the shore. The waterline was filled with tat. Tiny plastic toys, half an Oyster card, an entire coconut, plastic bottles, pieces of glass, a hinge, a screw, a laminated A5 page in a foreign language, a fragment of china, a bone. Viola squatted by the edge, hand deep in the water, playing like a child.

A man with a tight jaw, scrawny legs and a heavy-looking machine in his hands that hovered just above the ground was walking the length of the shore, right by the water's edge. He tutted at Viola, who paid him no attention, happily extracting something from the mud, cleaning it on her palm.

Enough, Gosia thought, and Viola's head turned rapidly as if she had heard. She looked at Gosia with pleading eyes. Five more minutes, thought Gosia and Viola smiled and turned her head back, dug deep in the slush. Gosia stood there, eyes closed, on a large flat stone, letting her trainers drip mud and brown water, while the sun beat down on her face, filling her with warmth and quiet. She had surrendered to the heat that was massaging her skin, to the sensation of prickling and tingling spreading down her body, to the build-up of sweat in her armpits, rolling down her ribcage. And then there was a sudden shift of colour and feel in between her eyes, from bright and brambly to cool and fleecy.

'Look,' said Viola. Gosia opened her eyes. Her cousin was standing just in front, blocking the sun, lifting Gosia's hand to deposit in it a small clay object. It looked like a funnel, with elaborate decorations carved on the outside and dark and tarred interior, stem missing.

'It's a clay pipe,' said Gosia. She'd seen these before, maybe in primary school. Definitely when they had come to London on a trip to visit a museum. 'The most common find on the shores of the Thames,' the guide had said as he had passed around a couple of examples.

Viola's face was vacant so Gosia pretended to smoke from it to make it more obvious.

'For you,' said Viola and folded it into Gosia's palm.

'I don't want it.' Gosia thrust her hand forward, giving it back. Viola's face trembled, the muscles knotting themselves into a grimace, and Gosia gave in.

'Thank you,' she said and put the clay pipe into her pocket. They walked on, towards this posh park.

The ice cream parlour is closing for the day. Another fifteen minutes and they'll have to start walking to the station to get Viola on a train back towards the allotments, Dad, fruit and jams. Gosia hesitated all day to ask any prodding questions, carefully assessing Viola's command of English and the extent of her vocabulary. She settles on keeping sentences simple.

'My mother and dad don't talk,' Gosia offers.

Viola considers the words and then she repeats.

'My mother and dad don't talk.'

Gosia keeps calm and tries again. This time using hands for support, pointing at herself.

'My mother and my dad do not talk, because my dad did something bad. Do you know what?'

Viola smiles a symmetrical smile that is rare and pleasant to look at as she says, 'My dad did something bad.' She smacks her hand with the other.

Dad never hit her mother, Gosia is sure of it. If anything, it was the other way around. Mother would often chase Dad around the house with a tea towel, whacking him with it on his back, on his head. She would clip them too, if they stood in her way or took Dad's side.

'A box from Poland arrived.' Gosia draws a square with her hands, indicates its journey from abroad. 'Mother opened it.' She does her best to lift the flaps of imaginary cardboard. 'And she saw something that made her very angry.' She pulls her face, she tries to make herself look scary. 'Do you know what was inside?' She points at Viola, at the air-drawn box.

Viola's eyes cloud and she bites on her lip looking inside the made-up container deposited by her knees. She finally says, careful to place the accent on the right syllable: 'Hi-s-tory.'

54

A small bathroom with a thin windowsill filled with Radox Nourish, Head & Shoulders 2 in 1, Tesco Everyday Value Sun Lotion SPF 15, Colgate Max White One, a cup with two toothbrushes with kinked bristles and Glade Pacific Breeze.

Beige tiles surround a small and shallow lime-green sink to the left, dwarf bathtub to the right in a matching colour. Yellowed plastic tubes are connected to the taps, imitating a shower. A lime-green toilet with a pink plastic seat sits straight ahead and, above it, a multi-edition print in a cheap frame: sunset by the sea with cliffs, boat and humans holding hands. A single loo roll on the floor.

Below the sink, a cupboard with a broken handle, and above, a square mirror glued to the wall. In front of it stands Lyndsey, repeating quietly in a mellow voice: 'I love you, I love you, I looove youuuu, I LOVE you, I L O V E you, I love YOU, I loooooove youuuuuuuuuu, I LOVE YOU, I love youuu, I love Y O U.'

Gosia stands by the door with her arms folded.

'Will you be long?'

Lyndsey's plump lips now silently make more oblong Os and Us to the mirror.

Gosia taps Lyndsey's arm.

'I need to brush my teeth, and I'm not moving your dinner plates out of the kitchen sink.'

Lyndsey's moist tongue now concentrates on Ls.

'It's twelve past, Lynds, I need to leave in a minute. I could do with a wee too. That's hard to achieve in a sink, especially one filled with your plates.'

Lyndsey's attention is on Is; she looks deep into her own eyes when each syllable silently leaves her mouth.

Gosia sighs.

'I'm going to be late. Do you mind hurrying up?'

Lyndsey now smiles with all her teeth and blows a kiss to her reflection.

Gosia threatens.

'I'm going to piss on the floor!'

Lyndsey moves. The two women silently squeeze past each other in the doorway. Lyndsey leans against the doorframe but Gosia shuts the door behind her, makes a paper nest on the toilet seat with loo roll and sits down to wee. Lyndsey starts talking. Her voice barely muted by the thin veneer.

'I think I'm gonna stop dieting. I'm not sure I can live without burgers or a midnight treat.' She sighs. 'I know my weaknesses and I accept them, and that's all thanks to you.'

Gosia watches the closed door and tries to pee on the side of the toilet bowl so as not to make a noise.

'You really inspired me. You told me, not once, not twice, that I have to embrace my thighs as they are. I thought you were just saying it to stop me whingeing but that article I read in the magazine you brought home last week changed my life. I've started the affirmation technique recommended in their "Soulful" section. I've been at it religiously for three days now, and I already see the benefits.' She chuckles. 'I thought it was just a load of bollocks that self-help books feed you with. And yes, yes, I know that I need to do it for more like twenty-five days. And that it's particularly good for people with high-pressure jobs, all these bankers and salesmen, but I think I must respond well to self-help. I'm just that type that's easily healed. Do you remember? That one day in the spa was enough for me to forget that swindler Sid.'

Gosia flushes and reaches for her toothbrush and toothpaste on the top shelf of the cupboard.

Lyndsey sighs some more.

'I really don't know what I'll do without you. It's going to be tough. Kev is great and all, but he would never buy a magazine like that. I thought that maybe I could drop in. How about monthly? To collect your old reading material. Because you know, just one evening reading those pages has totally changed how I see the world.'

Lyndsey inhales in a deep, satisfied way. Gosia's mouth is full of foam.

'Kev told me just yesterday that he can now clearly see that I'm the one to share with, not his mate Bob, and that we should move in together, so, I thought, I can't miss that opportunity. Men! Such an unpredictable lot. They're so fast to change their minds. So I'll be leaving at the end of the year, and, you know, we should keep in touch, because you are like a sister to me.'

Gosia takes the other toothbrush from a cup on the windowsill and starts rubbing off limescale from the tap handle while chewing on her own. Lyndsey shifts her legs, the floorboards creak.

'I better go now. I have two pedicures this morning and a few armpits to wax. Have a good one! Ta-ra.'

The front door shuts loudly. Gosia washes her hands, looks at the mirror.

'I hate you. I hate YOU. I H A T E you. I HATE YOU.'

55

The Bulletproof Guide to Sorting Out Your Life:
Work, Money, Free Time, Family, Friendship and Love.
STEP 89: How to Find a Home You Love

There is a common truth: your home is your castle. A place where you can recuperate after a long day, feel safe and comfortable. However, many of us find ourselves in dreadful living conditions - for example, sharing with people we do not even like - making home a prison. You need a calm and predictable private environment to be able to thrive in the busy and erratic public realm. A real home is worth all the money you can spend.

But how? How? *HOW?* We hear you shout. Big cities are not known for having an abundance of cheap and quality accommodation. The lion's share of your earnings are probably already swallowed up by the rent of a room that does not meet your expectations in a part of town that you do not even like.

Andy used to live with his ex in a small flat with a damp problem. The place smelt musty as soon as you walked through the door. That odour was definitely a telling sign of the relationship decaying: houses can give you hints like that. Your environment knows, long before you do, when things are going wrong and you should move on.

So, how do you find the house of your dreams? You need to know what you are looking for! It is all well and good having a vision of a villa with a swimming pool attached, situated just a short walk from Tottenham Court Road. This won't work. What you need is to visualise the qualities of your dream house, not just its physicality.

For Margaret, these qualities were: sunny, spacious, convenient and warm. This meant that when she was looking for a house she knew she needed a place that had south-facing windows, with more than one bedroom, close to all local amenities and transport links, and with double-glazing. With this knowledge, it was much easier to rule out all the red herrings that online searches and estate agents were trying to distract her with. It was tough, but she remained patient and did not jump at just any house. This meant she did not settle on the wrong place in the wrong area.

Staying focused, patient and ONLY viewing accommodation that meets ALL your criteria ensures that you will finally live in a place you love.

56

A windy and dry day, perfect conditions for airing woolly garments and drying sheets outdoors. A shabby estate agency on the street corner displays a large bespoke banner in the window: *We make your dreams come true this autumn at a reduced price.* Inside, a young, handsome, animated British Asian man ('Please call me Jas') with moisturised skin sits behind a large ergonomic desk with stylish cantilever legs. He wears a tight suit and describes the state of the economy and the reality of the current housing market to Gosia. Jas speaks with confidence.

'So, have you managed to list your requirements?'

Gosia is a bit distracted by the dots on his tie and his close resemblance to the man of her dreams. She is sheepish, the qualities of her dream home swim through her head.

'I always wanted to live somewhere green and safe.'

Jas is somewhat bewildered.

'Is that it?' He pauses, moistens his lips. 'A flat or a house? Number of bedrooms? Parking space? Generous back garden? Access to supermarkets? Maybe an appealing view?'

Gosia says, musingly, 'Yes, a tree would be nice.'

Jas suppresses a sigh and ruffles papers in front of him. He takes a minute, gives the sheets a few prolonged looks and finally replies.

'The market demand for affordable properties in quality neighbourhoods has tripled in recent years. Prices have soared and larger deposits are required. Would you consider renting with a partner? A boyfriend? A friend? An acquaintance?'

She opens her heart.

'Well, no. I'm here because I'm sick of sharing.'

It's a short-term solution. She was hoping to continue renting with Lyndsey until things developed between Vijay and her to a point where they could move in together.

Jas inhales deeply.

'And how much are you looking to spend?'

Gosia hesitates.

Jas looks at his watch, back at the papers and then at Gosia.

'Let's look at the cheapest option. Here we have a studio apartment in an ex-council tower block. It's rather cosy. Sixty-four per cent of the inhabitants are private owners. It has a separate bathroom and a corridor with generous built-in wardrobe. It's on the seventh floor. No balcony, but the shared landing is spacious and has a window that the current tenant uses for growing herbs. There is a fantastic community in the block, so I would consider it more than safe. People take turns to clean the landing, to lower the monthly maintenance costs. The view is spectacular! The flat is east-facing, so plenty of sun in the mornings. Now, it was renovated only four years ago and comes with an impressive spec kitchen. Granite worktop – a desirable finish – bathroom with white tiles, lino throughout. Finally, price wise, it's just fantastic. It's on the market for eleven hundred a month. There are the other usual fees on top: the agency fee, the reference checks. Landlord requires two months' rent deposit. We can even arrange a viewing for this week. It's a great offer, and perfect for someone who wants to live on their own!'

Gosia quickly calculates her financial situation. She has been working since she turned nineteen. She has been saving as much as she possibly can but certain life upheavals (a fine for the actions of her broken heart and the loans to her father) mean she has spent a good chunk of it. She stopped eating meat to bring her food bill down. She has only two thousand left in her ISA. Enough to go on holiday if she felt like it, or be ill or unemployed for a month or two. Her friends used to call her tight, but they are not her friends any more. She can be whoever she wants. Frugal. Until recently she was allowing herself little pleasures: chocolate with nuts and raisins, hair oil for her split ends, separate washing powder for whites and colours. Now she only splashes out on her pay-as-you-go phone.

Savings have always given her confidence; she felt prepared for the worst. Now she realises that it is a pathetic amount of money that will not even buy her a deposit and a month in a drab flat on the seventh floor where her vertigo would get worse, drive her mad and make her jump. She looks through the window, the bit not covered by the banner, onto a grey pavement filled with people in cheap shoes.

'I'm busy this week.'

Jas looks at the screen.

'How about the next?'

Gosia continues.

'And I would prefer a ground floor. I don't like heights.'

Jas looks at her, through her.

'Why don't you give us your number and we will call as soon as anything suitable comes up?'

'There is a place I'm interested in.'

She produces a Post-it with Vincent's address on it.

Jas looks it up.

'Ah, yes. Fabulous property. Lots of original features. It's an entire house but in need of modernisation. A bargain, considering prices in the area. However, it's for sale. We are talking in the region of over half a million. A rare opportunity. These types of properties are usually divided into flats. We've had considerable interest in it.'

Gosia interrupts.

'I wondered if the owner would consider renting.'

Jas looks at her suspiciously.

'And why do you think the owner would want that?'

'Apparently it has had bad press.'

Jas arranges his fingers into a little basket and places them on the table. 'What sort of bad press are we talking about?'

Gosia looks at his perfectly shaped thumbs.

'A murder. A man was killed in that house. Apparently in cold blood.'

Jas gasps.

'That's not true, according to my information. The owner died of a heart attack. Nothing more sinister took place. But may I ask who told you that? Very worrying to be hearing such news.'

She was right not to fill in the enquiry form with all her details. She can see the empty page among the brochures and printouts he has been feeding her this afternoon.

'In the newspaper. There was an article about it and the picture of the house matches this one.'

'We must be talking about another property. Some other unfortunate person.'

The bell by the door jingles and a couple in designer glasses enter. Jas shifts in his chair. Gosia gathers her things.

'You must be Alan and Claire?'

The couple nod. Gosia gets a weak shake of the hand from Jas, his business card and a reassurance that she can call any time she wants.

57

A drowsy, foggy morning on a back street leading towards a high street congested with traffic. People queue for a bus and mind their own business, sucked into the glow of their mobile phone screens. Gosia walks past them, towards a bakery where she can buy discounted bread baked yesterday. The queue's length matches the one at the bus stop but the people are different. Here, there are women with children wrapped around their legs, elderly people pushing their stability frames, rough sleepers with a handful of pennies. Gosia joins them, turns her head away from the traffic, hopes no one will recognise her. She definitely doesn't want to bump into Vijay under these circumstances. She only wants two loaves that she will cut into slices and freeze in adequate portions.

Her phone beeps. It is a new number, of a foreign sort, with +48 at the front. But the message that follows, there is no mistaking, has been typed by her dad.

> 'Gosia, my dearest, Viola's enjoyed her time with you. I knew you two would get on. She's going back to Poland tomorrow. She was a great help. Things are going very well. I found a distributor. Need extra £500 to make it work. See you on Sunday? Love, Dad'

The blood drains to her feet, she feels dizzy and fights the urge to hit a wall and howl.

Her phone beeps again and this time it's a message from Mother, clearly working her way through today's to-do list.

> 'Who are you bringing to the wedding? How about your cousin Seamus? He didn't make the guest list. Let me know ASAP. MUM'

She flexes the muscles in her hand, making a fist, ready to punch. Seamus, her distant cousin, is a bore, a hard-drinking chauvinist, known for explaining his point of view in a succession of racist jokes. They are blood relations removed far enough for her mother to entertain the idea of them tying the knot.

Gosia stares at the blinking screen. The only reply that comes to mind is simple though difficult: 'NO.'

58

The Bulletproof Guide to Sorting Out Your Life:
Work, Money, Free Time, Family, Friendship and Love.
STEP 292: How to Find the Love of Your Life

Have you practised your 'winning hearts' methods? Do you have considerable achievements? Have you learnt from your mistakes? If you can answer 'Yes' to all these questions, it is time to move closer to finding the love of your life. How do you do that? You take the first step!

Long gone are the days when women would sit waiting for men to approach them. Not many people decide to tie the knot and have babies before they are thirty, and, once you hit this landmark, you are exposed to all the infertility problems - your eggs become scarce/your sperm becomes wonky.

Margaret was thirty-five when she met Andy. She knew straight away that he was husband material and that she would marry him. It was his sense of humour and kindness that appealed to her. In the past, Margaret dated men with good looks, fat wallets and large egos. She learnt from her mistakes. She did not want to be just a pretty wife leaning on a successful man's shoulder; she wanted to co-author that success. So, when Andy landed on her ward with a broken arm and a mild head injury after falling down some concrete stairs on the way home from his late shift, she did not hesitate. She knew she had up to eight days to win his heart, and only if she swapped her shifts. However, it only took Andy forty-eight hours to realise that he was being looked after by his future wife. He immediately parted ways with his ex (Margaret did not realise that Andy was in a relationship, as the ex never visited Andy in the hospital) and he proposed shortly afterwards. Sounds like a fairy tale, right? But let's reveal that Margaret did her best to help her luck.

How? you may ask.

However crude this may sound, men are simple creatures. To win their hearts, all you need to do is appeal to their instincts and follow these three golden principles:

1. BTP: Be Their Prey

Margaret would stroke Andy's broken arm to both check on its healing process but also to build a connection through touch, but she would curtail the stroking as soon as she could tell Andy was enjoying it. Making yourself seem willing and available, but at the same time keeping the connection vulnerable is what counts, as men want to hunt.

2. BTF: Be Their Fan

Margaret would make Andy aware of his positive attributes and made sure she laughed her light, genuine laugh at all his jokes no matter how tiring her twelve-hour shifts were. Men's egos are fragile, they are not as sure of themselves as it may seem, so the more you do to make them feel good about themselves, the deeper they will fall in love with you, their ultimate champion. It is important to keep praise genuine. Men see through fake admiration surprisingly quickly, but sincere delight is not hard when you truly desire a man you picked to be yours.

3. BT: Be There!
It is all about presence. The moment you are out of sight, you risk being out of your man's mind. So, ensure you are close to him as much as possible. That you are the woman he looks at, talks to, listens to. Building that connection and sustaining it is the only bulletproof way of becoming a wife. If men are left on their own too much then their minds wander: they consider deviant options, like having mistresses or not marrying at all! Sustained presence by their side keeps them aware of your value in their life. Combined with genuine praise and your readiness to be devoured, the man you love will be yours forever.

Ensure you include these three elements in a relationship with the man you want to marry and he will offer you a ring within weeks. REMEMBER, be sure you apply this technique to the man you actually want to marry, or you risk divorcing soon after you tie the knot!

Let's reiterate. To make a man fall in love with you follow these three BT principles:

BTP: BE THEIR PREY
BTF: BE THEIR FAN
BT: BE THERE

59

A dry late-September evening with a sweet smell of autumnal rot in the air. It is still light on this quiet street on a hill. The bay windows of terraced houses do not have blinds down, allowing for peering in. The windowsills support ceramic pots with succulents, picture frames and wooden letters composed to read HOME. Fences are freshly stained in a calming shade of green.

Gosia stands for a few breaths by a rose bush that is already covered with horticultural fleece. She crosses the road and walks through the gate towards an azure door with a silver number 11 shining like a jewel. She peeks through the bay window, spots wooden floors accessorised with a rug in a multicoloured diamond pattern. She can imagine herself walking on it, its softness tickling underfoot. This sort of design, dynamic and geometric, must be inspired by art or fashion. It comes with a promise of luxury, clearly handwoven. She feels creative and open-minded just by looking at it. There is a large cactus in a decorative terracotta pot two feet from the window, spreading its branches liberally.

She first tenderly touches the door covered with three coats of paint, the brush marks almost invisible. There is no doorbell, so she counts to ten and knocks. She lets the air out through her nose, composes herself, arches her lips. The door opens gently and a man, tall and muscular with a large fluffy cat in his arms says, 'Evening.'

'Hi, I came to see Vijay.' She puts her shaking hands into her coat pockets.

'Oh, he's out tonight. Can I help?' The man strokes the cat.

She is not prepared for this. Vijay was in during all four previous Tuesday evenings, she followed him up the hill herself. She has a plan. That plan involves Vijay being home.

'I was . . . I am from . . . the gym. Vijay's membership has lapsed.'

'Oh, right.' His voice is surprised.

'And I . . . and we are . . . conducting informal visits. To learn what may have caused it.'

'I see.' He looks her up and down. She is not in her gym gear. She wears that nice slutty dress underneath her coat, gold eyeshadow and carefully applied red lipstick. She hopes no lace sticks out. She has no clipboard, no flyers, no cheap merchandise.

'It normally takes just a few minutes.' She moves back. 'We also have a "Welcome back" offer that includes a free session with a personal trainer.'

'Well, he won't be back until late tonight, but why don't you give him a call?' The cat meows, stretches its paws and lunges to the floor. It walks to Gosia's feet.

'Oh, we tried, but the thing is, his phone number goes to his old workplace. Hence visiting in person.' They both stare at her legs; the cat rubs her shins. The man's voice softens.

'Please come in, I don't want the cat out on the road.'

She walks across the threshold, steps on Moroccan tiles, gently closes the door.

'Sorry about that, I hope you're not allergic?' He points to the cat circling between her legs. 'Percy just loves stockings.'

'It's OK.' She smiles.

'Give me a sec, I'll just get you Vijay's card.' He disappears deep into the house.

She takes two more steps and has a quick look into the front room. There is a blue velvet sofa in front of a fireplace and above it a striking painting of naked bodies. Three or more, white and black, having sex. She turns her head back just in time for Vijay's flatmate to emerge from around the corner with a slim piece of card in hand.

'Here you go. He's normally on this number from 10 a.m. He might be up for it. I'll mention it to him.'

She takes the card and a step backwards.

'That's super-helpful. Thank you.'

There is a silent commotion by the door. Her, confused how to open the lock. Him, trying not to let the cat get out. She waves goodbye, stupidly turns the wrong way and has to head up the hill in the uncomfortable shoes with fashionable heels. She stops at the top, holds the card gently and takes it in: a drawing of a spine that looks a bit like peas in a pod, below it Vijay's name printed in mint green. She walks home the long way.

60

A corridor in a 24/7 fitness centre slowly filling up with human bodies in high-rise leggings with strategically placed mesh fabric that provides ventilation, and a side pocket that holds all the essentials. People hold their phones, flimsy A4 folders in teal with the FitYou logo on top, and reusable leak-proof water bottles with double-walled vacuum insulation to keep drinks ice-cold for (up to) twenty-four hours. Everyone is waiting for the evening course to start.

Gosia joins the queue to the water fountain with her bottle, a find from the end-of-summer sale at her local supermarket, reduced by 75 per cent and in canary yellow: a vessel that didn't pass any endurance tests and came with a warning to 'throw this bottle away if you see any signs of damage or weakness'. She stands in line and entertains herself by counting the number of people in designer trainers. Her folder and two pens are safely deposited in a tote bag on her shoulder. There is a heavy panting behind her. She turns her head.

'Howdy!' Steve, who she nearly razed to the ground, gives her a smile the size of a panoramic dental X-ray, accompanied by a wave. His hand is clutching a bottle that matches hers – in canary yellow and with a large dent in it.

Gosia nods her head for hello. He keeps his eyes on her face.

'How was your week, Gosia? Looking forward to the class? Have you seen these hilarious pictures in the pack? I was howling with laughter. Couldn't believe "downward-facing dog" was a fitness pose. I had to google it.'

She curls her lips. He laughs.

'I'm loving this course. Feel healthier every time I open my folder to check the exercise routines. Do you think it will be fun today? It said "nutrition" so I assumed it would be about food, but why are people wearing their running outfits? Do you reckon we'll talk about grub while working out?'

She points her eyes to the ceiling, raises eyebrows. He gives her another grin. He is the only person in the corridor wearing casual clothes: bleached jeans and a shapeless T-shirt.

She fills her bottle to the top and walks away to stand closer to the door, leans against the concrete, takes a small sip. He moves to stand next to her. His bottle is half full. He takes a swig.

'Yuck. Don't know about you but there's something off-putting about water. It's just too plain. I read you're supposed to have two litres of it a day. I mean, how? Through a drip?'

Gosia smiles. He looks at his bottle. Lifts it to his eye level.

'Every time I take a mouthful I imagine it's lemonade, zesty and sweet. Is that what you do?' He points at Gosia's bottle.

She gently shakes her head for 'no'. He considers his bottle some more.

'I spent the whole morning looking at these suggested menus. Nothing about them is exactly mouth-watering. Chicken, eggs and oats. Oats, chicken and eggs. And that vegetable that they push on you: kale. Where the heck does that even grow? What's wrong with a good old potato?'

Despite herself, Gosia is amused. He is mid-flow.

'Do you think you'll introduce all this birdfood to your breakfast? I ask myself, why would I want to sprinkle seeds on toast? And you know what?'

He is looking at her, his lips on pause.

'What?' Gosia says her first word.

'I've always been confused by this talk about coffee being good for you, protecting your heart and bowels from cancer, and so on. Every time I have a sip of my caramel latte with cream on top I think to myself, There's something dodgy about this.' He checks to see if she is listening. Gosia encourages him with a mute nod. 'And there it is, in this folder, black on white, spelled out: "Coffee is good for you but only if you have it black!" I mean, they should have that written on the menu as you walk in to place your order. I tried it today. Americano. Black. It smells like burnt tar and tastes like cleaning detergent. Is this how you have it?'

Gosia nods her head for 'yes'. He sighs.

'I thought so.'

61

The back garden of a semi-detached house in a small town adjacent to Greater London on a nippy grey day with no rain. A prominent apple tree grows by the fence. The tree's branches are heavy with fruit and the reddest apples lean into the neighbours' garden. The neighbours, two white, heavy-set men with facial hair, reach from a single ladder and pick the prime crop. They drop the apples into scuffed cardboard banana boxes and converse in a foreign language.

Mother and Gosia stand by the kitchen door that opens straight into the garden. Mother smokes a cigarette in a series of short, hostile inhales. Gosia smells trouble. They watch the neighbours.

'They haven't asked for permission,' Mother says in an irked whisper.

'It's on their side. Why would they?' Gosia offers in a flat voice.

'You're just like your father. Never concerned with what is right,' Mother spits out.

'You ruin your health over nothing,' Gosia soothes. 'You have too many apples anyway. These would rot.'

Mother sucks greedily on her cigarette.

'I'd like to be asked for permission that I'd kindly grant. Is that too much to expect?'

Gosia considers the question.

'Maybe it's different in their country. Maybe there is no need to ask.'

Mother snorts. The smoke escapes through her nostrils.

'They are Polish, Gosia!' she mutters. 'They're Catholic and should know their manners!'

'How do you know?' Gosia can't decipher that from their speech, and she knows that to her mother's ear any foreign language spoken by white men with moustaches must be Polish.

'I once asked your father to translate some of their arguments to me,' Mother whispers, her breath fuggy. 'All summer they burnt meat in the back garden. Night after night, sausage after sausage. There are seven of them living next door. All men. They talk so loudly.'

'And what did Dad say?' Gosia is curious now; Mother has not mentioned Dad casually in the last six months, although there is ongoing evidence of him trying to woo her: another bunch of roses, this time accommodated in a jug; a tray of jars filled with chutneys, stashed in a kitchen cupboard, a simple label attached to each: 'Siobhán's Pantry. Produced by OFF'.

Mother raises her eyebrows.

'You know him, useless like that. His translation made no sense, unless he was making it all up. He told me that they're builders, and that there was a lot of good-natured banter.'

Gosia watches the men.

'Sounds believable to me.'

Mother gives her a stare.

'Daddy's girl. You're always on his side.'

Gosia bites her lip. Mother pokes her arm.

'You would never believe what a coward your father is.'

She takes a long drag on her cigarette, smiles knowingly.

'One of those men came in to say hello when they moved in. His accent sounded like your father's, so I called him over. I said, "Stan, come and talk to your compatriots." They stood there, in the doorway, the man explaining himself in his broken English. He said that sometimes they may have deliveries and would we sign for them if they're at work. Stan agreed, shook the guy's hand and closed the door. So I asked him, then and there, "Why didn't you talk to him in Polish?" And you know what he said?'

She does not wait for Gosia to guess.

'He didn't want to make any assumptions about their nationality!'

Mother sniggers. 'I know him better than he knows himself. Since they allowed these hordes of people from Poland and Czechoslovakia and wherever else, your father doesn't want to mix with that crowd. He thinks he's better than them, escaping to live here earlier, and now he's embarrassed by his countrymen – ashamed to be one of them.'

She sucks hard at the filter tip.

'I see why. Look at them.' Mother points at the men struggling down the ladder. 'Primitive sort. Live like cattle in that house. Two to a room. You never see them washing their sheets.'

She squashes the remains of her cigarette in the metal ashtray balanced on the windowsill.

The men approach. Each carries a box full of apples, their smiles wide.

'She-von!' calls the taller one.

Mother stiffens hearing her name mispronounced.

He lifts the box and balances it on the rickety fence.

'She-von. You have good apples. One box for you, one box for us. OK?'

Mother doesn't move. Gosia walks to the fence in a few quick steps.

'So kind of you, I'll take these. Thanks for clambering up the ladder, and I hope you enjoy your apples.'

The man smiles broadly.

'Good apples. Sweet apples. Sweet like She-von!'

He winks at Gosia's mother and walks into his house.

Gosia struggles with the box back into the kitchen.

Mother's eye follows the taller fellow with a prick of interest and then she sighs.

'Just when I thought I was done with all this cooking there is more to do!' She cleans her hands on the apron. 'Fetch the knives. These must go on the hob today. I won't be making jams on a Sunday!'

62

A training studio in a 24/7 fitness centre. A wall of mirrors opposite the floor-to-ceiling windows with a view of the multistorey car park and a slim concrete walkway between the buildings. In the room, a group of people in tight-fitting, breathable activewear rest on large stability balls. An energetic instructor in a vest with a large tattoo of an eagle on his back adjusts a bony girl with pink hair. It is a diverse gathering of tall and short, lean and podgy, black and white. Above the instructor's head hangs a big banner covering the upper half of the mirrors with the slogan 'Local jobs for local people provided by your local gym' and a row of multicoloured logos beneath.

Steve is rolling on his ball next to Gosia. He's accompanied her to all of the evening classes, like chewing gum stuck to her shoe, embedded in the sole, too tough to remove. Now he offers her a running commentary of what's going on around them. She endures it, and thinks of him as her private portable radio as he shares his insights.

'I've heard that lack of experience is one of the biggest hurdles when trying to get your first job in this industry. So I had a grand idea! How about I train you and you train me? And we can be each other's success stories!'

She rolls and suppresses a comment.

'The other option would be spending some time shadowing successful personal trainers. But man, can you imagine that in practice? I feel like a shadow often enough already!'

He is beginning to grow on her, or maybe she is just giving in to his semi-permanence by her side. She finds his narratives entertaining but, for now, she decides to keep a straight face.

'I guess I could always try to find work as a gym instructor, but how?'

She allows herself a sympathetic nod. He belches.

'Pardon me. Too much protein for lunch! Where were we? Ah yes, so I think going freelance is my best bet. Flexible hours will correspond well with my varied lifestyle. Don't want this job to kill my work–life balance. I want it to support my larger goals.'

They readjust on the balls and follow instructions to move to another restorative posture.

She breathes out. He breathes in. They look ahead.

'Such as?' she asks.

He cranes his head and gives her a satisfied look.

'Living a happy, fulfilled life free of unnecessary drama. Spending my free time on the dance floor, lost in music, mastering my car wash send-out.' Steve tries to move his legs and arms to an imaginary tune. 'And I think I'm getting better at navigating away from other people's fracas. These days I calmly watch friends getting married, although I find it a truly sad story. "Happy ever after" is such propaganda. How can you expect one person to give you dinner *and* an orgasm? Personally, I don't think I could maintain intense feelings for just one person "till death do us part". At this stage of my life, I'm into short-term relationships.'

He sighs.

'My cat is the love of my life. Humans, by comparison, are rather tricky. Mood swings, depression, affairs, mortgages, adoptions, mess. I want it nice and easy. I've done the hard work of figuring out who I am and how I fit into this.' His arm draws an extravagant half-circle in the air. He loses balance. Gosia makes a weak, uncommitted and unsuccessful attempt to hold onto him. He hits the floor with a loud thump.

The instructor stops. The group crane their heads. Steve just lies there contemplating the ceiling. The instructor makes his way towards him.

'Are you all right?'

'Just having a rest, as instructed. Suffering from a bit of an arm ache.'

The instructor smiles and helps him up from the floor, patting his side.

'OK. Let's finish for tonight. I expect you to familiarise yourself with the other ball exercises in the handout and prepare your unique routine for next week.'

The group roll their balls to the storage unit hidden in the wall.

Gosia asks, 'But why fitness?'

'Why? You don't think I can flex my muscles?' He lifts up his meaty arm.

'I can't see you having a passion for it.'

He laughs.

'Surely that's something I can develop! This is where the future is. I think pregnancy fitness is the next huge thing. Look at all these yoga classes for expectant mothers. Oversubscribed! It's a ripe time for someone to offer a set of more energetic poses for greater vaginal flexibility that doesn't involve all that humming.'

He kicks the ball into the cupboard. She kicks hers in too.

'There's a huge market out there. All these lasses who pop out offspring at regular intervals trying to keep up with super-fertile celebrities? They don't know yet how much they need it. You just need endorsement from one of those famous mothers of five that make parenthood look like a fancy holiday. Stick her on a poster and voila! You'll have pregnant women queuing around the block.'

She wrinkles her nose.

'You could do something you actually enjoy.'

He stops. Turns to her.

'Like what? IT? I've been told fat people like to hide behind a screen, but that's not for me. I need human contact! Customer service? I can't stand permanently dissatisfied moaners. Working as an escort? There's a limited amount of blokes who pay well for a blow job delivered by a porky. I'm good here. I did my research.' He points at her. 'Not everyone wants to train with a celery stick.'

She raises her brows.

He continues.

'Other overweight people for example: the owners of malfunctioning thyroids, people stuck with tyres round their waists because of the side effects of the pills they have to pop for their long-term illnesses. Or the flabby army that no one cared to educate in their teenage years about the virtues of veg and the evil side of burgers! I'm sure they would develop clinical depression with you in the room. I'm a normal bloke. Harmless, overweight, on the hairy side, leisurely dressed, a bit loud and with a fortifying sense of humour. People will love working out with me.'

She puts her hands on her hip bones.

'Wouldn't clients be worried? Shouldn't you be living proof that they could look better?'

He grins, loops his arm through hers and she lets him walk her towards the changing rooms.

'Darling, where have you been? People want to *feel* better. Sure, some want to have muscular triceps and flat tummies, but the majority treat it like a trip to a community centre. You have a chat with your mates, watch people nude under the shower, swap rude jokes, sip energy drinks, find your next date – you may even lift some weights! This is not an Olympic Village. Here you can be any size, and people still compliment your new tight Lycra shorts.'

She has actually seen it herself. Chatty Ryan comes in every Friday and spends his entire time talking to people in the corridor, rarely accomplishing an actual workout. Aunty Bess, one of the oldest members of the gym, dates Fabio, an energetic Sicilian who she met in the jacuzzi. Louisa C forged many a friendship by the soft drinks machine. Chubby Mattie, Mary-Ann, Patrick and Phyllis have all been training for months, many with the help of a PT, and their folds and flab remain untouched. But they have a spring in their step, there is clarity in their eyes and a sense of purpose as they walk through the door. They look content and settled. All this for £19.99 a month is a bargain.

Steve pauses by the door, his arm still linked with hers. Moist hairs, which clamp together like wet dog's fur, graze her smooth skin.

'How about you? What really brought you here?'

She looks into his blue eyes, an unexpected pool of kindness. There is no music, the corridor is empty and she can only hear the heartbeat in her eardrums. She replies in a timorous voice.

'Love.'

63

A small bedroom gridlocked with furniture. A tangle of brown parcel string and newspaper cut-outs on the wall. A Post-it with the word 'suspect' is placed in the middle. A list of three numbered names below:

~~1. Bulgarian cleaner~~
2. Neighbour
3. Unidentified visitor.

The bed is stripped of linen and the mattress is covered in large yellow stains. Naked pillows are stacked by the wall. Gosia sits on the floor and reads.

I put on 2.5lb this week alone and I know it's all down to stress. Only Mars bars soothe my nerves.

Kev hasn't proposed yet, but it must be soon. We agreed my moving-in date for December and I made it clear, in between the lines, not once or twice, that I don't want to just move in together and give the whole of myself to him, without him making it plain obvious that he wants to commit too.

Mum always says, 'Only move in with a man who has offered you a ring.'

It's only two months from now but there's been no talk of a romantic weekend away, and I couldn't bear it if he proposed in the corridor or in a chippy. There'll be a wait to get the ring adjusted to my size, too, and I want to wear it for Xmas, so it has to be soon.

It didn't help that Vincent's son came in again. He was livid! As soon as I opened the door he started shouting that the sale fell through, that now people go directly to the estate agent to spread lies, that he's sick of dealing with it and being dragged into this neighbourhood.

He stood there in his flashy suit with clenched fists and I felt sorry for him. I told him they would find out soon who killed his dad and this would make things better. But it only made things worse.

'It wasn't a murder. I told you, it wasn't a murder!' he was shouting. And then he called me a stupid cow and left.

I didn't say a word to Kev, so as not to pull him away from the investigation. I'm sure he would abandon it as soon as he knew how badly I was treated.

Kev has made fantastic progress. He's had three separate Bulgarian women clean his flat. He was really chancing it, leaving knives about on the kitchen counter, but nothing happened. He said that they were efficient and cheap, just cleaned and left. He is adamant a Bulgarian cleaner couldn't kill Vincent. Kev says that they don't have it in their psyche, they are very task-oriented, meek and weedy. A guy like Vincent with all his strength and weight would crush them. Kev thinks it took someone stronger, someone who would have trained for it. And there can't be that many people training and living locally.

GG reacted surprisingly well to the news. She didn't tell me what her plans were but I saw her bank statements and I know she can't afford to rent this place on her own. We don't see each other much as she is out most evenings. Kevin thinks she is up to no good.

Gosia puts the diary in the top drawer, underneath a pile of synthetic pants in pastel colours, and leaves.

64

The Bulletproof Guide to Sorting Out Your Life: Work, Money, Free Time, Family, Friendship and Love. FAQ: What Are the Best First Steps to Finding the Love of Your Life?

We appreciate that sometimes it's hard to know what may constitute an appropriate first step. Seeing a man that meets your husband criteria is rare enough and it is hard not to want to jump into his lap and propose yourself. That's a no-no. Remember, the man must think he hunted you down. Men are predators and predators do not eat road kill.

Appropriate first steps: do not reveal to a man that you fancy him, so avoid inviting him for a coffee! Instead, think of other reasons why you should drink coffee together.

Maybe he runs a business and you can offer invaluable marketing advice? You will come across as a person concerned with his business aims and oblivious to his charms. While you create a strategy to sell his new range of products, you make subtle moves that work on his psyche. Scheduling weekly in-person catch-ups to be a constant in his diary, complimenting him at every opportunity and creating spaces of vulnerability that will make him hunt you. Be his prey, be his fan, be there.

65

A 24/7 fitness centre during a dead hour after the lunchtime rush, and before the post-work mob. A display board advertises: 'NEW offer – a selection of power drinks, a perfect refuel after your work-out, available at the introductory price of £3.99.' As part of her continuous professional development, Gosia tried the whole range: banana, strawberry and chocolate. She subdues the burps. The artificial flavours sit heavy on her tongue.

She turns the music down a notch, searches her purse and extracts a slightly bent card with a pea pod on it – the mint background, the straight font arranged into words she knows by heart: *Dr Vijay Kumar, Chiropractor*. She has memorised the number too. She has waited for long enough not to come across as desperate. Now she dials confidently, taking a long breath through her nose.

'Yes?'

It's him.

Gosia peddles the gym: 'Good afternoon, I am calling from the FitYou Centre. We have noticed that your membership has lapsed and would like to see if you are interested in joining us again.'

'Oh.'

It's definitely him.

'We have a range of interesting offers for returning customers. We include a freedom pass to all of our classes, a complimentary power drink and, most importantly, a series of sessions with a trainee personal trainer.'

She has thought it all through; she will create a bespoke training programme that he won't be able to say no to, and develop a relationship based on mutual trust and understanding. She has only a few weeks until her brother's wedding – that dreaded Saturday in October is looming closer, and at a push she could see Vijay six times, enough for him to get to know her while working on his personal goals. Joint workouts would bring them closer together and it wouldn't be creepy inviting him to be her plus-one. She pauses. He needs to take it all in.

'Thanks for calling, but I'm afraid I don't have time to think about it.' He sounds distracted.

'We could arrange a better moment. This could be combined with your first visit, a complimentary session and reacquainting yourself with the space.' Her voice is soft and light, all petals and feathers, but her belly contracts with anticipation and the overload of protein powder.

'How much is it?'

There is a pinprick of interest that she is gentle not to squash.

'Nine ninety-nine for the first three months.' She is going to subsidise his membership. She's done the maths, she can afford it.

'Listen, this is a very bad moment. I've got lots on and the whole gym thing,' she hears him pursing his lips, 'I don't think I can take it on. Thanks for your call, though.'

'I understand.'

Rule number one: always agree with your client, drummed into her by the checkout job. She applies it in life.

'How about if I check in with you in a few days, at a better time? We can do morning or evening.' She is tender, sympathetic and flexible.

'No, I'm fine.' His voice is tensing up. 'No need to call. Thanks again, and please take me off your list. Bye-bye now.'

He doesn't wait for her to respond and the line goes dead. The silence is deep and hollow. Gosia closes her eyes, feeling the void in her head and the heaviness in her stomach. The phone prickles her fingers and she slams it down. She stands like that a while longer, with blood draining to her ankles and a new dent in her stitched heart.

66

A council-run library on a wet day. The reading area is used as an impromptu canteen by a group of ramblers hiding from the heavy rain. Rounds of lukewarm tea are poured from thermos flasks, alongside rustles of aluminium foil, crumbs of cheese on the dark blue carpet, and the zesty smell of freshly peeled tangerines.

Gosia sits by the gleaming screen. Her head in her hands.

RichardMutton_PoetForDarkTimes wrote: 'Book your space here for the long-anticipated book launch of my new collection of poems.'

Rich_M wrote: 'I have voiced my outrage at this person's page and the poor attempts to write poems about her feelings on a number of occasions. This is yet another example of substandard writing, trashy language and dire imagery. I urge you once more to stop, you've littered the world of poetry enough.'

KarenStevensWrites wrote: 'There is something deeply moving about your "clumps of heartache" as well as "lumps of woes". The scenery that you open with these words is rich to enter. However, the poem finishes too early for me. Maybe you could expand? Create another verse? But I know that writing from a raw place can't be easy. See my poem *Hole in the heart* here.'

TORM3NT wrote: 'You inspired me to write my manifesto *Life with a drill.*'

Raw

Life is a bitch
Drills holes in concrete plans
Spills water
Blows sand
Sprinkles salt into a gash

Heaps of weeping
Buckets of sorrow

Life is a joke
Cackles in the first row
Mocks lines
Scorns signs
Rolls in the aisles

Clumps of heartache
Lumps of woes

67

A staff toilet in a 24/7 fitness centre situated at the back of the U-shaped counter, accessed through a yellow door made from chipboard. The exclusive use of the toilet by staff is enforced by a silver, push-button, keypad lock. Entry is granted after pressing down a correct line of six digits and twisting the lever the right way. The toilet is not an ideal location to be accessed when stressed, in a hurry or when carrying anything in your hands.

Gosia waved Janelle into the reception area as soon as her phone started ringing, the word 'Mother' on its screen, Gosia's heart in her throat. She pushed the phone into her pocket and waited for Janelle to walk behind the counter. Janelle took her time. Gosia stepped from leg to leg, faking an urgent toilet trip.

'Just for five minutes,' she said to Janelle and headed for the yellow door. It took her two attempts to get the code right and once she was through, she bolted herself in.

The phone rings again and Gosia answers, stuck between a sink and a hand-dryer with adjustable speed and sound-controller.

'Finally!' Mother's voice is impatient, magnified by the toilet's tiled interior. 'How are you?' she asks, and Gosia's heartbeat accelerates. She hasn't slept much since the phone call to Vijay backfired. She keeps her body erect and eyes open thanks to an overdose of instant coffee, eaten straight from the jar and dissolved on her tongue. Her brain is a muddle of random dark thoughts colliding into haphazard visions of a bleak, unbearable future.

'I'm at work. Is it urgent?' Gosia attempts to deal with phone conversations with her mother the same way she handles random approaches from call centres.

'Your distant cousin Seamus has popped in. A surprise visit,' Mother says, her voice glazed with glee. 'I've been telling Seamus about your new career and he wanted to have a word.' Mother hiccups with excitement.

The phone changes hands; there is a faint noise of twins in the background shouting and playing with musical instruments. Tambourines?

'Seamus,' says Seamus. The timbre of his voice suggests the lack of a girlfriend and a bloated sense of self-importance. Gosia hasn't seen him since Bernie was doing his A levels and Seamus was tasked with helping him with maths. She expects a bald patch and a triple chin.

'How can I help?' Gosia's voice is professional, removed.

'I hear you made an interesting career move. Would be keen to learn more about it. Maybe a little workout together?' He chortles. Her mother's laugh rings in the background.

'I'm very busy, I'm afraid,' she says matter-of-factly. 'And I am sure your local gym would be able to offer you an introductory session.'

'But,' Seamus's voice is low and tempting, 'I thought we should get to know each other a bit better before Bernie's nuptials. Because, you know,' Seamus' vowels are slimy, 'I'm really delighted to be your plus-one.'

'Oh,' Gosia sits on the loo for stability. 'There must be some mistake. Maybe Mother didn't get my message? I've already invited someone.'

'Someone?' Seamus titters.

'Someone?!' Mother repeats, her voice erratic.

'Someone,' Gosia confirms. Her statement final.

A clamour by the phone, the mouthpiece badly covered up with a tense palm.

'There must be some mistake. I'm sure she meant to invite you, Seamus,' Mother pleads.

Seamus, distant, probably already lacing up his shoes, offers in a hurt voice: 'I can't see myself as a third wheel.'

There is a noise of rushed kisses delivered in the proximity of cheeks and doors opening and closing.

'Who is it?' Mother shouts into the phone, and it's hard to tell if she's excited or angry.

Gosia closes her eyes to summon the right image, to give an adequate description and to suppress the tears. Vijay is full of desirable adjectives: handsome, educated, open-minded, wealthy, good-tempered, kind and generous.

'A lovely person, full of charm and personality. An exceptional man.'

Mother sighs.

'What is all that good for? Seamus may not be exceptional, but he has a stable job and no dependants.'

'I'm not into Seamus, Mother.' Gosia's toilet break extends into its eighth minute. Her palms sweat. Janelle's patience is limited.

'Oh yes, I know.' Mother releases bitter notes. 'You are not into anyone decent. You've always been into trouble.'

68

The Bulletproof Guide to Sorting Out Your Life: Work, Money, Free Time, Family, Friendship and Love. STEP 9: How to Come Across as a Strong Person

Your worth is directly related to what people think when they see you. Coming across as a strong person is paramount. You do not have to be funny, interesting or cheerful in the eyes of the crowd if you are strong. All these other qualities are helpful once you develop a way to display your strength, but they are not *necessary*.

Strength in women manifests itself differently than in men. For a man to come across as a person of strength, it is often enough to show up shaved, bathed and in a suit. Women do not have it so easy. Clothing and grooming play their role but, on their own, rarely work. Women, apart from a confident stride, well-fitted dress, hairless legs and a pair of killer heels, need an entourage.

A woman showing up on her own to an important event comes across as weak, lonely and not worthy of anyone else's time and attention. Women know instinctively that they are read differently (and to their advantage) in a group and often attend social and professional gatherings in company.

It is important to select your support circle carefully. You definitely want to be the prettiest person in the group if you are attending a singles' night out. You definitely want to be the person talking if you are at a business meeting. Be careful not to be overpowered by your crowd and end up being a support structure for someone else: meet your aims first.

Margaret learnt it the hard way. She invited two of her colleagues to go with her to a professional development training session subsidised by her workplace with a view to gaining new skills and asking for a pay rise upon completion. However, all three of them were committed, fast learners and all three of them requested better pay from their boss while presenting certificates for their obtained qualifications. This did not lead to a happy ending. Margaret was not granted better money.

If Margaret had invited two colleagues who had attended but not completed the course, her position would have been different: she would have been perceived as an exceptional and strong person, not one of many.

Carefully curate your entourage before conquering those parties!

69

A small cafe on a struggling high street serving quality coffee and savoury pancakes at unbeatable prices. Large-scale paintings reminiscent of *The Children's Illustrated Bible* cover the walls. Pastel hues of the murals contrast with the black and white tiled floor, and shiny aluminium bistro tables are enhanced by salt and pepper shakers.

Above the counter, next to a busy menu, hangs a multi-edition print of a seaside sunset. Gosia stares at the couple with their feet in the water, captured in the right-hand corner of the print. She ignores the cafe owner who made comments about her arse and is still trying to catch her eye. She is sipping black coffee in the company of Steve. She is keeping his spirits up while he eats a third potato pancake. Concentrating on Steve stops her from indulging in her own heartache.

Steve called her this morning. He read an article about 'The 10 Things No One Tells You Before You Become a Personal Trainer'. The future is not looking good, he announced, and asked her to join him for a second breakfast.

Over the plate of rich, fried food, he listed the burning problems: PTs get less healthy as they have no time to train themselves, they drink gallons of coffee, are asked to offer fitness advice in their spare time to mates, make people feel guilty for eating iced buns, date other PTs, always have the washing machine on and never, ever go on holiday. The cafe owner keeps winking in Gosia's direction as he cleans the table behind Steve.

'You can't believe every fad the internet spits at you,' she says thoughtfully as Steve chews. He is swallowing too quickly, trapping air in his stomach, troubled by his thoughts. A bit of pancake filling falls on his bobbling jumper. Gosia quickly flicks it away.

He stares at her finger.

'It was mine, for later,' he says in a steady voice.

'Should I go and fetch it?'

He nods.

Gosia surveys the floor, gathers a piece of dirt, an indistinct dark mass. Manure? Decaying insect? Filth? and offers it to Steve on her palm. He gathers it into a tissue with the air of a ritual. Folds it neatly away, puts it in his pocket. The cafe owner, disgusted, walks to the other side of the counter. They high-five silently behind his back.

'You don't seem very upbeat either.' Steve is chewing with his mouth open. 'What's up?'

Gosia circles the rim of the cup with her index finger, not letting her eyes go soggy.

'Just having a bad week.'

'How bad is bad? "Will never smile again" bad, or "Will be back to normal by Monday" bad?'

Gosia shoots him a sharp, stabbing look.

Steve protects himself with a fork.

'No offence, just want to know where we stand. If you're in need of flowers, wine or motivational quotes.'

'I'm OK.' She feels hot and exposed.

'Oh, come on. What is it? You look like a drained pipe.'

Gosia circles the cup a few more times.

'I'll be fine.'

What she needs is a new plan to approach Vijay, but her ideas supply is running low. She will go to Bernie's wedding without the man of her dreams, she decides, and she will have a good time.

'Sure you will. You've got me!'

Steve winks, stirs in his seat and triumphantly raises his fork. 'Forgot to tell you, Barnaby is coming back to town. I told him about the gym and he wants to join! He's in need of a way to boost his energy without relying solely on chocolate!' Steve guffaws.

'Who's Barnaby?' Gosia asks.

'Haven't I mentioned Barnaby? He's my best friend, the finest person on earth, positive as a licked battery and always ready for a party.'

Gosia thinks she saw them together a long while ago in the supermarket. Steve forgot to mention that Barnaby looks like an affluent social entrepreneur, a white T-shirt underneath his sharp suit, his body radiating with confidence as if he has just walked out of a successful business meeting.

'He used to live round the corner but then moved abroad for work. Now he's back for winter, working on a new project. He is SO. MUCH. FUN. You must meet him. If he can't lift your spirits no one can!'

Steve glows just talking about him.

Gosia stares at his plate.

'How did you meet?'

Steve shrugs.

'We went to the same school, but actually only became friends through dancing. Barnaby's a lindy hop king, so we've spent many a night swinging on the dance floor.'

Gosia digs some more.

'I see, so he's like a dance teacher to you?'

Steve puts the fork down. Cleans his fingers on a cheap, coarse paper napkin.

'He's a friend, someone you can lean on when things are tricky.' He looks at Gosia pointedly. 'And yeah, he helped me master a move or two. But the main thing he taught me is not to squash myself into narrow boxes.'

'What do you mean?' Gosia cocks her head.

'You know, like all those boring forms that ask you if you are this or that.' Steve pretends to mark an invisible rectangle. 'Barnaby made me question who I am, how I want to talk about myself.'

'Question what exactly?' Gosia enquires.

Steve lists on his fingers.

'Sexuality, gender, nationality, ethnicity. You name it.'

'Question how?' Gosia narrows her eyebrows.

'By exploding what you are told is "normal". Boom!' Steve pretends a bomb is going off underneath his hands.

'I've never seen it done.'

Steve laughs.

'Oh, Gosia, you're so sheltered sometimes. Have you never heard of someone questioning themselves and doing it out loud?'

She is puzzled.

'Questioning in what way?'

Steve squeezes his eyebrows together.

'Never felt like experimenting? Testing who you are? Listening to all those fuzzy feelings that you have inside? Never thought about stepping over the limits?'

She is instantly reminded of Mother, who frequently told her to control her anger, to smile, to please, to 'be more ladylike'. The limits were spelled out in a harsh, unforgiving voice and she was expected to obey them. 'Be a girl' in her mother's tongue means to be in the service of other people.

Then she thinks about all the awful jokes about lesbians, men in dresses and upturned stools that Andy would start retelling after the fourth shot of vodka, and how angry it made her. How uncomfortable it was sitting next to him when he was showing off his hostile side. And how she was lost for words, when she told him to stop and when he asked why, and then teased her in front of their friends, asking if she wanted to 'experiment'.

Andy would assert himself frequently and in all manner of situations that he only 'drinks like a man', 'thinks like a man' and 'behaves like a man'.

She realises now that she has packed away and stored in unlabelled boxes in the attic of her body a lot of uncomfortable feelings and oddly shaped, half-finished thoughts. Maybe Steve was right, maybe she should go through those boxes.

Steve leans in to touch Gosia's hand. 'It's never too late. In the meantime, you have to meet Barnaby. He changed my life.'

Gosia smiles.

'Sure.'

'Splendid!'

Steve beams. He stretches and reveals a large hole in his jumper just below his armpit. Then goes back to his plate, scoops up some more of his food. Watching him comforts her, softens her. She likes his company and for the first time in ages she feels listened to when she speaks.

'What are you up to on the twenty-seventh, later this month?' Gosia asks. 'It's a Saturday.'

'I don't plan my life weeks ahead! Don't know yet. Probably nothing much. Might jog 5k and try to get a runner's high.' He snorts.

'Come with me to my brother's wedding.' She locks her eyes with his.

'Is that an invite or an order?' He packs the rest of the pancake into his mouth.

'It's an offer. You don't have to, if you don't want to.' She puts her hands in her lap. Clutches her fingers together. She can imagine smiling at the party with Steve in the room, his good humour helping her forget about her aunt counting out loud, for the benefit of the gathered family, Gosia's remaining childbearing years.

He lifts the cutlery in the air.

'Why would a woman like you,' he jabs the fork in her direction, 'want to go to a wedding with a guy like me?' He pokes the air, pointing at himself.

'Let me think . . .' She pauses. 'You make me laugh, have great dancing moves and you're never, ever tempted to pat my bottom.'

He consults with the ceiling.

'Deal. Is it a formal affair or can I come in my sweatpants?'

70

A compact double bedroom overlooking an insipid street in a small town not too far from London, but not too close either. The closed door displays discoloured and creased collaged images cut out from cheap magazines from the previous century. The youthful face of Julia Roberts grins in the centre, surrounded by photos of bright flowers, butterflies, pictures of guitars and surfers interwoven with some hand-drawn sketches of furniture.

The metal frame of a double bed is pushed against a wall marked with the dark outlines of timber, where bunk beds used to stand. A flowery bedspread from a budget shop, and three velvet heart-shaped cushions in clashing teal cover up the mattress. On the right-hand bedside table sit pictures of twins in cheap chrome mounts, at different stages of development. On the left-hand bedside table, there is a single image in a heavy wooden frame of a couple looking lovingly at each other's foreheads.

In front of a large mirrored double wardrobe stand Gosia and Chrissy. They try on matching dresses for their brother's wedding.

Chrissy moans excessively as she pushes the zip past her hips. Gosia's dress hangs on her, boldly exposing her flat chest, excess material folding on itself in places where the expected breasts are supposed to fit. The dresses are light and flimsy, made from 100% polyester in sickly-sweet pale pink.

'We look like restored virgins,' says Gosia.

Chrissy groans and forces the zip up the side of her ribcage.

'I'd rather wear something that blends in with the surroundings,' Gosia says, smoothing the fabric that clings to her tights.

'I told Mum not to buy them from a catalogue,' says Chrissy, her face flushed with effort. 'But you know how she is.'

Gosia just nods. Their parsimonious mother made them wear each other's clothes throughout their childhood, when Bernie's wardrobe was not to be touched. This is one of a few occasions when they have been given a dress each. Gosia has already pre-selected a charity shop to donate this heap of synthetic resin to.

Chrissy sways in front of the mirror, trying different modest poses. Gosia sighs and sits heavily on the bed.

'It looks OK,' she offers to Chrissy. Their eyes meet in the mirror. Chrissy points at herself.

'I look fat and don't even dare to sit down in case it splits. I'll have to eat dinner by the bar!'

Gosia laughs.

'You look cute. Duncan will love seeing you in it.'

'Can't wait to see him, to be honest.' Chrissy tints red again. 'It's so odd. We're married and have kids, but because he's away so much it feels like dating!'

Gosia nods encouragingly as Chrissy continues.

'I don't get it when people say their marriage has gone stale. I'm, like, over the moon whenever he's home. But there's never enough time to do all the things we want to do and the boys, you know, they love having their daddy to play with. Having grand-parents is great for them but it's not the same, you know, they need a solid role model. I worry sometimes that they'll think men need to be away all the time from the family, that this is normal.'

Chrissy's voice trembles. Gosia speaks quickly.

'But it's just for a while, right? Till you've saved up to get a place of your own and can move out from Mother's, right? And he's been working offshore for three years now, so you must've saved a bit?'

Chrissy sniffles gently.

'But the prices constantly go up, Gosia. There was a house we went to see; beautiful home with four bedrooms and a big lush garden and it was snapped up, like, instantly.'

Gosia rubs her sister's side.

'Maybe you can get something smaller to start with?'

Chrissy perks up.

'Oh no. I don't want the boys to share. It's OK for now, they're still little, but in a few years they'll need their own bedrooms. I know you and I got on fine here' – Chrissy points to the walls – 'usually.'

Gosia winces.

The room was a stage for their long, bitter rows and weeks of sulking. Disagreements over clothes, cosmetics, books, pencils, posters, bags, shoes, swimming costumes, pillowcases, shelving units, cleaning, time spent in the bathroom, friends, boyfriends, church, music, alarm clocks, Saturday jobs, future plans. But mostly there were vexing and gory wars with Bernie, stationed in his larger room next door. The bloodiest battles and the most hurtful clashes took place in the corridor when their mother was blatantly unfair, always giving Bernie what he wanted.

Gosia stares ahead.

'Don't worry. You'll find the right house and finally get bored of your married life.'

'That's all I dream of,' says Chrissy.

71

A small bedroom crowded with objects. Dirty laundry unfurled on the bed. A selection of cardboard boxes crammed against the wall. Gosia sits on a pink, heart-shaped cushion with Lyndsey's diary in her lap.

I lost 1lb thanks to my new regime of having only lemon juice with hot water for breakfast.

Mum thinks it's a good time to move in with Kev and she keeps reminding me to keep my secrets because men don't need to know everything. 'Never let him see you pee, poo or wax,' Mum said – what wise words! She also said that I should never reveal the weaknesses of my heart: 'They're better off thinking that they are the only one.'

Mum's a hero. She remarried four times. Always for love. Richard is a great guy, I can see why she prefers him to Dad. Dad never wrote poetry for Mum, never gave her a foot massage or brought champagne home. Mum and Richard eat out, like, all the time. She often texts 'Went to Frankie & Benny's' or 'Great night at the pub!' or 'Loving these large lattes at Costa'.

Me and Kev will be just like them. We will drink bubbly, watch a good film and snuggle up on a large sofa.

I told Kev I need to go on a week's course to learn new nail techniques this winter but the truth is that I've booked a week's intensive slimming holiday. I read testimonials – people lose tons of pounds. A whole week on green juices and plenty of exercise suitable for the unfit. They measure you before and after so it's clear what you've lost. And it's literally in the middle of nowhere, so you can't even sneak out for a KitKat.

I took a week off and booked it; my heart was pounding as they only had a few remaining places. I got on, though! I sent through my history of failed diets and it was so reassuring to hear that that's normal. They said many of their clients had tried nearly everything and it wasn't until 'Juice Diet Intensive Away' that they finally managed to slim down.

Vincent's son came around again with his attitude. Thank god Kev was in, as I had just popped out to get us bacon butties.

I came back and saw them by the door. Kev was going, 'This has nothing to do with my missus' and Vincent's son started undoing his shirt sleeves, and Kev did his 'block the door' pose, and my heart raced because no one has ever fought for me before.

It was like on a film! I was sorry I didn't wear my floral dress with a V cut at the back. It spoiled it that I couldn't stop thinking about the food going cold.

Vincent's son said he would do his best to ruin our sale and it was only then that I realised there was a 'For Sale' sign in our front garden with 'ground floor flat' on a small board stuck to the bottom of it.

It came as a bit of a shock, but I know my guardian angel is looking after me, blessing me with a room in Kev's flat at the right time.

I said nothing to GG; I thought she would notice. Then, three days later, we both got a letter from the landlord. It simply said that our contract was coming to an end, we couldn't renew it and we'd have to move out before the end of the year.

I'm worried for GG because she is not herself lately, all gloomy and quiet in such a loud way! She also keeps filling the kitchen bin with used tissues. I bet it's her tears, not pads. I'm sure she menstruates like she eats, in droplets. I think this is all to do with her brother's wedding. I'm sure she's dreading it.

She said nothing but I could tell.

I asked GG what she was going to do and she said that something would come up!

GG never leaves things to chance. I smell a rat. She's acting like she's hiding something.

So I spied on her and searched her room for clues. Not proud of it but I needed to know for mine, Kevin and Anna's sakes.

I looked through her stuff. There was nothing under the mattress or taped to the back of the drawers. But in plain view, on her little table there was an empty plate and a sharp knife. The darkest place is under the candlestick, so I picked the knife up with my woolly glove and put it into a plastic bag.

I followed GG the next day but there was nothing unusual, apart from the fact that she walked to work the long way, through the park, and it left me breathless and with two big blisters on my heel.

I came back later, after work. I went into the gym and pretended to eye the leggings in their shop and chatted to a friendly receptionist. She told me without too much prodding that GG went to the library. This didn't surprise me. Since Margaret took Andy's laptop, GG would probably sleep at the library if they let her.

I was about to leave when the receptionist said that GG would be back shortly for her course.

I asked lightly what course it was and she said a fitness instructor course. I thought straight away that GG must be plotting something.

So I waited some more, had a pumpkin spice latte and a rather slim slice of cake at a cafe around the corner.

I went back and the receptionist was like, 'Oh, she's back now, in the yellow workout room,' and she let me stroll through the corridor and I spotted GG by the water fountain laughing her head off.

It came as a shock to be honest, a short chubby man with the face of a hog was making her roar. He showed her some bum wiggles, whispered something in her ear and she was nearly flat on the floor.

The world will never cease to surprise me – GG went for a misfit. I never thought she would do that, she's too shallow. I think she must be desperate. The news left Anna speechless. Kev thinks that this is to throw him off the scent.

Gosia puts the diary away, behind the DVDs in blue sleeves on the top shelf, and leaves.

72

The Bulletproof Guide to Sorting Out Your Life: Work, Money, Free Time, Family, Friendship and Love. STEP 10: How to Feed Your Creativity

Nutritious food, quality sleep and regular exercise are essential for keeping you fit and ready for your perfect life, but are not enough on their own. Your perfect life requires you to connect to your creative side. It is your creative mind that is responsible for excellent ideas and life-changing decisions, and that's why you want it functioning at its best.

Creativity needs regular stimulation to be sharp and switched-on, for ideas to flow and for solutions to arrive. It is not just with apples and carrots that you feed your imagination. You have to take yourself into places and be among people where ideas are generated. These will depend on what type of creative mind you want to foster.

Do you want to open a secret dining club in your garden? Going to upmarket markets to sample quality street food and a wide variety of artisanal produce will provide you with a sensual experience that you can recreate in your kitchen. This will translate into excellent meals for people dining near your hydrangeas and enable you to launch your career as a chef.

Feeding your senses feeds your creative mind. Smells, colours, sounds, textures and tastes contribute to the development of your ideas, open up your creative chambers and help you fly.

However, do not be surprised to find it hard to begin with! If you've starved your creativity of nourishing experiences, it might take a while to gain it back.

Andy, although clear in his ambition to write, needed a long restorative weekend at a spa with Margaret to help him reconnect with his artistic mind. The sublime mix of yoga, massage, nourishing diet, swims, walks and romance brought him back from the brink of extinguishing his dreams.

Andy and Margaret quickly discovered that they require restorative weekends away in order to keep their energy high and their ideas sparking, therefore they will prioritise these over anything else. It occasionally requires difficult decisions, like cancelling family dinners with the in-laws or meet-ups with friends, but they are prepared to make these sacrifices in order to put themselves and their creativity first. Looking after their fundamentals and feeding their talents allows them to be caring, loving and patient with others.

You may not know what will best feed your creative mind straight away and it might take a while to find a way to reconnect with your artistic side. Be patient! Be committed!

73

A well-lit and generously sized basement room in a bookshop in the city centre normally used as a cafe. Tables stacked by the wall and chairs arranged for a monologue. A waiter, tall and thin, in casual clothes and with a strained smile navigates the room with a tray full of sparkling wine in tall, plastic glasses. Gosia takes one. She arrives with minutes to spare before the official speeches of the book launch begin.

The room is rammed with serious-looking people in jackets and ties. Women wear high heels. The people are mostly old. Gosia quickly locates the author, a man in his sixties, with a hair transplant and the smile of a cheater. He stands in the vicinity of a table, on which his books are arranged in stacks for a quick sale. Each copy has been affectionately wrapped in a yellow ribbon by obedient female hands.

So this is the face of a guy who for the last few weeks, if not months, advertised his forthcoming book under each of her poems. Gosia has never read his work and has never been to a book launch before.

Another man, young and lively, attracts the crowd with a booming voice, delivered via a microphone. People take their seats.

'Ladies and gentlemen, fellow poets, my name is Derek Smith and I'm the administrator of Poetry Platform, a free online space for poets. It is with great pleasure that I welcome you to the launch of Richard Mutton's book of poetry, *Poems For Dark Times.*'

He lifts a copy of the book above his head and waves in all directions a burgundy cover with embossed gold letters.

'This is an essential read in this turbulent world. An exceptionally well-put-together selection of poems that attracted crowds to our online platform, which I'm sure many of you are part of. If not, please speak to me if you would like to know more, or wish to join this supportive poetry circle and read fresh poetry daily.'

There are a couple of enthusiastic whoops and nods.

'We are, however, here to celebrate this particularly great achievement. Richard Mutton is known to many of you as a prolific poet. He joined our poetry platform three years ago and took it by storm, regularly publishing and actively offering invaluable insight into other poets' work. It's fantastic to see how far he's come, having his work launched in this superb location. Can we have a big round of applause for Richard's wife, Doris, who coordinated this event?'

A woman sealed to the book-selling table waves her hand weakly. People clap.

'Richard, you said you have a few words to say.'

The man points at the author. Richard walks towards him, extending his hand for the microphone. He holds it firmly, centimetres from his mouth, his other hand busy gripping his book.

Gosia takes a sip. The wine is sharp and fizzy. It goes up her nose and rushes down her throat.

'Thanks, Derek. I'm really happy to be here. I didn't think this would happen so soon, and it wouldn't have been possible without my beautiful wife, Doris.' He doesn't glance at her. 'I spent months searching for the right publisher, but this work,' he holds the book close to his heart, 'is ahead of its time. I've been refused and, to put it bluntly, not taken seriously. That hurt,' he shakes his head, 'as you can imagine. But a man never gives up.' He punches the air with the book. There is weak applause. 'After extensive research I concluded that the best way for this work to be made available was to self-publish. I dedicate this collection to my wife,' he indicates her location vaguely with his hand, 'who is the biggest supporter of my work. Thank you, darling.' He continues to address the crowd.

Gosia notices a woman, closely resembling Lyndsey, joining the author's wife by the table with two glasses of wine.

Richard, like a prophet, extends his hands.

'I have dedicated my life to poetry. This is my vocation. This is my obligation to the world.' He brings his hands down, looks seriously at the crowd. 'To become a poet, one needs to commit to the task. It is a precious and tender world, a delicate one, so it is with a heavy heart and aching mind that I observe the pollution of it by amateur poets that soil the world of poetry with their half-baked work.' He looks at the crowd with his small, greasy eyes. 'If I can give you one piece of advice, it's to commit. Don't take poetry on board as a hobby. It is not a hobby, it is hard work, one that can't be undertaken by many.' He scans the rows. 'It is a struggle to be seen amid the waves of mediocrity, so I am humbled by the amount of support I've received from people reading my poems online, the ones that I now present in this collection. This would not be possible without you, although I must stress poems do not write themselves. This book cost me many sleepless nights, but I am delighted to be able to offer it to you.'

It must actually *be* Lyndsey. The way the woman shifts her weight from hip to hip and the speed with which she knocks the wine back leaves Gosia in no doubt. Richard finishes his speech.

'Tonight, there's a rare opportunity to acquire this book of poems at a reduced rate of only ten pounds and, if you have time and are able to wait, of course I'll sign it for you! Don't rush to the table all at once, though, there are enough copies for everyone. Please spread the word: I am going on a book tour in the coming weeks and will be visiting towns around the country. The full details are available from Doris,' he points his hand again towards the table, 'and online. Thank you for coming tonight. Your support means the world to me.'

There is some clapping, but most guests stand and rush towards a waiter with a tray of canapés. A few shift to the table with books, obscuring Gosia's view of most-probably-Lyndsey. A swarm of women attack Derek, who dishes out his business cards.

Gosia drains her wine, abandons the glass on the floor next to her chair and stands up to leave. She turns around and faces the bar. There, next to an empty bottle of a cheap Prosecco, stands Kevin, his hand firmly in his pocket, his other hand nonchalantly holding a glass of wine. Its contents have wet his shoes. He is pissed. His eyes are locked with Gosia's chest.

'Oi,' says Kevin, 'long time no see.' He hiccups. 'Killer.'

'Pardon?' Gosia cocks her head.

'Killer, look!' Kevin points his finger at her. He slowly sways towards Gosia.

She is holding his drifting gaze, and for a moment wonders if she should return to fetch her glass and offer a full set of her fingerprints to Kev as a goodwill gesture.

'I'll catch you,' Kevin slurs, walking past her, 'later.'

Gosia spins on her heel and makes quick steps towards the exit. At the staircase she turns around and catches Lyndsey staring directly at her. Kevin's arm rests heavily on her shoulder, her lip-glossed mouth wide in surprise.

74

A red bus congested with tense, tired and tender human bodies after eight hours of work in a city centre. The bus proceeds slowly, in a series of hiccuping moves. The horn on the bus beeps frequently.

Gosia boards it reluctantly but her shopping is heavy and she doesn't want to cart it all the way home on foot. Her tote is filled with large bags of split peas, dry beans and premium-quality rice sold at half price. She edges her way towards the top deck ready to hunt for a seat when she sees a familiar haircut squashed against the windowpane downstairs. She pushes through the crowd to be certain. It's him.

The man of her dreams is in a seat next to a woman in a floral jacket, his eyes closed, his earphones in. His hands calmly folded on top of his leather satchel. The faint noise of people talking escapes from his earphones and travels in her direction. He never fails to spend his free time expanding his horizons. He must be listening to one of these irresistible podcasts that allow you to connect to the vibrant lives of accomplished professionals and learn from their mistakes.

Gosia carefully manoeuvres herself until she is standing just a metre away, abandons her shopping at her feet and holds onto the metal bar with both hands for stability. She trembles. She hasn't seen him for ages and it's been over a month since the fatal phone call. Her eyes take in his smooth brown skin, the gentle slope of his nose, the perfect curve of his neck. And his lips. Lips that she wants to suck into her mouth, kiss urgently, violently.

The floral jacket has moved, obstructing her view and only then does she realise that the woman is leaving, motioning for Gosia to step aside. She does. The seat becomes vacant. The urge is so strong. She pushes herself into the empty space, trips on her shopping bag tangled by her feet and her left hand plunges forward, a bit too far, onto his thigh. He opens his eyes. She gasps and retracts her limb.

'Sorry, so sorry,' she says in the wrong voice. The voice of someone who would like to take it all back, when she would like to take it all further.

He shifts, gives her a distracted nod and closes his eyes again. He clearly doesn't recognise her, but should she be surprised? They haven't seen each other for a while, she must have slipped from his mind.

She sits down next to him. The contours of the right side of her body are communing with the contours of the left side of his body. She is all heat and liquid, ready to spill. Her hand, the hand that rested on his thigh, tingles.

They sit like that for a few stops. Her mind on a spin cycle, unable to construct a sentence that would make sense. Words – 'a drink', 'you', 'like', 'would' – not falling into the right order. Her shopping, an awkward ballast, twisted between her legs. She hasn't washed her hair today, is wearing old leggings, a dirty hoodie and no make-up. It's all wrong. It's all perfect. She closes her eyes, tilts her head towards his shoulder and is about to gently rest it against him when a woman, all wrinkles and rain cover, sitting in front, in a seat at a 90-degree angle to theirs, speaks.

'Long day, huh? Ready to nod off? Good to have a man to protect you and not worry that someone could pinch your purse.'

Gosia melts. They look like a couple, destined to hold hands, raise children and live in each other's pockets. He doesn't stir while she enthusiastically bobs her head.

The woman gives her a smile with all her false teeth arranged in two perfect rows, clicks the stop button and hoists herself up, her left hand adorned with a fat golden wedding ring.

'In this world, a good man is worth more than a good woman,' she says, looking straight at Gosia. 'But only because they die quicker and then women go sour.' She shakes her head and shuffles to the open door.

The bus empties. Gosia is a long way past her destination, but she doesn't want to go home any more. She resumes her plan. She inhales deeply to take in the smell of his luxurious fabric conditioner, a complex and seductive cedar-wood scent available in 1-litre bottles at an eye-watering six pounds. A biodegradable formula that makes ironing easy and the environment happy. He still buys it. She still inhales the undiluted version during her shopping trips. Smelling it on him is different, better. The fragrance is lighter and mingled with something else, something earthy and a bit balmy – his sweat.

She closes her eyes and tilts her head.

He taps her on her shoulder.

She turns to face him. The flesh of his lips is light pink and recently licked, moisture glazed on top. He moves those lips once, then twice. She finally hears him.

'My stop.' He repeats, 'It's my stop.'

She stands up into the aisle but he only moves an inch, his foot blocked by her shopping. She has to bend down to fetch it and pauses there to gather the bag's handles, her head in the proximity of his trousers' zip, his groin at her eye level. Her face is right there, next to his tight bundle. She trembles with internal fireworks and, with difficulty, stands up.

He takes a step, then another and is stationed by the exit, waiting for the bus to stop. She stands mute in the aisle, the bag in her hand, gawping at him. He catches her eye and mouths one word in her direction before leaving. It could be 'Bye' or 'Hi' but she settles on 'Mine'.

75

A small bedroom choking with cardboard boxes, half filled with poor-quality belongings stacked by the wall providing a slim access route to the bed. The investigation matrix is busy and confusing: the string criss-crosses the wall, while Post-it notes overlap each other. Gosia stands in the doorway and reads Lyndsey's diary.

I put on 5lb. Halloween is just around the corner so I've decided to enjoy myself although I avoid fried chicken and chips. Still, I couldn't say no to a triple helping of Anna's pumpkin pie. Afterwards, I couldn't do the zip up on my trousers and had to buy a new pair for work. I went for a tight-fitting look that shows off my shapely knees.

Richard had his book launch in a fancy bookshop in town. Mum got cases of half-price wine at Costco and Kevin was so happy for Richard that he got totally wasted. Later, Mum took us to an Italian place down the road for dinner but Kevin couldn't hold a knife and fork. We ordered pizzas.

Richard wasn't too pleased with Mum because she only sold twelve copies and he printed five hundred. The crowd thinned once the wine was gone. Free booze attracts anyone – even GG showed up. I must have blabbed about this launch to her but I don't think I gave her the address. What a creep! She must be listening in on my phone chats with Mum.

I wanted to stay for tiramisu, but Mum booked us a taxi home and told me to put Kevin to bed.

I made bacon and eggs for breakfast and slipped paracetamol into Kevin's coffee. He never takes it 'cos pills are for the weak-headed', but I learnt that trick from Mum and it works a treat, just need to add extra sugar. Within an hour he was perky and could speak full sentences.

I asked him then and there, no more beating about the bush, when we were going to get married.

He looked at me like I was someone else and then held my hand in his for a very long time, and after that he told me that he didn't believe in marriage.

I was shocked.

SHOCKED.

S H O C K E D.

S

H

O

C

K

E

D

Have I wasted my life waiting for him to be ready?!

I couldn't say a word.

He said that his parents are each other's worst enemies living under the same roof and he didn't want that for himself.

He talked about my mum and all her husbands who, apparently, make her a laughing stock, and wasn't it better to take the days as they come, one at a time?

I was S O A N G R Y.

L
I
V
I
D

I almost packed all his things and told him to go.

But sitting on my bed I saw clearly the size of his love in the lengths of string attached to the wall. The lines nearly made a heart shape.

He will change. I know it. He just needs time.

I went back and threw my arms over him and took him to bed but he wasn't able to get it up so we lay there, like married couples do. He fell asleep with his head in my cleavage.

I didn't mention it to Mum. She keeps searching for a ring on my finger. I told her we will move in together because this is what modern couples do. But I have stopped taking the pill.

Gosia puts the diary away, back inside the clammy pillowcase stained with flaxen discharge from an unidentified orifice and places it on top of the synthetic duvet.

76

The Bulletproof Guide to Sorting Out Your Life: Work, Money, Free Time, Family, Friendship and Love.
STEP 4: How to Understand Who You Are

You may think you know yourself through and through. You spend all your time with yourself after all, so what is there to understand? What is there to find out, you may ask?

Knowing your heritage is an important factor in figuring out your abilities, strengths and talents. If you understand your ancestry, you are at an advantage: it holds keys to recognising your potential.

Margaret only appreciated her strong mission to help and care for others when she found out that her maternal grandmother was a childminder during the war. That insight was important as it allowed Margaret to acknowledge that caring was written in her blood, and thus informed her choice to leave her job in a hospital setting to care instead for her readers. Knowing that it was 'care' that she was good at, not 'nurse-type care' was crucial in moving her energy from low-paid, demanding, undervalued work towards the career path that brought with it fulfilment, joy and monetary return.

Andy, thanks to an insightful conversation with his great-uncle, learnt about his own ancestors who were known for regularly putting words on paper. His great-grandfather, for example, had a journal in which he kept track of expenditure and income, but in the margins there were frequent notes about the weather and local affairs that might be affecting his smallholding. That was a fortifying insight as it showed Andy that an ability to write was already in his DNA - he just needed to give it space, energy and commitment to flourish.

The awareness of gifts and aptitudes that run in your family is a helpful tool to figure out your own capacities and ensure you are putting your energy into the right places. How do you go about it? You seek people with that knowledge! There must be a family member that remembers stories about your predecessors. Find them, visit them, encourage them to talk about the past and learn from this experience - this will help you to fully acknowledge the extent of your own talents.

No family members left? Do not despair! You can always go ahead with a DNA test that will reveal your ancestry. YourDNAmatters.com is our recommended service. Quote 'AndyandMargaret' at checkout for 2 per cent off.

77

A spacious ladies' toilet, tiled in shiny lime green, in a large, out-of-town hotel positioned strategically near a motorway exit and usually frequented by attendees of regional retail conferences. There are multiple cubicles and a row of sinks with large, splashed mirrors above them. The soap in the dispensers and the loo roll are both running low. The dim light flickers. Decorative fake flower arrangements in glass jars sit haphazardly by the rims of sinks.

Gosia washes her hands and watches her flushed face in the mirror. Her feet are sore and spilling out from faux-leather, timelessly chic, pointed-toe patent courts in nude. Shoes picked by her mother to match her polyester dress, two sizes too big, adjusted with an army of safety pins and a belt.

The wedding is nearly over. Many uncommitted guests left in pre-booked taxis shortly after the first dance. Her mother's long stares were their only goodbye; Aitziber and Bernie were too consumed in their practiced dance moves, silently counting to eight, stiff in their desire to show off.

These guests had already lived through the lengthy speeches, the slim portions, a sickly-sweet wedding cake and one round from the overpriced bar. Gosia, too, watched them leave.

Stalwart friends and family members stayed to sway for hours of cheap popular music especially produced for 'these sorts of occasions', to be sung out of tune into each other's collarbones.

Mother endured Dad by her side for the sake of group pictures and to avoid any rumours. Gosia was surprised. Her father looked dashing in a new suit and shiny shoes, acquired with Gosia's money. His hair clipped, his moustache moisturised. He hovered within proximity of his wife, offering his arm or his handkerchief, inviting her for a dance. Mother followed with a hard to read expression on her face – a mixture of amusement, regret and wonder, perhaps?

Gosia sighs at the mirror. She has danced with her father, both slightly drunk on a mixture of sparkling wine, rum, vodka and Coke. Dad held her in his arms lightly as they danced to three songs on the trot in a mixture of fluid moves and intricate steps. Gosia had forgotten how well he leads and how aptly she can follow.

Before they parted, both out of breath, her father touched the side of Gosia's face and in his spry voice with its slightly misplaced accent said, 'I am so proud of you.' A single tear gathered in the corner of his eye and she looked away.

'Thanks, Dad,' was all she said before walking towards the drinks counter to sober up with a pint of tap water.

Gosia observes an intricate pattern of dried-up droplets covering the mirror. When looked at from an angle and with one eye slightly shut, they make the shape of dancing feet.

The dance floor was sparsely populated when a lively jazz number started blaring out of the speakers and Steve, in his vibrant floral shirt bursting with colour, entered the room. He saluted

Gosia and wriggled his way towards the centre where Bernie was dancing monotonous circles with the aunts, bending his knees to the tune. Steve bowed in front of him and extended his hand, asking for a dance. Bernie squawked and tried to sidestep him. Steve smiled, whirled around, attached himself to Bernie's back and steered him away from the group. They danced a wild dance in which Steve expertly led Bernie through a series of elaborate twirls. Bernie tried to make it look fun, badly concealing his shock and surprise. They finally found a shared rhythm and waltzed around the room a few times in a mixture of feral moves that made Aunt Clara pant and wheeze from the sidelines. Steve let Bernie go and started his solo routine filled with proficient scissor kicks and dazzling boogie drops, encouraging Bernie to join in and follow. A small crowd gathered to watch and clap. Bernie's attempts looked flat next to Steve's effortless bends and the rhythmic moves of his hips that got whoops from the audience. Steve marked the end of the song with a wet kiss on Bernie's hairy face. Bernie laughed and, unexpectedly for Gosia, gave Steve an awkward hug.

Gosia is drunk, hot and tired. She runs cold water on her wrists and fights the urge to splash her face. It took an hour and a half to apply the make-up and it's still in place. She wants to maintain a proper look till the bitter end.

She looks pretty in the mirror. She must have disguised any signs of doubt underneath a double layer of foundation. The infrequent blasts of cold breeze from an ancient air-con surround her and she swims in a calm ocean of fulfilled everyday life. In the mirror frame, there is a radiant promise of happiness of her own. In the corner, almost out of sight, touching the horizon, floats Andy's raft. She sees him holding the stencil in his hands, shouting in her direction.

In this alcohol-infused moment, she feels no regrets. From the other side of the mirror arrives Vijay on his yacht, beckoning to her to jump in and go with him far out into the sea. His hand movement indicates it all: his feelings for her, his invitation to make love on the deck under the naked sun.

Viola walks in quietly, on her tiptoes. Throughout the evening they have relied heavily on a worn copy of a Polish–English phrasebook that Viola has kept in her hand, phrases highlighted in neon yellow.

They navigated between a celebrations section (*Cheers!*) and eating out pages (*A bottle of house wine, please*). It took Gosia a while to realise that the phrasebook didn't have an option to ask just for a glass. She calmly watched Viola knocking back the glasses of wine in large mouthfuls and promptly emptying the contents of a bottle of sour Chardonnay. Viola's face had gently twitched between refills.

Steve asked Viola a number of questions about Poland, starting with weather and food, and moving towards nightclubs and the queer scene. Gosia acted throughout as a translator from English into basic English.

'But could I hold my beloved's hand while walking down the pavement?' Steve asked, slurring his words.

'Boy-boy, hand-hand, city, walk, Poland, good?' said Gosia, looking expectantly at Viola.

Viola sighed, hit one hand with the other, while replying, 'Boy-boy, walk, no good.'

Steve raised his voice, slightly drunk, shouting across the table for twelve, now occupied just by the three of them.

'Violence! Gay people being attacked! How very backwards, how unfair!' He scrunched up his face. 'And women? Can you live a fulfilled life as a woman in Poland? Enjoy equal pay, equal share of domestic work, support in child-rearing?'

'Wife, work, good money, husband help?' Gosia translated.

Viola shook her head.

'Wife little money. Husband go away. Wife sad.' She looked at Gosia with her fearful eyes. 'You dad wife very sad.'

'She is,' Gosia agreed, looking at her mother, who was busy instructing the catering staff to package all uneaten food into freezable portions, gathering platters from tables herself and moving slices of ham into neat piles.

Now in the toilets, Viola gives Gosia a shy, craggy smile in the mirror and places her handbag on the sink. She dips her small hand into the mouth of her bag and produces an expensive water spray in an aluminium bottle.

'You want?' Viola asks, offering the container on her palm. Gosia nods. She takes it, wraps her arm around her cousin, holds her face next to Viola's and sprays them both with droplets of pure French water. They sigh with pleasure and then giggle like teenagers, their faces lit up with glee. As they embrace, their breathing synchronises and Gosia's internal apparatus to care for her kin is fully activated. Tonight, being part of this family feels like a gift, not a burden.

Through the laughter and thin mist, she notices Aunt Clara hesitating by the loo's entrance, her face bemused. Her aunt chooses to turn and leave, as Gosia moves to shield Viola from the disapproving gaze.

78

A generously sized kitchen in a semi-detached house. Seventies cabinets compete for attention with eighties tiles. There is a brand-new white fridge-freezer in the corner, covered with fridge magnets advertising famous streets: Oxford Circus, Abbey Road, Pall Mall, and seaside towns: Southend-on-Sea, Blackpool, Scarborough, Margate, Great Yarmouth.

A white plastic tea-splattered kettle sits next to a four-slice toaster covered in crumbs. The kettle boils. Mother in her apron brews tea in a large metal teapot. Gosia and Chrissy, both in their matching wedding pastel dresses, refreshed with an odour-eliminating spray, are drying up cheap china cups and saucers. Aitziber's parents, Alaitz and Ganiz, have just left.

'What a shame that Alliance doesn't speak English!' Mother says to the teabags floating in the pot. 'I really felt there was a lot more we could have discussed. She has the face of a woman who knows. I took an instant liking to her.'

She squeezes the bags with a spoon and shakes her head. The whole family watched with surprise at how well Siobhán and Alaitz managed to communicate using their hands and eyebrows alone.

'But Bernie. My Bernie. Oh, my Bernie boy. He's leaving! I can't believe that's what Itchybeer was planning all along!' she sobs.

Chrissy places her hand on mother's back and pats her gently.

'He will be OK, Mum.' Her voice suggests otherwise. 'Spain is great, and a lot of English live there too. He'll have some company for sure, and I bet he'll travel back home often!'

Mother's sobbing grows heavier.

'But my grandchildren.' She inhales. 'They may not even speak English! They will grow up foreign and I won't get to know them like John and Paul.'

The teabag in the pot bursts from over-handling and mother drops the spoon into the boiling tea.

'I'm too old to learn that Spanish, and now they tell me that they also speak something else! Basque! I mean, how could I ever learn two languages?'

She takes a step to sit on a nearby chrome chair with an orange vinyl cover, wiping it with a tea towel first.

'I thought Bernie would buy a house next door. Move in and start a family, but here we are. They're only just married and she's already four months pregnant. It didn't show, thank goodness.'

She wipes her brows with the same tea towel.

'I thought you couldn't fly if you were pregnant. I told her that. I went up to her and said, "I am pleased to have another daughter but you mustn't fly. It's bad for the baby."' Mother raises her eyes up, searches for approval. Chrissy nods obediently. 'But she wouldn't have any of it. She's taking a ferry if she must, but the baby will be born in Spain!' She sighs, shakes her head. 'She isn't as nice as before, now that my boy married her.'

Gosia volunteers, 'He looks happy.'

Chrissy adds, 'Spain is a perfect holiday destination. We can all go and visit!'

Mother dries her eyes with the corner of the apron.

'It was a beautiful wedding, and so lovely of Itchy's parents to come here today. I wanted to welcome them to the house, so they see how we live. How family is important to us.'

She rubs her hands on her thighs.

'So many people came to the service. I don't think Alliance and Gunit realised who was who. Who was important. All those friends of Bernie's in fancy suits with their fancy wives. Is that what decent women wear these days? Your father couldn't stop gawping!'

Chrissy and Gosia exchange a look. Mother and Dad shared a hotel room and returned together to the house this morning to partake in the preparations. Alaitz and Ganiz had endured an afternoon tea by the low table in the living room with polite smiles. Bernie had accompanied them. Aitziber was busy returning unwanted presents. Once they were gone it was Dad himself who offered to wash up, but Mother did not think his skills were adequate and told him to take the twins to the swings. The boys shrieked with joy and they are not back yet.

Gosia lifts up the cup she has just dried, 'Where are all these from?'

Colour returns to Mother's cheeks.

'I rented them out. With scones you must have cups and saucers. We would look common serving tea in mugs. They'll collect them tomorrow.'

Mother gives Gosia a studious look.

'Now I only have you to worry about. I didn't mention a word to Aunt Clara, that you were coming along with a guest. Just before the service, as soon as she got to the pew, she was asking about your Andy. So I said, "Clara dear, Andy is long gone. Gosia is an independent woman, happy to concentrate on her career. She's training to be a fitness instructor. She's coming along with a guest, who is also training for the same qualifications."'

Mother pauses dramatically.

'And then you arrived with that *friend* of yours and Clara had her eyebrows raised till the end of the evening. That shirt with all those obscene-looking flowers! Those filthy moves on the dance floor! I saw him grabbing Bernie's buttocks!'

She raises her voice. 'And Aunt Clara said, "Is our Gosia training to be gay?"'

Mother stands up.

'I told her, "Clara, my daughter is perfectly normal," but she was looking at me like she knew better.'

Gosia puts the cup down gently.

Mother attacks, tea towel in hand.

'So tell me, I want to hear it from you. Are you a lesbian now?'

79

The staff-only area in a 24/7 fitness centre. A small and windowless room with a dwarf-kitchen worktop and essential accessories: a plastic kettle, a toaster with an overflowing crumb tray and a 17-litre-capacity microwave designed for reheating cold cups of instant coffee. The room doubles up as an extra storage area, with a floor-to-ceiling metal shelf, housing FitShop stock organised in neat rows.

It is the fifteen-minute mid-morning break, and Gosia and Steve sit on foldable plastic chairs at a collapsible table. Each have a white, durable mug in front of them with the FitShop opening hours displayed on the side.

The tea is too hot, and Steve keeps blowing at the murky surface while swiping through dating profiles on his phone. Gosia reads an excerpt from an article out loud.

'"Dorothy, a manager at a large manufacturing company in England, believes her career opportunities were severely restricted by her weight. 'I joined a new company and was very overweight, wearing a size 26. I was excellent at my job but I wasn't meeting important clients. I was hidden in the back room and doing all the donkey work. At the time, I didn't realise why that was. I thought I just needed to build my network'."'

Steve keeps cooling his tea, while considering a picture of a bare, muscular chest. Gosia takes a deep inhale.

'"Then Dorothy started losing weight, down to a size 8. Suddenly, she found she got more opportunities at work: 'Within twelve months of losing weight, I'd gone from managing three people to managing 150 people. I was hanging out with the senior board members and was often invited to meetings with key customers, who I never had access to before. It was a lift in my career'."'

Steve sips, burns his lip, pants like a dog. Gosia continues in an even voice.

'"But I didn't give any thought to the reason until a male colleague said that overweight women weren't suitable for putting in front of customers, and thus confirmed that being fat was holding me back at work. That's when I realised it's just all about looks. As someone who's worked so hard to get my qualifications and build my networks, I feel that's deeply unfair. I was shocked when I observed that I myself favoured the slimmer people in my team. That's how deeply ingrained this mentality is'."'

'Are you reading this for my benefit?' Steve asks calmly.

Gosia lifts her head up.

'God no, it just never occurred to me that people may have it hard that way.'

Steve nods knowingly. They drink small mouthfuls, cool tea on their tongues.

'It's like you have to get slim to get prizes in life,' adds Gosia.

'Oh yes, darling. This world is built to accommodate the thin and pretty.' Steve laughs a small, bitter laugh.

Gosia extracts her thoughts.

'What a vicious circle. If you want to get healthy and are overweight you will probably lose determination in a day. All these fitness regimes are aimed at thin people. The FitYou leggings range only goes up to size 16.'

Steve's face lights up. 'Blimey, Gosia, are you considering this as a business opportunity?' He gives her a look. 'You would have to beef up for that. No one would trust a company sympathetic to obese people with someone as thin as you at the top.'

Gosia laughs.

'I don't think I want to run a business.'

'But why not?' Steve is visibly surprised. 'You've got what it takes!' He counts on his digits. 'Personality, looks, brains, manners, ideas! Look, I've run out of fingers!' He chuckles.

'I don't know.' She checks in with herself for adequate reasons.

'Don't get me wrong, but the way you measure out the amount of hummus you put on your carrot seems to be how you approach your life in general.' Steve hides behind the mug. 'You only bite so much and you never let yourself go.'

Gosia stares at him, suppressing a growl. She divides her hummus pot into three portions because of its cost. She does the same with nuts, chocolate, coffee and other expensive foods. She would love to eat 500g of yoghurt in one sitting but she can't afford to develop a taste for it. She knows that small expenditures add up and can quickly push you into debt. She fears debt most of all possible personal cataclysms.

'If I were you, I would want it all,' says Steve.

'And what is the "all" that you want?' Gosia barks, her cheeks burning.

'My own fitness centre for people like me – lazy but wanting to stay fit!' Steve paints the picture with the use of his hand. 'LazyFit, I would call it. It would be all about pleasant exercises that give maximum effect with minimum effort. A business promoting tasty diets, flattering clothing and a sense of humour, not just something for women or men or the disabled or the fat. Fitness for the lazy!' His arm is mid-air, his cheeks are red, excitement erupting from him.

'It sounds excellent.' Gosia gives him a tight smile. 'Needs some major adjustments to meet reality, but I like it.'

'Do you?' Steve's face is like a puppy's. 'Would you consider being my business partner? Split fifty-fifty and we can share all the nasty chores.'

Gosia checks the time.

'Let me think about it.'

'No pressure.' Steve's voice is flat. 'But just so you know, I have a queue of intelligent and good-looking women wanting to come on board, so maybe give it some thought during your international trip?'

'Sure.' Gosia fights the urge to touch Steve's shoulder. She pins her hand to her knee. Steve has wormed his way into her life. His presence is convenient. It's easy to be around him, his company doesn't require her being on high alert, constantly watching her words, worrying she is either not enough or too much. But at the same time she keeps him at arm's length, blowing cool air on their connection, just in case he has a capacity to hurt her. 'I'll think about it.'

80

A small airport, advertised as London-based but situated fifty minutes by train from the city centre. Low-fare airlines promote their deals on large banners polluted by obtrusive colours. The shopping area gulps down travellers as soon as they repack their oversized cabin bags and overflowing fluid-allowance plastic pouches.

Gosia beeps while walking through the checkpoint and is meticulously touched by a frowning woman in a navy-blue uniform, who is in need of treating her perm burn. Gosia's bag has also been searched and now she squeezes boxes of loose tea in between her tops and jumpers, rearranges her second pair of trainers and positions the plug adapter for Europe, lent to her by her manager Sasha, strategically at the top.

She obediently walks the slalom between perfumes, mascaras, premium whiskies and over-packaged chocolates before hitting the heart of the waiting area with an inadequate number of seats. She buys a cup of bitter coffee to get a seat at a small table adjacent to a cafe. She is quickly joined by a young professional with a skinny latte who uses the whole surface for his silver laptop and does not ask her if she minds.

She is here too early. Sasha told her a few horror stories about delayed trains, long lines for security check and scenes at the gate.

She panicked and took an early coach. She has been here for hours. She has already read a magazine, seamlessly combining fitness, diet, fashion, beauty and aspirational talk. She carefully studied proposed workout routines using core-strengthening sliding discs that would have fitted in her hand luggage. They tried them at the class a few weeks ago. Steve wobbled, fell head first and nearly lost his front teeth. She completed the routine gracefully and it was much harder than the ones outlined on these shiny pages.

It is a shame that Steve is not with her. He got on well with Viola and now she thinks he would have been an asset and a distraction during a trip to this unknown land. But she doesn't know her family in Poland, and the thought of negotiating new relatives makes her heart race. She is splurging her remaining savings on this trip. She has nightmares about her empty bank account, the warning message 'NO FUNDS AVAILABLE' blinking in her mind. On her return, she will have to get by on rice and split peas, instant noodles and custard powder for a month.

Her father had a tear in his eye when she mentioned to her parents that she was requesting annual leave to visit Dad's motherland. She still hasn't told them that she needs to move out of her flat and is in a dire situation. She shouldn't be spending money on holidays, but it felt good to announce a rekindling of family connections abroad just after Mother vented her anger at Steve and pinned Gosia to the wall with her bizarre assumptions.

Gosia stayed calm and explained that she could be friends with whoever she liked and didn't want her family peering into her sex life. Mother went mad, accused her of rampant behaviour, slapped her face for speaking back, took a Valium for tea and asked her to leave. So she left. The humiliating slap embedded itself in her cheek and she rubbed it frequently. Her family, people she would sacrifice herself for, calmly watched her leave.

Gosia informed them, before closing the door behind her, that Viola, in her imperfect English, had invited her to visit Poland and promised to be her host and guide. So here she is, waiting for a flight bound for a city whose name she struggles to pronounce, her tongue stuck somewhere between 'rock' and 'claw'. She paid a small fortune for the ticket.

But it is an educational trip and therefore worth all that money. She might understand herself better, she might have an important and enlightening realisation about the direction her life should take. She will meet her family – distant, removed, almost never talked about – but family, nevertheless.

She needs to rethink how to approach Vijay and she hopes that being away will give her clever ideas for merging her life with his. She boarded the same bus on four consecutive evenings, always dressed for the occasion, but hasn't bumped into him since. She wants to suppress the ache in her ribcage, soothe her molten heart and be ready to meet him not by accident but on her terms.

She takes a sip of her coffee and instantly spits it back. Her gate number comes up on the screen and the swarm of travellers rush towards a slim corridor behind the toilets. People are funnelled down the narrow passage; bags on wheels are dragged over fellow passengers' feet. She makes it to the gates and instantly knows which queue to join, the queue where every other man reminds her of her dad.

It's the roundness of the face, prominence of the nose, fullness of the cheeks, thin lips and striking moustache, gaps between the teeth, quick glances to the side, stocky upper body, bawdy laugh, flat fringe and moist forehead often partly covered by a cap.

She is embraced by the crowd, assimilated into the herd.

A woman behind asks her a question in a foreign language and clearly expects a reply.

Gosia mumbles, 'I don't understand.'

The woman shrugs her shoulders, exasperated. She stops someone else, raises her voice, demands answers. A young man, with Gosia's father's eyebrows, bushy and pronounced at the centre and plucked by the sides, offers explanations and points to the start of the queue.

The queue itself regularly breaks its boundaries. It expands and contracts from one person to five standing in bundles and semi-circles, flapping their arms around, fanning themselves with passports and holding onto their bags with their thighs. There is no clear line to it. A young airport hostess meanders through the sea of passengers, who ignore her efforts to check boarding passes and advise on luggage allowance.

By the time she gets to her seat on the plane she overhears a number of times a word her dad shouts in moments of distress, pure rage or ill humour. She finally understands that it's a swear word used in an equally throwaway manner as British people offer their 'fucks' and 'shits'. She locks it in her mind alongside *tata*, *mama* and *daj* – three Polish words that she vividly remembers from her childhood.

When Bernie was born and Mother wasn't coping, Dad took her frequently to a local park to feed the ducks and only spoke to her in a language that sounded like the soughing of the wind, the whistling between the branches. A language heavy with sorrow: repentant, fast and harsh.

A rush of warmth and cosiness spreads from her guts. She is comforted by faces that look so familiar. She shares the row with women tending to their offspring. She finds their round chins and low foreheads reassuring. They share common Eastern European features.

Before take-off she reaches for her phone and sends her dad a text. Her heart enlarged with a sudden surge of heat.

'Flight on time. Poland, here I come! Love you.'

81

A living room in a high-rise block, with the view of a foreign city centre in the distance. Open vertical blinds reveal a windowsill hosting a selection of cascade orchids planted in durable plastic pots. On a small coffee table, empty cups and saucers made from tempered glass sit next to highly polished crystal wine glasses full of red wine. An established succulent in a stubby pot fights for space with two empty wine bottles.

Gosia and Viola lounge on the sofa. Each cradles a cushion. Gosia fights a hiccup. On the floor, barefoot, clothed in a cropped cotton vest and skirts pulled up to the tops of her thighs, sits Zuza, their cosmopolitan cousin who has just returned from India and is now mid-explanation.

'Women who shave give up their sexual powers. Just here,' she points to the bush of her armpit, 'are produced smells that make men go mad.'

Viola nods. Gosia considers her shaved underarm, often covered in a rash from her diligent razor activity.

Zuza continues, 'If you want to attract the right guy, you have to let these smells work. Not everyone who sniffs will go for you. Nature is clever like that!' She holds Gosia's gaze. 'When you remove it all, it's like a diversion on the road. The guy is searching for other clues. Gets lost, loses interest, sits in a traffic jam and ends up in another town altogether.'

Zuza laughs noisily. Viola joins in although Gosia suspects that she doesn't follow.

'And here,' Zuza points to her crotch, opens her hips wide; the skirts roll higher up revealing lacy pants and black curls of pubes spilling down her thighs, 'is your greatest resource. The home of passion, desire and lust.'

She links her legs into a half-lotus position.

'If you want to keep a man, you need to use it sparingly. Don't just offer it all at once. Don't try to choke him up with your pheromones.'

Zuza lifts one of the wine glasses, takes a long sip.

This is the third new cousin that Gosia has met in the space of twenty-four hours. Yesterday afternoon, Viola collected her from the airport and took her to this flat, furnished with hand-me-downs. Sleeping on the pile of sofa cushions was surprisingly comfortable.

Today, after a walk through the old town, they had lunch with the children of her dad's brother, Jan. Her dad and Uncle Jan don't talk since their disagreements over the inheritance.

Dorota and Arek changed their weekend plans to make it to the city and never mentioned the money that Wujek Jan kept to himself. Over a portion of boiled potatoes, pork schnitzel and beetroot salad, they got to know each other.

Viola's abilities to translate were limited. They relied on pictures clearly displaying their spouses and children. Gosia underestimated the importance of the low-quality images that she had on her pay-as-you-go-phone. Mother and Dad with John and Paul, Chrissy and her eating cake, a wedding shot of Bernie and Aitziber were all met with squeals of joy. She understood that her cousins felt she looked like her dad.

Gosia went quiet when Dorota in her earnest English asked, 'You, husband?' She hesitated.

What simple words could she use to explain the complexity of the situation with Vijay?

How could she describe her mission to win his heart without sounding mad?

How to phrase her conviction that with Vijay she would be whole?

How to translate her own heart's feelings into a single hand gesture?

How could she announce that she was here, in this city with an unpronounceable name, to find her inspiration and an infallible way forward? So she paused, and Arek concluded on her behalf.

'*Feministka.*'

Feminist, sure. But later Zuza explained that in Poland that's on a par with being called a dyke.

Lunch was lengthy and heavy. They finished with coffee and layered creamy cake that congested her throat.

This is when Viola announced that Zuza was back in town and eager to meet up. Arek's face clouded over, and Dorota made elaborate hand movements and produced many whistling words, of a harsh and desolate quality, that quickly extracted them both from further afternoon plans. Arek insisted on paying the bill and they left. Zuza is their decade-younger half-sister and Gosia deduced that they don't get on.

Viola and Gosia navigated the cobbled streets to a lively bar where Zuza was drinking a green smoothie, dressed in layers of skirts and tops, just back from India, not used to the cold. Her face long and dark, eyes close together, her English heavy with an American accent – left over from years of living in Florida, first as an au pair, then as a wife.

'I used to think of it as a mistake,' Zuza overshares, 'but we parted without fights. We don't bother each other on Facebook and don't expect any further contact, so now I think of it as a gift.'

She still lives off his money, travels the world and acquires wisdom from different cultures.

'But I have a feeling that I'll settle soon.'

The certainty in Zuza's voice caught Gosia's ear. Zuza had what Gosia needed, a confidence in the way she held her body that life and people within it would bend to her will. This looked like a skill one could learn and it made Gosia buy two bottles of expensive wine and invite Zuza back to Viola's flat.

Viola didn't object.

Past the front door and with crystal glass in hand, Gosia skilfully brought the conversation back to Zuza's feelings of putting down roots in the near future, and she enquired about the source of this conviction between her measured sips.

It was like offering Zuza a Sunday sermon slot. Her monologue was impassioned and complex, full of references to people she had met, truths she had heard and experiences she had had.

It was in Darjeeling, the hill town of West Bengal in the heart of the North Eastern Himalayan paradise, where she started waking up to a foggy view of snow-covered Mount Kanchenjunga with a crack in her soul. In between the visits to the lush tea gardens and serene monasteries, she came across Rohit Negi, who uses the most authentic and accurate divination method of fortune-telling called Vedic astrology. His reading filled Zuza with calm and harmonised her inner discord. She started practising yoga, following Ayurvedic principles and living according to the words of wisdom that she acquired between Mongolia, Thailand, India, Florida, rural Poland, North Africa and a random visit to Basingstoke. The copious amounts of wine they had drunk during the evening was a small diversion from the chosen path of clarity and focus.

The visit to a fortune-teller was a substantial expense but it opened Zuza's mind to new possibilities. His words had offered her a future she couldn't have dreamt up on her own. She felt she had been given permission to live her life like she wanted and could look back on her experiences not through the lens of mistakes and failures, but accomplishments.

Gosia wants to know if she can get that without plunging herself into debt.

After a decade of being on the road, Zuza is ready to commit to geography. She can still afford to buy a smallholding in a remote part of Poland. She will make cheese and upholster furniture for a living. All she needs is a mature, polyamorous relationship that acknowledges the limitations of monogamy. She is into farmers. She can't place exactly by who and where she was advised to stop removing her body hair but, since she embraced it, her sex life has blossomed, her orgasms multiplied, and her lovers lingered.

'I bet my bottom dollar that when you two grow your bush you will have men queuing to get into your knickers.'

Viola shyly asks, 'Bush?'

Zuza switches to Polish. A cascade of consonants pronounced too close together, the whirlpool of shallow breaths caught in between the letters. She finally points at her nether regions, laughs a brutal laugh and makes Viola squirm.

Gosia sits back and traps the air in her lungs to try to kill off the coming hiccup. Could it be her blunting their pheromone connection with a razor and only being able to talk to Vijay remotely that had led to that catastrophic phone call? In her mind she revisits the tranquillity of his corridor, the calmness of his street. Their unexpected meeting on the bus wasn't the most conducive to the pheromone exchange, the blend of other people's smells and general tang of public transport dulling the senses.

This is when Zuza leans over, pats her calf and says in an assured way, 'It's good to wait and not put pressure on time. That's what the fortune-teller said. Leave it for a month or two and you will see, the man of your dreams will walk into your life.'

82

A sitting room in a small, detached house in the suburbs of a foreign city within walking distance of thick woodland, and just down the road from a newly built dual carriageway. Render by the windows is peeling off in fat strips.

The room is paralysed, choking with red objects and heavy brown furniture. A dozen ceramic figurines, pictures in solid metal frames, fake flowers in tiny coloured-glass vases and an old-fashioned box TV on the shelves. The corner of the room is blocked up with potted plants, trapped leaf to leaf. Gosia sits on the sofa with a warm shot of vodka and an old photograph in her hands.

Viola's mum, Elżbieta, keeps her moist eyes on Gosia and shakes her head in disbelief. Ciocia Ela (Gosia can't get her tongue to bend to pronounce Elżbieta, the full name) kept the front door open when kissing Gosia's cheeks for hello, as if she were hoping to spot her brother coming in behind her niece: Stanisław, Staszek, Stan.

Gosia's dad had visited Poland repeatedly in the nineties. He opened and ran an international business with his sister's husband, Zenon. The venture folded. Large debt affected both families.

Gosia's dad went bankrupt and her aunt filed for divorce. Viola's muted presence and involuntary spasmodic contractions of the muscles in her face are a testament to how loudly they argued, how much her aunt wailed, how hard Uncle Zenon hit his wife.

Ciocia Ela is paper-thin and full of wrinkly folds. She coughs a lot. Her hair is very short, clothes faded, complexion pallid, her English direct. Over the first cup of coffee, she tells Gosia in calm words that she has only months to live.

'Nice you parents invite me and Viola to Bernard wedding. My health bad and I don't go.'

She is using her time to put things straight: to ensure her ex-husband can't benefit from her remaining wealth, to instil in Viola a sense of self-worth, confidence and direction in life and, finally, to pass on family secrets.

The offensive photograph sits like burning coal in Gosia's palm. On it, her dad, young and handsome, with trimmed sideburns and a lush moustache, marries another woman. She is as far removed from her strong-boned mother as Gosia can imagine – petite, with long, dark hair and a radiant smile.

Ciocia Ela pours some more vodka, fills the silence.

'Long time ago. Staszek only nineteen. Very big love.'

Gosia's mind races. Did they have children? Why did Dad leave for England? Where is that woman now? Why does he never speak of her? Is it even true? Her chest is heavy with her aunt's revelations. She is unsure if they are even talking about the same man. She can't imagine her dad, a man who taught her to ride a bike, shoot with a slingshot, harvest gooseberries, climb trees and paddle in shallow water, being married to someone else. She was sure of the place she had in his heart, his first child, his first daughter. He has never favoured her openly, as Mother did Bernie, but she was always confident that his love for her was absolute. Now she questions that. Maybe he lied to her too?

Her aunt's eyes drizzle.

'But bad love. She sick in her head. She cut herself, she hit Staszek.' Aunt indicates with a hand gesture that it included the use of a knife. 'She go hospital. Forever.'

Gosia gasps and softens. She imagines a dismal building suitable for the isolation of a young woman affected by a severe mental illness.

Ciocia Ela, in simple sentences, adds that she used to visit – until Dad's first wife stopped recognising people, drowsy from all the pills. She died from heart failure stuck in a hospital room in early spring. Ciocia Ela received her belongings from the hospital as no other family members were found. She sent some of it to Gosia's dad. It wasn't much. Just one cardboard box.

Did her dad ever visit his first wife?

Her aunt shakes her head and in the strained, weak voice of a bad liar, talks of male hearts being built from a different tissue, helping them to forget and move on. She adds that the divorce in that case was just a formality.

Gosia turns the photo over. Her dad's first marriage started on the first of July, exactly to the day eight years before she was born, a birthday she now shares with John and Paul. She asks her aunt sheepishly, already knowing the answer.

'What was her name?'

Ciocia Ela is now crying fat tears, her face a shiny shade of ash.

'Małgorzata. Małgosia. Gosia.'

83

A well-lit street corner in a renovated neighbourhood of a foreign city. Wide streets with designated lanes for cyclists. Night buses frequently zoom past. Gosia and Viola stand with their hands in their coat pockets, Gosia's eyes locked on the third-floor apartment windows on the other side of the street. The apartment has a large corner balcony, elaborate metal railings with a leaves and flowers motif. The lights are on and occasionally a human figure walks past the windows.

Ciocia Ela gave Gosia three photographs of her dad with his first wife. A wedding shot taken in a studio against the plain background, their noses in focus; an image of Małgorzata and Stan sitting on a blanket in her aunt's garden, cherry tree in blossom, a book discarded on the grass, their eyes turned to the camera; finally, the image of them both standing on a balcony in a rented apartment. Ciocia Ela said they moved into it shortly after the wedding. She remembered the address but wasn't sure of the floor.

Gosia lifts the photograph a few times to compare the image with the building in front of her. The third, she is sure of it. The balcony is oblong and the railings on the two floors below are square. She fights her urge to press the buzzer and invite herself in to spy on her dad's previous life and inhale the air of a lost past.

They seem close on all three photos. Touching hands or calves. She wears well-fitted dresses with bold prints, thin belts around her waist, platform shoes. He is in flares and shirts with wide collars. Both slim, springy, smiling. She looks tiny next to him, her frame delicate against his muscular bulk. His face, unmistakably the face of her father, is smooth and rested. Not a single crease of worry on his forehead, no trace of sleepless nights under his eyes.

Gosia shudders. It is a cold November night and they have been standing here for a while. She touches Viola's shoulder and they start walking away.

Viola has been a scaffold for the fervour of Gosia's mind. During Ciocia Ela's monologue, Viola used her phone to offer translations: 'schizophrenia', 'hallucinations', 'psychotic episode', 'self-harm'. According to Google, people can live with these conditions, have a decent life outside a closed cell. Why didn't it happen for Małgorzata?

They reach a bus stop and Viola checks her watch. It is late and Gosia has an early flight to catch. Her mind races. She wants to know why she is named after that woman and why Dad has never talked about it. Małgorzata, with her petite body and broad face looks a bit like her, but she couldn't be her child. That woman, was she the love of his life? In photos she looks like someone you would want to spend eternity with, mysterious, complex, yet loving and sensual. It hits her then and there that her father has settled for second best.

She lets Viola punch the tickets, choose the seats and they silently travel back to the neighbourhood full of high-rises where Gosia will spend the night on the sofa cushions, staring into the ceiling until the alarm goes off.

84

An international fast-food restaurant with plastic chairs in bold colours and a menu offering free fries with every order. The establishment is situated on a struggling high street. The food is cheap, the queue for meals is five people deep.

Gosia sits in the corner; she hogs a desirable four-seat table benefiting from a plug for charging mobile phones. She has dispersed her belongings on three other chairs and discourages the crowd from joining her by laying her body on the tabletop.

Steve arrives, out of breath, just in shorts and T-shirt, with a green first aid kit plastic box in his hand.

'Where is this emergency?' he says between pants for air.

Gosia pulls her body up. She's crying, her eyes are red, thin slits.

'Where does it hurt?'

Steve places the box down, clasps his hand on top of Gosia's arm and takes a seat, crushing Gosia's hat with his bum.

'Here.' Gosia points to her head.

'Righty ho, I think I have something that can help.' He opens the box, extracts a small plaster and sticks it to Gosia's temple. She laughs.

'Now, we stopped that bleeding. Tell me what's going on. I thought you were going off on a jolly?'

She sighs. The moment her aeroplane had touched down, she switched her phone on and sent Steve a dramatic text, asking him to meet as soon as she made it back to the neighbourhood. She had punched buttons fast, through the tears. It didn't send but she only figured that out when Steve wasn't waiting for her by the station. She has spent the last thirty minutes in the corner of this room with its upbeat music and greasy smell of fried meat.

'My dad had a wife before my mother,' Gosia says. 'She went mad and tried to kill him.' Steve nods. 'They locked her up. Dad divorced her. And she died earlier this year.'

'Holy cow, that's gruesome.' Steve puts his hands down on the table, protecting the space. 'And you learnt all that in one weekend? What a thunderbolt! You must be dog-tired.'

'There's more,' Gosia adds in a morbid voice. 'He named me after her.'

'Ouch,' Steve says, and then pretends to catch his own word with his hand and eat it up. 'I mean, *wow*.'

'How can I be normal with that backstory?'

'But you're not related to her by blood . . . right?' Steve is making hand movements, pretending to connect the dots.

'I did the maths. I'm not.'

'So your chances to go mad haven't gone drastically up?' Steve offers, the corners of his mouth ready to smile.

Gosia stares ahead, her eyes vacant.

'Do you think your mother knows?'

Gosia shrugs.

'She does. The whole divorce thing? This is what must have started it. She found out that Dad was hiding this size of a secret from her.'

'But, like, how come he's still *alive* then?' Steve chances.

Gosia laughs.

'Divorce clearly benefits her more than a murder.'

Gosia thought it through. Her mother thrives on control so discovering her husband's first marriage must have caused an internal earthquake. Mother would never have agreed to this name if she had been aware of the ex-wife story at Gosia's birth. Gosia touches her cheek. The sensation of heat and tingling sits under her skin. Her mother's slap was delivered with precision, hard and fast, enough to make Gosia's head sway.

'Her anger, you know, maybe some of it is somehow directed at me, like it was my fault. I told you, we don't get on.' Gosia's chest hardens.

'People react differently. It must have been a shock to her too. Your mum doesn't strike me as someone who likes surprises. She comes across as a woman who wants life to be predictable,' says Steve in a gentle, calming voice. 'Just try to understand where she's coming from.'

'She slapped me,' Gosia points at her cheek, 'because I didn't dance to her tune. Is that what parents do? Just hit you when things get too much?' She sighs. 'Why doesn't she try to understand me?'

'She didn't leave you at the mercy of social services and foster families because of it.' Steve's voice is solemn as he presses his thumb hard into the plastic body of the table. 'You know, she loves you in her way. She worries about you.' He looks away. 'If you said sorry, she would welcome you back and cook you dinner.' He adds through his teeth, 'A toxic name is not the end of the world. Your mother is sober, and she didn't abandon you for a new boyfriend and a carefree life.'

Gosia stiffens. Her internal agony deflates to a pea size, hurtful and uncomfortable but mediocre. The tingling of her cheek compares weakly with Steve's pain. She opens the first aid kit, gets a plaster and sticks it to Steve's temple.

'You may need stitches for that one,' she says, 'but this will have to do for now.'

85

Gosia logs in.

> Kevin Harris added four new photos. 'House-cooling party!'
>
> 83 people like it.

Picture one: Kevin, Lyndsey and Margaret in Gosia's room with her leggings draped on their arms, giggling.

Picture two: Kevin in Gosia's leggings, the pink pair tight around his knees, his hairy thighs exposed.

Picture three: Anna waving Gosia's leggings above her head, eyes half shut as if in ecstasy.

Picture four: a group shot of Kevin, Lyndsey, Margaret and Anna lying on top of each other on Gosia's bed, laughing to the camera. The cameraman's blurry thumb in the right corner of the frame.

> Lyndsey Oates via mobile: 'LOL'
>
> Margaret Bark-Knight via mobile: 'Wild animals'
>
> Kevin Harris, Lyndsey Oates and Bruce Woodcock like it.
>
> Andy Knight via mobile: 'WTF! Take it down now!'

Gosia accumulates tears before letting them fall off the cliff of her face with a furious blink. She takes a screenshot, emails it to herself and logs out.

86

A kitchen with heavily stained, flowery wallpaper in vigorous yellow. The sink is piled high with dirty plates and cups. A small pot sits on the stove; porridge bubbles and sticks to the bottom. A white cup full of black coffee is placed on the dining table next to an empty bowl and a spoon. A clothes horse is spread out in the corner.

Gosia carefully arranges her freshly washed garments on the rickety metal frame. All her leggings in clashing colours, acquired for pennies in sales from a cheap retailer often accused in newspapers of making clothes in slave-like conditions, by children. She picks each item out from the plastic bowl and gives it a good shake before placing it on the line in accordance with her washing algorithm.

Lyndsey walks in, a gummy secretion stuck in the corners of her eyes, her pink PJs crumpled from heavy sleep.

'Hi,' she says.

'Hi.'

Lyndsey moves to the fridge, extracts a four-pint bottle of skimmed milk, picks up the last remaining white bowl with a large chip, and a bag of cocoa-flavoured wheat balls from the cupboard. She combines it into breakfast and searches with narrow eyes for a spoon. The only clean one is placed neatly next to Gosia's bowl. Lyndsey contemplates it for a few seconds, releases air from her lungs, carts her body to the sink and rinses one spoon with her fingertips. There are no tea towels and she shakes the water off the spoon before plunging it into her bowl. She sits down, takes a mouthful and asks, 'Good trip?'

'Good party?'

Redness flocks to Lyndsey's cheeks. She swallows and digs herself in deeper.

'Did you have a good time?'

'Did *you* have a good time?'

Lyndsey chews slowly on a single wheat ball. Gosia walks to the stove, switches off the gas and empties the porridge from the pot to her bowl, careful not to scrape in any of the burnt bits. She sits down and blows at the spoonful of cooked oats.

Lyndsey tries a new angle. The gentler voice of a person deeply concerned with the well-being of others.

'It must have been nice to visit your family abroad.'

'It must have been nice to party with your friends in my room.'

Lyndsey clots, her face goes white while her hand holds a spoon full of shapeless wheat. She says, 'It all happened so fast.'

'It all happened so fast.'

The trembling of Lyndsey's hand intensifies. She returns the mush to the bowl. Pushes her chair away and scrapes the floor.

'I don't understand why you're being so mean to me!'

'I don't understand why you're being so mean to me.'

She stands up now. Looks down at Gosia and spits her cereal out, 'You're mad!'

'You're mad.'

Lyndsey bawls. 'I don't want to live with you any more!'

'I don't want to live with you any more.'

Lyndsey visibly shakes, her hand claws the back of the chair.

'Andy was right to dump you!'

'Kevin is right not to marry you!'

Lyndsey pauses, looks in Gosia's direction and starts mewling. Thin tears cover her sulking face. She cries, 'Get out of my sight!'

'Get out of my sight.'

Lyndsey hyperventilates, releases a groan and leaves the flat in her pyjamas and slippers, without her bag or keys.

Gosia finishes her porridge.

87

A council-run library on a rainy day. The reading area is used as an informal indoor canteen. A variety of people pushed into zero hours contracts eat their sandwiches and wraps, boiled eggs, leftover rice and mackerel straight from the tin. There is no eye contact. The smell of damp clothes and pungent food loiters between the shelves. Gosia sits at the computer in the middle pinching her nose.

KarenStevensWrites wrote: 'Interesting concept of a toxic name but the poem doesn't explain enough what caused the toxicity apart from a brief mention of "origin". I would like to know more as I sense an unusual depth to it. Would love to learn which consonant is so harmful. This subject is close to my heart as I've struggled with my own name for a long time and only came to terms with being Karen Stevens in my late twenties, when my first marriage failed, and I returned to my maiden name and blessed it. Read my poem about that painful return here.'

Woman_with_feelings wrote: 'Shivers down my spine. *High-risk name.* I can only imagine the level of toxicity: Adolf? Joseph Vissarionovich? Mao?'

Rich_M wrote: 'Toxic poem by toxic poet. Toss it.'

Toxic

The poison released daily
Through my teeth
When I say my name

Each letter like a stab:
Hazard of vowels
Two harmful consonants

High-risk name
Of lethal origin
Venomous, Virulent

In search of an antidote I quarantine infected household
until further notice.

88

A small town with a weekly market day. The high street is filled with charity and discount shops. A workers' caff on one end and an old-fashioned tea room on the other. A large Conservative club with flags at the entrance situated in the middle.

Gosia arrives early. It's her first visit and she moves slowly through the crowd on the narrow pavement. Old people in mobility scooters speed in opposite directions, a string of young mothers with their children in pushchairs, faces full of snot, hands full of sweets. A young man with trousers covering just over half of his thin bottom jiggles in front of a pasty shop to music played from his mobile phone, sound distorted.

Gosia is here, in this town, temporarily, to jump into her future as a fitness instructor; she is not here to stay. She has a couple of hours to kill before her first fitness class is due to start. She woke up with a knotted stomach and has since developed shaking hands. She needs distraction. She gives in and walks into one of the charity shops that smells pleasant at the doorway. She finds an A4 lever arch folder in a delicate shade of green and with cellophane still wrapped around it. A volunteer by the till, a middle-aged man with a modest smile encourages:

'It's buy-one-get-one-free on all stationery and books.'

She is transported back to the supermarket. To team meetings where her loathed manager would run through a dull PowerPoint presentation outlining promotions for the week and new strategies to convince customers to buy more than they need. Who told this nice-looking man in a beige polo shirt to incite people to buy stuff they don't require?

She looks at him. They could be friends. He has that glow of a good person, someone who doesn't hurt others just for fun and she wants good people around her. She wishes she could find 'bad friends' with a quick search of her life and then simply click 'replace all'. She holds the folder in her hands. The one pound thirty for it will support research into a nasty illness and she will have somewhere to keep all her course handouts.

She nods and goes back to the dedicated stationery corner. She takes her time and finally picks another folder, in muted yellow, and returns with both to the till. The man scans the items.

Gosia is not an opportunist or blinded by random goods; she will give the extra folder to Steve. Does Steve like green or yellow? Has he sorted out his filing system? Does he have a shelf to keep this folder on? She is surprised that she doesn't know. Then she is surprised that she wants to know. The man offers a large plastic bag and gives her change.

She gathers her purchase in her arms and aims for the door. She turns around to see the man wheeling himself from behind the desk and moving towards the shelving area. He makes it all neat again as best as he can, straining to reach the upper shelves. He catches her looking and gives her a friendly nod as she leaves.

These days she functions on autopilot. Her father's secret and her mother's slap combined with her ex-friends' hostility sap her energy, making her physically weak and irritable. She is no longer capable of daydreaming, taking herself away into a scenario on the bus where everything goes right: Vijay recognising her instantly, offering her his seat or accommodating her on his lap. Him gently stroking her side, inhaling her scent, pressing his head into her lap. Her confidently resting her body against his, feeling his heat and the promise of wild sex as soon as they are past his front door.

A community hall, adjacent to an old church, is overflowing with opportunities printed on cheap, lurid paper. Once the morning watercolour class disperse with wet paper under their arms, Gosia has ten minutes to set up. The sound system is on its last legs and the wooden floor starved of varnish. She stacks all the chairs up and inadequately wipes the floor.

She stands in front of eight sixty-five-plus women with hair dyed in pastel colours and appropriately dressed in cotton T-shirts and loose trousers. Some adjust their hearing aids as she welcomes them to the class. Her voice levelled, their smiles encouraging. She has memorised her sequences but has her routine drawn up on a few sheets of A4, and she places it on the floor just in front of her feet.

She tells the group what to do and they follow. Jolly good wiggle of the hips, good stretch of the left side, tight abdominal muscles, energetic kick to the right side in beat with the music. The force of the screams of joy takes her by surprise. People go gently red, get hiccups, sip water, hold onto the wall, pant and giggle. A couple of ladies move to the side for a short catch-up and rejoin at the next sequence. The group is predictably enthusiastic about ABBA songs, and she is glad she was told to include some.

They clap for a full fifteen seconds once it's over and magic up small towels from their bags to dry their brows and armpits. They change just there, using chairs lined up by the wall, into flowery tops with low necklines.

A small-boned woman with carefully drawn high eyebrows and dolphin earrings comes up to Gosia. She is still feet away when she starts to speak.

'Dear, this was fantastic. Look what you have done to us! Awakened a devil!'

A friend of hers with matching eyebrows and a slight hump slaps Gosia's forearm hard.

'My lord, I haven't had so much fun since the Christmas party. You will be back, I hope? I can't endure that other teacher any more. The breathing exercises make me fall asleep and Maureen says that I snore like a pig!'

Women laugh. There is a lightness in the air despite the faint odour of a malfunctioning sewerage system. A radiant crowd looks at Gosia expectantly.

'Next week. Same time, same place. And please spread the word. I could do with at least five more of you.'

Maureen's friend raises her palm to her forehead.

'My lord, we can't multiply that fast!'

Women cackle.

Someone says that it's cake o'clock, someone else adds that Freddie has an offer on chicken wings, there is an announcement of a moved choir practice and Maureen, the owner of the dolphin earrings, proudly informs everyone that she is to hold her annual fundraiser in her house on the coming Sunday afternoon. They all leave.

Gosia rubs her slapped arm and smiles a victorious smile to a tall man in a fitted waistcoat walking through the door. He asks her in a sombre voice to vacate the room so he can set up for a wake.

The railway station is only a ten-minute walk away, but she has some more time to waste before the next fast train. She heads towards a small park behind the estate. She was told that there, on the edge, in a crumbling building is a library with an extensive local history collection, a dedicated youth zone, an impressive crime fiction section in large print and access to computers. She is going to check it out.

The treeless route to the park takes her through streets of shabby semi-detached houses with overgrown bushes in their front gardens. She develops a cold sweat walking past a driveway accessorised with an old Nissan and a selection of bins pushed to the fence. She turns her gaze away from the window boxes of dried-up petunias.

The warmth created by the success of her first fitness session evaporates. The Nissan looks too familiar. It's been only a week and she hasn't phoned home yet to demand answers and to find out the truth. She is telling herself that she is letting her questions mature so her phrasing could be underpinned by curiosity not accusation. But really she is waiting to recover, for wounds to form scabs, for time to tick away and make the memories distant and diluted, so she can look at it all as if it happened to someone else.

She nearly runs when the front door opens and a woman, her mother's height and build, leaves the house slamming the door behind her, a reusable shopping bag in hand. The air is still and Gosia stops breathing. The woman's hair is the wrong length and colour, and she treats the car differently to her mother. She doesn't light a cigarette or back out of the drive in a hurry, beeping at people on the pavement.

Gosia walks on, the cold sweat seeping into her clothes. If it was her mother, would Gosia run? If it was her mother, would Gosia be run over?

She will be commuting to this town weekly until spring. She will find a different route to the park or she will endure the slow train back into London.

89

The Bulletproof Guide to Sorting Out Your Life:
Work, Money, Free Time, Family, Friendship and Love.
STEP 13: How to Be Open to New Experiences

Same old, same old is never going to bring anything new and fresh. If you can't distinguish your Tuesday from your Thursday, it may be that a stifling routine is killing your creativity and enjoyment of life. What should you do about it? Shake it up!

New experiences are important to allow you to grow and develop as a person. Think about children and how they thrive on newness: everything is new to them. It is hard to recreate the awe of a two-year-old watching a ladybird crawling on their arm for the first time. As an adult you need to work much harder to find and expose yourself to new experiences. That's why we are here - to help you to find your ladybird!

Andy would only shop at ASDA. The calming green decor, the chill from the freezers and the predictability of the crisps aisle always neighbouring the beer aisle meant that shopping was easy. He was reluctant to change his supermarket of choice despite the fact that each visit would bring back painful memories of his ex, who worked for a rival shop. Andy would also never stray from his shopping list and kept it the same each week.

Margaret subtly influenced Andy's shopping decisions by exposing him to quality produce that she acquired in a high-street deli. In no time at all, ASDA's cheddar started tasting bland and chewy in comparison to the deli's Gouda - smooth, creamy and nutty.

Before long, Andy abandoned his weekly supermarket visits and started doing his food shopping at stores that focused on local, organic produce that changed seasonally.

Margaret made shopping fun; she made shopping an adventure! She stopped it being just a weekly ordeal of stocking up the fridge with edible goods.

Margaret's golden rule for keeping herself willing to experience something new is a rule of opposites.

Do you normally watch romcoms? Try a thriller! Email us with the subject *'New cinema experience'* at *savemoney@andyandmargaret.com* for a DISCOUNT CODE for £1.99 off a cinema outing.

Holidays by the sea? For a change, climb a mountain.

Tea drinker? Order mocha.

A fan of CrossFit? Sign up to yoga.

Enjoy the missionary position? Surprise him by switching to cowgirl.

Always buy roses? Purchase orchids. *Fancybloomstoyourdoor.com* offer same day delivery and <u>here is £0.99 off your first purchase.</u>

You may be sceptical. You know what you like. You may have tried Gouda in the past and hated it. Why should you care to keep your experiences diverse and new? What do you gain from it?

Let us remind you. It's to keep your mind flexible and creative – the two most important factors in sorting out your life on all the levels. Through this, you will become an open-minded, creative and exciting person that others want to be around. That reborn you is a you that has exciting work, enough money, enjoyable free time, a loving family, great friends and a loved one by your side.

90

Friday night. A swarming smoking area in the poky courtyard of a large, minimally maintained nightclub. All the walls are painted pink. A rainbow flag of polyester colours is erected on a metal frame and suspended from the first-floor window, where it flaps above the smokers' heads.

Gosia coughs and stumbles; she's had a number of bottles of beer and a couple of puffs of Steve's roll-up and now suppresses the sick gathering at the top of her larynx. The walls swim, her legs unstable. Steve waves his arms around, his white shirt tucked in, trousers kept in place with green and white daisy-patterned braces. Gosia wears Steve's vintage burgundy suit, quite a few sizes too big, bulky on her shoulders, kept in place around her waist with two belts. She only has her bra and pants on underneath. Steve convinced her that adding a shirt would suggest she was actually going to work. But all that air splashing around her ribcage makes her feel naked and exposed. She is watched by a couple: a man with a groomed goatee and a woman in a blonde wig wearing a catsuit. The woman waves to Gosia from afar and then blows a kiss. Gosia holds her gaze and then slowly looks away.

They stand in a circle together with Barnaby in a lush velvet suit, his eyes alert and heavy with professionally applied eyeliner. Barnaby's magnetic field pulls a constant stream of people in to kiss his cheek and lips. Men and women of all kinds touch Barnaby's body as if it were their own, express their delight and cry, 'Long time no see!' Barnaby is unfazed by all the attention.

Steve had brought his suit to the fitness club for Gosia to try on. He convinced her that going to the party in male clothes would bring her new and important experiences.

'You can have an evening off from being a woman ready for consumption! And there is nothing wrong with testing who you are,' he declared. 'We need to change your name for a start. Let's go for "Go", it's free from gender associations.'

'It's a verb,' said Gosia.

Steve shot her an annoyed look.

'What name will you go under?' she enquired.

'Steve.'

He smeared gel on her hair to make it go smooth, lie flat on her head and curl gently behind her ears. He encouraged eyeliner and mascara and a little bit too much blusher on her cheeks. He was strict on no lipstick, but he liberally applied it to his own lips.

'Stubble and lipstick create a desirable contrast,' he explained.

They danced underneath a sea of disco balls shimmering to the loud music pumping through a vintage sound system. Steve twirled Gosia around, manoeuvred her hips to the rhythm of the songs. They whirled, they laughed, they threw their arms in the air and sweated profusely.

But it was Barnaby and Steve who shone on the dance floor. They made their way to the centre of the bouncy floor every time a jazz standard came on and were absorbed in the music. Their bodies in sync, executing complex, flowing dance sequences with jumps and slides. The way they followed the tune looked nothing like the rigid dance routines taught on YouTube. Gosia watched enough lindy hop videos to grasp that what was happening in front of her eyes was an improvised delight, a manifestation of love for the dance executed by two people lost in the moment, lost in the movement. She was amazed and she was jealous.

Barnaby, celebrity style, is telling another story about his European adventures and holds his arm firmly and protectively at Steve's side. Steve, hungry for detail, leans in and loses himself in the ornate narrative. Gosia moves back a step, rests against the brick wall to keep vertical and to cool her spine. Her head swarms with random thoughts, her throat congests with stomach juice, her hand–eye coordination impaired. The woman in a blonde wig and a catsuit veers towards their circle; her hand slips over Gosia's hip, her lips attach themselves to Gosia's ear.

'Come with me,' she whispers. There is urgency in her voice as she entwines her fingers with Gosia's.

They swim through the crowd to a dark nook in a corridor, Gosia's back pushed lightly against the render.

'I'm Moira. I love your suit,' she murmurs and moistens Gosia's ear. 'What's your name?' she asks, her breath sweetly seasoned.

'Go.' Gosia lets the word out with a sigh. Moira's hand slips under the suit and gently caresses the side of Gosia's ribcage while rubbing her generous bosom against Gosia's elbow.

'Go,' Moira repeats softly. 'This is Ned,' she says, indicating to the goatee man who appears by their side and starts leaning against Gosia's thigh as Moira's tongue begins a deliberate journey down Gosia's neck. Her knee pushes Gosia's legs apart and a hand lands on her crotch. Gosia stiffens. She's never had sex with a woman before. She was told it was not right both at home and at her Sunday school. She remembers in vivid colours a dashing priest, known across the whole county for gambling away the portrait of Holy Mary with

Naked Baby Jesus, who would use elaborate adjectives to describe what happens in hell to people who indulge in such deviant behaviour. Her mother's face with a tea towel in hand appears next to an image of the dashing priest in his Volvo. 'Fuck you,' Gosia shouts in her mind, and shows them her middle finger as they drive away.

She returns to the here and now, puts her hand on Moira's bottom, bringing her hot body closer.

Moira's lips move up and start smooching softly around Gosia's mouth, and her hand makes its way past the flap, the trouser zip and the cotton of the knickers. She pauses to brush the short, pointy hair and then pushes her finger into Gosia's vagina, presses firmly at the soft flesh, plunges deep past the knuckles.

Gosia moans; she hasn't been touched like that before. She is hungry for a foreign tongue to massage her own, she's bored with climaxing on her own, collapsing onto her stiff fingers. The face of her mother swims once more past her closed eyes, but the alcohol in her veins calls for disobedience. She sucks Moira's fingers deeper into her vagina.

With her other hand, Moira finds Gosia's idle palm, limp and damp hanging by the side of her body, and moves it onto Ned's crotch, to a dazzling erection confined in his trousers.

Gosia gasps.

'Moira, dear,' Steve's sharp words sober Gosia up. 'Go is my date for tonight. Paws off my treasure.'

Moira extracts her hand and moves back. Gosia pulls down on her clothes, readjusts her trousers, feeling hot and faint.

'So, after all you've branched out, Stevie, my wonder?' asks Moira. She puts the finger that fondled Gosia's vulva into her mouth and licks it unhurriedly. 'She is so sweet,' she adds in a fragrant voice.

'We're in a deeply platonic relationship,' says Steve theatrically, holding onto his heart.

'You fool, you're missing out on a sugary pussy.' Moira rests her hand lightly on Gosia's breast and speaks in her honeyed way. 'Find us when you're bored with him. We can pick up from where we left off.' She kisses Gosia on the lips and leaves without giving Steve a second glance, Ned following her closely.

'Are you OK?' Steve's face is contorted into shapes of concern and worry.

'I'm fine.' Gosia pushes herself away from the wall.

'I hadn't noticed them hitting on you.' He shakes his head. 'I'm sorry.'

'It's OK. I'm an adult.' Gosia attempts to compose herself but nausea returns to her throat with the force of a tsunami.

'Darling.' Steve holds her floating gaze. 'You are drunk. And somehow I can't imagine you wanting to have a random romp in a corridor and then have no memory of how it happened.'

Gosia swallows and bats away a bleak memory of putting the thin and wonky cock of Ben_33 into her mouth.

'You don't know me.' She turns her head to the side.

'I know you enough.' Steve makes a step forward, folds her into his arm, gently pats her shoulder blade and says the magical words. 'Let's take you home.'

91

A large, unethical supermarket an hour before closing on a cold November night. The unsold bakery goods have already been tossed into milky, see-through plastic bags, the cleaning team is rubbing hard at the blackened baking trays and removing the sticky juices of slow-roast chickens from the deli counter.

Gosia is walking around purposefully, ticking things off her to-do list before heading home. The episode with Moira and Ned keeps appearing in her dreams. The new instalments, like a TV broadcast released every night, wait for her under the duvet. There, as soon as she closes her eyes, she kisses and fondles a number of people. Their bodies insert into her own. They murmur, moan and groan in unison; cascades of pleasure roam through her groin. She wakes up with her hand between her legs, in a pool of her juice. She isn't sure if she can get away with googling 'group sex' from the library computer and she doesn't want to ignore the desire to find subjects to experiment with in real time. Since Friday night, her orgasms are like explosions, and she suspects that, delivered by the hand of another person, they could have a nuclear strength. She has also decided not to beat herself up over the sweaty, messy imaginings that fill her mind and make her twist with pleasure.

But now, in the shop, she is back to thinking in pragmatic ways. She strolls through the aisles in search of bargains that she could wrap as Christmas gifts. She zooms in on small, light items. She plans to post them all this year. This is her chance to buy cheaper goods before the festive season prices arrive, and Gosia has given herself a strict budget with the intention of purchasing presents spelling out her love and commitment to her family without making them seem like an apology. Nothing lavish. The emphasis on thoughtful and useful objects. She thought about visiting, but that would mean accepting that she was wrong and guilty. It would be like telling her mother that she deserved that slap and offering the second cheek for more.

Since the wedding, Dad's stopped asking her for money and not being his personal ATM lifts a weight off her shoulders. She will call him some time soon, when her voice can remain still and aloof. She will assume the guise of an interviewer and prod him for all the details, for all the untold stories, to finally get the full picture unobstructed by her racing feelings. For now, she's arranged to meet up with Chrissy, to see how she's coping with all this mess.

Her basket holds Fairtrade chocolates, quality tea, a luxurious soap bar and a box of bath bombs. She moves to the household goods, clothing and toy areas hoping for some tasteful tea towels, a silicon spatula, dinosaur-themed jigsaws and colourful socks with a high wool content.

She takes a shortcut through a small but expensive and well-stocked section of baby clothing made from organic cotton and pays little attention to the tall and muscular man trawling through rompers. His breathing is exasperated. He turns his head, catches her eye, makes a step towards her with a handful of baby tops clutched in his fingers.

'Excuse me,' his face is wild, his voice is high, 'do you know the difference between a Babygro and a sleep-suit? I just can't distinguish between them.'

His chest looks different without a cat in his arms, a torso of muscles wrapped in a merino jumper finished off with a thick orange neck warmer. There is a flicker of recognition in his eyes.

'We've met, haven't we? You're Vijay's friend?'

She doesn't correct him.

'Yes, we have.'

'I've never been so happy to see a familiar face in a shop. Who knew that clothes for children could be so confusing! I've been looking, but it all makes no sense to me. Could you help?' He is pleading.

'Sure.' Gosia smiles the positive, understanding smile of someone who has spent hours listening to her sister's agonising puzzlement over the complexity of babywear. 'What are you after?'

He consults the notes on his phone.

'Six suits and six tops.'

Gosia nods.

'The suits, do you want them with feet or without?' She picks a couple of pairs, one ending at the ankle with a little elasticated band and one with a fabric foot.

'Ahhh.' His eyes widen. 'Let's go with ones with feet.' He abandons the pile in his arms on a sock shelf and picks identical suits from the rail Gosia suggested, all in calm grey with yellow detail.

'And tops, do you want vests, short sleeves or long sleeves?' She points to the helpful little drawings at the top-right corner of the packs displayed on the shelves.

He gives her a blank stare. Shakes his head.

'I guess short sleeves.' He picks two packs, each with three baby bodysuits in a busy geometric pattern.

'And the size?'

'Size? Right. It's for newborns.'

'All right, in that case you want these.' Gosia moves two steps down to an organic cotton section for 'newborn and baby 0–3 months old'.

He looks at the baby clothes in his hands, trying to determine the difference. Gosia taps on the numbers printed on the plastic hanger.

'These are for babies six to nine months old.'

'A minefield!' He gives her a big smile, deserts the clothes on a random rail and selects suits and tops from the right section. With the pile of ethical cotton in his hands, he exhales deeply.

'And it's full of hideous stuff!' She points at baby clothes that are made to look festive and shape newborns into Santas, Christmas trees or puddings.

'I'm surprised there isn't one to make you look like the baby Jesus!' he laughs.

'And at Easter it's all about lambs and chickens,' she adds.

'And nothing about crucifixion?' He chances it.

'I haven't seen that design yet.' She pretends to look around.

They hoot. A thin and invisible line of mutual understanding extends between them.

'Thank you so much! I'm so sorry, but I don't remember your name. I'm Matt.' He extracts his hand from under the bundle of fabric.

'Gosia.' She gently shakes his large, warm palm.

'Gosia, you are a godsend. I'll tell Vijay you saved my arse.'

They laugh exaggeratedly.

'Happy to help, any time.' Her heart hurtles.

He positions his feet to leave.

'Would be great to see you when you're next in the area. Ciao!'

He swiftly moves towards the checkouts. She waves the stupid little wave of a meek shop assistant while fighting an airlock in her throat. He turns the corner and disappears from her view.

Her hand prickles and she is too distracted to make any sensible shopping choices. Her basket dumped at her feet; her mind spanking along; her stomach enlarged with hope.

She replays the very first meeting with Vijay. Her sat at the checkout, scanning and snivelling, unable to control the tears silently running down her face; Andy's affair, the fine for her revenge and Anna's disgust with Gosia's behaviour piled on top of each other. And then a fresh white handkerchief, ironed and folded, appeared in front of her, delivered by the manicured hand of a handsome man. She took it. An electrostatic shock, gentle and tingly, passed between them. Vijay smiled at her; his perfect teeth shone. She wanted to take him to bed then and there. Instead she gave him the first of his 69 points.

Just as she'd thought she was lost in love's wasteland, she had stumbled onto the motorway of Vijay's life. Yes, she can be in the area, yes, she can find a way to see him. She exhales.

92

A library less than half an hour before closing time. The tannoy announcements are delivered by the branch manager in a high-pitched voice, snappy and cold, suggestive of a forthcoming breakdown. The queue to the self-service machine is seven people deep. A tall man in an old-fashioned green tweed suit is filling in his complaint form and monopolising the attention of the only customer service assistant by the information desk.

Gosia sits at the computer on the right engrossed in an instant message exchange with Zuza.

Gosia_Golab: 'Czesc!'

ZuZa: 'Gosia!!!! How's life?'

Gosia_Golab: 'I'm OK. You?'

ZuZa: 'With Mercury in retrograde I lay low and wait with my farm search. Two more weeks to go. You?'

Gosia_Golab: 'What's a mercury retrograde?'

ZuZa: 'Goodness!!! You don't know?!?!? It's the major communication havoc caused three times a year by Mercury's position. Complex stuff. The planet doesn't actually spin backwards from all I know but all the human stuff does.'

Gosia_Golab: 'How?!'

ZuZa: 'It's common knowledge that nothing will be settled successfully for the future during these periods. You can't plan and any plans you make will fall apart. During these weeks it's even hard to have a decent conversation.'

Gosia_Golab: 'Do you really believe in that?'

ZuZa: 'Gosia, the moon moves oceans and regulates my monthly bleeding. Who else do you suggest I trust?'

Gosia's ears are pierced by another announcement. A pitch higher, a notch louder: 'The library will be closing in fifteen minutes.'

Gosia_Golab: 'I stopped shaving.'

ZuZa: 'And? Are they already queuing around the block?'

Gosia_Golab: 'Who?'

ZuZa: 'Lovers! :)'

Gosia_Golab: 'The itch is unbearable. I want to scratch myself with a wire brush.'

ZuZa: 'It will pass. Just cover your bits in olive oil and cultivate with a bit of self-love.'

Gosia's fingers freeze. She offers an inadequate, basic laughing emoji. Zuza picks up from a new angle.

ZuZa: 'Saw Ciocia Ela this morning. She's so proud of herself, for "putting things right". I made her open windows and put crystals in the corners of that deadly room. I can't believe she blabbed to you about your dad's past.'

Gosia_Golab: 'Why?'

ZuZa: 'Not her story to tell. I guess Uncle Staszek still has a tongue?'

Gosia stares at the blinking screen, at the box where Zuza types her words.

> ZuZa: 'She's always been sour and I don't trust the intentions of bitter people.'
>
> Gosia_Golab: 'She's dying.'
>
> ZuZa: 'We all are, but not everyone's walking around spreading other people's secrets and sending old wedding dresses across the continent.'
>
> Gosia_Golab: 'She's dying right now.'
>
> ZuZa: 'Oh Gosia. Don't tell me that you are going to distance yourself from your parents on the back of her news?! If you do, she got what she wanted.'

'The library will be closing in five minutes,' the distorted voice howls through the speakers. The self-checkout machine beeps. There is a warning on Gosia's screen, three minutes left, and Zuza's pause is long and pronounced, the conversation box deserted. Behind Gosia there is a rush of human feet on worn carpet. She gapes vacantly at the large-print shelf by the window, at the long row of romance novels in glossy pink. She finally types.

> Gosia_Golab: 'Why would she want that?'

Zuza replies instantly.

> ZuZa: 'Ciocia Ela is known for her love of control and a very black and white world view. Look at Viola. The poor thing can hardly breathe on her own. Ciocia Ela excels at white lies too. She

claims that she was looking after Margaret but from what I know she visited her only once.'

Gosia_Golab: 'Margaret?'

ZuZa: 'Małgorzata is Margaret in English. Did I tell you that? Maybe not.'

Gosia stares at the screen. 'Małgorzata is Margaret in English' spins around her head and makes her nauseous.

ZuZa: 'I once overheard Ciocia Ela say that she wanted your dad to pay for what he did to her. She blamed him for her—'

The screen goes blank, jumps to the main log-in screen and then goes dead, its power cut off.

'The library is now closed. Please make your way to the exit,' the voice instructs the remaining library users.

The library assistant escorts an elderly man to the door. He has sat through the afternoon in an uncomfortable armchair by the radiator, the hair on the back of his head indented to match the chair fabric's pattern.

Gosia contemplates slipping under the desk, feeling with her foot the area covered with wires and plugs, ascertaining available space. She takes a deep breath and starts sliding down silently. She is tapped on her shoulder halfway down the chair. The manager's eyes wild, twitching with anger. She only uses curt words to ask Gosia to leave.

93

A council-run library, the slim forty-five minutes in between the opening and the Rhyme Time session. The buggy park still empty. Almost all computers are busy. Gosia sits at the one on the left and is slightly distracted by the loud conversation in the reading area.

R_M wrote: 'What's the big deal? All porn stars do it. Hairless pussies are far more hygienic! And what a threat! Is that what feminists think should happen? Violence? I thought it was all about not being abusive as apparently we (MEN) are!'

Derek_Admin wrote: 'Keep poetry platform free. Donate now.'

TheBestOf_Suzie wrote: 'I remove my pubic hair for aesthetic purposes, it simply looks neater.'

RichardMutton_PoetForDarkTimes wrote: 'Missed the launch? Buy signed copies of my just released book of poems here and join for the events during my forthcoming national tour.'

KarenStevensWrites wrote: 'Well done! Yet another punchy work from you! Excellent rhythm and a very interesting way in which you bring the everyday into the sphere of poetry. I love the specifics! Superdrug is my personal highlight. Could you develop the poem further with this everyday focus in mind? Add names of potions and lotions? Here are some ideas: "Grow strong", "Long & lustful".'

Rich_M wrote: 'Not signing online petitions means that we are definitely heading for a society in which people don't care what the state does. How can you otherwise protect and fight for your neighbourhood? We can't let those in power take over and change our leafy streets into a dump! Online petitions might be the only way for some (housebound, living in remote places, ill, working long shifts) to be part of a protest and to support activists' work. Don't break people's spirit! Remove this poem now!'

R_M wrote: 'Get your fat and ugly mug out of my sight!'

RM_1964 wrote: 'Pitiful work by a hairy feminist!'

Woman_with_hair wrote: 'Yes to hairy pussies! Sign the petition now!'

Open letter to men who want no pubic hair on women

Online petitions bore me
But I would sign one
That stops women from removing
Their pubic hair for men
Their vaginas look empty

If I heard men laugh
At hairy pussies
I would strap them to chairs
Remove hair on hair from their bollocks
For educational purposes

I look around Superdrug
For creams and lotions
That would help me grow
My pubic hair long and strong
There is a gap in the market.

94

The Bulletproof Guide to Sorting Out Your Life:
Work, Money, Free Time, Family, Friendship and Love.
STEP 20: How to Be Entrepreneurial

Entrepreneurship is all about seeing the business potential in the world around you. Some people are born being able to see a business idea in a pile of rubble, but the majority of us need to learn that skill.

Often, business ideas to follow and invest in are closely connected to your interests, as well as gaps in the market. It is this fine combination of the two that makes businesses succeed or fold. It does not matter if you are in a service or product market - you need to offer something unique and well-executed for it to survive in the competitive contemporary world.

It is often hard to see it yourself, and this is where getting a business assessment done by professionals could be crucial. Our rates are very competitive. Get in touch for tailored advice on helpme@andyandmargaret.com.

Let's look at one of our case studies - Lyndsey. She is a skilled beautician with an ambition to run her own upmarket nail bar. We assessed Lyndsey's business idea and how it fits into her life using our unique 300-step process, offering seamless synchronisation of all six important areas of life.

As part of our assessment, we closely researched the market: there are plenty of nail bars out there, so it quickly became apparent that offering something unique is key.

What is unique about Lyndsey's business? We concluded that Lyndsey's metallic finish to acrylic nails is not widely available. We also suggested she considered working directly on clients' premises during times suitable to them.

Armed with this advice, Lyndsey was able to make informed choices about her life, career and business idea. We are happy to report that outside of her regular job, she has started building a client base. Apart from extra money, this is going to be the source of her positive online reviews. The best starter client base is people you already know! Lyndsey, thanks to our insight, texted all of her contacts offering quality manicures at unbeatable prices as a rare introductory offer, and the bookings poured in.

It might be another month or two before Lyndsey gathers enough clients and is ready to jump in at the deep end – this will involve leaving her current position, taking out a loan and eventually setting up her own nail bar on a desirable high street. But she made the first move!

Working more hours and weekends will of course have an effect on Lyndsey's relationships. We assessed this area as well, optimising Lyndsey's diary to ensure she can continue having a loving and close relationship with her boyfriend Kevin as well as time to check in on her mum. Timetabling of romance may not sound romantic but Lyndsey reported having more love encounters with Kevin since she introduced the schedule. As you can see, we take care of all aspects of your life. You just have to live it!

Today it is Lyndsey. Tomorrow it could be you! We are here to help at helpme@andyandmargaret.com.

95

The staff-only area in a 24/7 fitness centre during a mid-afternoon break. The kitchen worktop is congested with white mugs containing leftover tea and coffee, the surface stained and sprinkled with crumbs. A single clean bowl with a small portion of muesli is lodged between the dirty dishes. Next to it stands Gosia. She cuts a banana into small pieces and adds it to her grain and nuts.

Steve flips through his handouts, now neatly stored in the light green folder. He gets bored and helps himself to a long-sleeved T-shirt stored on the metal shelves, removes it from the plastic bag and tries it on. He looks at himself appreciatively. Gosia fills her bowl with milk and moves it to a collapsible table. She sits heavily on a foldable plastic chair.

'You sure you don't want some?' Gosia asks, pointing her spoon at Steve.

'I told you. I had a big lunch.' Steve takes out his phone and uses it as a mirror. 'I think orange suits me. Do you think this would be a good profile pic?'

Gosia chews.

'I think you should keep it real. No fancy clothing. None of this fashion drama. Just wear what you usually wear.'

Steve sighs.

'I don't think social media wants it *that* real.'

'You don't know until you try.' Gosia smiles.

Steve removes the top and points at his regular vest underneath, shapeless and washed out.

'I mean, I'm already ugly. Wearing this goes beyond being eccentric.' Steve pulls at the cotton. 'I own a mirror, Gosia.'

She shakes her head, mouth full of cereal.

'I need to find my USP and I don't want it to be my gut.' Steve grabs his belly and shakes it.

'I think your USP is that you're actually working out, running 5k and gaining sweat patches under your arms at the end of it. And all the dancing you do, that's a full-on workout too!' Gosia taps her nail on the cover of a fitness magazine abandoned on the table. 'None of these fake smiles and tiptoe poses make your calves slimmer.'

'Really?' Steve takes a seat.

'Really.' Gosia points at the cover. 'Do you trust this person with a fresh blow-dry and a sunset in the background?'

Steve purses his lips for a 'no'.

'Why do you want to join them then?' she prods. 'A fake orange top is just the start. Three posts in you'll be looking for the perfect location. What's wrong with the view of a multistorey car park and people in coats on the pavement?'

Steve sighs.

'I don't want to become a poor and fat fitness star. I want it to be about a good life that involves easy but regular exercise, nice but nourishing food and comfy but flattering clothes.'

Gosia shakes her head again.

The triumph of her first fitness session has been reported far and wide thanks to Maureen, who personally called Sasha to express her excitement that they finally had been given an energetic instructor who didn't treat them like walking corpses.

Gosia Golab, Fitness Facilitator, she repeats on a loop in her mind. It has a nice ring to it. This would give her a new angle for approaching Vijay. She could be offering something her gym fails to offer – exercising in clients' homes. Making it convenient, beneficial and highly desirable. But she worries that on her own she might look too suspicious, helplessly in love. Kissing him by accident as he prepares to do a squat.

She rotates in her mind a new thought: *Gosia and Steve, Fitness Team*. It sounds even better, and why wouldn't you do what you love with someone else, especially with someone you really like? With Steve, she will be credible in Vijay's eyes: she will be establishing a new business venture.

'This doesn't feel that unique to me,' she says. 'Why don't we concentrate on exercises you can do wherever you are, whatever you are wearing and still having a good life? Working out on your sofa as you watch TV!'

'We?' Steve shrieks. 'We?!' He starts jumping on his seat and thumping the rickety table. 'Really, *WE*?' Steve does a little victory dance on the stool, his arm up in the air, his belly drawing circles. He whoop-whoops.

Gosia laughs.

'We. But we have to change the name.'

Steve's face goes numb.

Gosia explains.

'I looked it up. Someone is already using LazyFit, and it just sits too close to this.' She points at the walls of FitYou Centre.

'Right!' Steve rests his forehead on his palm. Taps his fingers on his head.

'Fit Slobs!' he yelps.

Gosia considers.

'It makes me think of pizza and sweaty foreheads.'

'But healthy pizza, right?' Steve looks at her, excitement filling his cheeks.

'I think it just sounds too wacky. I don't think people would take us seriously,' Gosia says with the last spoon of grain in her hand.

'All right, all right, how about Fitness Couch?' Steve's face is stuck in a wide grin. 'Implying that you can start at home, or wherever, really.'

'Great!'

'Let's set it up now. We need a picture!' Steve waves his phone in the air and, on cue, Janelle walks into the kitchen. 'Janelle, could you spare us some of your time and talent?' Steve pushes his phone into Janelle's hand. 'Can you take a snap of us?'

Janelle looks puzzled.

'Doing what?'

'Arm-wrestling!' Steve cries. 'I've read that during a single session you can burn a thousand calories!'

Steve positions Gosia's bowl on the edge of the micro-table. Janelle presses herself against the metal frame with camera in hand. Gosia and Steve lock their arms into an arm-wrestling position and look into each other's eyes jubilantly.

96

A cold, late morning in an infectious chain cafe that contaminates the country's minor train stations, serves bitter coffee from non-recyclable cups, tasteless pastries coated in icing and a range of tabloids. The cafe features an inadequate number of seats. All tables are supplemented with a single chair designed for lonely travellers striving to minimise their social interactions.

Due to engineering works on the main line, there is a bus replacement service running from this small town situated beyond the outskirts of the metropolis to the heart of the big city. Disoriented crowds tempted to do their Christmas shopping early (and take advantage of 30 per cent off this weekend only) curse in elaborate ways, push their bodies onto coaches and argue. Staff members made into easy targets with their high-vis jackets and orange hats band together on the edge of the pavement, infrequently issuing monosyllables.

Gosia and Chrissy take a window seat overlooking the haphazard coach loading and push two chairs together towards one single metal table. Its surface is kept level by a wedge of napkins under one of the legs. Their coffees steam up the glass of the window, revealing a drawing by a previous table user. A large penis and hairy testicles growing out of a flowerpot with a helpful arrow and the word 'cactus' fingered next to it. Chrissy pretends not to notice, Gosia clears it away with the fabric of her coat sleeve.

Chrissy pushes a plastic stirrer into her cup and moves it between the foam of the milk mindlessly, her eyes puffy from an earlier, spontaneous cry.

'Is it that bad?' Gosia chances it. It took a number of pleading text messages to get Chrissy to meet her at the railway station, away from their mother's house.

'It's horrible, and I really thought you were coming up to sort it all out.' Chrissy gives Gosia an accusatory look.

'I have nothing to say.' Gosia blows at her coffee.

'Just say that you're sorry. That's all she wants to hear.' Tears are pooling in Chrissy's eyes.

'But I'm not sorry.' Gosia takes a small sip of the murky liquid.

'She's your mother!' Chrissy's voice squeaks.

'She doesn't always act like one.' Gosia tightens the coat around her.

Chrissy pants, 'You, you, you . . .'

Gosia sighs, takes Chrissy's hand.

'And how is Dad?' The requests for money have stopped coming but there has been no effort to arrange the return of any of the cash she lent him. She has a piece of paper in her wallet with dates and figures. It amounts to a deposit for a new place.

'He's back. Moved home after the wedding but he's like a ghost. I barely see him. He is out before I'm up and back late in the evenings. He told us that now he's making chutney!' Chrissy shakes her head disapprovingly. 'He's taken the boys to the swings so I could come here, get you to sort things out with Mum.'

Gosia squeezes Chrissy's fingers. She wonders what words Dad used and what promises he made to worm his way back into the master bedroom.

'Chrissy, I love her, but I can't see her right now. Not after what she did.' The numbness of her cheek returns together with the piercing pain of her mother's accusations. 'I think it's better for me to have a bit of distance for now,' she swallows, 'and live my life how I want.'

Chrissy's mouth warps.

'Mum always said you were selfish. You know how she likes to exaggerate.' She inhales. 'Gosia, please don't prove her right!' Her eyes leak salty water. 'We're not free like that. Totally careless and offhand about what others think.' She sobs. 'Maybe you don't get it because you don't have kids!'

Gosia looks at the feet congregating on the pavement on the other side of the glass, a few turned to watch them. She moves her head towards the cafe. An older man, her father's build and size, sits at the next table reading through the sports section, a mound of empty sugar packets dumped by the side of his cup. He lifts his eyes, scrutinises the severity of Chrissy's distress and Gosia's bitchiness. The two-tone of the walls, the smell of burnt coffee beans and human odour, musty and stale, envelop Gosia. She wants to leave, push herself onto the next coach and never return.

Chrissy dabs at her eyes with an overused tissue.

Gosia says in a small voice, 'You can't control what other people think.'

Chrissy's face clots and thickens.

Gosia adds, 'There is no point worrying about that.'

Chrissy opens her mouth, draws a shallow breath. Gosia continues.

'And I feel so much better since I've stopped agonising over it.' She looks Chrissy in the eye. 'And if I had kids, I wouldn't want them to worry about it either.'

Chrissy's voice is measured and cold, tears soaked in the tissue's fibres.

'You.' She points her finger at Gosia. 'How can you leave me with all this mess?' Chrissy curls her hands into fists, places them on the table. 'Do you think it's fun living with Mum and Dad? To see them like that, pretending things are fine? To keep Mum from dwelling on her disappointments?' She flares her nostrils. 'I'm tired, Gosia. I haven't slept a full night's sleep since the twins were born. I've got no energy for any of that and I can't just leave, like you did.' She breathes through her mouth. 'All your weekend visits were upsetting anyway, always arriving in a mood and making Mum angry. Do you think I'll miss that?' Chrissy shouts as she stands up. Her chair falls to the floor with a loud bang.

Gosia doesn't care; in that moment she doesn't feel part of this family any more. This family that always takes and tells her what to do. They are not welcome in her new life, life with people who have great taste and open minds, who don't fill up their wallets with money-off coupons, who champion the best in her – people like Steve, who always makes her feel adequate, and people like Vijay, when she finally gets to be with him.

The cafe's clientele, arranged in a misshaped semi-circle, are peering for more, hungry for a fist fight.

Chrissy delivers her final sentence in her loud, high-pitched voice, for the benefit of the crowd behind her.

'Mum was right. You've changed! You are not one of us any more.'

She promptly leaves through the main exit, onto the empty train platform, parting the crowd.

Chrissy's words ring in Gosia's ears. Has she changed? Zuza told her that their surname, Gołąb, is the name of a common bird, and translates as both 'pigeon' and 'dove'. At the time Gosia was not sure how that could be possible: how could a word simultaneously speak of a peace bird and a flying rat? Now it's clear: they might be the same family but they are different species. Her plumage has matured, she is no longer an easy prey. She's shed that paralysing notion of always playing to other people's expectations; unwanted feathers that her family wear with pride.

Gosia leaves. She uses the side door, slips onto the coach, takes one of the last remaining undesirable seats at the back between teenage boys high on hormones and energy drinks. It starts to rain.

97

A manager's office in a 24/7 fitness centre. A small, cramped, windowless room with an imposing desk stacked high with paperwork. Sasha sits on the best-value, fire-retardant manager's chair made from Turin leather with comfortable padded arms and modern stitching detail. Her tight bum rests on deep foam cushioning, included for support and comfort. She fiddles with the chair's mechanism. The single lever that lets her adjust the seat height up and down and lock or unlock the tilt of the chair is playing up.

Above her desk hangs a picture of three young women spinning fearlessly on stationary bikes. Their faces are covered in foundation, smiles strained, teeth white. Gosia only now detects that the woman on the right is Sasha herself. At least ten years younger, not a crease on her forehead, biceps plump and pronounced.

Gosia stands by the door with a sheet of paper in hand. Sasha bends her upper body to reach a screw lower down on the chair. With her free hand she indicates for Gosia to walk in.

'Everything OK?' Sasha's voice is strained with effort.

'Just a quick one.' Gosia keeps her voice neutral. 'We have a person interested in joining the gym, and he wants to book some personal training sessions.'

'That's great!' Sasha straightens up; the back of her chair is sloping backwards. 'What's the problem?'

'He wants to book these sessions with me.'

Sasha tilts her head, processing Gosia's words.

'But you haven't qualified yet.'

'I told him that but he said it wasn't a problem.'

'Is he still here?'

Gosia nods.

'I'll speak to him.' Sasha stands up, puts on her poker face, removes an invisible speck of lint from her wide-leg trousers and makes her way to the foyer, marking the distance with quick clicks of her high heels.

By the U-shaped counter, sipping cold water from a disposable cup, stands Barnaby, in a deep green wool blazer and a soft pork-pie hat accented with a bright feather. He welcomes Sasha from afar with a gentle wave. An aura of good fortune and optimism revolves around him. Sasha extends her hand in a warm welcome.

'Sasha Koroleva, branch manager. How can I help?'

Barnaby takes her hand in both of his.

'Barnaby Basil Orlando Osborne, architect, Barnaby to friends.' He pauses, looks Sasha in the eye. 'I hear you're fostering new talent here and I'd love to book myself in for a series of sessions with this gifted PT.' He points at Gosia.

'I see.' Sasha extracts her hand, dips it into her trouser pocket, assuming a powerful stance she was taught at her leadership programme. 'News travels fast. May I ask who recommended Gosia to you?'

'I have my reliable sources.' Barnaby speaks in his soft, warm voice. 'And I wish to work out with the best.'

Sasha's eyebrows travel to the middle of her forehead.

'I see.'

'I'd be more than happy to settle for an introductory session today, right now.' Barnaby offers a smile, large and rounded. 'And ideally, I'd like a bi-weekly appointment at 6 p.m., so it slots in nicely to my day, just after I finish work.'

'Ah-ha.' Sasha takes a breath and prepares her reply using freshly acquired negotiation techniques. 'It's terrific to hear that you are ready to start immediately, but this presents a few logistical problems. Gosia's current role sees her looking after our clients here, at the reception area, and we can't release her from these responsibilities in order for you to have your introductory session. As you may already know, Gosia's not fully qualified yet and is therefore unable to take on clients. As for your request to start now, this minute,' Sasha takes in Barnaby's distinctly non-stretchy, non-sweat-absorbing attire, 'I feel that you are not quite dressed for a workout.' Sasha wears a victorious smile.

Barnaby nods. He plants his elbow on the counter; with his other hand he gently scratches his temple.

'How about if I buy my outfit from your well-stocked shop?' He points his finger at the sprawling display.

Sasha narrows her eyes, looks sideways at Gosia.

'As I explained, this won't help us solve our staffing issues.'

Barnaby is showing all his teeth, arranged in neat rows.

'Oh, I can't see a problem. Perhaps you could step in and allow us forty-five minutes for a one-to-one?'

Sasha takes a step back, this time to scrutinise Barnaby's legs. The ironed trousers and shiny shoes compliment the blazer and make Barnaby look like a TV presenter. She crooks a finger at Gosia.

'Please give us a minute. We'll be right back.'

She walks to the office, Gosia on her tail. Sasha closes the door as soon as they are both across the threshold and whispers:

'What is all that about? Are you all right? Is he stalking you? Or am I on *Candid Camera*?'

'I don't think so.' Gosia hesitates. 'I've met Barnaby before. I think it's a genuine request.'

'A genuine request?' Sasha growls.

'It may have something to do with Steve, a guy I met on the course. Barnaby and Steve are friends. Maybe Steve's recommended me?'

Sasha shoots Gosia a look.

'Right. So this simply can't happen.'

Gosia dithers. Sasha does her wrist motion, requesting more information. Words tumble out of Gosia's mouth.

'I told him that. He said it's either an introductory session with me or he's not interested in joining.' She exhales.

'I see.' Sasha calculates in her head. 'Let's meet him halfway.'

Gosia relaxes. Sasha opens the door and confidently walks back to the counter where Barnaby chews on a protein bar and flips through a fitness magazine.

'Happy to say that we can suggest a temporary solution,' says Sasha.

Barnaby swiftly lifts his head.

'Marvellous. I'm all ears.'

'We wouldn't want to keep you waiting. I know how it is. You're itching to start. Therefore, as an exception, we'll make it work on this one occasion.' Sasha looks Barnaby in the eye, drawing the line, flexing her fingers so they don't curl into fists. 'Gosia will be delighted to offer an introductory session as soon as you've completed the purchase of your sportswear and filled out the necessary paperwork. However, the regular workouts can only go ahead once Gosia qualifies. Until then you are welcome to book with a different PT, join our regular classes or use the gym at your convenience.'

Barnaby welcomes the news with a wide smile.

'Sasha, it is an unadulterated pleasure doing business with you.'

98

A mass-produced bed with a plastic mattress protector crinkling beneath the sheets. A bedside lamp that can be switched on or off from three different locations in the room; resting against it is a hotel breakfast menu. A print on the wall featuring a couple by the water's edge, their hands entwined, their gaze turned towards the low-hanging sun.

The light from the lamp is weak and yellow; it shines onto the bed, onto the bodies of John and Jennifer, in a close hug, asleep. Gosia is putting her pants on. She makes no noise.

They met in the hotel bar. It was easy to spot them, their eyes darting to the entrance with each new guest arriving, their cheeks flushed, their clothes daring, their hearts exposed. Jennifer in a very low-cut dress with no bra, John in a slim-fit shirt unbuttoned to the sternum. Gosia watched them through the window, assessing their skills. They were her age. It was their first time.

She approached them with confidence and said, 'I'm Jane.' They beamed at her, the smile of lucky lottery winners.

The conversation was flowing. So was the alcohol. They laughed a lot and talked about insignificant things while their hands shortened the distance between them. Gosia needed the loo, so did Jennifer. They walked into the disabled toilet together and behind the locked door, Jennifer attached her lips to Gosia's.

The smell of bleach was strong and distracting from the softness of Jennifer's tongue, hitting her own compulsively, quickly. Her hands travelled straight to Gosia's buttocks, squeezing her rear through the fabric of her slutty dress.

'Touch me,' Jennifer whispered and Gosia moved her hand between the open thighs, under the dress. Jennifer had no knickers on, her lady parts smooth, her hairs lasered off. Gosia's fingers dived in. Jennifer groaned and sat on Gosia's hand. Within minutes she was convulsing against the wall covered with a modern emulsion – washable, scuff-proof, protecting against mould.

Jennifer wiped and steadied herself by the sink. Their eyes met. In Jennifer's intoxicated gaze was a clear message of growing hunger. One come was not enough.

All three of them hastened to the metal lift.

'Kiss her,' Jennifer instructed.

John brought his face close to Gosia's, his sour mouth wrapped around her lips. He grazed her tongue. Jennifer put his hands on Gosia's body, lifted one of Gosia's legs and curved it around John's hip. The lift stopped and they spilled out into the sixth-floor corridor.

In the room, Jennifer took the director's seat, told them to take their clothes off, got John to burrow his tongue into Gosia's vagina, ordered Gosia to keep her eyes on her while she took out of her handbag a pink plastic dildo and began riding it vigorously.

It was obvious to Gosia from the first message exchange on the 'Three's a Party' portal that they were all in Jennifer's film, scripted to her desires. Desires not too dissimilar from Gosia's own.

For the rest of the evening, she was busy petting body parts, attending to open mouths and keeping shared tempo with her hips. Her mind only once managed to shape John's body into Vijay's and for a few minutes moved her from this budget hotel room to a boutique lodge on the edge of a lake in a tropical country.

Gosia locates her dress, shoes and coat. Gathering them silently off the floor, she slips them onto her body, checks for the Oyster card and keys in her pocket, and blows a kiss in the general direction of the bed before leaving.

99

A red bus bound for a city-centre train station crawling through the congested streets of Zone 3. The area downstairs is sardined with people ready for work. An aroma of fruity shampoo and lavender soap, a stink of tobacco and coffee breath squashed together.

Gosia and Steve have prime aisle seats on the upper deck by the front window. Steve's seat has a staircase behind it. He wears his usual outfit, old jeans and bobbly jumper. He keeps his back straight and his hands on his abdomen while lifting his thighs and creating a new, bus-friendly exercise pose: 'bus belly-crunch and bum upper-lift'. Gosia uses his camera, embedded in last year's generation of smartphone, to take a satisfying picture. She issues directives from behind the lens.

'Thighs higher. Back straight. Smile. Look ahead.'

Steve endures the session for the length of the high street until the person sitting by his side, a petite Asian woman in a beige coat, hidden behind his exercising body, taps his shoulder and stands up to leave. A tall white guy with a neatly shaved head takes her place. He rests his feet on the ledge by the window, spreads his legs, digs his knee into Steve's side and starts fiddling with his phone, earbuds tucked firmly into his ears.

Steve and Gosia swap places. She navigates around the obstructing knee, nods to Steve and sits with a straight back, arms lifted by her ears and bent like cactus branches, inches from the guy's face. He doesn't flinch. In her left hand she holds a water bottle, one litre of liquid in a canary-yellow container. She lifts both arms above her head, grips the bottle ends with both hands and starts moving her forearms up and down, methodically. Her triceps are tight and bulging below the fabric of her old top. A sleeveless puffer body warmer is zipped around her chest. She keeps her elbows close to her ears, careful not to let them flare out to the sides for maximum benefit. Steve holds the phone in position and presses the digital shutter.

The guy stops Gosia mid-move. His left earbud hangs down, the hip-hop beat bounces off his collarbone.

'What's this for?' His voice is curious.

Gosia turns her head to face him.

'We are working on exercise routines for everyday locations.'

Steve rests his face against her bent arm, and adds excitedly, 'It's a groundbreaking approach to fitness for anyone and everyone that can be done anywhere and everywhere!'

The guy nods. He points at Gosia's arms mid-flow.

'So what are you doing?'

'Exercising my triceps.'

Steve cuts in.

'We called this move "Bus bat-wings beater". It tones up your arms in no time.'

The guy nods some more, points at Steve's hand, gripping the phone.

'And the photos?'

Steve takes a breath worthy of a lengthy monologue.

'We promote it on our Instagram account. It's called Fitness-Couch. We're in the early stages of development but we have a good following' – four posts and twenty-four people, as Steve announced this morning at the bus stop. 'We have a different approach to the whole fitness world. It's genuine. None of that fancy Lycra, product placement and desirable locations.' He gestures to the bus, at least three rows behind them are now listening. 'Real people in a real city keeping fit when they can.'

Interest shines from the young man's face.

'So do you, like, run classes on buses?'

Steve's in his element.

'Not yet. But if you follow us on Insta we'll keep you updated when the bus classes start.'

The guy smiles.

'Sure.'

Gosia glows. Their business gains traction. FitnessCouch is now more than just an Instagram account. They took a series of photos on a park bench of their 'Nice 'n' Easy Everyday Bench Routine'. They produced two hundred business cards advertising their joint venture. They ordered a feather flag with a FitnessCouch slogan printed on the polyester, stitched with a double hem on the edges to make the sides strong and robust. The flag comes with a pole sleeve to keep it flying in the wind, and a sturdy base that can be filled with water – perfect for severe weather conditions when using the flag outdoors.

Gosia's confidence in her abilities is greater thanks to the impromptu introductory session with Barnaby. Fresh from spending almost three hundred pounds on the high-end kit from the FitShop, she took him on a tour of the facilities and did some small talk to break the ice. He answered only in monosyllables, as if his once-legendary eloquence and articulacy regressed the moment he donned his bright shorts.

She covered it all: asked him about his long-term and short-term goals, took his weight and height, measured body composition, checked blood pressure, assessed movement, cardiovascular health, muscular strength and endurance as well as flexibility, range of motion and posture. Barnaby was a picture of health, with a trim physique and defined six-pack, clearly following a rainbow diet low in sugar and trans fats. He looked like someone who already had a personal trainer and was merely here to compare her skills to theirs, to carry out a thorough appraisal. She felt assessed but wasn't sure of the outcome. Couldn't even tell what skills exactly Barnaby was inspecting: her PT experience, or manners, or ability to deal with stressful situations?

When she quizzed Steve about Barnaby's request to work out with her, Steve had just shrugged his shoulders as if it wasn't a big deal and quickly changed the subject.

A woman sitting one row down taps Gosia's shoulder.

'I love what you do. So fresh. What's the name of your Insta again?'

Steve's there before Gosia can process the question.

'At fitnesscouch. One word. All lower case.'

The woman smiles.

'I'll check you guys out. Keep going.' She starts descending the staircase. A tube stop for a fast line to central London is on the horizon and people start pressing their way towards the exit. Steve high-fives the guy and, along with Gosia, joins the queue for the door.

Steve can't contain his excitement, waves his arm from the pavement at the young man and is slow to follow Gosia to the bus stop on the opposite side of the road. He is compulsively refreshing their feed on the zebra crossing.

'Classes on buses! Just imagine. Gosia, we can pitch that to the mayor. Keep the nation healthy. Offer salvation to the army of all-collar workers!' He bounces as he walks. 'What a morning! And I thought you were mad when you said we needed to get on the bus by 8 a.m.' He beams. 'All the right people are on the move then. You really know our audience!' He squeezes Gosia's side. 'We can schedule the posts to coincide with the commutes. Inspire people to exercise as they fuss with their phones. It's a no-brainer.'

He offers her an arresting smile. Gosia gives him a hug and gently guides him onto another bus bound back towards their neighbourhood.

They stand downstairs next to the board fitted for the wheelchair users when Gosia blurts out:

'I know someone who works in start-ups. She's supporting new businesses.'

Steve's eyes double in size.

'You must be joking! We must meet her and tell her all about FitnessCouch. Get her on board. Get cash out of her.' Steve snakes against the board like a drunkard, intoxicated with joy.

'There is a small problem.' Gosia stops his board dance, pinning his chest with her hand. 'She's my brother's ex and a bitch.'

'Do you think she'd steal our idea?' Steve assumes his assertive position, a wide stance and raised chest.

'You've seen the Fit4All profile, right? We are not necessarily the first ones out there.'

'We are the best ones out there!' His hand, like Superman's, hangs suspended in mid-air. 'Let's meet her.'

Gosia hesitates.

'You sure?'

Picky Becky's business card sits at the bottom of her sock drawer, the language of business growth looking up at her every time she hunts for a matching pair. 'Accelerator programme' rubs shoulders with 'entrepreneurs' and 'scalable business model'.

'I'm sure.' Steve's face is flushed with confidence. 'It's a professional conversation, so let's assume her bitch side is for private use only.'

Gosia nods.

'I'll text her today.'

Acceleration is what she is after. The growth of their Instagram account brings her closer to Vijay. She just has to convince Steve that they need to do some home visits. Get people doing star jumps on their doorstep, get their heart racing to instantly lower stress levels. Then suggest local chiropractors connect with their efforts, figure out a narrative that would make it plausible. Maybe even name-drop Vijay's business. But she requires a bit of limelight first – people need to start talking about FitnessCouch by the water coolers. Then she can show up by Vijay's door.

She is ready. Her sexual experience is diverse and satisfying, her knowledge of her body deeper. What has she learnt from Jennifer's edit of a threesome? That she felt watched and kept her tummy flat, on a permanent exhale; that she was in service of someone else's cravings, fulfilling Jennifer's dream; that no one was concerned that she got rubbed a little raw and only orgasmed once. She kept the score.

Now her desire to devote herself to just one person is more intense and better informed.

100

A small bedroom with cream walls, frail furniture and a few tasteful accessories. A wool-rich, cable-knit throw on the bed, a small, fragrant candle on a floating shelf and a large peace lily in a sleek, understated white ceramic pot on the narrow chest of drawers. These adornments bring tranquillity and sophistication to any surroundings.

Gosia sits on a multipurpose laminate chair in punchy orange. She is wearing only a cotton vest and knickers. A heavily used towel in faded purple lies flat on the floor. One foot is in a bowl of soapy water placed on top of the towel, the other one bent and perched on the chair's lip, ready for clipping toenails. She works fast and cuts the nails in straight lines, scrutinises with her fingers the layers of old skin on her heel. She scrubs diligently with a double-sided foot file, directing fine shavings to land in the plastic bowl of water. Home pedicure keeps her feet attractive, her bank balance above zero and her socks without holes. Her phone rings.

She is not expecting a phone call but rushes to get it, wet foot forward. The phone is by the wall, charging at the only accessible power socket, its body buzzing against the laminate floor. The phone number is withheld. Gosia picks it up with her dry hand.

'Hello?'

There is an eerie silence typical of automated voice recordings and Gosia is about to push the red phone handle button when she thinks she hears her name.

'Gosia?' A barely perceptible voice sounds familiar in a complex and sour way.

'Yes?' She lowers her voice to match the hesitant whisper from the other side.

'It's Anna. I want to talk.'

'Anna?' Gosia's wet foot slides on the floor. She sits by the wall and holds the charger's wire in one hand, trying not to detach the cable from her phone; its battery is still low. She suppresses her surprise, her stomach knots. She inhales, searching for a neutral pitch.

'What do you want to talk about?'

Anna's voice recovers.

'I wanted to see if we could meet. Talk things through.'

Gosia can hear the familiar lilt, the tongue's inability to bend and enunciate 'r', although Anna has always treated her rhotacism as an asset.

'What things?'

It was Anna who took the proof of Gosia's revenge to the police and stood by Andy's testimony that they parted ways amicably, dividing shared belongings between them based on who bought what. In a room full of strangers, Anna confirmed, in her assured voice, punctuated by the speech impediment, that Gosia had unrealistic expectations of her relationships and often acted in impulsive, unpredictable ways suggestive of an underlying psychological problem. After that, Anna stopped answering Gosia's calls, blocked her on Facebook and warned her not to visit her flat.

Anna also informed Gosia that she had acquired all the necessary forms to apply for a restraining order if needed.

'It's been a long time. I've been thinking that it would be good to sort things out. Face to face.'

Anna's voice is businesslike, matter-of-fact, with not a prick of kindness. Gosia chews on her nail, looks at her feet.

'I thought there was nothing left to talk about. You chose Andy.'

Anna sighs, as if she had not been anticipating problems; a tinge of irritation colours her reply.

'Your letter made me think. Maybe I should've suggested that we met back then, when your letter arrived. But it's only now that I see it clearly, that it would be better if we talk.'

There is a pause, an obscure background noise, an inhale. Anna presses on.

'When would suit you? Maybe we could meet in the next week or so?'

Gosia's mind reels like a fairground, thoughts racing on steep slopes in fast open carriages, full of fear. She sucks on her lip.

'I'm busy next week.' She is.

Picky Becky's reply arrived almost instantly and they had trouble finding a lunchtime when they all could meet. Then Lyndsey announced on a yellow Post-it her earlier departure from the flat while committing to paying the rent till the end of December. Gosia is behind with planning her routines for her weekly class in the market town. She needs to cut her toenails.

'We won't need long,' Anna has clearly already prepared an agenda, 'and we could meet at Richie's.' Gosia has never been to the two-storey bar attached to a cutting-edge theatre located on the outskirts of the neighbourhood, near the tube stop where apparently coffee and cake costs the equivalent of the hourly minimum wage. The cafe beams a privileged light at all hours from the industrial light bulbs in the large windows.

She has her usual gap between her work shift and the evening course. This is when she likes to go to the library and prune the words of her verses. She is curious as to what Anna wants. Poems, she decides, can wait.

'Wednesday next week? Around 4 p.m.?'

'Perfect. In the diary,' Anna chirrups. 'See you then. Cheerio.'

She hangs up when Gosia is still halfway through her 'bye-bye'. The phone is silent but Anna's voice rings in Gosia's head like a booming sledgehammer. Her hands shake gently and she abandons cutting her toenails and peeling dead skin from her heels. She feels sick. She folds her body under the bed covers, only her damp foot sticking out.

101

A small bedroom loaded with sealed boxes with large writing in black, wonky capitals on the sides. 'PANTIES' reads one by the door. 'DVDS FAV' reads one underneath, 'SUMMER HATS' on the one underneath that. The investigation matrix can't be detected behind the cardboard stacks. The bed is made: a pale pink throw stretches out on top of the sheets, a faux-velvet heart-shaped cushion is placed in the middle. Gosia sits on the edge of the bed and reads.

I put on another 3lb but it must be muscle as it doesn't show and I did all this packing and box moving in recent weeks.

It takes it out of you, organising things.

Mum offered to pop in and help now that Richard is away touring the towns, promoting his poems. His poetry circuit is so supportive. People from all over the place invite him to come and talk about his work. It's an important tour of all the real centres of poetry production and he gets to meet this literary crowd.

Mum said he hates leaving London but needs must. He's been all over! First Hemel Hempstead, then on to Banbury and finally Grantham.

He sent Mum pictures of all the gorgeous rooms that he stayed in, with large double beds and wide baths. I asked her why she didn't join him and only then she told me that she had taken double shifts leading up to Christmas to help with the tour costs. I didn't know what to say.

GG and I aren't talking. It's not a shock that we don't get on but it was shocking how she attacked me. She was so aggressive just because we had some fun in her room! She said many words that cut me to the bone. I don't think I will ever be able to forgive her.

We avoid each other now and I vowed not to be nice to her over breakfast. It was me doing all the small talk anyway. So, I don't have breakfast any more to help with my weight and to avoid any face-to-face contact with GG. She is like a wild predator, ready to go for the throat, so I just dress and leave. In the evenings I eat dinner at Kevin's. We are back to fried chicken buckets because Kevin's kitchen is temporarily being used as Bob's storage space for all his music gear that he needed to move out from his studio at short notice. It's drums on hobs and kitchen units hidden under mixing decks.

Vincent's house must have been sold as there is a scaffold at the front and a large skip by the kerb. I'm so relieved I won't be seeing his son's face any more, but the builders are really cute and they whistle when I walk past.

It must be a tough time to sell. We had only one couple viewing the flat and it looked like they were spying for someone, asking unusual questions. They were not interested at all in where the boiler was, or if we could hear the neighbours through the wall. I mentioned it all to Kevin but he just shrugged.

I guess I am the one with the real detective flair. Two days later, the landlord came in person and he never visits. It was a rare evening when I was in, frying fish fingers, and he just walked into the kitchen with the key in his hand.

I screamed and he asked, 'What's going on?' And I said, 'Who are you?!' And he said, 'Martin.' And I said, 'What Martin?' And he said, 'Martin Martin, your landlord.' And I said, 'Thank god you are not a rapist.'

He sat down, although I didn't offer him a seat, and asked for a glass of water, although I was busy frying food, and he started looking around the room. I gave him water in the best glass and he said we had a problem. So I asked, 'What problem?' And he said, we are the problem.

I was shocked.

He said that since the flat went on the market there has been almost no interest in it and all he wanted was a quick sale. He was wondering why, since people buy much worse holes than this one.

He said that it took time, but he found the problem, and the problem was that someone on the internet said that this flat is a cathouse: two women to choose from, thin or fat, and a guy by the doors that checks out the clientele.

This left me speechless.

All I could do was eat my fish. This was a good move. My memory came back. I told Martin Martin all about Vincent's son's threats, his hostile face and intimidating behaviour.

He said that if we want the deposit back, we'd better fix the place.

I'm leaving. I don't want to have anything to do with it. I'm done.

Anna thinks I'm overreacting and Kevin was not happy either. There is not much room with Bob's stuff everywhere. I told him that if he loved me he would want me safe. I'm moving next week and I can't wait to get out.

Gosia puts the diary where she found it, inside a cardboard box marked 'DIARIES' stacked by the side of the bed.

102

A small bedroom with cream walls and disposable furniture, a cobweb arranged by the cylindrical lampshade. Gosia sits on a single bed. A thin pillow, with a yellow-brown flower motif, separates her back from the cold of the plaster wall. The other pillow is in her lap, ready to soften a punch. She picks a number on her pay-as-you-go phone, presses 'call' and holds the mobile close to her ear – but not too close.

'Hello?' says a booming male voice.

So it is true, Dad is back home and now even allowed to answer the phone. Gosia hesitates. This phone call feels simultaneously too soon and overdue but she has trouble parking nagging thoughts that wake her up at night, Dad's secrets floating in her mind, making her heart race. She misses him too and she finds it hard to admit, her dad being at once a liability and security.

'Hi, Dad.'

'Hello?' The voice can't hear and there is some commotion by the mouthpiece. 'Hello? Who's calling?'

Gosia's speech climbs up a few notches.

'Hi, Dad. It's me.'

'Gosia, is that you?' The voice is surprised but warmer.

'Yes, Dad, it's me.'

'Don't even think about passing her on to me,' says her mother in the background, loud and clear. Plainly hovering behind Dad's back.

'Shev-on, just stay calm.' Dad is doing a bad job of attempting to cover the mouthpiece. 'How are you, Gosia?'

Gosia shrinks back.

'I'm good, Dad. I'm fine. Do you have a minute to talk?'

'Me?' he hesitates. 'Yes, I do. We've just had lunch. You missed a nice pie.'

Her mother roars in the background.

'She wouldn't have been invited to have any! Ungrateful child!'

There is a door closing, her mother's muffled yell and then her dad's mellow breathing.

'What do you want to talk about?'

'I was in Poland,' Gosia starts.

'Hmm.' Her dad's favourite reassuring noise.

'And I met Aunt Ela.'

'How is she?' He perks up.

'Not too well, I'm afraid. Her treatments have stopped. They can't help her any more. She is very frail but she has this plan to put things right before, you know, before she goes.'

Gosia's voice cracks. Dad lets out a short groan. She tunes into a cheerful pitch.

'She was very hospitable, truly gutted to miss Bernie's wedding. We had a lovely afternoon with a lot of cake and a lot of vodka.'

Dad laughs. Gosia leaps in.

'She told me about you.' There is a knotted silence. 'And about Małgorzata.'

She can't be certain of her father's continued presence. The silence is hollow.

'So that was a bit of a surprise.'

She can now hear her father walking the length of the corridor, five steps between discarded coats and shoes, away from the living room but within the wireless phone range. Gosia knows that the signal drops past the front door.

'You never told me,' Gosia prods.

The footsteps stop.

'I didn't know that my name had any significance.' She keeps nudging. 'For a moment I thought that I might be her child, that this is why Mother hates me. But I guess she only found out last spring.' She pokes some more. 'And I'm just confused by it all.'

His silence hurts. She sighs.

'She was so beautiful. Aunt gave me some pictures to pass on to you. Do you miss her?'

There is no breath, no sound, no feelings.

'Such a tragic story. I wish I'd known about it. I wish I'd heard about her from you,' Gosia concludes, and squeezes the pillow. Her father is mute, just like her mother said – a coward. 'And Aunt Ela. Is there something unresolved between you? Could she want you in trouble?' She digs into his dirt. Her dad remains absent, a still life in the corridor.

'I met so many cousins. People travelled specially to hang out with me, which was nice. I think I might stay in touch with them, especially Zuza. I've never met anyone like her. She is one of these people that make you want to live your life more.'

'Hmm . . .' A distant enquiry.

'Things are OK, but not great. The landlord's selling the flat so I'll have to move again and you know how much I hate that.'

'That's not good, Gosia.' The voice returns and is concerned, the pacing down the corridor starts again. 'Have you found somewhere else?'

'Not yet. I have till Christmas.'

'That's only weeks away! You shouldn't leave it until the last minute.' His businessman-speak takes over. 'There must be adequate accommodation available. With your new job, maybe you can look for something nicer?'

'Maybe.' She feels weak now. Diluted by his generic advice and no mention of all the money that he owes her. Her fingers stone cold, wrapped around the phone.

'I'll come and help you move. Just tell me when.' The speed of his steps accelerates.

'There is no need, Dad. I don't have much stuff.' She stares at her belongings. She doesn't want them.

'I insist.'

Gosia can picture his creased forehead, his tensed lips, his worried eyes. The face of a man who won't give up the truth.

'OK, Dad.'

'Do you want a word with your mother?' Her father's voice is pleading.

She hesitates, her chest stiff, her cheek numb, and then there is a beeping sound, a warning of low funds on her pay-as-you-go phone. She uses the remaining time to prolong his agony.

'How is she?'

Her father drops his voice to a conspiratorial whisper.

'Well, as you can imagine. She feels hurt. She only wants the best for you. It might help if you two talk for a bit.'

She takes a deep, explanatory inhale.

'I don't know, Dad. Do you think that would change anything?'

He is quick to speak and starts with, 'I think it might . . .' and then there is another beep and the line goes dead and she can't hear the end of his sentence and she is relieved.

103

The Bulletproof Guide to Sorting Out Your Life:
Work, Money, Free Time, Family, Friendship and Love.
STEP 27: How to Sell Your Products or
Services Successfully

The best of ideas need to be presented in desirable ways for people to actually want your products or services. You can sell anything as long as you know how to attract your buyers.

Let's look at our next case study, Anna. Anna's sewing skills are fabulous and she makes fantastic cushions. We have been telling her that she could charge a small fortune for a handmade object in fashionable colours if she markets it wisely. We advised Anna to seek out an audience that invests in locally and ethically produced, quality home accessories in the spirit of 'slow fashion'. We warned her that if she promotes the same cushions in the wrong place or to the wrong people they will be seen as cheap, one-season sofa updates.

How to avoid your product being seen as a cheap, short-term-use-only item? Promote what you do and what you sell through the language of Luxury, Individuality and Exclusivity (L. I. E.). Even if what you sell is a one-use-only item, like loo roll or latex gloves – you can still apply the principles of L.I.E. and charge a premium for them.

Take us: Andy learnt that telling punters that he had a bulletproof method for changing people's lives for the better over a pint in a cheap pub by the North Circular on a Friday evening didn't bring him any business. The message did not register and he wasn't taken seriously.

However, when Margaret imparted the same exciting news to a friend over a glass of Prosecco in a lush hotel lobby one Wednesday afternoon, the friend requested more details and eventually became one of our case studies for this book.

What changed? Margaret delivered the information in the right way:

- With an emphasis on Luxury, Individuality and Exclusivity (L.I.E.)
- In a location that enhances the message
- During the time of day when people make life-changing decisions. (That time is never Friday night. You will have far more luck at a midweek lunchtime, when every day hurts and there is a willingness to spend, to change, to explore and to invest.)

Give your products what they deserve – a platform to become statement objects available to the select few who are prepared to pay for your skills and time, and who appreciate the unique beauty of a handmade product.

104

A cafe but also a restaurant and definitely a bar situated on three levels in the vast, elegant space of an old market building. Individual alcoves line the sides of an expansive room, neatly arranged on the mezzanine level, each booth furnished with velvet seats and mahogany tables. The bar on the top floor has been extended with a modern glass balcony, allowing anyone from below to peer up the waitresses' skirts. The cafe sits on the ground floor. Each small round table is supplemented with three to four metal chairs, made comfortable enough to perch on and uncomfortable enough to finish your meal promptly.

Gosia and Steve arrive early and are shown to the table Becky booked. They ask to be moved somewhere discreet. Steve points his finger at one of the velvet booths. The waiter informs them that these have been pre-booked at least a couple of weeks in advance.

They sit bang in the middle of the concourse, exposed to the entire room, squashed between other groupings busy with sealing their deals over platters of grilled king prawns and fat olives.

They start scrolling through the menu. Steve releases a low whistle.

'Is she paying?' He lowers the sheet and arranges his eyebrows into a question mark.

'I wouldn't assume so.' Gosia reads the menu concentrating on prices. The cheapest are the side dishes, starting at £6. 'She's always been tight.'

'But we are her clients, right?' Steve's eyes are large like two-pound coins and heavy with hope.

'We have a great idea and we're looking for support,' says Gosia, her lips pursing. 'She might offer us tap water. If she shows up.'

Gosia's phone did not switch on this morning, its plastic body didn't buzz when connected with the power lead nor when shaken or punched. If Becky cancelled, they wouldn't know. Gosia has her business card in her pocket – they can text from Steve's phone – but they've decided to wait until she is at least fifteen minutes late. Gosia needs a new phone anyway. A smartphone that can handle apps. She is saving up for one.

'Right.' Steve presses his foot against Gosia's shin and then gently taps it twice.

'What are you doing?' She moves her leg.

Steve lowers his voice to a conspiring whisper.

'Sending you a secret signal.'

'Why?'

He tuts at her.

'So we can communicate without anyone knowing!' He looks serious, slightly red in his cheeks, an overlay of worry in his eyes. This time, he kicks Gosia's leg with far more force. 'Double rap – yes. Single rap – no. Now you try.'

He extends his leg to make it an easy target. Gosia taps it with her foot, first twice and then once, and then Picky Becky arrives and insists on kissing their cheeks.

Gosia goes for a side of kale with smoked garlic and Cornish sea salt, Steve settles on a ham hock sandwich with a fried egg in a freshly baked focaccia accompanied by wafer-thin fries. Picky Becky opts for a three-course lunch from the set menu with a basket of bread, a glass of wine and a pot of coffee included in the price.

'I love FitnessCouch,' Picky Becky says just as her starter, mini crab cakes with watercress, arrives on the table with a glass of Chardonnay. Gosia and Steve sip tap water delivered in a glass bottle, chilled and garnished with lemon. Picky Becky speaks with crab lodged in between her teeth.

'There is a freshness to it that I haven't seen for a while. It's clever and funny and you are clearly passionate about it. Passion is the most important. It's so hard to make any start-up work without it.'

Steve opens his mouth but Picky Becky silences him with loud chewing and more words.

'Analysts predicted a few years ago that accessible fitness would rapidly gain traction in the mainstream market and the following of FitnessCouch is a testament to that – 570 real followers in the first few weeks, that's something.' She smiles. 'Of course, all the hard work is still ahead of us. I take it you haven't written a business plan?'

Gosia and Steve signal no.

'Conducted market research and found your target audience?'

Steve hesitates. Gosia sits mute.

'Registered your business? Opened an account? Employed an accountant? Started conversations with lenders, investors? Got yourself a business email and business cards? Registered the FitnessCouch trademark? Found out who your competition is?'

Steve perks up but Picky Becky ignores his sudden head nods.

'Starting your own business can be exciting, but it can also be one of the scariest choices you'll ever make. Because of the risks involved and the fear of failure, most people never follow their dreams.' She pauses to take a gulp of wine. 'Instead of letting these excuses control your life, we need to address them ASAP. If not, you'll never start your own business. One way to move forward is to work with a life coach who can provide you with actionable steps in getting started and I know the perfect person, and she charges affordable rates.'

Picky Becky places her cutlery neatly together on her plate and instantly a waiter walks out from behind a pillar and removes the offending empty dish.

'Alongside that, we need you to establish yourselves as authority figures and build trust among your potential customers. When they trust you, they'll be more likely to support your business and refer it to others.'

The main arrives with Gosia's kale and Steve's sandwich. Steve bites into his stack, Gosia dips her fork tentatively into a modest amount of greens arranged on a flat plate. Picky Becky sinks her fork into a twice-cooked pork belly with an onion and apple velouté while she continues to deliver her monologue.

'We need to get you some free publicity and ensure you're featured in some leading fitness publications, which will introduce your business to a new audience. Because if you want your business to succeed, you need to become a respected voice within your industry.'

She massages an onion ring in meat juices before folding it into her mouth.

'You can achieve this by creating content such as blog posts, podcasts, webinars, videos, infographics and case studies. I would suggest you do some guest posts on other platforms and start appearing at as many industry events and conferences as possible. I had a look and there is a big fitness event in January and we could get you a five-minute slot on the main stage for £250, a rare bargain!'

Steve chokes on his fries. Gosia drops the withered greens from her fork prong.

'Now.' Picky Becky abandons the better part of the pork on the plate. 'We need to think about your executive version. I thought about a subscription-only app and a bespoke programme for individual clients so they can practise in their limousines.' She has that satisfied smile on her face that Gosia detests. Steve stiffens in his seat; the metal chair rubs uncomfortably against Gosia's bottom.

'I drew up a shortlist of brands we should connect to and offer product placement. I think it would be good to start as gently as possible: water bottles, clothes, shoes, and then move towards supplements, fitness kits, destination.'

Gosia feels a series of kicks on her shin. She can't determine if they are singles or doubles. She tries to concentrate on the busy pattern of Picky Becky's top and faces away from Steve.

Picky Becky's plate is whisked off despite Gosia and Steve still eating. Her dessert arrives. A coffee pot, a slice of matcha mousse cake, a dainty china cup, a milk jug and a sugar bowl all protrude into Gosia and Steve's eating space. The bill comes too, in a leather wallet, placed against the napkin stand. Becky presses the plunger, pours herself coffee and adds a liberal amount of milk. She digs into the cake, licks white chocolate glaze off her finger and makes yet another point.

'And finally, I also have a few suggestions to improve your image. We want to keep it true and natural but it would enhance the vision of FitnessCouch if we made a few cosmetic changes.' Becky takes Gosia's hand in hers. 'Gosia, I think you could do with a push-up bra for a start; we can consider breast enlargements later. I think it will have a positive impact on the business from the get-go. Larger breasts attract larger audiences. That's a fact. There is an article about it that I will share with you. We need you to be comfortably a C-cup.'

Picky Becky delivers her truths in a matter-of-fact voice. Looking Gosia deep in her eyes, embedding her reality into Gosia's brain cells while gently pressing the soft flesh of her hand. She lets go and looks at Steve.

'For you, I suggest a little procedure: a chin liposuction. It's a quick way to get rid of fatty folds and enhance the overall facial appearance. It just involves the removal of fatty tissue under the chin, beneath the jowl and along the upper portion of the neck.'

Picky Becky demonstrates on her own face, embraces her jaw with her hands, gently stretches the skin.

'I've had it done twice. It's an instant face refresher. Takes a decade off your face in a quick walk-in, walk-out appointment. It causes minimal discomfort afterwards and it will help our target audience to like you better. Attractive people are taken more seriously, I have some stats about it for you to look at.'

She smiles the reassuring smile of someone who is comfortable with minor sacrifices.

Gosia's leg now receives an almost constant stream of blows delivered haphazardly to her shin and calf muscle.

'Finally,' Picky Becky looks at Gosia with shiny eyes, 'Gosia, I loved how you put it in your text.' She reads from the screen of her mobile phone in a haughty voice: '"A new approach to exercise delivered by a fitness freak duo." This will sell! People love quirky, peculiar and eccentric! I will be honest with you, I hadn't realised until I saw the pictures how bizarre you two look together. A fitness freak show you want to endlessly watch!'

Steve stops kicking, Picky Becky relaxes against her chair and sips her coffee while Gosia shifts uncomfortably.

'So what do you think?' Picky Becky asks.

'I only put it like that to attract your attention,' says Gosia.

'Well, it truly worked! I can envisage a poster campaign with you two showing off your freak sides.' Picky Becky laughs.

Gosia hardens. 'I don't think your vision aligns with ours,' she says.

Picky Becky reacts with a full-teeth smile.

'It is only natural for new start-ups to take a while to adjust to the reality of entrepreneurship. It's not a game for the faint-hearted. I brought some paperwork for you to sign.' She moves her leather handbag onto her lap.

Gosia shakes her head.

'No, you don't get us. We don't want to turn ourselves into a fake duet performing for a rich crowd. We have a vision and it doesn't involve a boob job or vacuuming a chin. We won't be working with you.'

Picky Becky narrows her eyes.

'Can I just make it plain and simple that no one walks out on me? I've already invested my valuable research time in your little *project*. Do you think you can just stand up and go?' she hisses. 'Oh no! You are a small fish in a big pond and I know all the sharks. If you don't join my programme I'll have no trouble finding another, better, *freak fitness duo* of The-Beauty-and-The-Beast type. That. Will. Eat. You. Up.'

Her right hand, like a clam, pretends to chew up all of Gosia's head.

Steve belches loudly, massages his stomach and speaks to Becky's forehead.

'Listening to you gives me indigestion.'

Picky Becky shoots seething looks at them both.

'I did you a favour. I don't usually take on high-risk clients with troublesome upbringings.' She looks at Gosia, hurt. 'This has never happened to me before. You will pay for it!'

Steve takes out his phone, clicks on the camera setting.

'What do you think you are doing?' Picky Becky's face looks confused.

'What do you think I'm doing? I'm taking a picture for our followers. Warning them about people like you,' he snaps.

Picky Becky releases a high-pitched squeak, snatches up her leather handbag and leaves without paying.

Gosia gathers her thoughts while Steve grabs the remaining cake and eats it in two mouthfuls. He pours more of Picky Becky's coffee into her cup and gulps it down. Then he checks the bill, extracts the right amount of cash from his pocket in crumpled notes and warm coins, arranges it into a neat stack and taps Gosia's shoulder.

'I need to go now. I'll get haemorrhoids if I sit on this chair any longer.'

She nods.

Steve adds in a flat voice, 'I know you mentioned that she's nasty but, holy cow, she is a monster. I can't believe you exposed us to her like that. *Freak fitness show*? What were you thinking?' Steve shakes his head. 'I'm ugly, short and fat, all right? I don't want to be telling everyone about it. And I've already told you that I do *not* want it to be my unique selling point!'

'I just tried to attract her attention, to give us a fighting chance. She gets loads of requests like ours, and I didn't say *freak fitness show*, but a fitness freak duo!'

Steve stands up, readjusts his belt.

'Oh did you not, Miss Perfect? Miss Big Brain and Flat Tummy? Miss "I Will Show the World How Open-minded I am Working Out with a Fatty"!'

'Steve!' Gosia tries to grab Steve's hand but he takes a step back.

'Hands off me. I am sick of it. Sick of being a spare part. An add-on. A distraction! You don't think I know why you took me to the wedding?' He hyperventilates. 'I might be short and fat but I am not blind, Gosia. You *used* me. Like some sort of cheap shield because you can't face your family alone! And now you brought this awful woman to the table and I had to sit through that humiliation with tight lips. God, I've had my share of awful people telling me horrible stuff. I don't need any more of that crap, so thank you for your efforts but I don't want anything to do with her or you.'

Gosia shivers.

Steve's face is red, his eyes are a little damp, his voice quivers.

'I really wanted it to work, you know. And I can see that I need some advice but ideally from someone with a conscience. I thought you got me.' He makes a hand motion as if he were cutting an invisible line connecting them both. 'I thought we were friends.'

Gosia's mouth is dry. She is pinned to the chair by Picky Becky's insults and Steve's words.

Steve leaves, abandoning Gosia at the table.

A mute waiter turns up and starts stacking plates, hoovers up the cash and takes away the stained tablecloth.

Gosia bolts for the toilets and locks herself in a cubicle. Above the sink sit two pretty bottles screwed to the wall: magnolia soap and rosemary hand balm. She squirts out liquids from both dispensers until there is none left and leaves the slimy dunes in the ceramic bowl, sliding unhurriedly towards the plug hole, choking it up.

105

A dark and narrow corridor with a lino floor and beige walls full of fresh marks and scratches. An old wooden coat rack with two coats; one large, bulky and pink, and the other well worn and black. The front door is kept wide open by a stack of brown boxes bandaged with parcel tape. Large, wonky writing on their sides is executed in black permanent marker: KITCHEN ESSENTIALS, BATHROOM ESSENTIALS, MAKE-UP ESSENTIALS, ESSENTIAL STUFF and DIARIES.

Gosia stands on the threshold of her room, a few steps from the front door, and shields herself from the cold with a four-ply acrylic scarf wrapped around her upper body. Lyndsey is carrying a box down the hall and panting heavily. She deposits it on top of the others. The stack gently sways.

'Why didn't you give them to the movers?' says Gosia.

Lyndsey holds her contoured face high, the make-up lifting her cheekbones to her eyebrows. She looks shocked at Gosia's suggestion.

'I didn't want my dearest possessions to be handled by some random men. You saw what they did to my furniture!'

The gashes in the wall are deep and dark. Lyndsey insisted that her bed frame needed to stay in one piece and couldn't be dismantled. It took three men to manoeuvre it around the flat's corners.

The moving crew were straining their muscles while Kevin, standing in the way, issued orders: 'Higher, lower, back, to the left.'

Gosia nods. Lyndsey massages her arms. Her phone beeps.

'He'll be here any minute. We're getting this lot into a taxi.'

There is a gentle knock on the door, and they turn their heads. A tall and heavily pregnant woman stands on their soiled doormat carrying a large, decorative tin of cookies.

'Yes?' says Gosia.

'Hi, sorry to bother you. I don't want to be a nuisance on Saturday morning but I'm a bit old-fashioned. We're about to move in,' she indicates a house across the street, with scaffolding all around it, 'and I wanted to meet my neighbours.'

They look at her, at her rectangular knitted dress in light grey made from ripple-textured merino wool with minimal seams, discreet slits at the hemline and clean edges tight around her belly.

'But no one seems to be in.' Her moisturised lips break into a warm smile.

Lyndsey moves a step forward and extends her hand.

'We are in. I'm Lyndsey. Nice to meet you. Sadly, I'm moving out.'

The woman shakes the hand. Opens the tin, offers Lyndsey a cookie.

'Oh, I see. Anywhere nice?' Her voice mellow and sweet, like a concerned doctor's. 'Home-made,' she adds. Lyndsey dips her hand into the tin.

'Moving in with my boyfriend.' She takes a bite, her phone beeps. 'He'll be here any minute.'

'Aww. How lovely. I'm Rosamund. We'll be moving into number 67.' She points again at the house, where some builders are busy hauling bags of rubble towards a skip.

'Yes, Vincent's place,' Lyndsey volunteers between chews.

'You knew him?' Rosamund leans against the doorframe, ears arranged for receiving information.

'Oh yes!' Lyndsey sighs. 'He was a charming man. Very outgoing and private at the same time. A generous neighbour and a real gentleman. They don't make them like that any more.' Lyndsey laughs the laugh of someone high on sugar.

'And what happened to him?'

Lyndsey concentrates on the cookie, considers its crumbling body.

'Accident,' says Gosia. 'Totally unexpected. He died on his way to hospital.'

'Oh.' Rosamund looks at them. 'So all these rumours about troubles of some sort . . .'

'What rumours?' Gosia is quick to react.

'I've heard that it was a murder. In cold blood.'

Lyndsey gasps. Gosia shakes her head.

'People!' Gosia offers.

'Exaggerate,' Lyndsey adds. 'He was a character, no doubt. Died a sudden death. His children dealt with his affairs. Lovely family.' Lyndsey extends lovely into three syllables.

'But what about a man being stabbed at home in this neighbourhood? I saw an article about it and the house in the photo sort of looked like the one we bought.'

'All the houses here look the same,' Lyndsey says thoughtfully.

'I wouldn't trust the newspapers if I were you,' adds Gosia. 'From what I know he was simply having breakfast, reaching for bread with his knife. He slipped and the knife went into his chest. I think journalists like to spice things up a bit and turn innocent events into something sinister.'

'Goodness.' Rosamund shivers in the doorway.

'A sad accident,' Gosia stresses.

Lyndsey helps herself to another biscuit. Rosamund shifts in the doorway.

'Well, I am so glad it wasn't anything menacing. We weren't sure what to believe. The police didn't release any information and the news coverage didn't fit with this peaceful location.' She points towards their street. 'But I burnt a bunch of sage around all the rooms just in case.'

'It's a really lovely place. As long as you get yourself double-glazing you'll find it warm and cosy.' Lyndsey smiles her nice smile, a fleshy raisin bit stuck between her teeth. Her phone beeps. 'Hard to believe I'll be gone in three minutes!'

'And how about you?' Rosamund looks at Gosia.

'I'm moving out soon too. This flat's being sold.' Gosia shrugs her shoulders.

'Ah, what a shame. Have you found somewhere new?' She doesn't wait for a reply. 'House-hunting is such a tiring operation. It took us months, and, in the end, we could only find a project house. We're having some building work done,' Rosamund circles her index finger around her house with its dull noise of drilling and hammering. 'We plan to move in in the New Year.' She massages her belly. 'It's only a couple of months until the new arrival.'

Lyndsey nods.

'It took me weeks to organise things for the move. What a job!' She exposes her shoulder for a congratulatory pat.

'I'd better be going,' says Rosamund. 'Just popped in to check on the building works and thought I might meet a person or two.' She extends the tin again and Lyndsey dips in for another cookie.

'So lovely to meet you both. Good luck with all your moves. Bye-bye for now.'

Rosamund steps back outside, takes the tin to the car parked by the kerb, a low vehicle, of a sporty type, with leather seats and a retracting roof. She switches on the engine and gives them a wave before pulling away.

Lyndsey shakes away the crumbs from her cleavage. Her phone beeps.

'He's just minutes away,' she says, but then turns to Gosia, jolted by a sudden thought. 'I never thought you would do that,' she says sternly. 'Lie about Vincent's murder like that.'

'It sounded to me like you were helping with the cover-up.'

'I had no part in it!' insists Lyndsey, her lip wobbling.

'Well, me neither,' says Gosia and goes back to her room, closing the door tight behind her.

106

A generously paved area in the vicinity of a bus stop in Zone 3. A rare mild December afternoon enhanced with the sun glowing a soft, forgiving light making everyone appear younger and prettier.

Gosia has set up a FitnessCouch feather flag in a heavy base unit filled with twenty-five litres of tap water. She had to bring it all in a wheelbarrow that the upstairs neighbours abandoned in the shared garden. The rusty sides of the cart left dirty marks on the shiny durable plastic of the water base. She stashed the wheelbarrow in a nearby bush, praying no one would take it.

She is waiting for Steve to show up as agreed (before the deadly lunch with Picky Becky), to conduct an outdoor event and present to passers-by an 'Easy weekend workout routine'. Standing next to the flapping flag on her own is unsettling, making her feel like a fool. With Steve here she would not have her guts in a twist; with Steve this exposure would make perfect sense.

She prepared some words of apology, carefully curated sentences in which she is taking the blame, acknowledging her offence and issuing genuine sorrys. As soon as Steve shows up she will action her 'Let's Start Again' plan and they can move on and leave the Picky Becky incident behind. In the near future they will laugh about it and learn from that mistake.

But Steve is nowhere to be seen. He also doesn't know the significance of the bus stop that Gosia suggested. She has never told him that this is Vijay's destination, that this is where he lands after a day at his practice in the city centre and, according to the website, today is his working Sunday. She's never told Steve about her deeply rooted love for Vijay either.

She half hoped that leading this outdoor session together, metres from Vijay's house, would be to her advantage. But now, with Steve no longer in the picture, she suddenly thinks that might be for the better. Steve could restart his serenades and alienate Vijay forever. That knot in her innards loosens; without Steve, this appearance is an act of courage in her ongoing fight for Vijay's heart.

She has their business cards in her leggings pocket and starts a warm-up as she sees a convoy of buses approaching. People stop, their curious eyes watch Gosia bend and stretch. She puts on the professional voice of a friendly, helpful instructor. Her approachable personality switched on.

'Tired of Christmas shopping? Try an instant-relief lower back stretch now!' she shouts to gathered spectators, and to her surprise a couple of people actually join in. She takes full advantage of it. 'It's a two-minute routine that strengthens your core muscles and improves your posture. You'll feel the benefits by the time you get back to your home,' she tells them as she gently adjusts their poses.

Gosia gives out the cards and from the corner of her eye sees the next round of buses drawing closer. She gets ready for the next round of interest.

She spots him as soon as the doors open, people spilling onto the pavement. His face bright, his leather satchel bouncing on his hip. Her magnetic pull brings him closer. He approaches her station, slows down his walk, lifts his head, their eyes meet.

She addresses him directly.

'Hi, nice to see you again.'

He stops. People look at them. She walks towards him.

'Please join me for an instant-relief whole body stretch. You look like you've had a busy day. Those shoulders could do with a bit of TLC.' She speaks directly into his eyes, pausing only once she reaches his personal zone, demarcated by the unmistakable warm, heady scent of cedar wood. 'Just lift your arms, grab your left wrist with your right hand and stretch the side of your body to the right.' She demonstrates. He smiles, puts his satchel down, lifts his arms in the air.

'Like that?' he asks.

'Almost,' she says and steps forward. Her hand reaches up to meet his. Her freshly showered body, mildly exhausted by the wheelbarrowing of the load, is moulding in his image. She multitasks – pulls gently on his wrist with one hand while the fingers of the other run down the side of his body, encouraging deeper extension. She is sure to start at his hip bone and gradually move her hand towards his armpit. He sighs.

'And now on the other side,' she says up towards his ear. He obeys and repeats the side stretch. She is dipping her hand as low on his hip as the circumstances allow, assisting with his stretch. His eyes close and he issues another loud sigh. Then he windmills his arms down and brays like a horse. She jumps to the side.

'That felt great!' He licks his teeth. 'Good to be reminded of one's body.' And then he adds, 'What is it that you do?' He takes in her face, carefully applied blusher, flicks of mascara, lip balm massaged into her pout.

She is on high alert. The hairs on the back of her neck are up, her internal organs ready to erupt, his proximity intoxicating.

'I'm from the local gym, promoting exercise on people's doorstep.' She whips her card from her pocket. 'Here's my number.'

'Nice initiative.' Her card in his palm. 'You are only ever as young as your spine!'

'You sound like you know a lot about it,' she teases, her voice a candy. 'If you are interested in working with us we offer bespoke programmes that fit within busy schedules,' she says lightly, hoping this message will filter down to his subconscious. 'Just give me a call.'

'Thanks for that.' He glances at his watch, 'Shit! Must dash, see ya!' He slips her card into his back pocket.

'Bye,' she replies. Her plan to invite him for a drink sits at odds with him hastily gathering his bag, making a move for his street on the hill. 'See you soon,' she adds.

He turns, looks at her once more, lifts his hand in the air for a gentle, royal wave.

She smiles a million-dollar smile, her teeth all diamonds, shining and sparkling with saliva gathered in her mouth. A voice, loud, hoarse and mocking, brings her back to the pavement.

'Is it my turn?'

She stiffens.

Next to the flapping feather stands Blake, the man from the library, a sneering smile on his red, peeling face.

'So all this self-improvement research has led you to wear Lycra and display your arse?' he asks.

Gosia exhales, controls her hands. People still watch, there is no point making a scene. She doesn't want to harm her brand with reckless words that she might regret later.

Blake is not giving up.

'Can I get that side-body massage that the other bloke received?'

He puts his arms in the air, sways to the right, pretends to stretch.

'Do I do it badly enough for you to adjust *me*?'

'Thank you for your interest, but we have finished our session for today.' She issues the words like a warning announcement and walks towards the bush. With effort, she extracts the wheelbarrow from behind it, carts it to the pavement and starts dismantling her station.

'So it's over now?' Blake teases. 'Looks less like FitnessCouch to me, more like FitnessCrotch, but not for every groin.'

She looks at him, her icy glare heavy with the promise of pain and slaughter.

He takes a step back.

'I was just walking past. Saw you and wanted to say hi.'

'Why didn't you start with that?' Gosia lets the water out into the kerb, where it glugs and gurgles. No one pays attention to them any more.

Blake shifts.

'Do you want a hand with that?' he asks. 'I can help you take it all back.'

'So you'll know where I live and start harassing me on my doorstep? No thank you.' She hauls the water base into the metal body of the wheelbarrow.

'God, you know how to make me feel like a wanker.'

'Maybe because you are one?' Gosia offers calmly and wheels her possessions away.

107

A two-storey cafe/bar attached to an experimental theatre and located by a busy tube station. The establishment is erected between a road full of worn-out council flats and a street of upcycled Victorian terraces. The management offers a 25 per cent discount on tickets for plays and events to people who can prove they live locally. The cafe/bar sells coffee and wine, cake and salad, as well as light warm bites, soups, tagines and arrangements of sharing platters. The tables are long and accommodate eight to twelve people, pretending all visitors are part of an extended family. The place is moderately busy.

Two people, barefoot, sip coffee by the bar and hug yoga mats under their arms. There are men with silver computers scrolling down Excel sheets. A line of industrial light bulbs hangs in front of the floor-to-ceiling windows, glowing the golden light of prosperity and good fortune.

Gosia walks to the first floor and finds Anna at the end of a large table for twelve. The table has a sign: 'Reserved for Anna for 4 p.m.'. The note is carefully handwritten on a small blackboard. Anna lifts her head from her phone and looks at Gosia approaching. She doesn't smile or wave or indicate in any other way that she knows Gosia and is expecting her to join her.

'Hi,' Gosia says and sits two seats away from Anna.

Anna grunts 'Hi' back and only now signals with her hand, freshly manicured, long artificial nails shaped into almonds and painted deep red, for Gosia to move up.

Anna's face has changed. The skin of her neck is sagging and the creases around her eyes are exposed by her foundation, one shade too dark and smudged around her hairline. She is dressed for a business meeting, in a suit and shirt.

Gosia has made no effort. She is wearing a Lycra outfit that she has had on since seven-thirty that morning when she left for work, underneath a zip-up fleece and an old black coat. She took a bus after her shift to avoid getting wet in the drizzly weather. She sat on the upper deck, stuck in traffic, thinking about Steve, who still hasn't been in touch.

Or maybe he has? Her phone, a dead plastic casket, has been discarded into the recycling bin for small electrical objects. She had taken it to a shop where a smiley guy with a heavy Indian accent told her it was 'gone'; some crucial mechanical parts had failed and it would be cheaper to buy a new device. He had removed the SIM card for her and had tried to extract information from the mobile. He delivered the bad news with the tightest of smiles. The data was lost. She only remembers one number by heart, the landline of her parents. She was too proud to look up Steve's details on the gym database.

As Gosia moves, Anna touches something in her suit pocket, scratches the back of her head and taps her ear. There is a low humming buzz of an electronic sort that distracts Gosia. It penetrates her consciousness.

Anna seems not to notice or mind; she clutches a phone in her hand as if for protection.

'So,' Gosia says.

'So,' says Anna.

The silence falls. Gosia tips her head. Tired. Not sure she has time for it.

'So,' says Anna. 'I wanted to speak to you about someone.' She straightens her back.

Gosia looks at her.

'About who? Andy? I have nothing more to say.'

Anna shakes her head slightly, as if worrying that her hair may fall out of place if she puts more energy into it.

'It's not about Andy,' she says.

Gosia waits but Anna doesn't continue.

'Who then?' Gosia asks. She could have been in the library right now, doing some thinking and figuring things out, not playing an odd version of 'Guess Who' with Anna.

'Who do you think I might mean?' Anna asks.

Gosia sighs.

'Anna, I don't have time for this.' She starts standing up.

'Vincent,' Anna hisses. Gosia sits down. 'I want to speak to you about Vincent.'

'I didn't know you knew him,' says Gosia, surprised. She thinks. She started cleaning Vincent's place after Andy left, when she needed money and was emotionally damaged. She can't recall if Vincent was part of their conversations when things were good. Would a person in a stable relationship pay attention to him at all? No, she didn't know who he was before those dark mornings of watching his sunken chest by the table, smelling his stagnant breath, ignoring his withered penis swaying above her from her kitchen floor vantage point.

'I know about what happened,' says Anna. 'I know about the murder.'

'Really?' Gosia is curious now. 'How come? Do you work for the police now?'

Anna smiles a thin smile.

'Do you know how it happened?' Anna asks.

Gosia doesn't know. She suspects, but she doesn't know.

'An accident, I've heard.'

'Gosia, you know it wasn't an accident.' Anna's voice is low and pressing.

'Well, I think he was killed by his cleaner,' Gosia offers bluntly. A little space somewhere deep in her lungs contracting.

'With this,' says Anna, placing a knife in a plastic freezer bag onto the table. It's an old-fashioned sort of knife, with a short, sharp blade and an engraved motif of a rose bush on the handle, its edge smeared in something white, that could be butter.

Gosia knows this knife. It belongs to her. She found it in a charity shop, paid 10p for it. She smiles and says, 'This will disappoint you, but that's my knife.'

Anna bows her head, executes a mini nod for yes.

'I know it is. That's why we are here.' Anna looks at Gosia expectantly.

'I'm not following.' Gosia is bemused and unsettled. Why would Anna keep her knife in a bag? How does she think her knife could be the one that someone pushed into Vincent's chest?

'You can tell me the truth, Gosia,' says Anna, in her heavy whisper. 'I know you did it.'

Gosia takes a moment to absorb this. She dissects Anna's words and then laughs.

'Anna, are you mad?' Gosia starts standing up again. She's had enough.

'Sit down,' Anna hisses and pulls Gosia by her hand. 'Don't make a scene unless you want me to call the police.'

Gosia laughs some more and pulls her hand out of Anna's grip. 'Call whoever you want.'

Her shoulders are seized by someone from behind and she is forced to sit down. She is startled, she cranes her head. It's Kevin. With a long wire sticking out of his ear. He stands behind her. His heavy hands now firmly planted on Gosia's shoulders.

'What do you think you are doing?' Gosia spits at him.

'Listen.' It's Anna again. Her voice commanding. 'We've got the evidence. We know it was you. We have a witness.'

The low-frequency throb intensifies and Gosia can't ignore it now. It spreads, giving her a sudden headache.

'What witness?' Gosia is confused.

'Come through,' says Kevin in an official voice, pressing the wire in his ear and speaking to the inside of his check shirt. Lyndsey appears, and takes a place on the other side of the table, a safe distance apart.

'Tell her,' Anna instructs while looking at Lyndsey, at her wobbly lip.

'I saw you,' Lyndsey says in an injured voice. 'I saw you walking from Vincent's house on the morning he was murdered.' She exhales wheezily, as if freed from a heavy obligation.

'Have you all lost your minds?' Gosia looks at them, at the thin wires sticking out from their ears. The buzz of electronic devices is clearly audible now and pulsates in Gosia's temples.

'You saw me outside the flat where I live and you have my knife as proof?'

Gosia's voice is growing loud. Kevin shifts, pokes her in her ribs and tries to shush her. But she is not having any of it: she uses her teaching voice now, well-pronounced and strong for the ease of the hard of hearing.

'I don't want to have anything to do with you and your crime fantasies. Leave me alone and go and investigate your deranged brains.' Gosia tries to step away but Kevin stops her by tightening his grip on her shoulders, hurting her.

'You can't leave. We are taking you to the police.'

'You must be fucking joking!'

But clearly he is not. The bar staff look their way, all whispers and eye rolls. Anna and Lyndsey's faces are smug. Kevin holds Gosia's body, squeezes her collarbones painfully. He barks orders.

'Stand up. Move right.'

Gosia shakes her head, releases a big sigh. Anna's face lights up, as if this sigh alone were evidence. Gosia is extracted from behind the table, held tight in Kevin's grip, her shoulder and arm in increasing pain.

Gosia was, in fact, by Vincent's door that morning. She faffed with the lock and helped the Bulgarian cleaner to get in. She must have left plenty of fingerprints on the wooden frame and the door handles, but she never crossed the threshold, she had nothing to do with it.

They escort her out, trying to push her down the street towards the police station, clamping their hands on her body, but they are either too inexperienced, or too excited to have nabbed her, and she manages to turn and kick Kevin square in the bollocks. She runs in the opposite direction leaving him on the floor, Lyndsey crouched beside him and Anna wide-eyed and startled.

108

A training studio in a 24/7 fitness centre. All the lights are switched on. Harsh halogen grazes the exposed skin of the attendees. In the room, a group of people in tight-fitting tops and leggings, leather lifting belts and supportive wrist wraps look at themselves in floor-to-ceiling mirrors. An animated instructor in a fitted vest with a large tattoo of a bird of prey on his back stands by the three-tier rack, made from heavy-gauge steel, giving out dumb-bell sets.

Above the instructor's head, covering the tops of the mirrors, hangs a big banner advertising a free training programme. The bottom section of the banner, containing a row of multicoloured logos, has been lifted, folded, creased and secured higher up to reveal more of the mirror and less of the banner.

Gosia walks in. She is very late. She scans the room in search of Steve. He is not there. The instructor acknowledges Gosia with a nod and signals for her to come up.

'All good?' he asks, not really concerned with Gosia's answer.

Gosia is hot, wet and sweaty. She ran all the way back from the cafe/bar with her coat in one hand and a fleece in the other. She is drenched.

'Where is Steve?' she asks.

The instructor looks at her blankly.

'Steve?'

'Steve, the guy that always laughs,' Gosia says.

'The fat guy with a loud voice?' the instructor checks.

Gosia just nods, enraged but empty of the strength to be verbally angry. Steve is so much more than this.

'He dropped out, I think,' the instructor says bluntly. 'Here, grab your set.' He gives Gosia a pair of dumb-bells.

She walks out of the room with the weights and makes straight for reception, where Janelle sits behind the U-shaped counter listening to some motivational podcast on her Bluetooth headset. She had seen Gosia running past a few minutes earlier and hadn't even given her a weak wave.

'Is it true?' Gosia asks.

Janelle wiggles her headphones clear of her ears.

'Pardon?'

'Is it true that Steve left the course?'

Janelle nods.

'He phoned this afternoon.'

'But why?' Gosia's voice panicked, her breath shallow.

'He said it was due to personal reasons.' Janelle looks at her hesitantly. 'But then he told me the truth.'

Gosia's head spins. The dumb-bells keep her vertical.

'How could you do that to him?' Janelle adds slowly, her eyes filling up with fire.

'Janelle, could you give him a ring?' Gosia places one weight on the counter, extends her freed hand for the phone.

Janelle shakes her head.

'No, I can't. It's not a work-related call. Data protection.'

'Janelle,' Gosia pleads, her eyes wet. 'My phone broke. I don't have his number.'

Janelle stares back, a blaze in her voice.

'That's unfortunate. Sorry to hear that, but I don't want to lose my job and I don't think Steve needs any more anguish at the moment.'

Gosia collapses with her chest against the counter, abandons the second dumb-bell on the floor and heads for the changing room.

In the humid breeze trickling from the showers mixed with the stale air of sweaty socks and tops, she cries. Her upper body shaking lightly, her collarbones tender and red, her soul tugged and wrenched. She doesn't stay long. She walks out into the rain.

109

A wet and windy night on a quiet street on a hill lined with terraced houses. Fences soggy with rain. Front gardens pooling with water. Bay windows with blinds pulled down. Faint yellowish lights glimmer. State-of-the-art, flicker-technology light, simulating the glow of real candles (to create a cosy atmosphere), seeps through the fabric of the blinds.

Gosia stands by a rose bush tightly wrapped in horticultural fleece and looks at the windows of house number 11. The lights downstairs are off, apart from a faint shimmer somewhere by the front window. There is clearly activity going on upstairs; she can see the outline of a human figure walking up and down, bouncing.

She crosses the empty road, navigates between parked cars and walks through the metal gate towards the door that looks pale and colourless, but she knows is blue. She traces the silver number 11 with her finger, its metal body gleaming gently in the light of the streetlamp, above it a striking Christmas wreath.

She peers through the bay window, spots bundles of wooden objects, short staves and planks, scattered on a rug. A large cactus in a decorative terracotta pot near the window has a chain of thin fairy lights wrapped around its prickly branches. It twinkles gently.

She knocks.

There is silence. No foot movement behind the door. She knocks again, but louder. She presses her ear to the wood and this time she can distinguish quick steps on the stairs. The wood squeaks.

'Yes?' It's Matt with his muscular chest and soft voice looking at her from behind the half-open door.

'Hi, it's me, Gosia. I need to speak to Vijay.' She looks at him. She holds his gaze until he recognises her.

'Gosia from the supermarket,' he says. The door is open wide now. 'What's up?' He looks tired and worn as he lets Gosia in.

She closes the door softly behind her. She knows she is a mess. Her coat drips water straight onto the doormat, a tough blend of coconut fibres. Her hair is stuck unattractively to her forehead in long wet strands.

'I need to speak to Vijay. It's urgent.' She shakes slightly, tired and cold. She walked up the hill in the storm, the wind beating against her. She is battered and bruised from Kevin's rough handling earlier in the day. Her mind pivots.

Matt watches her suspiciously.

'Sure,' he says. 'I'll get him. Please wait here.'

He walks away, his bare feet disappear around the corner and softly move up the stairs concealed by an L-shaped corridor. She doesn't dare to move off the mat. Her feet ooze rainwater.

There is a muffled conversation somewhere at the heart of this oh-so-comfortable house, two male voices speaking slow, velvet words in the cold night, starved of sleep. Footsteps, faster and lighter, are moving down the stairs. His footsteps.

Vijay emerges from around the bend. He looks dishevelled. His hair untidy, his navy top with a large whitish stain on its shoulder, his face covered in unsightly stubble, his eyes thin slits, drowsy and lacking their usual shine. Not like the man she saw just a week ago.

'What's this about?' He doesn't even look at her, really. He speaks to the space above her head. 'Are you one of my clients? Have I cancelled your appointment? I'm not back at work for another three months, but Naomi Hammond has taken over any urgent consultations.'

'No, no,' Gosia says, her voice barely detectable.

Vijay is looking at her now. His eyes slightly wider. He takes in her face; the wet hair strands stick to her chin.

'I came to say that I . . .' Gosia hesitates. The words are wedged inside her and she pulls them out, forces them into the chill of the corridor. 'That I love you.'

'Pardon?' Vijay is looking at her again. He takes a step back, lifts his left hand to his head for support or orientation. She notices, with a prong of horror slicing through her guts, the shine of a wedding ring on his finger.

A soft cry reaches Gosia's ear. The whimper of a new voice, uncertain of its magnitude and reach. The whimper of a tot. It appears around the corner, in Matt's arms. A little baby in a calm grey suit with subtle yellow detail. Matt bounces gently on his feet, moving forward with a bundle of organic cotton in his arms. He stands beside Vijay. Matching wedding rings glisten.

'All good?' Matt asks, looks at Vijay who shakes his head. 'Tea?' Matt offers and lifts his eyebrow.

'No,' says Vijay. 'We are done here. This woman is leaving. Right now.'

Gosia stiffens. Vijay's face gathers for a storm. His nostrils flared, his lips pursed for a spit, his eyes alert.

'I know who you are.' He points his finger at her as if she has stolen from him. 'You are from that dodgy fitness centre. Why are you following me around? I told you not to contact me again.' His voice is loud, and the baby starts to cry. 'How dare you come here, disturbing my family. Please leave. Now. And don't come back.'

Vijay walks past Gosia and, with a sharp move, releases the lock and opens the door. She looks at Matt. He stands there, muscular and mute, holding the tiny baby tightly, bobbing softly and looking at her with large, surprised eyes. Vijay folds his arms and protects the corridor, prevents entry to his family. The white stain on his top is clearly baby vomit. Gosia can smell its faint sour odour. She opens her mouth for some words of apology, but Vijay's bolted face makes her fasten her mouth and fold her tongue back. She walks out into the rain and rolls down the hill, pushed along by the gales.

She makes it home on account of some basic survival mode embedded in her legs. Autopilot directs her through the abandoned streets where currents of air move bins around and howl like stray dogs in the sullied alleyways. She is a walking lament. All tears and sobs, wet through to her bones, dripping with sorrow.

110

A bare room, big enough to accommodate four people, with table and chairs bolted to the floor and a window you can't see through. A man in front of Gosia is chewing spearmint gum. He maintains eye contact. He asks her questions that she duly answers.

'Do you know why you are here?'

'Why do your former friends think you murdered your neighbour?'

'Why did you not report your neighbour's inappropriate behaviour?'

Her ex-friends hate her and think she is capable of murder. She needed the money, so she endured Vincent's attacks on her hip with his groin. She successfully suppressed an urge to strike him with a hammer or press him to the floor and choke him with a tea towel.

'How did your relationship with Andrew Knight end?'

'Did you contact your ex-partner against his wishes?'

Andy left her. He took everything from her: their meagre, jointly acquired wealth, people and dreams. She doesn't miss him any more and is not bothered by what they had together: an annual trip to Rutland Water, monthly visits to a car boot sale, weekly fish and chips.

'What happened yesterday?'

'Yesterday?' Gosia doesn't want to remember but she explains in words she can barely access what took place at the bar, her peeling knife presented as evidence of a crime. She takes off her jumper, pulls her T-shirt to the side and exposes her bruised shoulder.

The man shifts in his chair, rests his hands on the table, links his fingers together, crosses his thumbs.

'What happened after that?'

She has already tried to forget the last part of the evening. She would like to extract it from her brain and dump it outside of her consciousness. She is silent.

'Did you visit the house of Mr Vijay Kumar?' The man pronounces his name differently to her, with an accent on the first syllable. It sounds wrong.

Gosia straightens her back. Looks at him, at his crossed thumbs.

'I didn't know where else to go. Who else to speak to.' She ducks her head.

The man asks more questions, all plainly structured to elicit a response.

'Have you met Mr Kumar before?'

'Did Mr Kumar give you his home address?'

'How did you know where he lived?'

'How many times did you visit his house?'

'Did you attempt to stage any meetings with Mr Kumar's family or friends in order to get closer to him?'

'Has Mr Kumar ever expressed any feelings towards you?'

The last question lands heavily on her chest, squeezing her lungs and causing an internal fire to spread around her ribcage.

'No,' she whispers. 'He has not.'

The truth is reflected in the shine of the laminate table, its scratch- and heat-resistant top designed for durability: she sought the man of her dreams to meet deep-rooted expectations planted by fairy tales with princesses in castles, bolstered by films, magazines, TV soaps, Mother and Aunt, church, her teenage friends, passing couples, adverts and books. She was taught from a young age that to be happy is to have a man. What a misunderstanding. What a joke. What a lie.

111

A small bedroom with cream walls, scarce furniture and adornments pushed against the walls. The curtains are drawn. A lonely plant, a large peace lily, renowned for its superstar qualities (helping to filter out harmful benzene, trichloroethylene and formaldehyde toxins from the air), its leaves drooping. Somewhere under the yellow-brown flower sheets and the wool-rich cable-knit throw tangled across the bed lies Gosia. She is not asleep, although she must have slept.

There is very little that will make her change her position or extract her feet from under the duvet. She left the bed earlier that afternoon only to use the loo and drink a pint of water. The dim light of the day has turned to dusk.

She cuddles a pillow, her mind foggy. She thinks in simple, declarative sentences: *It's late. I'm tired. There is no point. Life is a bitch.*

Her shoulders and arms hurt, deep purple marks around her collarbones in the shape of Kevin's fingers. That halfwit's hands imprinted on her flesh. She feels sick. That weasel with his criminal case, with his pathetic evidence and a pitiful witness.

The spearmint-gum-chewing detective interviewed her all the way through. He asked her to wait. She counted minuscule squares on the lino floor to keep calm and reached thousands before the detective returned. He told her she was lucky. Mr Kumar wouldn't be pressing charges but she may want to consider reporting a common assault. Her capacity for reply was low, so she just nodded.

Anna, Kevin, Lyndsey – they all stood there, looking pale, in the small and drab waiting area at the police station. The detective's parting words were: 'Do not play Sherlock Holmes at other people's expense.'

Gosia touched his arm.

'And how do I report the assault?'

That's when Kevin started crying.

She'd never seen a man cry like that. Her dad excels in a single tear pooling in the eye socket. Andy used to get teary in a dry-eyed way, when his football team was winning or losing, all the moisture dispensed through his nose. This was different. Kevin's eyes like two oscillating lawn sprinklers provided an even coverage in a two-inch radius, salty tears jetting out for minutes on end at steady pressure.

The detective offered to take her statement straight away before the evidence faded away. She said she needed to rest first. He nodded and left.

Kevin at that point was pretty much on his knees, in convulsive spasms, saying on repeat, 'Please, no, please, no, please, no.' Lyndsey gathered his limbs off the floor and shoved him into a minicab.

That left Gosia with Anna, who was standing tight-lipped and whey-faced, eyes jutting out towards the exit.

'I feel a bit of a fool,' Anna said in a repentant voice.

'A bit of a fool,' Gosia repeated slowly. 'Not like a moron? Total muttonhead? A fucking twerp? A cunt?'

She wishes that she had had a longer list at the ready. Each word, like a slap, landed on Anna's face, distorting it. A police officer, an obedient audience, stood by the door, silently cheering Gosia along.

'I don't ever want to see you again,' said Gosia before leaving and heading back to the flat, and straight under her duvet.

Since she has woken up this morning, it is Steve she has thought about the most. How good she felt in his company, how she enjoyed his humour, warmth and generosity. And how she had let him down. She did say 'freak duo' in her text to Picky Becky. She said other things, too, that Becky did not quote. She wishes she could eat her words up.

She has never had a friend like Steve. None of the people she was close to before were that open and honest. Steve's hunger for life shines from his face. He wants it more than other people. He keeps grabbing at it. He taught her how to want more of it too.

Their joint venture was freeing and fun. It brought them together in a way she did not think possible. When she asks herself, when she is honest with herself, it is true that she sees Steve as the unconventional part, the anomalous half, making her the usual, the standard, the typical element of their team.

She feels sick with herself. She throws up onto the floor. The yellowish, watery liquids reek of acid. The sharp acerbic taste of her well-preserved sense of privilege and normality spreads across her dry mouth. She gags again. Her stomach cramps and a new bout of sick, thicker and creamier, lands on the floor. It lasts for a few minutes but these minutes feel like years, each burst of vomit violently emptying her gut.

Gosia looks at the sludge cooling by her bed and can take it no more. She cleans it up with her slutty dress; slime catching in the lace, leaving slippery smears behind. She puts the fabric straight into the outdoor bin.

It's dark outside. There are stars. The world keeps silently moving.

112

A heavy morning already stained with coffee. The street is quiet, thick mist wrapping around the gate. Gosia sits in her room and stares at what was once Vincent's kitchen window. She woke up early, strangled by the clammy sheets, her heart racing, her hands shaking. She thought about Vincent and her chest tightened, because she didn't want to think about him any more.

Yes, she had seen the cleaner that morning. Gosia had been walking back from her night shift at the supermarket just as the cleaner arrived at Vincent's door.

They had met before. Her name was Penka. Her English had been basic and she was timid. Gosia had shown her the ropes and wished her good luck.

But, that morning, Gosia simply asked her how things were. She kept the words plain and apart; she wanted to be understood. She wanted the cleaner to know that she cared. Penka nodded. Her body wrapped in a thin coat. Her eyes red, her small hands holding the key to Vincent's front door.

'Lock,' she said and extended the key in Gosia's direction. It was a tricky lock and sometimes Vincent bolted himself in from inside, keeping his cleaner waiting. Gosia fitted the key into the hole and manoeuvred it up and down until some mechanical tension loosened up, the key turned and the door opened. Gosia stepped back,

Penka thanked her in bows and blessings and disappeared behind the heavy wood.

She saw her a bit later, carefully drawing the kitchen curtains. He had always asked Gosia to do the same but she had refused.

There was forever the heavy smell of burnt toast in that kitchen. Vincent loved scraping away the charcoal with a blunt butter knife. He would probably have hummed one of his post-war songs and tried to catch her eye, while Penka wiped the floor. Gosia could bet that he was sat in his usual way: legs spread, bare-chested and hairy. He must have already grabbed her buttocks at least twice, and Penka would have patiently swatted him away with a tea towel.

She cleaned the floor with small, harsh movements. Gosia saw her once before with her hands clasped around the mop on the porch. She recognised that shallow breath.

Perhaps Penka's eyes were fixed on the ketchup smudges running down the kitchen unit and hitting the floor. He always had hotdogs for supper.

Vincent would be slowly spreading chunks of butter on bread, looking around and sighing excessively. He often, purposefully, forgot the marmalade. He would stand, the hand towel wrapped around his loins no doubt landing on the floor. He'd chortle, swaying his shrivelled willy as he walked to the fridge.

She would look away.

He would move the jars around.

She would scrub the tomato sauce off the tiles.

'I've run out!' he would say. Shut the fridge. Expose his hollow chest. Scratch his thigh. Move towards her.

The floor would have shone but Penka would surely pretend she hadn't finished yet. She'd have trained herself to leave without warning, before he'd have a chance to press himself against her for a goodbye kiss, the smell of his stale mouth making her gag.

She'd hold the mop firmly. Her eyes would accidentally alight on the knife, beckoning her over. She'd check the curtains, mute fabric covering the window tightly.

She only came here to clean. He had no right. She'd looked him in the eye, told him not to approach her. He ignored her. Laughed at her shaking hand, at the pathetic length of the blade. He'd moved closer. She was scared. There was no time to hesitate.

Gosia has never doubted that it was Penka, that she killed that man. Gosia would have done the same if Vincent had ever pushed things further. She would have twisted the knife into his chest, to be certain. She had quit instead. Was she a coward?

Now the thought of wanting Vincent dead makes her feel embarrassed and uneasy. She shudders. She has never been told what to do with difficult emotions, how to acknowledge them and let them pass. Mother would smoke a cigarette. Dad would leave the house. Bernie would shout. Chrissy would cry. Nobody would talk about it.

And so here she is, alone. Holding onto her raw soul, her dirty parts exposed, and no clue what to do with them next.

113

A firmly shut door in front of a council-run library at 8.50 a.m. A librarian has arrived. He had walked past Gosia earlier, letting himself in, while leaving her standing in the punishing rain until they officially opened.

A gutter above an old, narrow portico is leaking. Water bleeds in a heavy stream, slides down the wall towards the pavement and rushes down the hill. Gosia watches it go.

A man in a sturdy oilskin jacket approaches. He halts close to Gosia, shortening the distance in a way suggestive of an existing intimate relationship.

'Hi,' says the guy, his face red and raw. He smiles. 'Long time no see! Continuing with your research?'

Blake keeps standing there, inches from Gosia's face, close enough to make them look like an item. Close enough for Gosia to smell his cologne. She is about to step back when he takes out an umbrella from his cavernous pocket, opens it and holds it above Gosia's head.

'I'm done with the research,' she says. 'You were right. It is a load of bollocks.'

He laughs.

'That's interesting you say that. What put you off?'

She shrugs. Droplets roll off the umbrella onto her shoulders, seeping into the soggy coat.

'It's all about being like everyone else – a couple! And then . . .' she uses her fingers to list the rest, 'A couple of kids, a couple of bank accounts, a couple of houses, a couple of cars, a couple of holidays a year.'

Blake nods.

'What's not to like?'

'What do you mean?' Gosia searches Blake's face for a smirk.

'That's the best deal, right?' He seems serious. He copies her and uses his fingers to count. 'People want family, security, home.'

'It's a lie, Blake. A big, fat lie.' She stamps her foot as she says it. 'But people use it like a blueprint. If you miss out, you are a loser. You are out. And,' she inhales, 'throughout that book, it's me being used as an example of someone pathetic and warped.'

Blake's face softens. He touches her arm, she feels the warmth of his hand through her waterlogged coat. 'That's a load of baloney. You've got what it takes to have it all.'

She doesn't escape his touch, but she doesn't fall for it either.

'You don't get it. I don't want it all,' she says firmly.

'What do you want?' Blake moves an inch forward and his hand travels up to her shoulder. It might be a sleazy rub or one full of misplaced hope, but she welcomes human contact and what sounds like a genuine question. It's been days since she talked to anyone. She is hungry for touch; she suspects Blake is too.

'I just want to love myself,' she says, looking Blake in the eyes. 'What do you want?'

The librarian opens the door, looks at them both with confusion and concern. Watches Blake's hand on Gosia's body, arches an eyebrow, straightens his own sleeve, clears his throat.

'Morning,' he says to them both.

But Blake ignores him and holds her gaze. There are droplets of water, rain or tears, gathered all around his eyes. He moves his hand off her shoulder, slowly steps back and folds the umbrella.

'I want you to be my wife, breed with me a couple of kids, divide our time between a remote Devon farm and a town house in London. Maybe holiday a couple of times a year in, let's say, the Alps and the Algarve. And ideally drive matching four-by-fours. Would you rather go for black or silver? Your choice.'

Gosia makes a weak attempt at a laugh. Should she be amused, flattered or scared?

'Sorry for being such a wanker the other week,' he adds. 'I promise to leave you alone. There's my witness.' He points at the librarian. Gosia, startled, just nods.

114

A manager's office in a 24/7 fitness centre. A poky, airless room with an inconveniently large desk swamped by files and folders. Sasha sits on the edge of her leather chair, pressing her rump into its deep foam cushioning. Above her desk hangs a picture of three happy young women spinning gallantly on stationary bikes, their eyes glistening. Today, Sasha looks nothing like the younger self displayed in the photo. The bags under her eyes are heavy with concealer, her hair is unwashed and gathered into a thin, messy bun on top of her head. She doesn't smile. She looks at Gosia.

When Gosia arrived this morning, she was told to make her way straight to Sasha's office. Janelle, stationed at reception, opened her mouth and then closed it and pointed, flight attendant style, towards the manager's office.

Gosia sits in the designated chair, which is pathetically small and flimsy in comparison to the manager's. She doesn't dare look into Sasha's eyes.

'I'm afraid there's not much I can do,' Sasha says in the measured voice of a fair person. 'Mr Kumar phoned last week and outlined your trespassing in great detail. He went straight to head office, bypassing our branch. So, as I'm sure you understand, it leaves me with no choice but to dismiss you.' Sasha lets her words settle. 'I'm very sorry.'

Gosia just nods. She expected repercussions; not least for missing her three eight-hour shifts the previous week. That must have been a headache. They are low on staff.

But she underestimated Vijay's outrage; she stupidly hoped she had only come across as a bit lame and harmless. She takes in the loss of her job calmly but she tries to detect from Sasha's tone of voice how much of the fine detail Vijay has gone into.

'Head office gave clear instructions. You are dismissed with immediate effect. They have convinced him not to go to the press with it.' She pauses. 'So there is no harm to the business.' She exhales. 'You'll be paid this month's salary in full, if that's any help.' Sasha tries to make eye contact, catches Gosia's flat gaze.

Gosia is grateful though she can't show it at this minute. Her internal parts are haphazardly kept in place with what feels like Sellotape.

'And I'm sure I can give you a reference that omits this transgression,' Sasha continues. 'Nothing too colourful, but enough to gain you employment elsewhere.'

'How about the course?' Gosia asks. She is surprised that the words make sense. That she formed a sentence.

'The course.' Sasha searches the wall behind Gosia's head. 'Ah, the fitness instructor course. Let me check.' She dips her head into a folder in front of her, pushes some papers around and finds what she is looking for. 'You'll need to join the gym, like the rest of the cohort.'

She taps now on her computer, flips the papers.

'Feedback from the group you teach is excellent. I can't see why you shouldn't finish. Continue as usual. The transgression, as I gathered,' she pauses, looks at Gosia in a concerned way, 'was to do with a misplaced infatuation and breach of data protection caused by these strong feelings. I wouldn't want to class it as habitual abuse and a threat to the wider community.'

Gosia feels her face filling with blood, radiating embarrassed heat. So, does everybody know she was wrapped up in platonic love for a man she didn't realise was gay?

'I spoke to him,' Sasha adds, 'later in the day. He was . . .' She hesitates. 'He was outraged.' She sighs. 'He said they had just adopted twins and he needs to protect his family.' She licks her lips. 'Basically, he wants you as far away from them as possible.'

Gosia nods. The pressure in her skull is hard to withstand. The veins in her throat rhythmically pulsate. She stands up and her eyes fill with celestial bodies, comets with tails of gas and dust zooming in all directions.

Sasha moves around her desk, extends her hand and holds Gosia's cold arm. Sasha hasn't slept much. Her skin is tight around the bones of her face, dry patches of eczema on her neck, a couple inflamed and raw. Sasha's voice is warm and kind.

'It was such a pleasure to work with you, Gosia. I wish you all the best.'

Gosia leaves. Janelle is waiting by the U-shaped counter with a bag-for-life full of Gosia's paraphernalia – her favourite mug, her spare top, her course folder, her trainers. Janelle places the bag on the floor, takes a step back, doesn't offer a hug or a wave, hides behind the counter and keeps her distance. Gosia gathers her stuff and squeezes her innards so as not to spill them on the ground.

The day is grey and humid. Water still leaks from the clouds. Gosia walks away.

115

A cold morning in a council-run library with a temporary heating system implemented while a broken boiler is being replaced. Small, old, domestic oil heaters are distributed evenly around the room and emit an inadequate amount of heat. The faint smell of burnt dust loiters in the room. The library is deserted but full of notices stuck to available surfaces informing of the heating failure and circulating apologies that the regular events and classes are being cancelled. The lone librarian deals with injured books at the desk, woolly hat on.

Gosia is the only computer user; she is seated at the screen closest to the oil heater. She is mindlessly scrolling through comments, her hands encased in gloves.

Rich_M wrote: 'This cheered me up no end I must say. I assume this hopeful title celebrates the long-awaited end of this pseudo-poetic journey and a fast disappearance from the poetry platform.'

KarenStevensWrites wrote: 'Written in a visual and visceral way. The triangle of durations of a cigarette, a film and a day created a very pleasing if sad and disquieting image that speaks of an individual end as opposed to the grand end of the world. This work provoked me to write a new poem *Terminus* that can be found here.'

R_M wrote: 'Rubbish. Redundant. Remove.'

TheBestOf_Suzie wrote: 'This poem touched me at a time in my life when I find myself anticipating unexpected events that will turn my comfortable life upside down. As a young mother of a young child I constantly find myself lost in a vicious circle of worry: what about the environment and climate change? What about jobs for future generations? On top of it are the daily worries. Is my husband safe at work? His retail consultancy position sees him covering large patches of the country in an old vehicle. This morning, when I tried to reach him on his mobile phone and couldn't, horrific images began flashing before me. With relief, I learnt that it wasn't the end of my world but just a mobile phone network failure. But this poem unnerved me and I don't know if it is a good thing, to feel so haunted by it.'

Woman_with_patience wrote: 'Punchy work. Clearly successfully scraping at the scab covering common fears. Even the crude comments of the sexist thickheads didn't spoil it for me.'

The end

It ends like a fag
with a stub
with thin smoke
a reeking smell that leaks into flesh
the end

It ends like a film
with a dark room
empty seats
an endless list of unknown names
the end

It ends like a day
gauzy light
porous air
the tar of sky in the east
the end

116

A half-empty corridor in a 24/7 fitness centre. A few people prop up the walls and navigate social media with their thumbs. They all wear versatile, finely textured leggings for outdoor and indoor training sessions, and soft, sleeveless tops that suck in sweat thanks to the technical properties of the fabric.

Gosia, on her way in, had passed by the FitShop display. Winter hats on solid metal stands, ribbed, double-layered beanies offering luxurious warmth. A section of runners' gloves in block colours. Fleeces made from thick, soft fabric enabling heat retention. All thrown together, among artificial holly berries and leaves, with neither taste nor thought, colours and textures clashing. She would have done it differently.

Gosia hesitates. The gym looks different. Hostile and alien. People she used to know don't even lift their heads, don't acknowledge her with a nod.

She stands for a long time by the water cooler, filling up her canary-yellow plastic container with cold liquid that comes out in a trickle. She makes bets with herself. If the water runs out before her bottle is full, she will leave this place and this course and never come back. She watches the dribbling stream, holding onto her promise, when something bright catches in her peripheral vision. She lifts her head. That high-tech outfit in statement colours can only belong to one person.

She follows, quickens her step, takes a sharp right and moves through the doors to a generous room all set for a spin class. Barnaby in the front row mounts his water bottle in the holder provided. Gosia makes her way straight for him, and, when Barnaby turns his head, she is already crying. Large, perfectly formed droplets cascade down her face. He just extends his arms and she folds her entire weedy body into Barnaby's, between the muscular flesh of his limbs, with her chin resting on the mesh of his high-stretch top.

She delivers some non-audible words into his torso and Barnaby directs her out of the room, holding onto her bones. They end up sitting on the floor, in a quiet nook away from any prodding gaze. Barnaby settled with his back against the wall and with Gosia's head in his lap, her middle convulsing, her weeping muffled by the fabric of Barnaby's garments. His hand is softly brushing her ribcage and the alcove shifts and recasts itself as it's slowly filled with a lullaby sung in Barnaby's dulcet voice.

When the song ends Gosia lifts her head.

'I miss him so much,' she says. Her face a pink and sticky mess.

'But he hasn't died, my darling,' Barnaby laughs. 'He's around. Angry as fuck, and still with your blade stuck in his back. But he is around.'

Gosia sniffles, removes the moisture off her face with the worn cotton of her sleeve. Her other hand is in Barnaby's warm and consoling clasp.

'Will he ever forgive me?' she asks in a bashful tone, searching for a 'yes' in Barnaby's eyes.

He hesitates. Voluminous amounts of air pass through his nose and there is a slight twitch of the carefully threaded eyebrows.

'It's complicated,' he offers. 'I've seen him hurt before and I've been telling him ever since to hold a bit more back, be a bit more reserved with giving his heart away . . . You know, assess people properly. He said he would. Then he meets you and tells me he made a true friend and a business partner. I was mortified, thought you were yet another pretty woman in urgent need of a gay best friend.'

Barnaby caresses her hand in a series of soft, soothing strokes.

'I advised him against starting any business dealings with you but it was too late.' He sighs. 'So I had to check out your credentials myself. I was relieved that you turned out to be a classy girl, solid, confident and open-minded. I read you as a trustworthy human and a staunch champion of Steve's. I liked your razor-sharp tongue and thought you'd use it to protect him.'

Barnaby says the words slowly, letting them release in Gosia's head.

'Steve is like a brother to me. I hate seeing him in pain like this. He's a mess, busy squashing his dreams. It hurts, you know?'

Barnaby looks into Gosia's eyes – between the puffy flesh. She nods. She knows.

'I know,' she says weakly, teardrops forming all over again.

'I was totally taken aback, thought it was just a joke when he called you his soulmate,' Barnaby says, holding her tight, gently rocking her backwards and forwards. 'I guess I'm jealous.'

'I think he's my soulmate too,' Gosia says through the salty drizzle trickling down her throat.

Barnaby moves her away from his torso, holds her gangly arms in his tender grip.

'Why don't you answer his calls then? Did you block his number?'

Gosia quivers.

'My phone broke. And I lost my job. And I have no money to get a new one.'

'Hold on.' Barnaby cocks his head. 'So, you really, really want Steve back?' His face fills with an expectant smile.

'I miss him so much.' She catches the air in inadequate amounts. 'I thought he would be here. At the evening class. And. That I'd get to say. Hello. And. That. I'm sorry.'

She stammers. Halts for breath.

'But he left. The course. And. I don't. Know. Where. He. Lives.'

117

A warm corridor with bright, fluorescent strip lighting on the ceiling. The walls swim in a seaweed colour and are disturbed at frequent intervals by the tiger-orange rafts of the flat doors. There are no windows. The floor surface is covered in a slip-resistant polythene material in dark smears of grey, resilient and durable. The notice stuck to the community board informs residents that the floor, recently installed, comes from a Nordic range, inspired by the Scandinavian, unadorned style, and is suitable for use in commercial kitchens, washrooms, changing rooms, entrance halls, stairs and corridors. It has proven to save up to 60 per cent in maintenance costs due to a pattern that successfully conceals dirt.

Barnaby and Gosia take the lift to the top and calmly walk past the algae-coloured walls. They stop at door number 111. Barnaby knocks lightly with his almond-shaped fingernail. He taps the surface with care. His arms migrate to Gosia's shoulders, embracing her like a gift. The door opens to reveal Steve, standing in his sweatpants and an oversized hoodie, biting his lower lip.

'You two should talk,' Barnaby says and pushes Gosia forward into the aperture of the door. Steve moves aside, letting her stumble over the threshold, onto the tiled floor of the poky hallway.

Barnaby waves his hand, blows a kiss and heads towards the lift cheerfully singing: 'Bye-bye, bye-bye, bye-bye.'

Steve closes the door, chances a look at Gosia and asks in a detached voice, 'What do you want?'

'I'm sorry.' Gosia keeps calm, forces her eyes to stay dry. 'I let you down. You were right: I did think of you as different, unusual, maybe even a freak. I sold you cheap to that awful woman.'

Steve sighs. His hand on the door handle.

'And I'm ashamed of it. And I know you must hate me, and never want to see me again.'

Steve nods.

'But I can't imagine not having you in my life. You are my best friend,' Gosia continues.

'Let me stop you there.' Steve moves towards her, his hand curled in a fist. 'And let's get this straight. You think I'm a monster, a freak that decided to tone up, and you want to be friends?'

Gosia hesitates.

'I didn't mean it like that.'

Steve sighs. 'I don't have time for this.' He circles her with his index finger. 'You are wasting my time. Please go now.'

'Steve,' Gosia pleads, 'I want to make it work.' She bites her lip. 'Yes, for a while I saw you as a loud, fat, obnoxious guy, always in my space. But that has changed! I was so stupid and so wrong.'

Steve makes a face, unamused.

'You're not that, Steve. You are a funny, smart, generous, caring man! I want you in my life and I want to be in yours.' She pauses.

Steve watches his feet intently. 'I don't think you're the right size for my life. Look at us. We don't belong.'

'But we do!' Gosia extends her hand. Steve steps back. 'We both want to be ourselves and be happy with all that goes on in our heads.' She cranes her neck to catch his gaze. 'But first of all, Steve,

I am very, very sorry. I'm such a dumb-bell. But I promise to do my best to never, ever hurt you again. Please give me another chance. I've changed. Or at least, I'm changing.'

Steve emits a long, deep, audible breath. The air is still, the light bulb above their heads hums at low frequency. Steve slowly lifts his blue eyes to Gosia, pearls of tears rolling down his cheeks.

'I need to think about this.' He reaches for the door handle and opens the door. With his chin, he instructs Gosia to walk into the corridor's jaws. 'Please leave.'

She walks out. Turns around. The door shuts tight behind her.

'I'll come back next week,' she says to the spyhole and waves goodbye.

118

A chilly, council-run library kept just above a limb-numbing temperature with an assortment of domestic oil heaters turned up high. The continuous low purr of the machines fills the air. The library is moderately busy with solitary users lingering within the heat radius. The notices stuck to the walls are now updated with the much-anticipated date of the installation of the new heating system. A pair of customer service assistants race trolleys full of books around the room decorated with handmade paper chains and cheap silver baubles.

Gosia blows warm air onto her fingers. She reads.

TheBestOf_Suzie wrote: 'This is the best poem I've read this week. A friend that can admit a mistake is a good friend!'

KarenStevensWrites wrote: 'A metaphor for friendship being a voyage on a ship appeals to me greatly. And how easy it is to sink an important boat like that! I feel your pain, I hope you can rescue your vessel. I wrote about my failed friendships too, thought of them as car collisions. Interesting use of transport as a way to speak of emotional closeness. See my poem "Crash!"'

Rich_M wrote: 'I can clearly see that you are high-risk. The way you talk about your friend is disgusting. No wonder he left you behind. I would too. Your poem is yet again another step backwards in our fight for a better and fairer society. We do not need voices that undermine that work.'

R_M wrote: 'With your mug you can only hope for a fat guy to do you.'

Woman_with_a_friend wrote: 'My best friend is the heat of my soul too.'

Love Letter to My Best Friend Who I Failed

It took a downward facing dog
To gaze beyond my navel
I saw That
Fat Guy
With a Loud Voice
Doing better than me

He started talking to me
About things in common
Short-fused
Muddy lives
With self-love deficit glee
Abused by significant others

It surprised me how easy it was
To be around him
Dream up
A shared dream
A ship of high hopes
But I failed us, sailed onto rocks

It took a downhill fall
To pierce my inner coat
Spill open
Loose change
Of my soul
Laid bare contents all cold

As I float I say those words

I'm sorry I'm sorry I'm sorry
I was wrong I was wrong I was wrong
I hurt you I hurt you I hurt you
My fault My fault My fault

In the ditch
I make myself whole
I see sky
I see sun
And I know
My best friend is the heat of my soul

I don't want to walk ahead
Without you my captain
My skipper
My friend
I'm high-risk
Please risk me again

119

An orange door. Green walls. A durable grey floor. Harsh overhead light. Stale air. A quickened heartbeat. Sweaty palms. Soft knees. A knot in the guts. A lump in the throat. A dry mouth.

Gosia knocks. Steve opens the door an inch. It's only been forty-eight hours.

'I wrote a poem for you,' she says to the narrow gap. 'That's what I used to do on a Wednesday before the course. I'd go to a library and I'd write poems.' The gap remains small. 'They are about all sorts of things. Like bad sex, or people who don't love me.' She slips an A4 sheet folded in half through the opening. 'And I wrote one about us.' The sheet is pulled out of her hand. 'It needs more work,' she adds quickly. 'But I wanted to show it to you.'

The silence falls. The light in the corridor goes off. The darkness is complete, save for a crack of light seeping through the door crevice, where now she can see a foot, bare and hairy, standing still on the tiled floor. She flaps her hands for a sensor to kick in, for the lights to flicker back on.

The door opens slowly. Behind it stands Steve with the A4 sheet in his hand, his face ready for a sob. She takes a tentative step forward, opens her arms slowly and then Steve embraces her.

They hug and cry, and then cry and laugh, and then smear away mucus with the backs of their hands.

They finally move from the cramped hall into a living room with single-glazed windows unobstructed by net curtains where city lights flicker and sparkle. Gosia gasps. But the usual sensation of whirling is not overwhelming her. Her inner ear feels surprisingly stable and balanced, as if her vertigo has switched itself off. She walks towards the window. Its sill supports an army of succulents planted in the brown plastic containers typically used by supermarkets to sell mushrooms. She gently squeezes one fleshy leaf and turns to look at Steve.

He stands by a sofa. A smile fills his round, unshaven face.

'Tell me what the hell happened to you. You look like you've been flattened by a truck.'

Gosia smiles, weakly.

'My life is a shambles. I managed to lose you, my job and my mind almost simultaneously.'

He nods and points at the faded sofa with a nest of floppy cushions in pale, washed colours. She plunges between the soft fabrics. A fat brown cat mottled with dark stripes settles in her lap and, instantly, she feels at home.

120

A drab kitchen with peeling, blemished, patterned wallpaper in jaunty yellow. A scruffy dresser, with oil marks on the woodwork, is pushed against the wall, its shelves vacant. A single window, splattered with washing-up liquid, frames a small, abandoned garden. Overgrown stems of a fruit tree poke through the fence into the neighbour's yard and a plastic sheet in bright yellow is tangled in the roots of a nearby bush. Broken flowerpots and an abandoned garbage truck suitable for children under five, made from safe, non-toxic materials, litter the paving stones.

A couple of chipped mugs with steaming black tea slowly mark the top of an extendable table. A white, mass-produced plate made of earthenware (dishwasher, microwave and freezer safe for everyday convenience), is filled with a slender selection of biscuits: custard creams and digestives lying in two straight rows.

Gosia and her dad sit on rickety chairs and watch the curls of tea mist dissipate into the kitchen air. The room is cold. Gosia is layered like an onion in blouses and fleeces. Her father in his thin, frequently washed polyester shirt designated for household chores, all wrinkly face, prominent moustache and gaps between his teeth.

'You don't have much,' Dad says in a grave tone, borrowed from his wife, scrutinising her boxed-up possessions.

'I don't need much.' Gosia chances a sip; the warmth of the cup spreads through her numb fingers.

They sigh and observe the walls and make small, considered movements, adjusting their bodies on the chairs, deterring the biting cold from their limbs.

'I can pay for your heating. It's unthinkable to be sitting in a place like this. You'll get a chest infection, or worse, in no time,' Dad says. He looks concerned, worried even, but doesn't extract any hard cash from his pockets, doesn't mention all the money he owes her. His eyes are observing the damp patches by the window where a furry growth of dark green fungi spreads like a rash.

'I can pay for it myself. Just being careful with money this month. As I said, I'm looking for a job.' Gosia offers a non-committal smile that could easily be adapted into a frown.

'Yes, you said.' Dad nods, registers the bare facts. His daughter, the eldest child, is moving out from this damp hole into a grisly high-rise. Steve's tower block is part of the sprawling estate on the other side of the high street, where the crime statistics are bound to be worse, and people more diverse, in a troublesome way.

She described Steve's house in detail, in an attempt to paint a picture of a calm household: two bedrooms with a generous lounge, a narrow kitchen, a tiled bathroom. A place where Steve has lived all his adult life.

'Steve?' Dad furrows his brows.

'Steve,' Gosia confirms. 'You've met him. He came with me to Bernie's wedding.'

Father's face remains creased and rumpled.

'Is he,' Dad swallows, 'your boyfriend now?'

She smiles.

'He is my best friend. We really get on. Not like her.' She makes a hand movement to indicate the other room that used to be Lyndsey's. Gosia is trying to keep Lyndsey out of her mind. The door is shut. She only had one brief look at the soiled walls, the scuffed floor, the voluminous coils of hair and dust in the corners.

'And will you be home for Christmas?'

The fact that he is asking suggests to Gosia that he anticipates a 'no'. She shakes her head, freed from the obligation of an obedient daughter. But there is a growing sorrow within her, trapped by the wall she erected to keep her mother away. Its hard, sharp shape is throbbing in her ribcage. Rebuffing a parent stings.

'I will miss you.' His voice is far from pleading. The voice of someone who would also like to escape the rigmarole of turkey and tension by the tree, TV on mute, sofa dramas and the sogginess of the pudding.

He had arrived earlier with a bottle of thinner, and a selection of paintbrushes acquired in a pound shop on his way to the flat, the bristles shedding already.

When she phoned, from Steve's phone, she mentioned to Dad that she might Polyfill a few holes and paint a wall or two. Since then she had read her contract. The terms she had signed were unrealistic. There is no way Martin Martin would give her deposit back unless she redecorated the whole place and splashed out on a professional end-of-tenancy cleaning service.

She would rather see the place rot. The decaying walls are feeding off her own decline, her fanciful imaginings and improbable undertakings. The fuzzy growth of mould is suckling on her prejudice and bigotry, her delusional thoughts corroding the beams. She is not sorry to leave it all behind. She had made a list of things that tie her to this place and she had disconnected from them one by one: utilities, council tax, bank statements.

'And what happened to that job you had?' Dad says in as non-intrusive a way as possible, in an attempt to keep the conversation going.

'I lost it,' she says flatly. 'There was a justified complaint and they sacked me. So I'm looking for something else.'

Dad chews on this.

'And your course?'

'I'm still doing that.' All her hopes are now pinned on getting qualifications.

'You know, when you were little, I lost a big business. Had to sack lots of people. That debt is,' he indicates a size with his hands and she knows he means thousands, 'I'll always have it.' He shakes his head and pendulous moustache. 'Thank god the house was in your mother's name.' He empties decades of resignation from his lungs in one long sigh. She has heard the story of his decline many times over from her mother. A story of a loser. 'And all because I took risks. Did you take risks?' His eyes on her.

'I broke the data protection law. But not for money.' She dithers, envelops the cup with her hands and seeks the right words among the stains on the floor. 'I thought I was in love.'

'Ah, love,' her father smiles. '*Miłość*,' he adds in the language of turbulent, rustling consonants. 'I loved like that, once, too. I loved her so much it almost hurt. It was such a strong feeling. She was . . .' He brushes his moustache, his chafed fingers stroking it in regular intervals. '. . . Exhilarating.' He smiles a broader smile, a gauze of moisture on the surface of his eyes. It's clear he doesn't mean Gosia's mother. 'I walked into a room and felt loved with the intensity of a furnace. It was breathtaking. Did you feel like that?'

It is a serious question, put forward with an open mind, with the hope of understanding. She shakes her head.

'I think it was my replacement strategy. A substitute of sorts. Like an instant coffee.'

She cites word for word Steve's diagnosis of her heart, delivered to her after a pot of tea and a series of large glasses of dry, red wine. Steve did not ridicule her, did not minimise the torment of her soul.

'You were alone,' he said, 'you invented that love to save yourself.'

Now it's clear to her that she succumbed to a self-inflicted delusion and it didn't even feel like love. It felt like a hallucinogenic trip; it was easier to pretend to love someone than be on her own.

Her dad nods.

'Not a good strategy,' he says, his eyes on her with attention and care.

'You gave me her name,' she says.

'I did.' He nods some more. 'And it suits you. You wear it so well.'

121

A spare bedroom in a council flat on the eleventh floor of a tower block recently upgraded throughout with new, durable, fire-resistant flooring. A solid wood bed frame with a white mattress cover, a simple pine wardrobe, a generous, oak-effect desk, a chair with an upholstered seat, all arranged for a warm reception. On the sill of a single-glazed window with an imposing view of the city sits a shallow ceramic dish of little cacti. Laminate floors sparkle.

Gosia and Steve move in boxes and laundry bags with bedding and clothes. A peace lily, all leaves intact, rests on the table.

'Can't believe this is all you've got. I haven't lived with a minimalist before,' Steve pants. 'I don't think I'd ever be able to downsize and live without my things.'

In his bedroom, twice the size of Gosia's, stand two wardrobes filled with retro clothing fit for the dance floor: shirts with wide collars, waistcoats with statement buttons, blazers in delicate shades of pink, blue and grey. One wall is full of braces hung on nails banged straight into the wall, creating a cacophony of patterns and colours. And finally: shoes. These are arranged onto a customised bookcase, each polished pair made from soft leather housed in a designated pigeon-hole. Many items look brand new or barely worn. Gosia takes in the collection slowly, appreciating the fabrics and the designs.

'You're obsessed,' she proclaims.

'I'm a collector!' He corrects her in an amused voice. 'I've been at it since I discovered lindy hop. It's got more sophisticated and expensive over the years. Some of it,' he points to a wardrobe filled with pieces concealed in see-through bags, 'is proper vintage stuff, worth good money. I think of it as a retirement plan!'

He clasps his hands and shines with pride.

'I really appreciate you letting me stay,' Gosia says in a small voice.

'I really appreciate that you'll pay the rent!' He laughs. 'I need a lodger these days, or they'll shift me to those depressing studio flats where you cook, sleep, fuck and pee in the same room.' He pats her side and winks. 'You're helping me out!'

'It's temporary. I just need to figure things out.' She says it like someone who's already settled.

'Take as long as you want. I could do with you being around.' He means it. She knows now when he's lying. He gets hiccups and wheezes for air.

'I like it here. You keep it nice,' Gosia says appreciatively as they stand in the micro-corridor separating their bedrooms.

'I'm glad you like my style. And I want you to know,' he puffs up his cheeks, 'if you try to introduce your sparse approach to the living room, I'll kick up a fuss.'

While Steve puts the kettle on and bustles around the kitchen, she lies on the bed and lets the terry sheet scratch her cheek, the smell of synthetic lilies and cold air locked in the fibres.

She doesn't take for granted Steve's capacity to forgive and embrace. She is careful with her thoughts and places them against the harsh light, searching her head for motivations to judge and call names.

'It's not about being a good student,' Steve said that evening, when he took his shield off and exposed his heart again, 'it's about being a decent human.'

Just above the bed is a window and when she lifts her head, she can gaze north onto the railways tracks, and the dual carriageway, past the car park and shops, at the rest of Zone 3 and beyond. The muddy park, the industrial estate, the neat rows of houses with generous back gardens and the sibling towers, silent and erect. This is her landscape; she doesn't know anywhere else like it. The town she grew up in filled her with a fear of over-familiarity. The caterwaul of small-town gossip and endless gasping for air exasperated her.

Sir Charles, Steve's obese cat, drags his belly onto the washed sheets and curls up next to Gosia's feet. She shifts on the bed and makes space for something new.

122

A crisp, sunny morning in a small park with an arbitrary distribution of trees and benches. A high number of dog walkers and pram pushers. The dogs tend to be large and toned, ready for a race. The prams tend to be grey, black or beige, robust and stylish. The pram pushers and dog walkers wear puffy coats.

There is a small congregation of children and adults by the weedy pond, throwing stale white bread at the greedy ducks. Excited toddlers shriek. Gosia stands next to Chrissy. The nephews, in matching outfits, balance on the edge of the pond, ferociously throwing balls of bread at the birds.

'Got ya!' cries John as he hits the floating target, the bread caught on the coot's back.

'Careful!' Chrissy shouts, and catches Paul's hood to save him from falling in.

Gosia stares at the dark green of the water, into the thin blue of the sky, onto the dull grey of the concrete path. A big, multi-coloured hoarding erected in the middle of the park is spoiling the view. It advertises coming attractions: a cafe by the pond, boating opportunities, accessible toilets, an all-year-round adventure mini park.

They walked here from the station. Chrissy had arrived on an early train, benefiting from the revised festive timetable. It's the first time she has made the journey with the boys. As they strolled up the hill towards the promised pond, Chrissy recalled in micro-detail Mother's Christmas preparations; the hams and the cakes.

The conversation has moved towards her womb, still unoccupied by a baby girl. Chrissy, in a twitchy voice, has shared with Gosia her investment in an expensive set of 'help-to-conceive' sticks, that she wees on in the mornings when Duncan is around, to help her determine her fertile days. She's had no fertile days so far and he only has a week of his break left.

'How would you bring up a girl?' Gosia asks, partly to change the subject. She catches herself worrying that Chrissy will start disclosing the most efficient positions to aid conception.

'How?' Chrissy lets the question boil and infuse. 'To be strong-minded and sure of herself. None of that princess stuff. Look where that got me!'

Gosia muses on it, forcing herself not to conclude too easily. Taking time is something she is learning to do. She applies multiple angles to situations, listens instead of issuing opinions; she poses questions.

She is about to ask Chrissy to clarify, to understand better what her sister is driving at, when she sees the man she thought she loved pushing a large, double-sized pram up the concrete path. Her heart doesn't stop but she pulls her hoodie up, takes a few steps back and covers half of her face with a scarf. He parks by the pond and is deep in conversation with his hands-free set.

'It's apparently common for them to be in sync. Yes, Mum, they're doing well. They're asleep now.' He checks the two parcels inside the pram. Tenderly covering them up with a sheepskin blanket. 'Yes, I know. I love you too, Mum. Speak soon.'

She doesn't find it hard to look away. His voice doesn't carry with it the tranquil frequency that she once admired. His body is just the body of a man, someone she doesn't know, someone she doesn't care about. Someone she certainly doesn't love. She faces the weak sun, closes her eyes, soaks in the rays.

'Careful!' calls Chrissy. A happy shriek from the twins follows.

The man that unknowingly polluted her dreams for months speaks.

'Does it get any easier?'

Chrissy sighs gently, flirtatiously.

'You get more sleep, but also more worries.'

The man that she mistakenly attached to her heart laughs a short laugh.

'Do I look that bad?'

Chrissy adopts an expert voice.

'Oh, no, but I still remember how it feels. Doing everything twice. Exhaustion and having no time for myself.'

There is a leaden silence. They must be watching the pond, the children, the ducks. The pram's wheels squeak in an expensive way as they move up and down.

'Boys?' Chrissy asks.

'Yes.' A short inhale. 'They're currently pretending to be sweet angels. I love them most when they're asleep. What a shame they don't do that at two in the morning.'

'Careful!' Chrissy shouts and quickly walks away.

Gosia opens her eyes. Her nephews are patting a large dog, fearlessly pulling on its tail. Chrissy apologises to the dog's owner.

The man, a father of two and a picture of whom she kept under her eyelids, stares ahead, his hands clasped tight on the pram's handle, his face drained.

She feels nothing. She checks her organs for trembling and excitement, for the heat of a furnace – but there is only a gentle prickling on her cheeks where the sun warms her. A small hand is touching hers. Her nephew pulls sharply at her index finger.

'Can we go now?'

All the ducks are gone.

123

A council-run library kept in the Christmas spirit thanks to frosty temperatures, an abundance of handmade paper chains and an array of mass-produced baubles made of a durable material that won't break if they are dropped. Soft tunes of carols recorded in the last century by pop stars of previous generations are playing through the tannoy. Domestic oil heaters with yellow cones positioned securely near them clearly mark the hot trip hazards distributed around the room. Sheets with information about the progress of the heating system repair are nonchalantly covered with notices of the festive opening hours. A customer service assistant wearing a Father Christmas hat issues armfuls of DVDs to entertainment-starved and conversationally exhausted families queuing and arguing about what to watch first.

All the computers are busy. Gosia sits at the most exposed screen, her chair's legs vulnerable to a casual kick from prying passers-by keen to read other people's screen content. She is not bothered by it. Her mood is light and her body pleasantly heavy, full of roast that she cooked with Steve for Christmas.

She checks her inbox. There is a message from *blake_is_always_right*. The subject reads '*Thought this would cheer you up*' and in the body of an email there is a single URL. She clicks. It takes her to andyandmargaret.com where the couple has announced their impending divorce and the splitting of their business. There is also a flashing 'NEWS' arrow that Gosia follows. It jumps to another website, margaretbark.com, publicising a forthcoming book: *How to Divorce and be Happy*, with only Margaret's name on the cover and a brand-new, weekly local radio phone-in where she will be dispensing advice to soon-to-be-divorced callers. It's called 'Margaret Barks'.

First, Gosia closes the browser's window, then deletes the email from Blake and removes Andy's contact details from her address book. This does not feel like enough; her online account is still contaminated. She clicks 'Delete all' and stares at the screen as her email archive is cleansed of all contents. When it's done, she is calm. She logs on to the poetry platform.

> *KarenStevensWrites* wrote: 'I've been following the development of your work from the very beginning and always sensed that you are maturing with every verse. This poem displays the transformation from a young, naive, people-pleaser type of a girl into a self-assured woman. I hope this metamorphosis arrives at a time when you are still blessed with good looks and can enjoy your new-found confidence before your body starts to sag and expand, and you are swiftly moved by society into the side lane for the old, the fat and the problematic. I've tried to express this condition that largely affects women after forty in my recently published book of poetry. It took me twenty-six poems to convey this fatigue through waving at the younger crowd, showing them that I'm still here and have no intention of going off into the woods. The book, titled *Half of Britain's Womanhood is Dress Size 14 and Over* is available now online as well as at the venues of my forthcoming national poetry tour.'

TORM3NT wrote: 'I would.'

Rich_M wrote: 'I'm trying to place where this obsession with body hair comes from. Have you ever seen a male poet spending that much time writing about hair on legs, any legs?'

Woman_with_ideas wrote: 'I'm disappointed by this poem, to be honest. It doesn't have the usual edge. It's removed of the conflict and thorniness that I have come to appreciate in your work. A bit bland. A bit self-congratulatory. Maybe poems written from a happy place are simply not that interesting?'

Rich_M wrote: 'Lost for words. Woman, go jump off a bridge.'

R_M wrote: 'Don't try to make me feel sorry for you. Try being a bloke. How is a healthy guy supposed to pull in these circumstances – if women don't wax, if they are all fat and wear socks to bed? You can't tell jokes to pretty faces about blondes in the workplace any more. Can't even get my daily fix of bouncy boobs this time of the year with everyone in turtlenecks. Life is hard and women know nothing about it.'

Woman_permanently_in_a_turtleneck wrote: 'Enough of the small cock attitude, boys! Write from every place. Always. Good on you.'

Would you?

Not so long ago I would
go blonde
get tanned
forgo carbs
forgo tights
wax
make an effort

seek a man
follow him around
show interest in things that bore me

so men would see me
so men would love me

Now I
spend time to
tune in
eat slow
wear clothes
breathe in
breathe out
smile
follow my thoughts
make friends with people that grow me

so I can see me
so I can love me

124

A large, 24/7, unethical supermarket, late at night. Gosia Golab and Steve Bennett stand at checkout number fourteen. They are thirty-two minutes into their shopping spree. The next time they visit the supermarket it will be a new year. Only a few lanes are open, and the self-service desks are closed due to malfunctioning software.

As they stand in a long line, they activate their 'exercise for queuing by the checkout' routine and take turns to snap pictures of themselves in their balance poses or squatting while holding the metal strip of the conveyor belt.

People watch. Some laugh. Some tut at them bending and lifting parts of their bodies, spoiling the clear view of operations ahead that allow one to estimate the time of departure from the shop. Some use their own devices to document this rare and odd occurrence.

It's Gosia and Steve's turn and as they pile selected products onto the conveyor belt, they lift each item in the air first, bringing it down to the chest, using it like a weight. They perform the workout with reduced-price sweet potatoes, two-for-one tinned tuna in brine, eggs, rice, lentils, a bag of ground coffee and a bottle of sparkling wine.

A man sits at the checkout. His large eyes shaped like oval kernels frame the earthy brown of his irises. His lips plump and dewy, his skin caramel, his posture erect. His name is on the plastic plaque: Yiannis.

Steve at the front gives the man at the checkout one of his arresting smiles, conveying his delicate nature, friendly persona and abundance of fun.

'Howdy,' says Steve as he places the bag of rice by the plastic divider separating their shopping from the previous customer. 'I'm sure you're wondering what we're doing.' He maintains uninterrupted eye contact with Yiannis, soaking in the ploughed fields of his gaze. 'I can reassure you, we're not here to harm any of the goods. We're just connecting the pleasure of shopping with the pleasure of keeping fit.'

'It looks interesting,' the man offers in the soft, well-enunciated voice of a radio presenter. 'Quite an unconventional way to exercise, though.'

'It's the future. Exercise to go.' Steve adjusts to his promotional tune, chest lifted, eyes sparkling. 'Life's busy. It's hard to make time to pop into the gym or go for a run. But pretty much everyone still has to shop for food or commute to work, so we offer exercise routines that work with everyday commitments.'

Yiannis nods politely, while scanning the items calmly. The beeps of the machine correspond with Steve's breathing.

'That's quite innovative, isn't it? Forty-two pounds and thirty-five pence, please. Do you have your loyalty card?'

Steve whips out his wallet from his back pocket, pulls out a piece of plastic and some rolled-up notes. He hands them over to Yiannis.

'It is! We have a staunch following online.' He beams at Gosia. Embraces her and leans gently against her side. 'People are clearly looking for new ways to integrate fitness into their daily routines.'

Gosia embraces Steve back, holding onto his firm upper body and rubbing his shoulder blades with fondness.

Yiannis watches them closely. He hesitates as he swipes Steve's loyalty card and neatens the notes.

Gosia plucks a cotton tote from her pocket and starts packing their food. Steve grabs the bag of potatoes.

'Here's your change.' Yiannis extends a well-kept hand with clean fingernails and passes Steve a handful of coins. Steve opens his fist and there is a slight brush of skin as their hands hover and their eyes flutter.

The machine spits out a receipt with a beep, and Yiannis redirects his hand, detaching the paper from the mouth of the printer. Gosia extends her hand to intercept it.

'Thanks, and see you very soon,' she says, her voice teasing.

'Yes, very soon. Happy New Year!' adds Steve, hugging potatoes to his chest.

Yiannis gives them an ornate wave, keeping his eyes on Steve.

'Happy New Year, and thank you for shopping with us today.'

As they leave Gosia scrutinises the receipt. Sixty-nine green points are firmly printed at the bottom of the statement.

'He likes you,' she says, catching up with Steve, who is walking at a swift pace. His face, like a soft pancake under a thin coat of sugar, radiates deliciously.

'Oh my god,' says Steve as he bounces into Gosia's side. 'I just spoke to the man of my dreams.'

END

Thank you

Ben Dunn, my agent, I would be nowhere without you.

Rosa Schierenberg, my excellent editor, Annabel Robinson, Maddie Dunne-Kirby, Rob Cox, Nico Poilblanc, as well as the rest of the great team at Welbeck.

My teachers: Joanna Murat, Teresa Mielniczek, Maria Korczyńska, Season Butler and Sarah May.

Early readers: Amanda Fostervold, Annabel Johnson, Franziska Oehme, Josh Baum, Louise Pack, Maiana Mendiharat, Marielle Uhalde, Timothy Smith, Tomasz Jedrowski.

Amy Pennington and Sahjan Kooner for all their wisdom and guidance.

My Faber Academy tribe: Alice Coubrough, Bhavi Teli, Chantal Korsah, Charlotte Biddle, Chris MacDonald, Ella King, Emily Green, Laura Lawrence, Lucy O'Hair, Natalie Cox, Saya Yada. You are my writing family.

Everyone who has worked on the publication, distribution or sale of this book.

Mama, Tata, Babcia, Marcin, Boguś, Marta, my friends, and my dearest Tom and Marysia.

Author bio

Ania Bas grew up in Poland and moved to the UK fifteen years ago to pursue her career in the arts. She has worked with the *Tate*, the *Whitechapel Gallery, Eastside Projects* and others as an artist and arts organiser. She graduated from the Faber Academy in 2018 and this is her first novel.